THE WORSENER'S TALE

Praise and Protest for *The Worsener's Tale*

'I nefer stael'd fromme Henry Oldryss.' *G Chaucer*

'Yis ʒou dide.' *H Oldrice*

'What, precisely, is a Worsener?' *Hapax Journal*

'I don't like you.' *Maiden of Fates*

♬My Government congratulates the author.♬ *Thrycian Ambassador*

'Chiedo scusa.' *M Polo*

'Viva Circumferentia! Viva Ferendes!' *Democrasi Party banner*

'The PRC will defend resolutely all purloined territory.' *Admiral Feng*

'Will no one rid me of this turbulent knight?' *T Becket*

'Call off the posse and you can have the fox.' *J James*

'Call off the hounds and you can have Jesse. Plus Frank.' *Reynard F*

'Correspondence pertaining to "Worsener" is now closed.' *Editor, OED*

'Correspondence pertaining to "Nymphéa" is now closed.' *Editor, London Tribune*

'I shall return.' *Nymphéa (Communicated by D MacA)*

'His Grace has no comment at this time.' *Spokesperson 1, Lambeth Palace*

'Spokesperson 1 is not authorized to speak.' *Spokesperson 2, Lambeth Palace*

'All of you! Shut up! This is dynamite! No one speak!' *Unattributed, SE1*

'To the Index!' *Papa F*

'To the Inquisition!' *Papa B*

'Leave my name out of this mess—I wasn't there!' *G Duquel*

'Lego et taceo.' *Elizabeth I*

'Après cela, le déluge.' *Louis XV*

First published 2024 by
FREMANTLE PRESS

Fremantle Press Inc. trading as Fremantle Press
PO Box 158, North Fremantle, Western Australia, 6159
fremantlepress.com.au

Cover images aarrows, Nick Photoworld, shaineast,
Foxys Graphic, serazetdinov
Designed by Carolyn Brown, tendeersigh.com.au

 A catalogue record for this
book is available from the
National Library of Australia

ISBN 9781760992514 (paperback)
ISBN 9781760992521 (ebook)

Fremantle Press is supported by the Western Australian State Government through the Department of Cultural Industries, Tourism and Sport.

Fremantle Press respectfully acknowledges the Whadjuk people of the Noongar nation as the Traditional Owners and Custodians of the land where we work in Walyalup.

THE WORSENER'S TALE

Robert Edeson

 FREMANTLE PRESS

For Lindy Jane Roberts

Nefer soule maked wrecched by sum wrong was ther
Desyred no its vengeaunce donne in Worsenpreyere.

Henry Oldrice
Th Pylgrymes Wey

This is an undone day. Summon
a Worsener to pray.

E Satroit
Requiem from *Damascene*

FOREWORD

I must first express my gratitude to the eminent historian A B C Darian, who has generously contributed a suitably repurposed Preface that modern readers will find invaluable for locating themselves within mediaeval language and story. Moreover, the new translation of Henry Oldrice's *Th Pylgrymes Wey*, accompanied by intriguing research annotations—in part, reproduced with permission in this volume's Prologue—is entirely the work of Dr Darian.

Without this historical resource, the extraordinary progress made by Richard Worse and his investigatory team in solving a series of attempted and actual murders in the deceptively tranquil village of Steeple Resting could hardly have been possible. More certainly, the repellent secrets of its ancient parish church would have remained undiscovered, perhaps for centuries more.

This Journal is intended to record for posterity those events, and to pay tribute to the ingenuity and courage of the men and women who not only brought long-overdue justice to victims of treachery, but in so doing restored honour to the great steeple of St Eke's, and hope and holiness to its famed bell-peal.

CONTENTS

PREFACE TO *AN ANNOTATED TH PYLGRYMES WEY*

I was delighted to learn that my annotated retelling of *Nyght of Stēpel Raest*, reprinted in this volume, was instrumental in the cause of justice—remarkably, both modern and mediaeval—as described in the pages that follow. Here, I offer also the Preface to that edition of the *Wey*, very slightly amended for the circumstances, in the hope that new readers might better appreciate the historical, and literary, antecedents to an intriguing contemporary drama.

Six-and-a-half centuries of audience slumber is more than any poet should endure before the waking-call of critical applause. Such has been the fate of Henry Oldrice, whose major work, *Th Pylgrymes Wey*, is only now receiving its deserved attention. In a case of belated fame falling strange[1], this has partly come about because of the *Wey*'s prophetic bearing on present-day events in the picturesque village of Steeple Resting, near Canterbury, England.

Of course, there has long been academic interest in the Oldrice manuscripts, but regrettably never of an excellence fit to appraise their author the equal of his near contemporary, Geoffrey Chaucer. This injustice is rapidly reversing, and it is a matter of some personal satisfaction that in offering the following work to the public I might contribute, even slightly, to his cause.

The translation here is based on my reading of the *Wey* in all available versions, in which endeavour I was greatly assisted by Lawrence Enright's modern prose treatment of the

Treutheim manuscript, that being the most complete extant. Indeed, I owe much to Lord Enright's erudition, the more so for an auxiliary compilation glossary of rare words, some uniquely Oldricean, made available online.

I am also most appreciative of discussions with Magdalena Letterby, who contributed so much to my understanding of early Church doctrine, delinquency, and discipline. Others deserving special thanks are Edvard Tøssentern for his freely shared encyclopaedic knowledge of linguistics, and Lady Isobel Beckoner for her poetic commentaries, as well as a most hospitable accommodation during my research stay in London.

I thank the Master and Fellows of Nazarene, Cambridge, for private access to the College library's Mediaeval Collection.

In the past year I have been the honoured recipient of a Regents' Fellowship in the School of English at Mount Sycamore, affording many hours of stimulating discussion with outstanding faculty and international scholars, both established and student. For this I am most grateful.

Lastly, as ever, the greatest thank you goes to my incomparable editor at UITA Press, Alison Pilcrow.

Where MS-Treutheim extracts are given, as below, I have modified the original slightly (for example, by judicious repunctuation, and standard substitutions for the obsolete letters[2] þ, ð, and ȝ) in order to improve intelligibility for a reader not schooled in Middle English. In doing this, every effort was made to preserve both the wit and music of Oldrice's poetry.

For those unfamiliar with the *Wey*, two further matters for comment are briefly addressed: that of mood, and the dating of MS-Treutheim. We begin, by way of example, with the introduction of the Abbess of Ruine (*Prologue* l.65):

From Normandie she wer and greatly fonned
Of Englis Hims she livd foure yeare in Lond.

The reader (or listener) in Oldrice's time, by virtue of public taste and inconstancy of the vernacular, would be excused for not noticing a word play, but the intention is immediately made clear:

> As well confessen to th ostel throng
> Affections for our worshippe songe.

If the case for scandal were still not apparent, this follows:

> Faire was she, betroth'ed trewe to God, but alswo thanne
> Bi-twenen Holy Prayers givd wyfliche offeryng to Mann
> So by orologe of Canon Houre her feyth an chasthede stayt
> Were efer perfyt suited this or thate.

In its time, this was sensational composition, and could be expected to draw the ecclesiastical charge of *Insultemente*[3], if not civil and royal censure. The important point to note is that a satirical intent is clear throughout the *Wey*, progressively sharpened as each pilgrim, with one exception, is introduced. That exception is the last, number 37, who rode, ever watchful to his best, as the party's rearguard:

> Ther was a pious book'ed man secrete in every thing
> Sum calld him Knyght an prēst an Worsener to Kyng
> He wered blak cope an rod arere eure waccheful to his
>   beste
> An sayed nought til dethe nyght of Stēpel Raest.

The unexpected shift in mood from irreverence to solemnity, and quickly to darkness, is one of the most startling in literature. (The abruption is made more evident in poetic voice by a metrical jarring in the last line.) Yet, it makes sense, partly because of an irreproachability attaching to the office of Worsener, but also given the tragedy shortly to befall their company on the eve of entering Canterbury. (We might, too, suppose an atonement benefit for Oldrice were he ever in need of divine forgiveness for all the *grete mockrie* that had gone before[4].)

Regarding chronology, there are two questions to answer. Mention of a Bischop Angren of Bruges within the pilgrim group dates the events in or before 1370, the year of his death recorded at Dover. Next, the lore attaching to the Kneeling Knight bloodstain in Canterbury Cathedral can be traced to 1369 precisely. In support of this, Wallis Pioniv in a Lindenblüten lecture entitled 'Henry Oldrice and His *Wey* with Numbers', suggests that the contested line

Thrette-seuen soule waeren tho of egal yeir

(*Prologue* l.17: 'Thirty-seven souls were they of equal years') encodes the year of interest, being 37^2 or 1369. (There are other instances of Oldrice being sly with numbers.)

Whilst 1369 seems widely accepted, at least provisionally, as the year of pilgrimage, the date of writing is less certain. No one has suggested this might predate the events depicted (such a concept, now commonplace, was limited to practices like divination), which leaves us with 1369 or later. What can be confidently asserted, though, on copyist style and linguistic grounds, is that *Th Pylgrymes Wey* was in the hands of scribes many years before the appearance of Chaucer's *Canterbury Tales*. The obvious inferences to be made regarding historical priority and originality—and appropriations, possibly—I shall leave to literary jurors more robust in argument than my peaceable disposition allows.

At this point it is customary for an author, having acknowledged indebtedness to the expertise of others, to conclude with a saintly *mea culpa* regarding possible textual errors yet to be discovered. This gesture is invariably disingenuous and would certainly be false in the current circumstance. Notwithstanding the sentiments of gratitude expressed above, I wish to make clear that authorities cited, presumed to have contributed their best, own full responsibility for any and every perceived shortcoming of scholarship in the work.

A B C Darian
Madregalo

---

[1] An aphorism due to Oldrice! (Laite fame fallès straungeli: *Me Meneth* IV l.222; transmitted through Elizabethan 'Late fame falleth strange', in several sources.)

[2] To be read *thorn*, *eth*, and *yogh* respectively.

[3] Peculiarly, lay-blasphemy, corresponding in gravity to secular *Sedicioun*.

[4] Decades later, Chaucer attempted the same with his 'Retractions'.

PROLOGUE

NYGHT OF STĒPEL RAEST

Being the conclusion of *Th Pylgrymes Wey* by Henry Oldrice,
tragically shortened by an unforeseen event.

NEAR CANTERBURY 1369

Of all the stopping places serving pilgrims who journey from London to Canterbury, Stēpel Raest has no equal in prettiness and comfort.

The spire of St Eke's[1], when seen from miles before, lifts the spirit of any traveller, for the village reputation is of good fare and warm bedding. Of course those things—the steeple and fine rest—gave this place its name.

This spire is a progress marker too, reminding the saddle-sore that next morning they dismount in Canterbury. That also lifts the spirit, for by now some would gladly exchange an hour's riding horse for a day's hard kneeling. But these are people genuine[2] in faith, and many aver, on first sight of that spire, to feel within them the nearness of Saints, who are here Thomas Becket and Augustine of Canterbury. There is certainly much holiness about Stēpel Raest.

Even the horses from that point become more eager in their step[3], perhaps aware they will soon be lightened of a human burden, just as those they carry will be also lightened of a human burden, which is the heaviness of conscience. For such riddance, done publicly, is the purpose of pilgrimage. By this reasoning, about riddance, we can say that horses too are pilgrims going to Canterbury.

The land of Kent is deceiving, though its people are not—you know the thieves and brigands on the *Wey* are descended from the North, or crossed from Normandy with the chill wind. I mean that when the steeple is first seen, as was described, there remain hours of travel, and many times the spire seems smaller after larger. That is strange advancement through a land, from one to another vision trick, but in the nature of those parts.

At last, the company reached Stēpel Raest, to great welcome, as if no similar column of confessants had ever been encountered. The church bell rang, village dignitaries came out, and many a hostelry servant, instructed to solicit custom, shouted out the glories of his place. But the pilgrims' constable of the day, whom you know was the college Praeceptor, chose their inn. It was called the Canterbury Bell, with beds enough for all. So to The Bell they went, led by messenger Hobble, that institution's winning advocate, first to queue before the ostler, look about the premises, then settle into lodging rooms.

At three hours after noon, the company were gathered up by the Praeceptor and led to St Eke's. There was held a service conducted by the vicar, giving thanks for their safe arrival. When this was over, the pilgrims wandered separately or in small groups, exploring the churchyard, the village green, and the variety of taverns and alehouses.

I should tell you about this churchyard, which is very beautiful, if we say that of a site of graves. The grass slopes down to a river, called the Anas here, and over that is a stone arch bridge, with fine yews all about. The headstone inscriptions are the saddest in England, even if that might be claimed of others, because to die a pilgrim is the most miserable destiny. There is one naming Simon Acolytēs, of whom you will be told.

I said there is a holiness about Stēpel Raest. From a distance, when the spire beckons forward and back as I described, those of fragile faith may think this truth illusory. But I assure you, once here, in the graveyard, looking up, you feel the certainty of God in the steeple of St Eke's.

They next assembled at six o'clock, to be seated in the great refectory at The Bell. There, supper was served, and it was the best in their journey, along with wine and ale and merriment. So the reputation of Stēpel Raest was not diminished. After some time the Weaver, who had been elected host of ceremonies—or truly stated, festivities—for their final night, ascertained that all had finished eating and were ready for a course of entertainment.

Now, about the Weaver, you know that he was cut from cynic cloth, and clever in his art[4]. He judged a garment's worth by the weight of human failing it concealed, and by that measure priced his fabric into silver. But more than master of the loom was he an artisan of homily, professing expertise in the business of a soul's repair, at least exteriorly. So he prospered selling sanctity to sinners; by which I mean a thin cloak's thickness of the semblance of it. Anyway he, this clever Weaver, stood up, gestured for quiet, and spoke to the others.

'You vagabond lot, you sorry scoundrels, feasting and carousing now, when in the morning you will hide your moral pocks beneath a shriving robe, and on still-drunken knees beg favour from a Saint. Alas, what companions have I had these days? What impureness have I supped with?'

He held forward his arms as in a benediction, but where now a priest would gaze to the ineffable and intone some mystery of his calling, the Weaver feigned to study closely his hands, one then the other, saying dramatically, 'And ... these stains. These tincture marks of Satan. I am corrupted by impenitence about me that is not my own. In truth I tell you: it is the contagion sin of his society, and that only, for which this sober child of God will seek tomorrow's pardon at the Shrine.'

The vagabond lot were silent, not knowing whether to be amused or chastised. But none then picked up a cup of wine. The Weaver continued.

'But I have observed one amongst us who is no wretch like all of you, but man of faultless spirit; who along our way has protected us from brigands by his presence and from God's wrath by his prayer. You know I speak of the solitary man, who wastes no word.'

The host now looked at the Worsener. 'Sir Knight, these fallen souls beseech, share with us your humour of whatever kind, for we approach night's ending, and our thirty-seventh Tale is rightly also ranked Knight's ending. We are, Sir, your obedient and grateful audience.'

With that, the Weaver resumed his seat. After some seconds the Worsener, who had been looking down throughout, rose at his place. He thanked the host for his words, but begged earnestly to differ in the judgement of others, saying he was honoured to be in the company of good people on a noble and Christian enterprise. He hesitated, as if weighing his words, and looked around the room. Then he added something unexpected.

'Good people but one, I say: the one whose design is not our holy end. For there is a wretched spy and felon in our midst. Of whom I speak I cannot tell, but know this: before you reach confession time his hand will smite us foul. Tonight I pledge his wickedness will be punished, whether in its hour of committing or on his Satan line a hundred generations forward. May the Lord have mercy on all who suffer harm, and may the Lord bless the good amongst you.'

He led the room in a short prayer to St Thomas Becket, asking for safety in the night and on the next day's ride to Canterbury. Then he began the thirty-seventh entertainment. It was not to be mirthful or ribald like its predecessors, and you will understand that those who listened were quickly sobered in their chairs.

First, he raised his arms, as had the Weaver, but more properly, as a priest would. But, also like the Weaver, he looked first at one hand, then the other.

'About the staining of hands, Master Weaver, have no fear; for God knows the origin of all things. Now on that subject, I can tell you of a well-regarded maiden, once in Saracen lands, who did in divination plunge two natural hands together into one same broth they named Augury Water. This was done in full view of her audience.'

He imitated the act in the air before him.

'And out might come one hand red and one blue, being left and right; or right and left; or two red; or two blue. But also front and back, being palm and knuckle sides, of either hand might differ so as well[5].'

He held up his hands again, turning them over for study.

'And by these signs she told the future of the curious, for both colour sort and men's destinies are numbered sixteen[6], and she was knowledgeable in their meaning. She was called the Maiden of Fates.

'But that is a tale inside a Tale. Let us start where it is sensible to do so.'

37. Here Beginneth The Worsener's Tale

From Venice, there was a philosopher-priest called Christianus del Oscini, and I describe events around one hundred years before tonight. But let us start where it is sensible to do so[7].

As an infant, he was named Lorenzo, and was silent for his first five years. But when he did begin to say words his family was much astonished, because he proved gifted in any language spoken before him. Also, his memory for every fact and experience was unequalled.

For this promise of peculiar genius he was given schooling under patronage of the Doge. That was in holy matters, in languages, and all the sciences. At twelve he won a *Sapienza* debate against a great rhetorician of his city; the event was in public and adjudicated by those listening.

At age sixteen he was found to speak the language of the birds, and this attracted great respect, for all would wish to know their thoughts. It was said that he was most happy when in discourse with the swints, which are the holiest of birds[8], and likewise in his presence their song would become the sweetest ever heard.

Next he was summoned to Rome by His Holiness the Pope, who was incredulous of reports, and set a test. Three scholars read before the boy different texts, but all at once, as if competing for attention. One spoke Latin, one Greek, and one Arabic. This was for about three minutes. Then the Holy Father asked Lorenzo to repeat each passage in turn, and also render it in vernacular. So he tested concentration, memory, comprehension and translation together in a most unfair way. This task Lorenzo accomplished with great precision, such that the Pope recognized him to be a miraculous youth, and supported him through monastic training. This education would prepare Lorenzo for a temporal life devoted to reason and good, and spiritually for life in the service of God.

About then, because of his devoutness, and because of the Godly nature of his gift, he came to be called Christianus, and we will not hear of Lorenzo again.

Now, it happened some years later, when few remembered Christianus because he lived in scholarly seclusion, that Venetian merchants brought news of a remarkable thing. In eastern lands was found a winged, owl-like[9] creature, called *ghoghnoos* in the Persian, or generally by travellers *Phlox*. Without warning, this Phlox would appear instantly in the presence of a holy person, whom it then accompanied closely, observantly, and in total silence. This vigil might last hours or days, until quite suddenly the creature would cry shrilly in a strange language, perhaps in torment some said, and dissolve in brilliant flame[10] leaving no trace but a sweet perfume[11] in the air. According to a trusted, Latin-speaking Samarran chronicler, were the Phlox to return to the same place, that event would occur on its sixteenth day of absence, the cycle of apparition, vigil, utterance, and dissolution repeating as before.

The officers of the Church in Rome were greatly interested in this phenomenon, which appeared to recapitulate the suffering, sacrifice, and resurrection of Christ, and this they would desire to promulgate widely as a mystery of the faith.

Moreover, it was possible that the creature's speech conveyed some prophecy, or commandment to humankind. And so the Holy Father, being troubled by these concerns, thought of Christianus—for who else in Christendom might understand the cry of the Phlox?

For the second time Christianus was summoned to Rome, and charged to journey east as papal ambassador to witness the Phlox and interpret its message. If that contained an instruction of any kind, Christianus was given liberty to follow as best he could, and return to Rome with news however God saw fit.

So Christianus, now twenty-seven years of age, in the year 1269, set off with a retinue of assistants to the region of Samarkand, whence the last Phlox reports had come. All the way, he spoke freely to inhabitants, for either he knew their language or acquired it quickly. Some whom he met, on hearing of his errand, desired to partake and so committed their service and fortune. Amongst those, I mention now Simon Acolytēs of the English Priory of St Ignorius at Constantinople; and Antiochus the Memorious from Damascus. Also, Matteo Lusco, a navigator, joined them in Acre. He was one-eyed. Also, Vesalio Leche, a respected physician, came, but he was first to perish. His assistant, the apothecary Pestle, was the second.

On this travel Christianus saw the Maiden of Fates, about whom you have learned, and was much puzzled. And this is how I know about her.

Near Samarkand, he enquired of the Phlox, and hired guides. But as he drew closer, their people became less welcoming. They had heard he knew the language of the birds, and did not want the creature understood for fear its talk professed the Western faith. Such was their weakness of belief. So they were not helpful. The guides deserted, along with men who were paid to guard the caravan. Soon a party of bandits attacked their camp at night, but withdrew in terror because of this happening.

There is a saying in some parts that a mountain moves not

to a prophet, but the prophet must move to the mountain. Something like the first did happen that night of the brigands. The Phlox came to Christianus, cried its message, and set itself aflame. Christianus heard the cry, and understood. But he stayed in that place thirty-two more days, to hear twice again the Phlox so he could be truly certain of its meaning. The third time, he answered in the language of the creature, saying he would do its bidding. Anyway, regarding the brigands, it is argued that the Phlox came to save Christianus from certain murder, but you know that cause and coincidence have slight distinction in the faithful.

Nevertheless, news of this spectacle most surely spread forward and back along the Silk Road, as the merchant route is known, for never again was his caravan attacked, though that is common heathen practice in those countries.

And so it was that Christianus and the papal retinue headed further east, through the fabled Kingdom of Thrycia, where fireballs fill the night sky and the people sing where we would speak, eventually to Khan-balik[12], the capital of the Great Khan, who was at that time Kubilai. For this is what the Phlox instructed, and what the Holy Father had sanctioned him to do.

Now two years had passed in finding the Phlox, and another two passed before they reached the Mongol capital. But their welcome was great. Kubilai Khan was a cultured leader, desirous of knowledge about the world, and he feted these ambassadors of the religion from the west.

For a year, Christianus stayed in the Great Khan's palace, teaching as well as receiving instruction in the Chinese and Mongol ways. But he was always perplexed about what he should do, for the Phlox had instructed him to come to this place but given no reason.

It was during this time that by chance another party of Venetians, who were named Polo, arrived at the court. You will believe there was mutual delight in the discovery of countrymen so far from home, but we learn that their relations proved only cordial. This was because for the scholar-envoy his quest was spiritual, and for the other it was mercantile, which is not Godly. You know, then, we find in the Polo journal no mention of Christianus, nor his marvellous travels, nor even his presence in Khan-balik. This is a great slight to the messenger of Rome and a disservice to God and history.

One day, Christianus was walking alone in the palace garden[13], and as was his habit chose to sit on a bower bench for the contemplation of Nature and the Divine. This time, instead of entering an attentive meditation, he was drawn into a deep sleep—the state of inexistence called in the Greek κῶμα—in which he had this dream.

The Phlox alighted beside him and spoke. It told Christianus that God was pleased with his unerring faith whilst deprived of guidance for this past year; now his instruction was to be made complete. His final destination was not Khan-balik but far south to the Circular Sea[14], into the *Centrum Mysticum*[15] of the world; there he would truly begin his work for the Lord. If Christianus prepared a ship of passage, and took leave of the Khan, a company of swints would escort him across the waters.

And when Christianus awoke, he found the bower filled with the sweet perfume, and was thus assured his counsel came from Heaven.

So it was that some months later, when the seas were favourable and the wind from the north, Christianus bade farewell to Kubilai and set out in a vessel newly constructed in the Venetian manner. This ship he named *Bethlehem*, and her complement was drawn from his entourage.

As promised by the Phlox, they were guided by a tidings of swints, appearing as a golden, cruciform cloud before them. On seeing it, all knew that the holiness of their mission could not be doubted.

On the forty-ninth morning, the swints were joined by

four black birds, larger than any the Europeans had seen, which circled their ship for the rest of the day. During the afternoon the sea calmed, became darker, and gave off a scent more gloriously citrous[16] than salty. At sunset, the party made landfall, and hove to so that their course to shore would be effected in daylight. During the night, the inhabitants of the land stoked a great beach fire, giving comfort and bearing to the mariners adrift in the darkness of the perfumed sea.

At dawn, three swints alighted on the prow, and Christianus was called to speak with them. Their directions for safe progress he was able to interpret and convey to the boatswain and master of sail. In this way they navigated into a calm bay, and anchored. All the while, the four black birds circled above, though mysteriously seeming to vanish and reappear at will[17].

With the *Bethlehem* made fast, a shore party was mustered and set out for the beach. This included Christianus, of course, as well as Simon and Antiochus. These I will now call the Three, as they remained normally together.

They landed where the night fire had burned, and hauled their lighter up the beach. About forty men, women and children were gathered to receive them, but first the Three kneeled on the ground for a short prayer of thanksgiving. During this, a swint came to perch on each one's shoulder. To their hosts this was surely a sign of peace and goodness. The Three stood up, and Christianus spoke.

'I am named Christianus, and I have been sent by the Holy Father in the service of God, for what reason I do not know.'

The swint on Christianus' shoulder sang to him, and Christianus answered, and the swint sang again, and Christianus answered. The people of the land were much amazed by this stranger's communion with the birds. One woman, whom they later learned was called chieftain of fishers and acted, as Venetians say, in the capacity of Podestà[18], stepped forward. Her hands were outstretched, holding a large yellow crystal[19] as if it were a gift. The words she spoke were unlike any language

Christianus had heard[20]. The swint advised Christianus that he should reach out and touch the crystal, and touch only, as it was not a gift but a totem in their ritual of welcome. So was established a peaceful harmony between the delegation from Rome and the people of the Circular Sea.

Over the following weeks the Three, and many of their crew, lived on the land, well cared for by their hosts. Christianus worked hard to master the new language, sometimes assisted by the swints, and was most interested in its unique qualities. He discovered[21] that much of their people's thinking, and verbal expression, was predicated on what were surely cultural superstitions regarding a mythic sea creature. He didn't fully understand the nature of this motivation, never having encountered such a strange and pervasive determinant in any other language. Anyway, this creature, or fish, they called *kenijo*[22], though it had many names, and that was all he learned of it.

Again, Christianus was perplexed by what he should do, as he had been in Khan-balik, and entreated God for guidance. One morning, his prayer was answered, not by agency of the Phlox but a thrice of swints. They told him to make preparations for a journey into the centre of the land. There he would be given audience with the most holy Empress of the swints, who was not of their kind, but an ancient woman, and she would relate the spirit history of the world. This he was to record for the benefit of men, who came late to life on Earth and were ignorant of the Creator.

And all this came about. For five hundred days, on a royal hill in the middle of a vast plain in the forest, the Three rendered into Latin the words of the Empress. We know this included a chronicle of the True Prophets.

This testament they named the Book of Swints, though also they said *Documento*, and it was now Christianus' solemn duty to deliver it to Rome.

So from the country of the Circular Sea they sailed south, through the Malay Straits, then to India, then to Arabia. In Hormuz they sold the *Bethlehem* and joined a traders' caravan to Baghdad, and on to Jerusalem. On the way, which accounted for two years, the company fell into many adventures, as you would understand if you travelled in their place.

But we are following the life of Christianus, and the journey of the *Documento*. Alas, in the holy city of Jerusalem, it was God's will that the messenger of Rome who spoke the language of the birds should be struck down by the ague. And so, in his thirty-seventh dutiful year, Christianus del Oscini breathed his last. This happened at the Sepulchre of Our Lord in the presence of the Phlox, which shed tears as it shrieked. That fact was witnessed by the gathered companions.

Beside this occasion, the Phlox had not appeared to Christianus since his dream in the garden of the Great Khan. Nor has it visited any other mortal from that time on.

Now after all these years the papal retinue was much diminished, by sickness, by loss at sea, by temptation, and by seizure, ransom and murder, which are common treacheries in Saracen and Mongol lands. The remaining few resolved to sail from Acre to Venice, with the able Matteo Lusco their navigator and a complement of Levantine sailors. It is impossible to think they journeyed without the *Documento*, but we cannot be certain of events as that sacred text was carried in secrecy. Whatever the case, it was not received in Rome.

The eight winds were not clement, for their ship never arrived. Nor did all perish as was first believed. We know this because after a year Antiochus was found in Rome, sick of mind and deprived of his memory. We know this also because after another year Simon Acolytēs, whom no one had supposed to be alive, died on our Saint's pilgrimage at this very place, in the holy steeple tower of St Eke's, whence today our prayers ascended to the Almighty.

Good pilgrims, I beg forgiveness for a Tale miraculous but sorely ended, that being because I know nothing further of the Book's fate. Yet I promise that all you have heard, being what occurred and what was spoken, and about places, and about creatures, is the testimony of those noblest Three amongst God's Servants, and they were Christianus who understood, Antiochus who remembered, and Simon who kept record.

I say to you, remain always believing in the workings of the Lord. Beseech Him this night, of all nights, and in this place, of all places, to strengthen your faith, so on the morrow your confession will be true, your spirit purified, and your heart made ever open to the mysteries of Heaven. Amen.

May God be merciful to the souls of Christianus the Blessed, and of Simon Acolytēs, and of Antiochus the Memorious, and of all who brought the *Documento* westward, for that was the Lord's bidding. And let there be anointed new Servants who are strong and wise, that the Book of Swints should be restored to light and finally delivered in peace and holiness. Amen.

Here Is Ended The Worsener's Tale

Amen. With that appeal to God, the Worsener thanked his host and those present for their forbearance, and begged leave of the company. All remained quiet, for they had not previously heard a Tale of such gravity. So they did not burst into chatter, or take up drinking, or harass the innkeeper on his kitchen skills, as had been their practice. Instead, feeling chided by the Weaver, and humbled by the Knight's story, they retired, singly and pensive, in preparation for the entry to Canterbury.

You know it was their custom that the evening's host would also serve as pilgrims' constable the following morning. So it was that before dawn the Weaver roused the company, checked harnessing and stores, and settled payments. But when they were all assembled ready to leave, the solitary man was not to be seen, and his horse was still with the ostler. They searched the inn and called his name, which I now tell you was Geoffrey Magnacart[23], who was indeed Knight Worsener to the King. Next Hobble, runner for The Bell, was dispatched to look about the streets, but he returned without news.

The Abbess suggested that, being devout as the Knight certainly was, he might be lost in worship at the Stēpel church, so the Weaver led a group through the village to St Eke's. They found the nave and chancel deserted, but an unfamiliar odour drew them to the steeple tower. Looking through the sexton's open doorway they saw the Worsener, whose back was to them, kneeling in prayer as the Abbess had anticipated. So they were naturally reluctant to rouse him. But after much hesitation, because their departure was now felt urgent, the Weaver quietly entered and advanced around the kneeling figure. What he saw caused him to collapse in pallor to the floor. The Worsener, serene in death, was supported upright by his longsword, and this had pierced his heart.

The others rushed forward to assist the Weaver, and confronted the same. They too were stricken weak with horror at the grievous find, and all fell to their knees in solemn commendations for their companion's departed soul.

And when they could later speak of the sight, they said three things: there was no trace of villain about; all recalled the pungent smell of Hades in that tower; and the Worsener bled not. He bled not on his tunic, nor skin, nor sword, nor on the stone beneath him.

But we know that bleed he did, and by intercession of an Angel his mortal spill completed holy pilgrimage—for that same morning it appeared by miracle upon the obsecration steps before the great altar of Canterbury.

Now all who visit there and gaze upon Th'Imperishable Stain[24] affirm that what they see is a vision of the Kneeling Knight, and are likewise given to fall in prayer in sympathy with the martyr Geoffrey Magnacart, and in admiration of the workings of Heaven.

And this, faithful reader, must be your heart's commandment also.

Here ends *Th Pylgrymes Wey* by Henry Oldrice
as nothing worthier could follow.

---

[1] In *Anselm's Industrie of Antes* there is mentioned a trite witticism amongst English bishops to the effect that in granting benefice to this parish, they were directing a vicar to Eke out a Living. (The jest retains currency, not for quality of humour, but through occasional citation in scholarly debate concerning the historically proper pronunciation of the saint's name. See note to Chapter 28.)

[2] The ME text has a Latinic word play here, relating *kneeling* and *genuine*. Further similar instances will not be noted.

[3] Characteristic from thereon and, as is well known, later named *canter*, from the context.

[4] There is omitted here a mysterious Passage present in MS-Oxford (but not Treutheim) which, because of multiple hapax legomena and opaque symbolism, cannot confidently be translated. Enright surmises that it further extols the Weaver, insofar as his art expands the world (abstractly, in our thinking, 'space') from line to surface (being yarn into cloth), and analogously (by *lengðe an brede th Holi-wrappe*) extends the canopy of Heaven. The reading is considered ingenious but too speculative to be authoritative.

Equally ingenious, but more radical, is the suggestion due to Franz Hebe that the lines conceal an Author's Confession: namely, that Oldrice himself was present on the pilgrimage—thus explaining accurate reportage of historical persons such as Bishop Angren and Geoffrey Magnacart—but has disguised himself textually (and textorially) as the Weaver, a quite central figure who is generously described in every way except biographically. (A natural equivocation about the unmasking could explain why it appears in one MS and not others.) According to Hebe, the narrational praise (and cynicism) afforded the Weaver is self-referentially ironic; and here, for example, *Holi-wrappe* wishfully signifies something protective (a notional garment, presumably) against censure for deception. Hebe's thesis has been savagely attacked as naïve (unreasonably, in this writer's opinion), most notably by Geras and colleagues who seem to favour a retiring defeatism over intellectual adventurism. Even so, it is worth keeping in mind Enright's droll observation that the Oxford Passage calls not so much for translation as decipherment. Finally, whatever meaning they might convey, the lines in question may not actually belong to Oldrice, but be attributable to a zealous monk or a mischievous copyist.

[5] A literal case of legerdemain, with assistance from pH. Out of sight, she would have an accomplice rub citrus juice or vinegar (citric and acetic acids, respectively) into the skin she chose to be red, and potash water into that she wanted blue, the difference not being evident to the eye. Then before her querent, and with suitable solemnity, she would immerse these apparently normal hands into the Augury Water (effectively, an indicator solution: very likely pomegranate juice, or possibly some litmus congener), and they would emerge coloured accordingly—acidic red and alkaline blue. (Potash, crude potassium carbonate K_2CO_3, is alkaline in solution. 'Alkali' is from al-qali, the ash, this being of plant matter burned in a pot. 'Potassium' for the element ultimately is derived in this way, the suffix –ium here signifying metal.)

[6] If she exhibits both sides of both hands there are sixteen possible combinations (Oldrice's use of sort in this line, instead of kynde, is a deliberate connection to sortilege) of red and blue. The reader can confirm this heuristically, or by summing combinations, viz. $\sum_{r=0}^{4} \binom{4}{r} = 16$.

The corresponding fates are speculated to number the eight principal winds together with return and not-return alternatives. There are many competing explanations, including a probably spurious connection to days of the Phlox. (Note that from a theatrics point of view she is unlikely to choose a degenerate outcome—all red or all blue—as this would lack miraculous impact; hence in practice her suite of destinies reduces to fourteen. Irrespective of that number, in the presence of the Maiden of Fates the first law of divination should be observed, which is not to consult an oracle who doesn't like you.)

[7] Repetitions of this type (other examples are 'So', 'You have learned' and 'You know') are a rhetorical habit of Oldrice.

[8] Here it is opportune to correct an egregious heraldic misrepresentation regarding the three birds depicted on the City of Canterbury coat of arms and, earlier, the arms of Thomas Becket. For no sound historical, ecclesiastic, or artistic reason their armorial progenitors became identified as Cornish choughs, despite the singular holiness and characteristic thricing behaviour of the swint arguing that it is most certainly the species figured, or intended to be so. Moreover, a commentary in Clavenger's Almanack of Errants citing as authority Bede, no less, and instancing inter alia thriced swints on the seal of St Ignorius, a vexillum of (the Christian) Constantine, countless illuminated manuscripts, and Becket's own papers,

should have settled the matter three centuries before the City's philistine embrace of the chough travesty.

[9] Possibly a temporal incarnation of the Counting Owl, a senior chthonic figure overseeing progression of souls through the Underworld.

[10] Hence φλόξ, flame. Capitalization in the Roman as a reverent form is invariant. Here, the Greek alludes to flame colour without presuming fire, as no ordinary signs of combustion (such as radiant heat or ash) are recorded. We can only conjecture a process of reversible *manifestation*, between material embodiment (the evidence for this being odour molecules and vocalization) and some form of coherent, dissipative emanation, of unknown mechanism.

Regarding obvious parallels between the Phlox of witness testimony here described and the 'phoenix' of fable, I am indebted to Edvard Tøssentern for the following origination argument. Since the natural may beget the mythic, but not vice versa, the attested Phlox must certainly have revealed itself in earliest antiquity, though literary references over subsequent centuries inseparably confuse the two.

[11] Many came to believe this 'sweet perfume' to be the breath of God, and that the sinful could be purified by nothing more than enthused inhalation. (In those parts the corporeal depiction of God or prophet is not allowed but, in a failure of imagination by their originating dogmatist, the *smell* of both escaped prohibition.) In the absence of actual visitations—and in the nature of religious ecstasies generally—the Godly scent was hallucinated into existence for mass consumption, notably in dervish rituals, fiery prayer, and (understandably, given the intent) hyperventilation manias.

The Western Church, being less averse to representation and the sensual but disinclined to whirling and howling—in fact, cathedral exertions of any kind—adopted incense, quiet breathing, and plainsong as decorous substitutes.

Whilst on this subject, there is a rigorous scholarship corroborating the assertion 'no trace but a sweet perfume'. Early mediaeval legends predictably emerged claiming the fantastical, for example, that a glowing or jewel-like ember-egg persisted from which the Phlox was fully reborn. To the modern intellect, these embellishments, like the phoenix itself, are obvious fictitious imports. All but the fact of 'perfume' have been forensically discredited.

[12] Now Beijing.

[13] Undoubtedly a *hortus conclusus*, comfortingly sized to Catholic horizons.

[14] Now South China Sea, a mislabelling. Despite bellicose territorial larceny by present-day communist China, this sits entirely within the maritime borders of the Ferendes—by proclamation of that nation's founding queen, Rep'husela. 'Circular Sea' therefore remains the preferred designation.

(The origin of this name, based on the maximum perimetric flight of royal Asiatic condors, is explained elsewhere. Perhaps more consequentially, that defining radius of the realm most certainly described an arc through what is now viewed as mainland China; the eastward interior of that arc is therefore properly a western province of the Republic of Ferendes. (An ancient Ferent-language name for these stolen lands was aptly rendered into Latin by the Scottish explorer-scientist Thomas MacAkerman: *Circumferentia*.) The eventual forfeiture of this continental sector by the People's Republic will reverse an illegal—and brutally defended—annexation, and is widely viewed as a geopolitical inevitability. Meanwhile, to Beijing's perennial annoyance, Madregalo appoints every year a symbolic Governor-in-Exile of Circumferentia, who functions essentially as a cultural ambassador raising international awareness of the occupation. Intriguingly also—and another needle in the dragon's toe—in modern Ferent the ancient name for Circumferentia back-translates to 'Property Theft', as laid down in the Ferende criminal code, further impressing on national consciousness the Sino-imperialist historical injustice. Such a socially-determined, emergent redefinition, it is worth pointing out, exemplifies Tøssentern's widely quoted aphorism that, before all else, language is memory.)

Elsewhere in the region, historians interpret the Japanese seafaring tradition of appending *maru* ('Circle') to the names of vessels plying these waters as evidencing centuries of that people's acceptance of the Rep'huselan maritime claim.

[15] Identified with modern (archipelagic) Ferendes (note 14).

[16] Indeed; subsequent European geographers named this body of water the Bergamot Sea. In Ferent, the scented air is called *muriatika*, translating to 'spirit of salt', though this same English term in Western chemistry refers to something very different (and wholly pungent: hydrochloric acid). The olfactory phenomenon is believed caused by seabed micro-effervescence of aromatic volatiles originating in bacteria within the ocean floor. Tradition has it that seafood harvested here is subtly infused with a citrous flavour imparted by these marine prokaryotic bergamot analogues.

[17] This observation is diagnostic of the Asiatic condor.

[18] Approximately, 'mayor'.

[19] Almost certainly a volcanic josephite.

[20] Unsurprisingly. Computational linguistic analysis has failed to identify a common parentage connecting Ferent to any other language; it remains in a class of its own—an *orphan clade* in Tøssentern's systematics.

[21] This author agrees with Lord Enright, who admits to difficulties in rendition here; we draw on modern cultural concepts to convey efficiently the evident sense.

[22] Weaver fish. Their existence was documented by Europeans in 1816.

[23] Pronounced Marnacourt. The Magnacart crest, shared with the Misgivingston family since the thirteenth century, comprises in part three swints (see note 8 above).

[24] Imperishable in the firmament perhaps, but not underfoot. In the early sixteenth century, a hapless novice, poorly tutored in his cleaning duties but ably equipped with a scouring broom, and eager for the notice of his Cathedral superiors (he certainly attracted it), took pride in re-brightening those holy steps of every old Stain. Such was the fate of our only manifest sign of the one true miracle since the time of Christ—to be sluiced away in a lime-water bucket.

1 NEWS FROM STEEPLE RESTING

[Monday]

Bring spent spent hours to the waiting giants
Who Milton-serve, yet stand in spelled defiance.

A precise translation, but Satroit's language typically is allusive. Who could know the poet's intention?

Still, it was never meaning, intended or not, that caused those lines to stay with Worse. It was something non-literal, set apart from the telling, at once fascinating and foreboding. Like ripples in liquid uncertainty.

Which came to mind now, because of Millie. Her mother had telephoned from England, and instead of the usual family catch-up chatter conducted from a comfortable lounge chair, Millie was standing across the room, looking very concerned, and saying almost nothing.

Charmed listener: See! They set you free!

So much for an exegetic flourish to end. But Worse was listener enough to realize that the news from Kent was not good. He watched Millie, patiently. She said her goodbye, sending love, and lowered the hand holding her mobile.

She looked at Worse.

'He's okay, but Dad was coming home from Canterbury last night and found himself forced off the road by some monster driver who didn't stop. Rollover, airbags, everything. The police haven't ruled out that it was deliberate. They sent him by ambulance to hospital for a check over. He's home now, resting up.'

Worse moved to put his arm around Millie's shoulder. 'No serious injuries?'

'So it seems. Just a badly damaged, much-loved Saab.'

'He was alone in the car?'

'Yes.'

'And how is your mother?'

'She's fine. Worried.' Millie sat down on a sofa. She was still holding her phone. Worse sat sideways on the same sofa, looking at her.

'Something else happened. The same night, Dad's best friend died, in the church, of all places. Across the lane from my parents' house.'

'Suspiciously?'

'Mum can't say. He was alone, so the police and coroner are involved; apparently that's usual.'

Worse nodded, still looking at Millie. 'Was the friend someone you knew?'

'William Whencely. Yes. Will's been sort of extended family since I was at school. Dad and he were always doing projects together—local history, biography, interpreting old maps, tracing place names. Will was the trained historian; he owned an antiquarian bookshop in the village. Dad's a passionate amateur.'

'Have the police looked for a connection between the two events, do you know?'

Millie was surprised at the idea. 'No. Mum didn't say anything to suggest that. Why would there be?'

'Because a prior connection exists between William and your father, and because of timing. They're not two everyday events, dying and nearly dying. I have learned to view coincidence as a pointer to wrongdoing until proven not to be. In context, of course.'

Millie gave Worse a look she might afford a student submitting a theorem with a page of proof missing. Worse expanded.

'We should consider the worst case, which means the one with the most serious implications. You say your father and William were collaborators of a sort. Perhaps, unwittingly, they were researching a subject of extreme sensitivity to a ruthless third party. So, William was murdered, and on the same night an attempt was made on your father's life, or at least a strong message of discouragement was sent. That possibility should be explored.'

Now Millie looked almost disapproving. 'You do go through life with an extraordinarily high index of suspicion, Dr Worse.'

Worse was untroubled by the judgement. 'As would you, Dr Misgivingston, if your profession were intelligence analyst.'

He spoke quietly, with no trace of condescension, or defensiveness. And he refrained from voicing his following thoughts: First connect known facts in every feasible way, then progressively reduce the possibility set. Investigation by elimination, detection by discovery, was a standard teaching mantra. In matters referred to him, the gravest suspicions were, unhappily, the most often validated. Therefore, efficiency, and urgency, dictated he start with a worst-case hypothesis. Anything after that would be mild by comparison and generally less distressing.

He found Millie staring at him, as if physically examining a mental hiatus.

'Are you saying that my father's at risk, from criminals, in some way?'

'Almost obviously, yes.'

Worse took Millie's hand. 'Phone your mother back. Ask her the question that I asked you. That will be enough to set her thinking about your father's current safety. I doubt that protection is needed at this stage. If they wanted him removed, they would have used a more reliable means than sham road rage. It suggests that William was closer to the offending party's self-interest than your father is. That will be a helpful fact.'

Worse took his own mobile from a pocket. 'I'll see what

Victor can find out for us. Last night, Sunday night in the UK, are you saying?'

'Yes.'

'The road from Canterbury to ...?'

'Steeple Resting.'

'Oh, yes. And William Whencely: what church?'

'St Eke's.' She spelt the names, Eke and Whencely.

'Good. Tell your mother we're likely to be there in a few days. It's time I met your parents, anyway.'

'Really, Richard? You think I should go, and you would come with me?'

'Of course I will come with you. It's well known that Kent is wild and treacherous, with giants and trolls and misty woods and werewolves in moonlit churchyards. You managed to leave once, but we're not chancing it again.'

Worse gave no indication that he wasn't gravely serious.

'Anyway,' he said, 'I want to see where you grew up—try to understand your ... deviancies better.'

'Oh, what? You're the one!'

It was mock hurt over real relief.

'Besides,' Millie added, 'I've told you: I didn't grow up till Cambridge.'

Worse projected a pained worldliness. 'Nobody grows up at Cambridge. Did your mother say whether she'd spoken to Nicholas?'

'She's doing that next, accepting that my brother is sometimes difficult to contact on the research station.'

Worse stood up and moved to the balcony. Watching the evening traffic thirty-three floors down, he phoned his friend, and closest colleague in the police department, Inspector Victor Spoiling.

—

Ten minutes later, Worse finished the call and re-entered the lounge room. Millie was still sitting on the sofa. She looked up.

'I got back to Mum. Things seem calm at home. Dad's not

particularly concerned for himself. He's hugely upset about Will, of course. The police have made no comment to them about connecting the car business with William.'

'Fine,' said Worse. 'Victor sends his regards. He will look into both matters for us. He did ask the sensible question of whether your father had any known enemies.'

'Dad's a retired GP, for heaven's sake. It's a village. People love him,' said Millie.

'That's what I thought. I basically said that.'

Worse joined Millie on the sofa again. 'You do realize that what you are saying reinforces the theory that it was your father's connection to William that attracted jeopardy to his person?'

'I follow your argument,' said Millie.

'When I told Victor that we would go over to give support to your parents, he offered to arrange introductions and for me to have a visiting officer's rank, so I can join the investigating team and have full access.'

'Join the team? Take over, don't you mean?' said Millie.

'Strangely, Victor implied something similar. I don't know where you people find reason for such meanness.'

Millie touched the bridge of her nose with a forefinger. 'Oh look! In front of our eyes.' She leaned toward Worse and embraced him.

—

Emily Misgivingston had arrived in Perth to take up a one-year visiting professorship in her field of mathematics. Having met and briefly stayed with Worse on a previous occasion, he had offered her temporary accommodation in the adjoining vacant apartment, which he also owned. The understanding was that within a few weeks she would find her own place nearer the host university, and move on.

It was an understanding at odds with destiny. Out of that unruly, compelling place called the heart there came to each a realization of attraction, of curiosity, and then desire. Instead of leaving, Millie moved into Worse's apartment, and their cohabitation trial became a relationship.

There were complications. Millie was a Fellow of Nazarene College, in Cambridge, and lectured in Rodney Thwistle's department there. Worse was committed to his police intelligence consultancy in Perth, to collaboration with Victor, and to other lifelong friendships. They discussed how their future together might unfold, but for the present, inside their contentment and the unworried optimism of new love, hemispheres apart seemed no distance at all.

—

Worse employed a full-time housekeeper, who was accommodated in a small unit elsewhere in the same Grosvenor Apartments building. Hilario Wotsan, trained as a first-class steward on cruise ships, suited Worse's lifestyle needs perfectly; he had proven to be uncannily endowed with efficiency and discretion. Worse called him with the news that he and Millie would be travelling to the UK in the next few days, and likely away for a fortnight.

An hour later, walking into their bedroom, Worse found bags ready and a selection of his own clothes laid out for approval. In separate piles were travel documents, toiletries, and device chargers with UK adaptors. Millie's things were untouched. Neither had seen or heard him working.

—

Millie's academic responsibilities in the Perth department were not yet onerous, and she was able to take leave without difficulty. Meanwhile, Worse organized their flights and transfers.

After a call from Victor, he sought out Millie in the bedroom, where she was now sorting clothes to pack. She spoke without looking up.

'I'm thinking I should appoint Hilario packer plenipotentiary for me as well. You seem to have it too easy.'

'You should, you should. He works miracles. Of course, he may need in-service training in the matter of ladies' smalls. I would think he's never had reason to master those ... delicates.'

Millie turned to Worse with theatrical shock. 'Why, Richard, you surprise me,' she said.

Worse grinned. 'I've heard back from Victor. It seems the police are conducting unrelated investigations into William's death and your father's vehicle attack.'

'Attack? That's a powerful conclusion. Where did that come from?'

'From thinking about it,' said Worse. 'They are suspicious about William, though. There's no established cause of death yet. The next step will undoubtedly be further advanced toxicology. All the same, it seems they will release his body for burial in the coming days.'

—

Worse and Millie flew direct Perth to Heathrow, arriving early morning. A pre-booked airline chauffeured limousine was waiting to take them on the ninety-minute transfer to Steeple Resting.

As they negotiated minor roads leading toward the village, Millie seemed to recover from her long-haul tiredness; she became increasingly animated looking at the scenery. Eventually she exclaimed, 'There it is, Richard!' pointing to the spire of St Eke's. Worse caught a glimpse of it, and said so. Millie was delighted for him.

He wasn't really confident of seeing it again until their car pulled into Old Forge Lane and stopped outside the Misgivingston house, directly opposite the church.

Whether it was waiting by a window, precision calculation, or paranormal sensing, both her parents emerged from the house before Worse had his car door open. Millie jumped out and hugged her mother, then father, then managed both together. Worse, who had conversed with them many times on video calls, shook hands with Philip, and was given a restrained embrace by Veronica. Philip helped with bags, showed them to their bedroom, and announced that when they were settled in, tea would be available in the kitchen at five minutes' notice.

—

'I hardly remember a thing. Not because of concussion. From the speed of it all. I couldn't see anything, except bright, very bright, headlights coming up behind, then passing, then crossing in front of me and its brake light coming on as it forced me over, off the road.'

They were sitting around the kitchen table. Worse and Millie had been keen to get a first-hand account of the incident.

'Could you say what sort of vehicle it was? Sedan, van, estate?' asked Millie.

'Unfortunately, no,' said Philip. 'Well, perhaps a van.'

'Any sense of its colour? Light, dark?' she asked.

'Light, I would guess.'

'I take it that you have no dashcam,' said Worse.

'Again, unfortunately no.'

'Do you know if there was actual contact between the vehicles?' asked Worse. He was hoping for the possibility of paint analysis.

'I don't think so.'

'On your drive back, did you notice anything odd, a vehicle stopped off road, bad driving, anything at all?' asked Worse.

'I'm afraid not,' said Philip.

Worse pushed his chair back from the table, but sat forward to speak.

'You said headlights, Philip, then brake light, singular. Are you telling us there was only one, that the other was out?'

'My God, Worse, I wasn't counting.'

Worse caught a *Relax it a bit* glance from Millie. He softened his voice, even if the underlying fact of exact interrogation remained.

'I'm sure you weren't. But it's the asymmetry that you would sense, subitize, even under duress. And, just now, your unconscious spoke the singular when, with no extra cost in syllables, it could have been "lights".'

Worse paused, allowing time for the argument to steep. He looked at Millie. Her eyes were fixed on Philip, which Worse took as permission to continue. Even so, he would inject a little community plural to dilute his role as chief examiner—after all, he did see himself as a sort of probationary son-in-law.

'Tell us this, Philip: If you were forced to choose between one brake light and two, what would it be?'

Philip stared at Worse for a few seconds, before closing his eyes.

'I believe I would answer one.'

2 THE FIRST EVENING

[Thursday]

'Well, Worse, let me say it again: What a delight it is to meet you in person, and to have our daughter back from the Antipodes for a time. Notwithstanding the seriousness of your visit.'

During introductions that morning, it was established that Philip would address Worse by surname, and Veronica would use Richard.

Philip raised his glass. 'Quench'n'temper.'

They all sipped their drinks. Millie directed a perceptible eye-roll to Worse.

'Don't mind Philip, Richard. Sometimes he speaks in riddles.'

'The toast?' said Worse. 'It was fine. Surely a riddle is the most holey of holeys in any fine home.'

Worse paused, apparently to consider the problem.

'A call to moderation. Pleasure with restraint,' he continued. 'Or perhaps a steeling cry before some knightly charge. Were there blade makers in your family, Philip?'

'Yes, Worse! Yes! You have it! My grandmother ended a dynasty of cutlers in Sheffield by marrying an Oxford rogue who gambled her fortune away, leaving little but that family toast. In my study there are archive boxes of company records and some heirloom pieces that I plan to sort through one day for Millie and Nicholas. Are you familiar with the history of steelmaking, Worse?'

Worse picked up a dessert spoon, rotating its hallmark into view. 'Very little after eighteen-ten[1], no.'

Philip took a few seconds to process the answer, then chuckled as he reached for his glass.

'Oh, very good, Worse. Very good.'

Millie sent a glance of exasperation to her mother, but

secretly she was pleased that Worse and her father were relating, even if on some arcane matter.

'Actually, my metals interest over the years has been in bell casting,' said Worse. He omitted mention of gun barrel steels and projectile alloys. 'I hope to examine the St Eke's one while I'm here. Photograph the foundry stamps; perhaps take a surreptitious scraping for assay and isotope signature, if you think your Kentish musicians wouldn't detect a change in timbre.'

'Worse, that would be unforgivable vandalism ... never once perpetrated in the Home Counties.' Philip's expression changed from faux outraged to conspiratorial. 'However, I'm sure an innocuous little thieving party could be organized. For the tiniest of scrapings, you promise. We'll need to poison the steeple bulldog, of course.'

'Philip, that's not very funny,' said Veronica.

'I just meant figuratively: evade, incapacitate harmlessly ... circumvent, as the situation required.'

'Bulldog?' asked Worse.

'A verger, named Mansion. Then there's His Reverence, the choleric Canon, named Simony. Charm won't work on him; he doesn't know about it. Your choice is subterfuge or authority. And Worse, don't do anything on your own. We need to consider that the *Stēpel Malison* may have re-emerged with William's death.'

'Malison?'

'The Steeple Curse. In the Middle Ages, some famous pilgrims met untimely deaths within those walls.'

'They were murdered? In the St Eke's tower?' asked Worse.

'Almost certainly. Will and I have been researching some of that history. According to contemporary accounts, the spire of St Eke's was reputed to project great sacredness to pilgrims, a sort of *Salvator Mundi* in the Kentish distance. Only it seems to have housed a dreadful profanity as well. Not advertised to the faithful, of course.'

'Tell Richard about the swints, Philip,' said Veronica.

'You know that swints alight exclusively on holy ground, church belfries and so on, all over Britain,' said Philip, addressing Worse.

'All over the world; I do know,' said Worse.

'Not here. Not St Eke's,' inserted Veronica.

'Records go back centuries,' said Philip. 'It's part of the *Malison*.'

'You subscribe to a curse, what, seven hundred years old?' asked Worse, with no hint of incredulity.

'I'm not saying that. I'm simply reporting that others have. Generations have,' said Philip.

'Well, we've lost Will, in a bizarrely similar fashion,' said Veronica. 'Philip, you are not to enter that tower. Millie and I forbid it.'

She reached out to Millie for support.

'No, Dad. Leave matters to the expendables.'

Three expressions of mild shock were turned on Millie.

'I mean professionals, obviously ... I'm tired.'

Worse looked at Millie but spoke absently. 'You know, we can see that steeple from our bedroom window.'

No one responded. Veronica pushed her chair back.

'Returning to the theme of cutlery, it's time we put some to use.' She moved toward the kitchen.

'Can I help?' said Millie.

'No, darling. Next course, yes, but relax for now. Try to teach your father the difference between sensible and dispensable.'

—

'Worse, I know you're a Magnacart. You don't seem aware that one of the prominent pilgrims murdered in the steeple was a namesake: Geoffrey Magnacart, in 1369.'

Worse stared at Philip, shaking his head slightly. Philip continued.

'The best account is given by Henry Oldrice, who was evidently on that particular pilgrimage and wrote about it in *Th Pylgrymes Wey*. When I was at school, some were lucky enough to study it—my own misfortune was to be cast into the Chaucer stream instead. Vastly inferior. Anyway, Will and I have been reading that period as part of our research into the history of St Eke's.'

'That was your project together?' asked Worse.

'Well, it began as the story of Steeple Resting, but it soon became clear that most of the unmentionable scandal in our past was concentrated beneath that spire.'

'And, needless to say, it was the unmentionable that those two most wanted to mention,' said Veronica to Worse.

'Was there pushback from the Church when that became your focus?' asked Worse.

'Not really. Not the Church as such. The staff themselves were often unhelpful, though. Mansion, for one; he seems to have entered the world congenitally obdurate.'

'Was anyone positively helpful?' asked Worse. 'Actually encouraging?'

'There were some. In fact, many, to be fair. And Will had a gift with people; gentle and diplomatic, able to share his enthusiasm for history.'

'You will miss him, Dad,' said Millie.

'We all will,' said Veronica. 'He was a lovely man.'

Philip just nodded slightly, and the table fell silent. They were remembrance seconds.

Worse waited before changing the subject.

'What more do you know about Geoffrey Magnacart?' he asked.

'First, tell me this: your name, Worse—how did that enter your Magnacart line?' said Philip.

'It's never been certain. Not by marriage. The family legend is that an errant ancestor was judged worse than bad but better than worst, and ultimately set free in the world labelled accordingly.'

Philip kept looking at Worse. 'Do you know what a Worsener is?'

'Satroit presumably did; there's one in tomorrow's requiem,' interrupted Millie.

'Not really,' said Worse. 'Taken literally, one given to worsen matters, I thought.'

'True for some, quite the opposite for others,' said Philip.

'An avenger, of sorts, are you saying?' asked Millie.

'That seems likely, at least partly so, yes,' said Philip, 'though the exact meaning of the word, and nature of the role, have been lost over the years. Anyway, Oldrice states quite unequivocally that Geoffrey Magnacart was a King's Worsener. It occurs to me that your name might be explained by usage shift from the title of office, in which case you are a descendant of that order of knighthood.'

Millie grinned at Worse. 'Richard Magnacart Worsener ... Sir Richard, to be proper!'

Worse looked unimpressed. Millie wasn't finished.

'Now you'll have to do knightly deeds.' She raised her right arm, wielding an imaginary sword. 'Quench'n'temper!' she cried.

—

'Philip's retirement passion is philology,' said Millie. 'And history. Why he read medicine is the great family mystery.'

They were finished eating. Millie had rather proudly introduced Worse to her mother's academic and personal achievements; now it was her father's turn.

'For the vocabulary, naturally,' said her father.

'Dad! That isn't true.'

'And the hubristics,' he added. Philip leaned towards Millie, his voice bordering on tragedian. 'And for the metaphysics; of illness and despair.'

He sat back. When he spoke, it was difficult to gauge his seriousness.

'Imagine: a word for every fragile human part. Another for every ailment of every part. And all of these in tenuous bondage to a fat companion dictionary of hope-remedies—named, memorized, and half discarded in a physician's lifetime. What could better define the human condition?'

'He's just being tendentious, Richard,' said Millie. She

scowled at her father. 'You were known as a brilliant and compassionate family doctor in these parts. Why would you pretend that wonderful person away?'

'Ah. Compassion. I have discovered it to be an arrangement of letters like any other.' Philip addressed Worse. 'Millie tells me you're medically trained. What did that arrangement spell for you?'

He reached for his wine glass, holding it without drinking. Worse was given no time to reply.

'My experience has been that one day I was young and the next old. In between was a restless long night of working and worrying. And, I suppose, compassion.'

Philip's voice had dropped, to almost inaudible at the end. The bonhomie that began the evening was extinguished, replaced by this thinking man's revealed introspection: deeply personal, confessional, and regretful.

Veronica and Millie looked extremely concerned for him. They probably also felt some awkwardness that such a baring of the self was happening in front of Worse, who during this time had been observing Philip silently.

Eventually, Worse spoke.

'Poetry, perhaps.'

The others looked at him, expecting some explanation, which didn't come.

'What do you mean, "poetry"?' said Millie.

'Might better define the human condition.'

There was a moment spent relocating the thread. For Millie and Veronica, this delivered a certain relief that the conversation was drawn away from the anguished, back to the intellectual.

Something similar happened for Philip, whose face lightened with renewed interest. He was the first to speak.

'Possibly, Worse. But for poetry, you still need words.'

It was an assertion, but also questioning.

'And yet, for compassion, you don't,' said Worse. He looked at Millie, signalling I've had enough for tonight.

Millie stood up.

'My arrangement of letters spells "tired". I'm going to bed.'

'Yes, so must I,' said Worse. 'That was a wonderful meal, and conversation. Thank you, both.' He looked at Philip. 'I look forward to hearing more of those ideas.'

'Sleep well,' said Veronica. 'There's no rush in the morning.'

Worse thought she was probably pleased to have time alone with Philip.

'Oh Worse, before you go,' interrupted Philip. The seriousness was still there, but the subject lighter. 'Why is a riddle the most holy of holies?'

'Ah!' said Worse. 'The riddle in the griddle is the griddle in the riddle.'

—

'Don't mind Philip, Richard. He wasn't himself tonight.'

They were standing on opposite sides of their bed, undressing.

'Oh, I like him; he's complex,' said Worse. 'He obviously enjoys playing with challenging ideas. Is he genuinely cynical, about medicine particularly?'

'He's not a cynic at all. He's a natural enthusiast. That was all completely out of character.'

'Had he been drinking, do you think? Was it disinhibition? That's an occupational hazard in the profession.'

'No. He doesn't. Didn't you see? He likes to pick up his glass, but almost never drinks from it. It's always been his way.'

'Yes, I did see that. Of course, a plausible explanation is that meeting his daughter's choice of partner has leached all happiness from his heart.'

'No, no. He likes you, I can tell.' Millie bent over to step out of her briefs. 'My concern is that he's become depressed. I need to talk to Mum about him.'

Worse turned serious. 'But you must have noticed that depressive introspection, the negativity, didn't come through until near the end, when you began to talk more personally about him, medicine and the history interest, and so on.'

They both processed the observation.

'So, why would he abruptly behave out of character in front of me?' asked Worse.

'I suspect you had nothing to do with it. He's coming to terms with losing Will. He's grieving. They were close, and the history projects they shared were very important to Dad. Now he's facing the shock of learning that his friend was probably murdered. That must raise doubts about his own safety; particularly whether the road rage business was more sinister than he took it to be.'

'As we have doubts,' said Worse, lying down.

'And it's all happened in the setting of recent retirement. That's been a huge thing, to give away his professional persona. There's a normal grieving around that too. Not to mention the instability; anxiety about what to do from now on, fundamental questions about identity, direction, purpose in life, meaning[2].'

'Yes, I'm sure there is. I understand that. But grief and loss and anxiety are very different matters from depression. As you said, that's the possibility to address. When you talk to your mother, make sure that he has his own regular GP. I would start there.'

They were both quiet for several seconds.

'Tomorrow is the funeral, Richard. Remember, you're performing.'

'I hadn't forgotten. We're going to rock this parish.'

Millie had pulled down the bedclothes on her side but paused before getting in, looking at Worse. He loved her complete lack of self-consciousness around her own nudity.

'By the way, where did that griddle business come from? Dad looked more confused after it than before.'

'Ah, a classic riddling triumph, then. I confess: I composed it for the occasion, over dessert,' said Worse. 'Don't you think most people would prefer to go to sleep partly puzzled rather than have all the mystery of their day explained?'

Millie grinned, pointing a finger at Worse. 'You evil, evil man,' she said, slipping into bed beside him.

'Puzzle me partly, then.'

---

[1] That is, 18/10: percentage content of chromium and nickel, respectively, in iron—being a common specification for flatware stainless steel.

[2] A meaning facetiously reimagined by Wallis Pioniv, Rede Professor in Logic at Nazarene, in a valedictory for an opinionated colleague. Of their shared academic passion, he asked: Why is it that we have logic?

> Because logic allows us to extend our knowledge of the world—to assert true statements—by reasoning, rather than by observation. Indeed, were logic sufficiently powerful, we could all sit at home, never venture out, and still claim to know everything. This, I am told, is already a favoured style of modern retirement naturally suited to certain individuals.

3 MORNING BRIEFING

For much of Millie's childhood, the Misgivingston house on Old Forge Lane had, as was usual for a village solo general practice, an attached surgery and dispensary with separate street access for patients. When the demands of the community required that Philip invite in a partner, the whole operation was relocated centrally to larger, purpose-renovated premises just off the market square. After Millie and Nicholas had left home for university studies, Philip and Veronica returned the old surgery to more domestic functions, including a large guest bedroom having a private sitting area and bathroom at the front, with the separate entry preserved. Within the family, this converted east wing was still referred to as 'the Surgery'. It was where Millie and Worse were housed.

Behind the guest suite were storage rooms and other utility spaces, and at rear two generously sized home offices for Veronica and Philip, both having southerly aspects over open fields.

Since Philip's retirement, the paraphernalia of new interests had rapidly supplanted medical texts and journals in his study. Some historical research materials he had accumulated over the years, but much of his newest library was acquired under guidance from William, or been gifted or loaned by him.

From now on, being in that room would forever remind Philip of his friend. But before those feelings could find their equilibrium, there was a duty to discharge: to explain William's death, to identify perpetrators, and to see justice done.

—

This morning, Philip, Worse, and Millie were meeting in Philip's study. Most available wall space was taken up with bookshelves. The curtains were drawn open, offering a view of the fields and a blue sky. Philip caught Worse appreciating the vista.

'We've been fortunate. Nearly all the new housing is on the other side of the village, towards Canterbury.'

'I was thinking it's a fine day for a funeral,' said Worse.

There were two sofas facing each other, with a coffee table between them. Worse and Millie sat on one, with Philip on the other.

'Could we begin, Philip, with you telling us when you and Veronica last had contact with William, in person or otherwise?'

'Will was here on the Friday evening, working in this room, with me.'

Philip paused, looking around his study.

'He stayed for supper with us, then left around ten-thirty.'

'What arrangement did you have to see each other after that?' asked Worse.

'It was left informal. We were always calling in on each other for research chats.'

'Did William mention any plans that he might have had? Anything on the weekend, for example?' asked Millie.

'He only spoke about the reading he needed to do. But that was typical Will. He spent his life reading.'

'Millie, do you have further questions on that?' asked Worse.

'Not for now.'

'In that case, can we move on to the evidence for William's death being homicide, rather than natural or misadventure?' said Worse.

Philip nodded. 'The post-mortem toxicology is suspicious but not yet definite. As I understand it, there are abnormalities that need further analysis. They are obviously confident enough of getting an answer that they released his remains for burial.'

'I will chase that up shortly,' said Worse.

'The other thing is,' Philip continued, 'Will's shop was found burgled the day his body was discovered.'

'That's the bookshop, right?' said Millie.

'A very out-of-the-ordinary bookshop. Antiquarian, first editions, and so on; cadastral and other historical maps; manuscripts, even some illuminated ones. Selected modern works also, but not a lot. It's in the square. Will had a flat above it.'

'Any leads on that, CCTV, witnesses, for example?' said Worse.

'I haven't been told of any.'

'Do you know what went missing?' asked Worse.

'Unfortunately, no. I wasn't completely familiar with his holdings in the first place.'

'Had he ever been broken into before, over the years?' asked Worse.

'I'm sure, never,' said Philip. 'The average villain has no idea of the worth of that kind of stock, or how to pass it on for cash.'

'I imagine not,' said Worse. 'Can we visit his shop?'

'We can. I have a key, and the police seem to be done there.'

'Excuse me, team. Sorry to interrupt.'

It was Veronica, at the study door.

'Richard, there's a stern-looking courier out the front with some packages for you, and a quite admonishing refusal to let me sign for them on your behalf. He wants to see you, sight ID, get your signature, and photograph you holding the parcels. What are you into, the atomic secrets trade?'

Worse stood up and smiled, with a non-committal tilt of his head.

'More ... experimental literature, speculative science, ulterior fiction.'

Veronica looked bemused. Worse elaborated.

'Atomic secrets are last-century, worthless in comparison.

These days, it is authors who imperil humanity, and also preserve it. Excuse me.'

At the door, he thanked Veronica and turned to the others.

'We shall have another riddler in the house, Philip.'

Philip looked blank, turning to Millie for help. She shrugged.

—

A few minutes later, Worse returned, holding the packages. He put them on the carpet at his end of the sofa.

'Bad books, for later,' he said, without further explanation.

As if he had never been absent, Worse continued. 'And other evidence?'

Philip took a moment to re-assimilate.

'I believe there were threats,' he said.

Worse sat forward. 'What form did they take?'

'I should first say that threat is my idea. Will didn't think it was so, and showed little interest. He certainly never reported them to the police.'

Philip fell silent. Millie sensed Worse's impatience, and offered assistance.

'What form did they take?' she asked.

'Calling cards, through the letter flap at the shop. Will gave me the first one, a few weeks ago, for my opinion.'

He lifted a manila folder from the coffee table in front of them, removed a business card, and handed it to the space between Millie and Worse, saying 'Exhibit Alif' as he did.

Worse took it by the edges, turned it over to ascertain that the reverse was blank, then read the only type on the obverse.

'Al-Sedeqim.'

'Arabic?' said Millie. She looked at Philip.

'Not, actually. Intended to imitate Arabic, I would say. My diagnosis is a Latin corruption. *Sedecim*. What does that mean, Millie?'

Worse sensed something inquisitorial in Philip's tone; it brought to mind a black-gowned Latin master towering close with fierce eyes, and he felt an oddly visceral relief when she answered confidently.

'Sixteen'. Millie enjoyed this small triumph with her father. 'I'm a mathematician, and it's a number,' she said, as if an explanation were necessary.

'Is it a particularly interesting number?' asked Philip.

'All numbers are particularly interesting,' said Millie. 'As you might say of all words.'

Philip looked pleased. Worse realized that he was overhearing old business between them. Philip was the philologist and Veronica was the mathematician, and Millie had followed her mother. Millie's brother, Nicholas, had taken both routes. He was a mathematician working in the Ferendes for the Cambridge-led Language Diversity Initiative. Worse knew him well.

'Sixteen certainly seems of particular interest to the party who sent it,' said Philip. 'That was the first card. All the following ones were identical to this.'

He handed over a second card. Its only printed content was 'XVI'.

'What do you think sixteen means, in the context?' asked Worse.

'I think, to avoid suggestion bias, that I should leave that hypothesis for each of you to form independently,' said Philip. 'Then we compare.'

Worse valued this discipline in others. He held up the cards.

'May I keep these, for now?'

'Yes, Worse. I could be wrong, of course. About threats, that is.'

Worse moved the discussion on.

'Could you give us the timeline, Philip, of William's discovery, estimated time of death, involvement of the police, and so on?'

'So, Will was found on the Monday morning, just after eight, by Mansion. He phoned the Canon in Canterbury, who contacted the police. A team arrived at the church at nine twenty, brought in the coroner, and conducted enquiries, as they like to put it. Simony was here before the police, at about eight forty-five.'

'Was Simony cooperative, do you know?' asked Worse.

Philip smiled. 'I believe the Canon would be viewed by many in this parish as incapable of being civil, let alone helpful.'

'But not obstructionist?' said Worse.

'Who knows?' said Philip. 'He's probably capable of subtlety, even if it's not in evidence.'

'The dangerous kind,' observed Worse. 'And time of death?'

'Not precise at present; ten o'clock Sunday night to three in the morning. The ambient cold in that tower is difficult to estimate, especially the flagstone floor temperature. The police set up thermometry recording for a few nights. Apparently, they may also refine that five-hour window after doing some advanced chemistry on their samples.'

'How do you know all this, Dad?' asked Millie.

'Through our village keeper of the peace, PC Rence; he's a reliable source,' said Philip. 'I should have mentioned: Rence was at the church too, joining Simony at about nine am, I think.'

'Presumably there were services on that Sunday?' asked Worse.

'The usual programme. Evensong finished at seven thirty. The church was empty and dark from soon after nine o'clock.'

'Evensong conducted by Simony?' asked Millie.

'As far as I know,' said Philip. He looked at Worse. 'Veronica and I are not regulars, as Millie would be aware.'

'Was William a regular?' asked Worse.

'He was an occasional. He made, shall we say, secular visits; astutely timed to avoid services. His interest was in the heritage, architecture, and so on.'

'Do you know how he got to be there on Sunday night? Did he have a car parked in the street, anything like that?' asked Worse.

'No car,' said Philip. 'Will lived in antiquity, in many ways.'

'He had no mobile phone?' asked Millie.

'No mobile. A fixed-line relic in the shop met his needs.'

'How long would it take to walk from William's flat to the church?' asked Worse.

'Fifteen minutes, for Will, I would say,' said Philip.

Worse stood up. 'Not sixteen, then. If you will excuse me, I'd like a little time to collect my thoughts before the funeral. Thank you for all that, Philip. You two carry on. Had William been in good health, generally, do you know?'

'As far as we were aware, excellent,' said Philip. 'Will always walked from his place to ours, whatever the weather, no matter the time.'

'How was the weather on Sunday night?'

'Clear, I think. Crisp.' Philip gestured for Worse to remain for a moment. 'I mentioned the Henry Oldrice text last night. I strongly suggest that you two read this.'

He lifted up a volume that had been obscured under files on the coffee table. 'Some background to Steeple Resting. Relevant, I believe. I'll give it to Millie.'

—

Worse collected his packages and left. In the Surgery sitting room, he chose a chair under the window, sat down, and thought about Philip's information. He arrived at two conclusions: nothing that he heard was surprising, and foul play was a certainty.

He opened the first package and scanned its contents. They included an up-to-date account of the police investigation along with photographs, statements from witnesses, and a preliminary coroner's report with laboratory findings and a schedule of toxicology studies yet to be finalized. The summary finding was 'Unnatural Death. Hydrogen sulphide implicated.'

Parcelled separately within this package were a warrant card conferring power of arrest, weapon licence, and a list of contacts within Kent Police and New Scotland Yard. He was afforded the courtesy rank of Adjunct Chief Inspector, and supplied with business cards for introductions.

Worse knew what was in the second package before opening it: a Totengräber 9, and a full ammunition clip. He held the barrel up to daylight, checking the sight; they were never defective. This weapon was unused, and not from a police armoury. He had Victor Spoiling in Perth to thank for that, and for enabling the access he was now provided.

He thought of his friend. Wherever Worse travelled in the world, Victor seemed able to arrange for all his investigatory and personal protection needs, deploying an influence far exceeding his rank of Inspector. Worse never fully understood why this was so. He knew that Victor was unusual for a police professional, having published many papers and some monographs on logic, ethics, criminal psychology, and the role of police in society. But, as Worse understood it, these were better received in philosophy departments than police academies. He determined, one day, to interrogate Victor and expose whatever secrets might explain the deference he enjoyed. When he had tried that in the past, the response was always of the form, 'No, no, Worse, it is *your* fame that achieves these things, not mine', a blatant formula of charm, flattery, and untruth that pleaded no further trespass on the matter.

For now, he simply sent a previously agreed coded message confirming the safe arrival of his parcels, and set about reading.

—

'What's all this?' Millie entered the sitting room.

'Kent Police case file on William's death, thanks to Victor,' said Worse. 'Hydrogen sulphide was the cause, I'm certain.'

Millie looked grateful that it was Worse doing the reading.

'Well, hurry up. There's more homework to do. Philip's given us this to study. I've read the ending.'

She held up the book that Philip had produced when Worse was leaving the meeting earlier. He caught the title: *An Annotated Th Pylgrymes Wey: Translation and Commentary*, by A B C Darian.

'Darian? Really? He doesn't go away.' The tone was slightly complaining. In the past, Worse had considered his privacy invaded by the historian.

'I know. The "Seer of the South", some are now calling him,' said Millie. 'Still writing, despite allegedly being locked down in Madregalo, evading extradition calls from offshore culture warriors, not to mention detain-and-disappear orders from the nearby dictatorships.'

'You sound sympathetic,' said Worse. 'Madregalo's not such a bad place. Anyway, the last I heard he was hiding away supposedly working on the long-promised Great Ferende Novel. How inflammatory can that be?'

'I haven't a view. But I'm guessing there's some monetized mythologizing around him, probably invented by his publisher[1]. Artist exile is a romantic notion, these days—exploiting the genuinely tragic. Many profess it.'

'Do I detect a newly acquired cynicism here?'

'Well, if so, Richard, I've learned it from you.'

'I think I'm pleased.'

'I'm simply saying, looking at the preface in this, it appears he's travelled very nicely indeed, thank you, on fellowships and research visits.'

'Mm. I'm not surprised. Mythology is a delicate titration,' observed Worse, 'easily misjudged; not always relatable.'

'Titration?'

'Yes. Of deception into credulity. To an endpoint translucency where the subject can see, but not see through.'

Worse hesitated. 'In theory, there's the making of a perfect false alibi, for example.'

He paused again. 'Actually, when you think about it, that is precisely the base alchemy of fiction[2] generally, given and received, don't you agree?'

Millie wasn't sure. She placed Darian's volume on the coffee table and pointed to it.

'Perhaps so, but this is different. However questionable Darian's credentials may be, Oldrice himself is no wizard of lies in the way you're suggesting. It feels entirely factual. As you will find, Richard, when you read about your presumptive ancestor, Geoffrey Magnacart, in the final chapter. The thirty-seventh Tale.'

If Worse had been the source of previous cynicism, it vanished from his face as he looked down at Darian's book.

Millie gave him a few seconds, before continuing. 'Also, here's my mother's copy of *Damascene*, for this afternoon. Are you ready for your performance, Richard?'

'Yes, I'm ready.'

---

[1] The author records, under advisement, that Ms Alison Pilcrow, for UITA Press, denies categorically this or any similar promotional artifice concerning Dr Darian.

[2] Worse seems unaware that his 'alchemy of fiction' recapitulates (at least, in certain aspects of imagery) an earlier cosmology having an aristocratic (no less) imprimatur. In 'The Origin of Story', from her collection *Aliquots*, Isobel Beckoner portrays the whimsical enchantress Fabula regulating the tap of a Divine Burette of Make-Believe—dispensing from on high exact measures of fancy and falsehood into the once-barren, realist realm of Mortals. The very pleasing quality of Fabula, for most, is that along with strife and drama, she sends wonder and laughter to the world.

4 REQUIEM FOR THE MURDERED

[Friday]

Draw close the whispering shore. That difficulty
is more a remoteness of the mind.
Now turns the earth to my hiding-spade, before
an arc's thought, or mourning substance weighed.

This is an undone day. Summon
a Worsener to pray. Wind the ghost
in porphyry cloth, with lutesong recitation
for its rite. Slow the light to walking pace
Enough to sew the rents of purpose in my stay.
and in the step of constant evening place
unnatural cause and bloody consequence upon
that near imagined coast.

Then listen by my swollen ground.
Within its thousand shallow artifacts of protest
I keep a stolen breath. It is for accusation.

Millie began, reading the part of orator, while Worse, standing
beside her at the lectern, voiced the plaintiff interjections.
For the closing lines, he looked up from the text, his delivery
rasping bitterness into the words of William Dale Whencely,
deceased.

When finished, he continued surveying the congregants as
if searching out an individual for *accusation*. Even Millie felt
discomfort. She placed a hand on his shoulder, persuading
him to their places in the front pew. As he walked, Worse held
Satroit's *Damascene* close to his heart—the way some might
carry a prayer book in that setting.

They sat down. Their audience, perhaps unsettled by this bold stranger's interrogating stare, and, as happens, possibly affected by irrational guilt, remained silent. Millie whispered in Worse's ear.

'I think that went well, Richard.'

Worse was looking at the casket, and didn't respond.

—

The Reverend Canon Simony, eyes fixed on Worse as if beholding the actual Devil for the first time, was slow to rise from his ceremonial faldstool. The delay gave opportunity for the brethren to begin an indecorous murmuring that persisted until His Reverence raised an arm, bent at the elbow. It might otherwise have been a village traffic warden's gesture to stop, but was here given Inquisitional gravity by a brimstone glare and the billowing sleeve of a white surplice. All chatter ceased on the instant.

'Let us pray.'

—

Through the centuries, the graveyard of St Eke's has expanded eastwards as well as over the River Anas, which here is narrow but deep, into the parish meadow on its northern bank. When Worse and Millie emerged from the church, the cortège was at some distance, about to cross the twelfth-century wheatstone[1] bridge to what is termed the North Ground. Millie's father, as a pall-bearer, walked beside the coffin, but Veronica had waited, and the three fell in at the rear of the line of mourners.

'Picturesque, isn't it?'

Millie was looking at a white, four-post canopy tent on the other bank. Next to this, contrasted with the green lawn, was a pile of black earth. Two gravediggers, resting against shovels thrust into the ground, stared at the procession. They wore white-collared shirts with black waistcoat and tie.

'For the living, yes,' said Worse.

'You don't imagine the porphyry-sheeted ghost looking down to share the spectacle?'

'I do not.'

Worse's reply was slightly sharp, and Millie was silenced for a few seconds. But she had more to say.

'At least the invocation's answered. A shore is close. And those would be Satroit's hiding-spades, I take it.'

'Yes. Indeed. Hiding-spades and a meaning of turned earth,' said Worse.

Veronica looked at Worse, touching his elbow. 'An apposite reading you chose, Richard, given the circumstances; and well delivered, both of you—more sentiment in a short phrase than our esteemed Canon can command in the whole Lord's Prayer.'

'Well, that compliment belongs to the poet,' said Worse.

'Oh, I think you two can share in the appreciation. By the way, I'm still not sure what the Worsener reference means.'

'No,' said Worse.

—

The burial site was high on the sloping riverbank. Worse and Millie positioned themselves uphill, from where they had a view of the open grave, the Anas, and beyond it the fabric and spire of St Eke's. Veronica moved to stand beside Philip.

The interment service was conducted by Canon Simony. At their distance, Worse was aware only of fast monotone prayers of commendation accompanied by dramatic swooshes of the surplice. As the coffin was lowered on royal purple straps, Martin Allegorio's *Committal of St Anthony* resonated from an ageing portable CD player. Philip touched a handkerchief to his eyes.

When it was their turn, Millie stepped forward to take a rose from a flower basket proffered by a funeral company attendant; she dropped it onto the coffin. Worse followed, but chose to throw a scoop of earth. He stared into the grave for several seconds, contemplating the random scatter of black soil on the white coffin lid: its mystery was rudely ended by an explosion of rose petals thrust by a pushy mourner next in line.

—

Worse and Millie joined her parents to walk back over the bridge. They were headed to the parish hall for the traditional exchange of memories and condolences over refreshments.

'Speaking of the picturesque ...' said Worse.

Millie smiled. She was becoming accustomed to the long caesura in Worse's conversation.

'... do you know of Hans Sucher's *Memo Szenario*—said to be the essential directors' guide?' He didn't wait for an answer. 'Scene 13: Funerals should take the form of burials in bleak and beautiful settings. Quite like this one. They offer more poignancy per frame than the off-camera cremation. Bonus emotives for light drizzle and a sea of black umbrellas. Extra points also for a veiled woman, solitary, standing at a distance.'

Millie nodded thoughtfully.

'There's something else, of course,' said Worse. 'Burials allow the plot device, the drama, of an exhumation further along. The alternative, raking through cremains, would never work.'

'Cremains?'

'Cremation remains, ashes; as opposed to buried bones.'

'You've made that up.'

'No, I haven't. I wouldn't. It's the least beautiful word in archaeology, surpassing even decoffination.'

'Decoffination? You've made that up.'

'No, I haven't. Do you know how to identify the archaeology majors in a campus canteen?'

'They carry spades?'

'They order decoffinated caffee.'

Millie eye-rolled a visible groan.

Worse paused, in pursuit of a thought. 'Cremains or bones. Perhaps we should choose our physical afterlife depending on the concept we prefer: portmanteau or synecdoche.'

Worse paused again, this time for review. 'Or, meanings aside, which word most appeals to the ear: mellow French or sharpened Greek.'

He ended the digression by looking at Millie. 'Anyway, burial's the selling storyline in film. According to Sucher, only the grand, ceremonial funeral pyre can compete, most exquisitely with a climactic, selfless act of suttee—that, of course, would be your role, in this instance.'

'Richard!'

—

As they walked through the old graveyard, the church bell sounded. Worse excused himself, saying he would meet them later at the wake. He left the gravelled path and made his way on the grass between ancient, weathered headstones to the north-west door of St Eke's.

Inside was a table displaying pamphlets, maps, and newsletters of interest to parishioners and visitors. He stopped and looked at several, selecting one on the architectural history of St Eke's and one on the church bell, paying for them with coins to the honour box. Then he moved to sit on the rearmost pew on the south side of the nave, filing his acquisitions between the pages of Satroit.

Up in the chancel two women churchwardens were sorting wreaths and floral bunches from the funeral, placing some on a flat wooden barrow. These, Worse surmised, would be wheeled to the gravesite, there to become—in a blameless paraphrase of St Augustine[2]—an outward and visible sign of a mortal's earthly passage, which is brilliance into decay.

The women were quiet in their work, and he wondered how close they were, what they were thinking. Worse himself thought this: there would likely come a day when one performed the equivalent task for the other, and he briefly entertained approaching them to share the pathos. Of course, he would not do that; faith and fatalism find no comfort in each other, and this was a church, it had to be remembered.

The bell-ringing stopped. A minute later, Worse heard squeaking hinges behind him. He turned to see Mansion, the verger, emerge from the sexton's door to St Eke's tower.

'Hello,' said Worse as Mansion passed his pew, walking toward the choir.

The greeting wasn't returned. Worse watched as Mansion mounted the chancel steps to extinguish the altar candles using a long-handled snuffing cup. He moved to the pulpit, appeared to sort service papers, then conferred with the women before making a call on his mobile phone as he left through a vestry door on the south side.

One of the gravediggers entered by the north-west door, passing Worse without acknowledgement as he proceeded to the chancel. There, he exchanged words, inaudible to Worse, with the women before taking up the flower barrow and wheeling it through the same priest's door.

Worse had come to the church for some solitary, reflective time, and to relive the funeral service as a non-participant, to spectate from the back of the room, as it were. Instead, he was left musing that the working traffic and mundane activities of a church in recess were quite intriguing. The thought was reinforced when, just as he stood to leave, Canon Simony burst through the south-west door.

It was an entrance befitting a fugitive, as no doubt he was, thought Worse, escaping the insufferable tea party that is a stranger's wake. As he swept past, Worse offered a greeting. It probably wasn't helpful that this included a raised hand holding his volume of *Damascene*; whatever the case, the Canon showed no warmth or even recognition.

Worse decided that there was no polite sociability, or more importantly assistance, to be had there; he would go about his enquiries unannounced. He walked over to the entry leading to the basement of the tower. The door was sprung shut, decorated with an unshot wrought iron bolt on the outside. As anticipated, it squeaked loudly when he pulled it open.

Inside, it was quite dark, the only natural light filtering through belfry windows and steeple louvres high above, and further attenuated by a platform below the bell. Worse was impatient to look around, and sought out a light switch near the door.

As he expected from the church exterior, the space was roughly square. Strictly described, it was gnomonic, as the north-west corner was walled in with a square-sectioned, chimney-like structure having an entrance through which were visible the lower treads of a spiral staircase. The floor was everywhere irregular, rounded flagstones, more worn and polished toward the room's centre where the bell rope hung. The air was musty. Worse stood against one wall to survey the whole.

The door squeaked, more loudly than before.

'What are you doing in here?'

It was Mansion. Officiousness never moved Worse, and he ignored the question.

'Describe to me exactly where you found William Whencely's body.'

'I'm not telling you that, or anything else.'

'And yet, you have,' said Worse. He turned his back on the verger to look around, but continued. 'I suggest you cooperate, if only out of self-interest.'

Though Worse spoke mildly, he knew his statement carried threat.

'Get fucked.'

The door slammed shut with all the force its rusty hinges would allow.

A very Anglican withdrawal, thought Worse, suited to some reimagined Protestant schism—perhaps a staged *Henry VIII*, distilled into expletive gems for the modern audience concentration span.

Using his mobile phone, he set about photographing the room, while inspecting its features in detail. The manila bell rope looked old, being blackened and greasy at grasping height, though its ferrule of crimped copper was recent. His eye followed it upward until it disappeared through a large gap in the timber platform below the bell.

Attached to the south wall, just inside the door, was a rough bench; on it was an antique wind-up clock timer, two sets of industrial earmuffs, leather gloves, and a clipboard holding typed sheets of rosters. Worse picked this up and flicked through the pages, noting the names or initials of bell-ringers other than Mansion. Further along, against the same wall and reaching to the corner, was a dusty stack of about thirty wooden folding chairs—a silent statistic, Worse concluded, of declining congregations.

On the west wall, opposite the door, a substantial oak wardrobe was fitted between the chairs and the staircase. Worse inspected it. The base was flush to the floor, and he wondered how it had ever been moved into place. The double doors were warped, their natural state being ajar. Inside were old vestry garments and faded liturgical banners on hangers. Above these, a high shelf stored laid-down candlesticks and assorted altar cups in need of silver polish, if not a complete electroplate. Altogether it was, thought Worse, a kind of purgatorial waiting place for passed-on furnishings of the sacrament. In his mind, he labelled it the Wistful Wardrobe.

The door from the nave squeaked, even more loudly than before.

'May I help you?'

It was Canon Simony. He had removed his surplice.

'Yes. Indeed. Thank you,' said Worse pleasantly. 'Could you show me the position of William Whencely's body when you first saw it?'

'I wasn't the first to see it.'

'No. That was the King's player, according to the initial police report.'

Simony looked momentarily puzzled. Worse would not accept evasive word play.

'I shall clarify: my question related to when you first saw the victim's body, not when the body was first seen.'

'If you've read the police report, I have nothing to add.'

'A conversation at the scene is far more informative than a statement on the page, I've always found,' said Worse. 'I would very much appreciate ... your assistance.'

Again, the phrasing hinted at unstated consequences. The Canon hackled up.

'You must leave. This is property of the Church.'

Worse offered no sign of acquiescence, until he spoke.

'Yes, it suits me to leave.'

He had been looking around the room as he spoke. Now he addressed Simony directly.

'But even on property of the Church, you surely know that in the hierarchy of sins, murder outranks trespass.'

Unable to contain his irritation, he added, 'Or is that not the understanding at St Eke's?'

'Will you stop going on about murder! The poor man had a heart attack. And, I might say, the reading you two perpetrated was an outrage. Despicable. Satroit's writing is the Devil's work. Half of the parish is in shock.'

'With respect, Canon Simony, you need to adjust your thinking. William Whencely's death was not natural. Which makes this ...' Worse gestured to the walls around them, '... property of the Church, most certainly a crime scene. And as a crime scene, in the matter of trespass, it is I who can order your leaving.'

Worse delayed a few seconds to read Simony's reaction, before moving past him toward the door. He pointed at the light switch.

'Have you been made aware that the electrics in here are unsafe? Not the cause of death, reassuringly, but this place does need rewiring.'

---

[1] Presumably a misrender of 'whetstone', consistent with accounts of passing Crusader knights praying at St Eke's before honing their blades on a special Anas bridge capstone—lubricated for the task with pilfered font water. (Along with others in a small walking-tour group, this author was directed by a village history guide to a fine examination of the quite indifferently weathered said capstone, declared to be 'rutted in Jerusalem holiness' by the practice.) Despite all this, regarding the bridge's material description, proposals dating from the time of Dr Johnson for a reversion to the obvious have met with determined resistance, most recently by a local activist group calling itself OhHo, reportedly, if abstrusely, a contraction of Ohmage Homage.

[2] Of Hippo, not Canterbury.

5 WHENCELY'S WAKE

[Friday]

By the time Worse stepped from St Eke's south-west porch onto the path leading to the lychgate, he was annoyed with himself.

His enquiries into William Whencely's death would not be advanced by having bad relations with church figures, and he resolved to rectify matters. He would make an appointment to speak with Canon Simony, apologize for any perceived discourteousness, and explain more fully his role as a specialist crime analyst.

It would be an opportunity to make clear the very considerable investigative powers that the position carried. Moreover, he could share just enough forensic information to convince the Canon that Whencely's death was indeed unnatural and warranted a comprehensive criminal review. If that didn't elicit cooperation, the conclusion was straightforward: His Reverence would become a person of greater interest.

At the gate, he turned west on Old Forge Lane, heading toward the parish hall. On his left, across the road, was the Misgivingston house, with Veronica's car parked at the front, just ahead of a local bus stop.

To his right was the Old Vicarage, now converted to offices and meeting rooms serving community and charitable organizations, as well as the needs of church administration. As he approached, he saw Mansion leaving the building, walking out to the lane. Worse adjusted his gait to ensure their intersection; he was determined to test out the new policy of friendly appeasement.

'Hello,' said Worse.

The response was a dark glare.

'Off to the hall?'

That was ignored.

'You know, I would be very keen to watch some bell-ringing one day. Even have a lesson, if you would be agreeable.'

Worse was repulsed by the insincerity in his own voice. Even so, this was a peace effort, and he persevered.

'And I hope to see the bell itself, if I may. I've always been fascinated by bell metallurgy and casting.'

Mansion found himself walking in the same direction at the same pace with a man he wanted to avoid. His escape was effective and boorishly non-verbal. Without a word, he stopped, turned, and headed back toward the church.

—

The parish hall was modern, in a 1960s sense of modern, set back from the road with a paved area and a square of lawn in front. Some mourners were leaving as Worse approached the door. They exchanged looks of polite recognition.

Inside was a spacious vestibule, with a trestle table holding hot water and coffee urns, along with stacks of clean cups and saucers, and milk jugs. As if captured in a kitchen wonderland version of Go, these were everywhere invaded and surrounded by thoughtlessly abandoned used cups and side plates holding biscuit and sandwich detritus, and sodden teabags.

Worse, ignoring the dilapidation, stopped to serve himself tea. As he was manipulating the hot water urn valve, a woman appeared beside him.

'Never an appetizing scene, after the elders' tea stampede, I'm afraid.'

'Oh, it's fine,' said Worse, adding unnecessarily, 'I was delayed.'

He was tempted to share that making enemies on the way proved time consuming.

'I wanted to thank you both for your reading today.'

'It was a privilege. May I pour you something?'

'No, thank you. Perhaps I should introduce myself. I'm Angela. William was my husband.'

Worse was surprised; he had not been made aware that Whencely was married.

'I'm sorry. My condolences, Angela. I've heard only wonderful things about William.'

'Well, you and I haven't spoken until now.'

That was callous. Angela apparently sensed Worse's momentary imbalance, and smiled.

'I don't really mean that. William was a good person. But we found good-person reasons to separate about eight years ago.'

Worse looked at her, nodding sympathetically. Angela continued.

'Eight years apart. And yet today I feel like a widow. His widow. It's a strange business.'

'I don't find that strange,' said Worse. 'It was an identity-in-waiting. Unremarked till the moment it's lived.'

Angela looked distracted by the thought. She moved her head, indicating a change of subject.

'Of course, I've known Millie since she was in school. It would be lovely if you both came to tea. I still live in the village.' She gestured at the trestle table. 'I think I can put together something less chaotic than this.'

'That would be very nice. I look forward to it. Speaking of Millie, I should go inside to find her.'

Worse looked toward the entrance to the main hall.

'Actually, I saw her leaving with Philip and Veronica about ten minutes before you arrived.'

Worse placed his teacup on the table, completing the encirclement of an unguarded sugar bowl. All the while, his copy of *Damascene* had been tucked under his left arm, and he now retrieved it.

'In that case, I might join them at home. I'm glad we've met, Angela, and my condolences again.'

'I'm glad too. I'll call the house with an invitation.'

—

Worse walked through to the kitchen, led there by voices. He found Millie and Veronica sitting at the table, an unopened bottle of wine and four glasses between them.

'What happened to you?' asked Millie. She pulled out the chair next to her. Worse sat down.

'I was busy thrusting my friendship into the grateful arms of St Eke's.'

'And?'

'Hard to judge,' said Worse. 'So far, one hostile verger, one angry Canon, an ill-mannered gravedigger, and two self-absorbed churchwardens. I was thinking I should return tomorrow with a fresh approach.'

'That sounds like a hard-won realization, Richard,' said Millie. She was smiling. 'Would you like some wine? We waited.'

'Thanks. Maybe later. I need a little thinking time. You start.'

Worse was actually pleased to see Millie spending time with her mother, and was keen not to curtail it, partly in the hope that Millie could gain some understanding of Philip's behaviour of the previous night. He stood up.

'At least one person was nice to me. I met William's former wife at the wake. She's going to call at some stage to invite us to tea.'

Millie looked at Veronica, and Veronica looked at Worse.

'That's very kind of her,' said Veronica.

—

Worse went to his and Millie's bedroom and lay down, his head propped up by several pillows.

He had found the interaction with Angela a little odd. That foul play was the cause of William's death had, until now, been tightly suppressed, which is why Satroit's requiem had been a controversial choice. And there was nothing in the case file to indicate that police had conducted any kind of interview with her, let alone shared their suspicions. Yet she had thanked him for that reading, without expressing curiosity about its theme. Could she have completely missed the point?

Worse put that enquiry to one side, and picked up his mobile to scroll through the day's photographs of St Eke's tower. His attention was drawn to the lower steps of the internal staircase leading to the loft and the bell. *Stēpel Malison* or not, he would be returning for further inspections.

He got up from the bed and stood before the window, looking out across the street to St Eke's, imagining himself back inside that tower, being William Whencely, an inquisitive scholar harmless to everyone except his killer, and probably unaware of who that was to be, and why.

Worse's gaze moved to the right, where part of the North Ground could be glimpsed beyond the old headstones. He was saddened; from the steeple to the grave was the length of one man's last journey, from living to remembered, retraced by another at the speed of a glance.

Something else came of the thought: a rising slight, but definable, anger. Worse knew the feeling well; invariably, it was about injustice. His plan, made just an hour before, to apologize to Simony and employ polite ingratiation, was summarily cancelled.

6 CANON SIMONY

Worse arrived at 8.00 am, entering by the south-west door. A churchwarden was vacuuming carpet on the chancel steps; otherwise, the place was deserted. She didn't hear Worse opening the bell tower door.

He switched on the mains light, but this time he was equipped with a powerful torch. From the doorway, he directed its beam systematically around the space. He estimated the area to be five metres by five, and confirmed this by pacing it out. Then, torch pointed down, he examined the floor, walking boustrophedon for thoroughness. There was no litter of any kind, and Worse concluded that the place had recently been swept clean. The maintenance had failed to include the floor beneath the stack of folding seats, which was visibly dusty. A census of lost souls inside the Wistful Wardrobe revealed no recent arrivals or departures.

Satisfied with his survey, Worse entered the spiral staircase. The stone steps were mortised into the containing walls, which were square, while centrally they were shaped to form a stacked, round newel. At their narrowest, Worse judged the width to be about forty-five centimetres; it would be quite difficult for two adults to pass each other. The risers were uncomfortably high, and Worse was surprised at the steepness of ascent. Every so often there was a slit opening to the main tower that offered a meagre share of its own inadequate electric light.

The staircase emerged onto a wooden platform, though the masonry stair enclosure extended upwards a further few metres where, at plate height, it supported two thick oak beams, the other ends of which were corbelled into the opposite wall. From these beams the bell was suspended. There was natural light here, provided by large vertical unglazed bell-openings, built for peal projection, on all four sides.

Worse walked around the bell to where the rope traversed the platform in a gap large enough for a person to fit through. He reached up to touch the bell, ringing it softly with a tap of the knuckle, then set about examining the timbered floor, finding nothing of note. On the south wall, he spent some time taking in the view, seeing over the Misgivingston house to the fields and orchards beyond. He turned, moved to the centre opening on the east wall, and hoisted himself onto the sill for a better look down. It was wide enough to be dangerous, and for safety he grasped a lightning conductor on the outside edge. The drop was sheer, ending at the slates halfway between the gable ridge and the crenellated parapet capping on the south wall of the nave.

Worse reversed his body into the tower, and looked up. The beams yoking the bell were out of reach; immediately above them was the octagonal base of the timber-framed, tapered spire with its nailed slate roof and panels of wooden louvres. Worse studied that interior, then decided it was time he should return to ground level for his appointment with Canon Simony.

–

'I would like to keep today's interview largely informal,' began Worse.

It was a contradiction of the serious and disarming, and implied there would be more to come. Simony showed no response, beyond what appeared to be a normal countenance of irritation.

'You are free to make your own audio recording, if you so wish,' continued Worse. That rather punctured the promise of 'informal'.

They were seated on the rearmost pew, where Worse had been the previous day when Simony chose to ignore him.

Worse selected it as a signifier of their power reversal.

Simony launched straight into his unhappiness with developments.

'I must tell you that I strongly object to this intrusion on my time. My diocesan superiors have been informed, and have asked me to express their displeasure.'

Worse was unmoved. 'Your diocesan superiors may themselves be summoned to interview, depending on my findings. Then you will be able to compare displeasures.'

Worse placed his torch on the pew between them. Simony glanced at it, evidently curious about its purpose.

'Is that a recording machine of some sort?'

'It is a torch. I will record in my thoughts.'

As if to reassure, Worse picked it up, flicked the switch on and off briefly, and placed it out of view behind him.

'Disregard the police statement you previously made,' said Worse. 'It was deficient in respect of questions not asked, I presume out of deference. That will not be an issue on this occasion.'

Simony bristled, but said nothing, as if it were dawning on him that he had no power at all.

'On the evening before William Whencely's body was discovered, you conducted Evensong?'

'Yes.'

'In this church?' The detail was intended to warn the Canon that any clever deception in his answers would not be effective.

'Yes.'

'At what time did you leave St Eke's?'

'About nine o'clock.'

'Where did you go?'

'I drove home, to Canterbury.'

'Alone? And directly, without stopping?'

'Yes, alone, and directly.'

'Did you notice anything unusual on the drive home—stopped vehicles, for example?' Worse was thinking of Philip's attacker.

'No.'

'Where were you, between nine fifteen that evening and eight o'clock the following morning?'

'At home.'

'Can anyone corroborate that?'

Simony had not been asked to provide an alibi by the Kent police; he was no doubt beginning to realize the seriousness of these new proceedings.

'My wife, Cecile.'

'I shall need to speak to her,' said Worse. He moved on.

'Who was still at St Eke's when you left that evening?'

'As best as I remember, my pastor, a warden, and the verger.'

'No parishioners?'

'I don't believe so.'

'How well did you know William Whencely?'

'I would say, not at all. He was not a congregant. Some years ago, I believe I visited his business in the village in search of a book.'

'Do you remember what book?'

Simony looked surprised at the question. 'Yes, I do, forgettable as it was. A work from a professional irritant of the sacrosanct, by the name of Darian—recommended to clergy solely to advise its prohibition from our parish libraries.'

Worse offered no opinion.

'Do you know people who were close to Whencely?'

Again, Simony looked surprised.

'I take it you know Whencely was married in the past. His former wife, Angela, is a bridge partner of my wife. Angela still lives in the village but rarely mentioned Whencely, as I understand it.'

'Where do they play bridge?'

Yet again, Simony showed surprise by the turn of questioning.

'In our community facilities next door, the Old Vicarage as it is now called. On Wednesday evenings.'

'Are you a bridge player?'

'I prefer chess.'

'But not bridge?'

The precision of answer sought by Worse was becoming clear.

'No.'

'Does your wife drive herself to Steeple Resting for bridge club?'

'Often. She shares driving with some of the other Canterbury players.'

'Are you in a community chess club?'

'No.'

Worse stood up.

'Thank you for that. We'll resume our conversation in the coming days. Now I want you to show me the position of Whencely's body when you first saw it.'

Worse was aware of the humiliation that Simony might feel in returning to the same request of the previous day. They entered the bell tower. Simony advanced a few paces and stopped.

'About here, I would say.'

'What was the position, the posture, of the body?'

'Almost foetal. As if he were kneeling, then fell to the side, to his left.'

'Try to imagine him kneeling before falling sideways. Can you say which direction he would have been facing?'

Simony considered.

'His back would have been to the door, I think.'

'Did Mansion show you in, and remain with you when you first entered?'

'Yes.'

'What time was that?'

'Eight forty-five, or so.'

'And the police arrived?'

'At nine, I would say.'

'And who was that?'

'Constable Rence, from the village. He called his seniors in Canterbury, whom I had also called from my home when I received the news from Mansion.'

Worse looked back at the floor.

'Was there any object in Whencely's hands or about his person when you first entered?'

'No.'

'Such as a mobile phone, a torch?'

'No.'

'Could you have missed something that was there?'

Simony considered once more.

'Not in his hands. They were clasped; fingers interwoven.'

'As if in prayer, are you saying?'

'Prayer or supplication. That was what I saw.'

'Your verger was here before you. Is it possible that he removed anything from the scene?'

'I sincerely hope not.'

'You said that Whencely was not a congregant. But had he been spending any time around the church, in the grounds perhaps?'

'Not to my knowledge. It wouldn't necessarily have drawn any comment. We often have large groups, tourists, history clubs, and so on, visiting.'

'As the celebrant of St Eke's, do you have much cause to be in this room?'

'Rarely. It's the verger's domain, traditionally.'

'Before the morning in question, how long would it have been since you were in here?'

'Months. Possibly even five or six.'

'And for how long have you served this parish?'

'Six years, in my current capacity. I was also here as an assistant when still in theological training.' Simony glanced at the dusty pile of folding chairs. 'That was thirty-odd years ago, when congregations were larger.'

During the time that Worse had been exploring the tower, he was trying to imagine the detail of Whencely's movements, and what might explain them.

'Do you have any idea, any hypothesis, as to why Whencely

would be in here in the middle of the night?'

'I do not. The event is extraordinary. Quite beyond my experience.'

Worse stepped back toward the door.

'Thank you again. Now perhaps you can assist with Mansion, who has not answered my messages. Would you be good enough to instruct him to come for interview at eleven o'clock. And if you have influence over him, you might advise him to be cooperative. As you have ascertained, we are no longer conducting a conventional investigation. Niceties will be limited to the deserving. What is the name of the warden whom you said was still in the church when you left?'

'That was Mary. Mary Coppicer.'

'How can I contact her?'

'She's here most days, in the church or the Old Vicarage. The parish offices will have her contacts if you require them.'

'And the pastor?'

'David Fielding. His details will be with the office as well.'

'Thank you. Speaking of names, have you ever wondered about Mansion's?'

Simony hesitated. Worse wondered if the subject of names carried a special sensitivity for the Canon, given his own.

'Not really. Other than that John 14 naturally comes to mind.'

'Yes. I expect it does,' said Worse. 'Where does Mansion live, can you tell me?'

'The Church provides a subsidized flat, at the rear of the Old Vicarage.'

Worse held the squeaky door open for Simony to exit. As he passed, Worse spoke.

'Have you personally ever felt unsafe, or threatened, for any reason, at St Eke's?'

Simony looked taken aback. 'No. Goodness no.'

Worse simply nodded. He offered Simony a business card.

'Please take this, and call me if you wish to add anything, or have any concerns. Do not disclose the content of this interview to any other person. That includes your wife. By the way, with whom do you play chess?'

Simony needed a second to process the instruction followed by an apparently disjunct question.

'Cathedral colleagues, usually. Also, occasionally, with parishioners in this village. One is very good. He's improved my play, for which I'm grateful.'

'And that is?'

'Xavier Grimly.'

Worse was genuinely surprised. 'Grimly, of automaton fame?'

'I believe so. It's not a subject we discuss over chess. I don't know how talkative his automaton might be, but Xavier is a man of long silences. Typically, apart from occasional tut-tutting when I make a move, a game will pass with fully two apologetic words: Check and Checkmate.'

7 GRIMLY

When Simony had left, Worse unfolded one of the stored chairs and placed it at the entrance to the spiral staircase. He sat with a view of the squeaky door, the feeble mains light just inside, a fire extinguisher on a wall bracket, the sexton's shelf, the dusty seat pile, the Wistful Wardrobe, and the bell rope. In the centre of his field of vision was the position of Whencely's body when found.

Simony's description of the scene accorded with what Worse had learned from police photographs. But Simony had arrived before the police, and Mansion had arrived before Simony; obviously, Worse was keen to speak to Mansion.

For now, Worse sat there, thinking. The final seconds of Whencely's life were sculpted into that death cast: facing these stairs, fallen to knees, hands clasped, collapsed leftward.

Worse's challenge was to unmake the sculpture: rewind the seconds, effect to cause, that cause to its cause, and so back to the reason for Whencely being there, then back further, to why he received threatening cards. Then back further, even to the Middle Ages if Philip's reference to the *Malison* proved of relevance.

In considering this problem, Worse was aware that he had been presented with a peculiar fortuity: Simony's mention of Grimly[1]. In theory, the automaton was the ideal co-investigator needed to unravel all possible causal strands and identify a conditionally optimal one. Not that it was an assistant in any ordinary sense, like a detective sergeant to whom a task could be delegated. Worse knew that the work ultimately remained with him. What Grimly offered was the right way of thinking, and a ruthless discipline not to stray from it.

—

Ten minutes before eleven, Canon Simony phoned Worse to report, apologetically, that he had been unable to contact Mansion regarding an appointment for interview. Worse thanked him for trying, and asked if Mansion would normally be quick to respond to the Canon's texts or calls. Yes, he would be, was the reply; this was out of character.

When that call was finished, Worse phoned Constable Rence and instructed him to locate Mansion and hold him at the village station for questioning, if necessary under arrest.

—

Worse decided to use the time to visit the Old Vicarage and introduce himself to parish staff. As he approached the entrance, Simony was leaving. They both stopped. Worse detected the first warmth in the other's demeanour.

'I'm sorry about Mansion,' said Simony. 'He's normally reliable.'

'Are you concerned about him?' Worse asked.

Simony took time to answer.

'I'm not sure.'

'We will find him,' said Worse. 'When is his next duty at the church?'

'The midday Angelus, I expect. Unless he's handed over.'

Or unless Rence has him detained, thought Worse. Simony turned to move off.

'Well, good day,' he said. 'You will find Mary Coppicer inside, if you wish to speak to her.'

—

'My husband came to collect me at nine-ten. That's usual for a Sunday night. He walks me home.'

Mary Coppicer and Worse were seated on opposite sides of a card table in one of the vacant clubrooms. For Worse, facing across green baize had little to do with bridge or any other game. It was indelibly connected to something even more competitive, more wily, and certainly less pleasant: the viva voce examinations of student days. He blocked the negative associations.

'So you actually left, when? A few minutes after that time?' asked Worse.

'Not a few minutes. Straightaway. I can't keep him waiting. He doesn't like churches.'

'Was there anything out of the ordinary about Evensong that night? New members of the congregation, for example?'

'No.'

'Would you recognize William Whencely if you saw him?'

'Oh yes. I see him in the village. He wasn't at Evensong.'

'What time did the Canon leave?'

'Nine o'clock, as always. Very regular, our Canon.'

'And who was in the church when you left?'

'David. That's David Fielding, our pastor. And Michael Mansion, the verger.'

'Was there anything unusual outside as you were leaving? Parked cars, people around whom you didn't recognize, that sort of thing?'

'No. Everything seemed completely normal.'

'When you actually left the building, where were Fielding and Mansion, exactly?'

'David was going into the vestry. He waved to me from the door. Michael, I'm not sure. I supposed he was in the bell tower because he hadn't said good night.'

'Do you ever have reason, as a churchwarden, to go into the tower?'

'No.'

'Thank you for your time, Mary. Why does your husband not like churches, may I ask?'

'I didn't mean all churches. Just St Eke's, really.'

'Why St Eke's?'

'Because of the Steeple Curse. Not even the swints visit.

That's why I don't go into the tower. My husband won't allow it.'

'What does your husband think would happen to you?'

'The Curse! Like poor Mr Whencely. Killed by it!'

—

David Fielding was not on site. Worse requested his phone number from the office secretary, and called him. They arranged to meet at the Old Vicarage the following morning.

Worse was introduced to another churchwarden, the florist Sylvia Hurt, whom he recognized to be the second woman, along with Mary, tending to chancel matters following William's funeral service. She had not been at Evensong, due to ill health.

—

Worse checked his watch as he crossed Old Forge Lane. Midday, and no bell. He entered the house by the main front door, and once again found Millie and Veronica talking in the kitchen. Millie stood up to give him a kiss, then waved her arm at a collection of ingredients on the table.

'I offered us as joint chefs for tonight. Mum's in Canterbury this afternoon. I thought we could have the famous Worse lamb pappardelle, ready for seven-thirty.'

She turned to her mother. 'You'll love it. It's the reason I live with him.'

Worse smiled in resignation. 'Your daughter has mastered the alembic arts. She can distil both insult and compliment into the one brief remark.'

'I daresay that's the reason you live with her in turn,' said Veronica. 'The retorts.'

Worse enjoyed the play. 'Yes, but not entirely. Pappardelle will be fun. How has your morning been, Veronica?'

Worse and she had not seen each other before he left for the church.

'Busy. I'm still supervising two doctoral candidates. One this; one that,' she added, enigmatically.

'Missing the other, then,' said Worse.

Veronica smiled. 'My good fortune. We were just planning bread and cheese for lunch. Okay with you?'

'I'm setting it out,' said Millie, stepping over to the sink counter. 'How did things go across the road, Richard?'

'An improvement on yesterday. The verger's absconded, it seems.'

'Suspiciously?' asked Veronica.

'We'll see,' said Worse.

'And did you speak with the Canon?' asked Millie.

'I did. I have concluded he is a good person. Though, oddly, every time I asked a question, he seemed surprised. Why would that be?'

'I imagine he's never before encountered such a tangential fellow,' said Millie. 'I certainly hadn't.'

She sent a raised-eyebrow look to her mother. Veronica smiled and turned to Worse.

'And did he give surprising answers?'

'Only once. Millie, have you had a good morning?'

'Excellent. I've been working backwards through the Oldrice book—the translation by Darian that I showed you yesterday. You must read it, Richard. Especially the last chapter. Especially the editorial notes.'

She carried bread, on a board, to the table.

'In fact, you will read it after lunch, without delay,' Millie continued. 'I insist. We will share thoughts at three. You will be pleased.'

It was Veronica's turn to raise her eyebrows, toward Worse. 'You will, will, will,' she murmured, and mouthed, 'Three o'clock'.

'Then I will,' said Worse, placing slight stress on the last word. 'Where's Philip?'

'He's been in his study all morning, sorting out the insurance claim on his Saab. Plus repair quotes and all the rest of it,' said Veronica. 'It's an old car and parts are scarce. Personally, I think it's a write-off.'

'I don't envy him,' said Worse.

'Whom do you not envy, Worse?'

Philip came into the kitchen, pulling out a chair to sit. He was looking at Worse.

'Many,' said Worse. 'By the way, I was told this morning that XX Grimly lives in Steeple Resting. Is that correct?'

'Xavier? Oh yes. He's treasurer of our antiquarian society. Xavier's been our guest a number of times, hasn't he, Veronica?'

'He has. An extremely quiet man, I would have to say. There are no wasted words with Xavier. On occasion a meal has passed like a séance.'

'That may give a false impression, Veronica,' said Philip. 'In fairness, we could reliably expect two words: Thank and You. Would you like to meet him?'

'I would indeed,' said Worse.

'If we had known, we could have introduced you at the funeral,' said Veronica. 'He was a pall-bearer for Will.'

'Out of interest,' said Worse, 'why do you enjoy his company?'

'You said yourself, Worse, that for compassion, one doesn't need words. A striking insight, equally true for many virtues.'

'Many emotions,' added Veronica. She sounded less ironic than before. 'Xavier is expressive in wordless, in gestural, ways, as you will see. He's a thoughtful man. We like our interactions.'

---

[1] Grimly's Automaton, or Grimly, is a hypothetical being endowed with human faculties (sensorium, psychomotor function, language, memory, reason, model construction, will) any of which can be partly or totally deleted and reintroduced in arbitrary order. The precise faculties, suite of precepts, and resources available to her (by convention Grimly has feminine gender, apparently—in a chromosomal whimsy—after the initials of her inventor, philosopher XX Grimly) under prevailing experimental conditions are together termed a *Grimly compiler*.

Grimly acquires knowledge by instruction, enquiry, observation and heuristic, and inference. She is strongly motivated to identify and explain unfamiliar phenomena, within the limitations of her compiler.

A philosopher asking 'What would Grimly think?' seeks to deconstruct implicit assumptions underlying explanation. Equivalently, if not obviously, Grimly forces any solution path to reinitialize to first principles. The modern techniques of precept deletion and hidden bifurcation theory owe their origins to Grimly, as do many novel counterfactual analyses in the history of ideas. Recently, two Grimlys in argument were used to settle the worrisome Inevitability Conjecture in consciousness studies.

Standard textbooks of epistemology addressing the compiler-dependence of human knowledge generally introduce Grimly with a series of arresting 'What is?' thought experiments. One example: Given a telescope to examine, different Grimlys infer it to be an instrument that (1) acting instantly and at a distance, causes an object to reversibly enlarge; or (2) acting instantly and at a distance, causes an object to shift closer; or (3) acting instantly and insensibly, causes Grimly herself to shift closer; or (4) has no real effect on object size or translation, but alters only a corresponding image, consistent with a theory of lenses and the laws of refractive optics. Importantly, Grimly (the philosopher, not the automaton) urges us to consider the possibility that conclusion (4), whilst in accord with current belief, may itself be replaced—for example, were hidden bifurcations to be discovered in its inferential composition.

8 CONNECTION

Lunch was light and informal, picnic-like, seated around a kitchen table already crowded by various ingredients and cookware that Millie had laid out for making the evening meal.

Veronica left for Canterbury soon after. Millie went with Philip to his study to help sort some family documents. Worse made himself comfortable in their private sitting room, and phoned PC Rence for news about Mansion. It seemed that vehicle and phone tracing placed the verger in Ashford, where he was known to have a cousin living. Rence asked if Worse wanted him arrested.

'No. At this stage, I would rather wait to see if he returns of his own volition. But I do want his location constantly monitored, plus a report of his contacts. If the cousin has a police record, I want to know. Also, could you obtain a warrant to search Mansion's flat in the Old Vicarage. Tell me as soon as you have one. We'll do it together.'

Worse had previously spoken to Rence about Philip's recall of the vehicle that forced him off the road. There wasn't much to go on: pale colour, single brake light. Without being asked, Rence offered an update: there was no progress in that matter.

When that call was finished, Worse phoned Simony. The Canon had heard nothing from Mansion. A bell-ringing roster using volunteers had been urgently arranged by the parish office, and churchwardens were generously stepping up to cover other duties.

That done, Worse picked up the Oldrice volume, and relaxed into a lounge chair to read. He hadn't forgotten the deadline set by Millie. Following her advice, he started with the preface then skipped to the last chapter.

Before long, Worse was sitting upright, concentrating, referring back and forth in the text, engrossed in Darian's copious annotations. At one stage, he got up to collect a pad for making notes.

—

An hour later, Worse was still sitting there. He had swung his chair around to face the window, through which he could see across the street to St Eke's and its silenced bell tower.

The book was on his lap, open at Oldrice's last paragraphs where the finding of Geoffrey Magnacart's body is described. Worse wasn't reading now, though one hand semi-consciously held the book from slipping to the floor.

He was thinking, fully absorbed, staring at the church, imagining the last hours of the knight-priest six and a half centuries before.

And in that state of reverie, Worse became aware of a sensation of being connected—an existential connection to another person, of a kind he had never experienced: ancestral, distant, and calling. It was as if a part of him had become Geoffrey, seeing St Eke's as he had, entering the tower only to confront some overwhelming adversity.

There was something else, more disturbing. At first indefinite, free-floating like a puff of anxiety, it fluttered in and out of comprehension before settling upon him as a heaviness, slowing his thought, holding him still in the chair, and fixing his gaze on the steeple of 1369.

Worse tried to resist the unknown. But gradually, as if from a delicate, unstoppable self-unwrapping of the heart, he was confronted by its meaning as a moral burden. It was obligation.

—

A noisy car on Old Forge Lane restored Worse to the present. He thought of William Whencely again. For the investigator who joins facts, to whom coincidence was the name for inferential failure, or at least an unsatisfactory resort to indeterminacy, the similarities were pronounced: St Eke's tower, night, unwitnessed killing, praying position, mystery. Place, time, method.

He was immersed in these thoughts when Millie burst in, looking extremely happy.

'I have news,' she announced, but stopped on sensing Worse's state of mind.

'Are you okay, Richard?'

'Yes. I'm okay.'

Millie waited for more.

'I am okay, really.'

Millie continued looking at him. Worse elaborated.

'That Oldrice chapter describing the pilgrims' final night sets you thinking. I find it strange ... for me, the actual Worsener's Tale is more revealing of Geoffrey than the Christianus history that it's about. I mean, why did he choose to tell that? It wasn't light entertainment. In the end, it was more a sermon; like a long parable of quest and catastrophe. What was it about the story that presumably carried great personal meaning for him?'

Millie perched on the side of Worse's chair, one arm around his shoulders.

'I wonder the same, Richard. I've no idea what we should take from it. Although ...'

'Although what?'

'Well, the Tale did return his audience to Steeple Resting, to St Eke's, in the person of Simon Acolytēs. Maybe there was special significance in that, for Geoffrey.'

'Or he simply thought it an apt story for where they were, and the occasion,' said Worse.

'Mm. Then again, perhaps it was just what you suggested— allegorical to his own life journey: Christian faith, duty, obedience, privation, mortality.'

Millie paused. They were both reflecting on the heaviness of themes. Worse put the thought into words.

'Weighty matters for the times. Nowadays, we can read it lightly. Not then.'

'True. Oldrice himself reports that its pessimistic tone sobered up the gathering, which for a party night must have been quite something.'

'It rather sobers me as well,' said Worse.

Millie squeezed his shoulders. 'Of course it does. And we're together in this, Richard. Remember, wherever a Magnacart appears, there's a Misgivingston connection[1] as well. You told me that.'

Worse nodded. He brightened. 'There is. Well, what's the good news?'

'Nicholas phoned Dad earlier. He's coming to England as well.'

Worse was delighted. Nicholas and he had shared adventures, and conversations, over the past few years. Moreover, Worse had since come to realize that Nicholas, as Millie's caring brother, had sensed the beginnings of attraction between Millie and him, even before they themselves were aware. Now there was a part of Worse that wanted Nicholas to see, first-hand, how well suited and happy they were together.

'That's wonderful. I was hoping he might. We haven't seen enough of him lately, have we?'

Worse leaned forward to place Oldrice on the coffee table. Then he turned in his chair to hug Millie. She slipped off the sidearm onto his lap and kissed him.

Five minutes later, Worse peeked at his watch.

'We should end this affair before it gets out of hand. I have an appointment with my governess in ten minutes, and I dare not be late. Shall I make tea before I meet with her?'

'Good idea. Include Philip; you and the governess can take over his study for a conference room.'

Worse collected Oldrice and his own notes, and headed off to the kitchen. He called out behind him.

'When will Nicholas arrive?'

'Day after tomorrow, midmorning. He'll drive himself from Heathrow.'

---

[1] Referring to a thirteenth-century sacred compact of *Famille Oblige* commanding in perpetuity each family line to defend the other as its own. (See Prologue, note 23.)

9 THREE O'CLOCK

[Saturday]

'My first question to you, Philip, is: How old is the steeple tower that we see over the road? And when was mention first made of the *Malison*?'

'The tower is Norman, completed in 1116. What you see is original stonework. The timber spire is later; anyway, that's been rebuilt over the years, for the usual reasons of decay, lightning, fire. This one is eighteenth century.'

'So, in 1280, Simon Acolytēs died in that actual bell tower, according to Oldrice?'

'That is what he states. And Simon's grave is in the churchyard.'

'And in 1369, Geoffrey Magnacart died in that exact same room? Is that your understanding?'

'Yes.'

'And the *Malison*?'

'Less definitive than architecture for dating, of course. The Domesday Book makes reference to a "Derke Chapelle" on the site, predating our building, obviously.'

'Remind me,' said Worse.

'1086,' said Millie.

'Of course,' continued Philip, 'Derke Chapelle could mean anything. But the swints were gone before then, so it's a reasonable supposition. Anyway, by the time Becket died in 1170, the curse was definitely established, and named the *Malison*. It wasn't widely spoken of, presumably to protect the Church. At the time, there was a school of belief that Becket's spirit chose St Eke's steeple to ascend to Heaven, as a parting gift of exorcism for the place. It didn't work, as we have seen.'

'Well, perhaps without that blessing, things could have been worse.'

Worse's remark drew a glance from Millie. She had become sensitized to hearing his name in common speech.

'Obviously, Canterbury wasn't pleased with the idea that their noble son should prefer an exit by some provincial back door, as it were, bequeathing no more than a cadaver to the Cathedral,' said Philip. 'They didn't lend credence to it.'

'I can imagine,' said Worse. 'They would rather commercialize the spirit. It doesn't decompose with the rapidity of a corpse.'

Philip and Millie seemed surprised at Worse's level of cynicism.

'It does make one wonder, though,' continued Worse, 'did Becket have some special connection with the village, with St Eke's? Did he ever visit here, is it known?'

'Worse, you do have antennae for the mystery of things,' said Philip. 'There were rumours in his lifetime of night visits by coach to St Eke's, with a guard of knights on horseback—'

'Worseners?' asked Millie.

'We don't know,' said Philip. 'Everyone would be in some form of disguise, in any case.'

'Was it to pray?' asked Worse.

'Well,' said Philip, 'It was to St Eke's he came, not to some sordid lodgings in the village, if that's your line of thinking.'

Millie grinned. 'Yes Richard! A governess, no doubt.'

Worse was unperturbed by the imputation. 'Be realistic everyone. He's a saint. Saints are human. Humans are flawed[1]. Why would he come to St Eke's when he had a whole Cathedral to himself? And Philip, how do we know of those rumours?'

'I only know from Will. He was of the view that there were accounts of the Becket visits in deeply hidden Church records.'

'An English Apocrypha,' mused Millie.

'In Canterbury?' asked Worse.

'Canterbury, Rome, Avignon—we've no idea.'

'Was Will researching that subject especially, do you know, Dad?' said Millie.

'I don't know about especially. Will had a lively interest in everything historical.'

Philip's grief came near the surface as he said this. Worse changed direction.

'When you spoke earlier of a "school of belief", about Becket's ascension, did you mean that loosely, or was there a formal group, a sect, of some kind professing and promulgating that idea?'

'Very likely there was, though it's not clear who it might be, or for how long it persisted. Perhaps more than one. Remember, even by the fourteenth century, it was an undeveloped, very uncertain, splintered social fabric, destabilized by the Crusades, military failure, plagues of whatever kind everywhere, antagonism between sovereign and Church, and class. Not only that, in 1369 the Caroline War with France broke out. There were the usual monastic orders, Benedictines and so on, often competing for recognition and support, along with the various mendicants, abbey-based groups, reliquary sites, heretics—we had everything. Plus communities of monks and nuns and other ecclesiastics from the Continent. Enemy spies included, no doubt. There was a surprising amount of movement.'

'As in Bruges and Ruine with Oldrice,' said Millie.

'Exactly,' continued Philip. 'And, of course, there were many religious chivalric orders: for example, the Templars were around till early in the century, followed by who-knows-what legacy groups enjoying their wealth. Then we have the Knights Worsener, a particularly select and somewhat secretive lot. Even more secretive was the Order of Merciful, who began benevolently enough supposedly as physician knights. Another sect was the Sedites, who apparently survive in various orders still. There were also minor groups like the strictly observant Solemnists and a shadowy lot called the Hriddists. I can't tell you anything about those two.'

'Were you and Will researching any of these, Dad?' asked Millie.

'Oh yes. The Oldrice account is a major source for Steeple Resting pilgrimage history at that time, so we were naturally curious about Worseners. William also found the Mercifuls of great interest and made them his subject.'

'Are the Mercifuls described in *Th Pylgrymes Wey*?' asked Millie. 'I haven't managed to get through it all yet.'

'Mentioned, not described. Their relevance is that there were Mercifuls chapels along the way, starting in London, though none here. Will found that a little odd.'

'Did Will share those research findings with you?' asked Millie.

'Absolutely. He had colleagues at the British Library who sourced and copied materials for him. I was able to benefit from that as well. Several of those people were at the funeral.'

'Let's come back to the *Malison*,' said Worse, 'and consider opposing interests here. Clearly, the established Church would wish the idea away. Who would have benefited from promoting that fear?'

'Any number of parties, possibly. Though not the Worseners, I would have thought, unless Geoffrey Magnacart was a rebel of some kind, to be rid of,' said Millie. 'After all, his death would have reinforced the curse.'

'Philip, I take it from your strong recommendation that Millie and I read Oldrice that you think those events of 1369 might have bearing on our investigation into William's death?'

'I do, Worse.'

'Good,' said Worse. 'I find the parallels striking. Then are we agreed that advancing our understanding of the deaths of Simon Acolytēs and Geoffrey Magnacart may help with solving William's murder, and vice versa? Millie?'

'I think we are agreed.'

'Yes,' added Philip.

'Millie. Can I ask what elements in the Oldrice text or Darian's annotations stood out for you as possibly being of relevance?' asked Worse.

Millie consulted notes on her smartphone. 'I'll list them

without elaboration, to start with. The number sixteen in the Maiden of Fates passage. The Worsener's reference to a "wretched spy and felon in our midst". We have an unnamed vicar of St Eke's who welcomed the pilgrims. The references to odours, being the "sweet perfume" of the Phlox and the "pungent smell of Hades" in the tower. The *Documento*, if it really existed. Why Geoffrey might have gone to the tower in the middle of the night, and equally, why William did so. Finally, the Oxford Passage discussed by Darian.'

Millie put down her mobile. 'They were the outstanding points for me.'

'Thanks, Millie,' said Worse. 'Philip, on the subject of sixteen, you said that William advised that all the cards arriving subsequent to the first were of the X, V, I sort?'

'That's what he said. I only saw the first two.'

'Do you know how many he received?' asked Millie.

'Not exactly. I suspect that he was reticent in telling me as he knew that I considered them possibly threatening, and he didn't.'

'You should know that an X, V, I one was found on William's person when he died,' said Worse. 'In his jacket's side pocket.'

'What else did they find?' asked Philip.

'His wallet,' said Worse.

'No keys?' asked Millie.

'No,' said Worse.

'So, we might imagine a killer who planted a calling card, then possibly used the stolen keys to gain entry to the bookshop later in the night,' said Philip.

'Leaving a card is a rather ritualistic thing to do, don't you think?' said Millie. 'And somewhat daring.'

'Will might have had it with him, from home,' suggested Philip.

'Possibly,' said Worse. 'But his pockets were checked to steal his keys and presumably anything else of interest. In which case the card was left on him. Otherwise, it was planted. Either act is deliberate.'

'Why would they do that?' asked Millie.

'It's not an uncommon practice,' said Worse. 'Sometimes, with serial killers, it's a signature, a form of claim on the act, motivated egotistically. In the case of organized crime, it's a statement of power. With William, I would take it to be a warning specially directed to those who would know the significance of sixteen.'

'Which suggests that should be something we determine without delay,' said Millie. 'Dad, are there other sources describing the Maiden of Fates, and the sixteen futures of an individual?'

'Undoubtedly there are, but I'm not acquainted with any. Darian must have pursued that literature, given what he wrote about her, the chemical subterfuge and so on.' Philip paused to consider. 'I could enquire of Will's London colleagues about it.'

'Wait,' said Worse. 'Let's be cautious. Imagine for a moment that William made a similar enquiry, and that his curiosity, reported through one such contact, sparked concern in our hypothetical organization, leading to the X, V, I threats and ultimately his murder.'

Millie was nodding slowly. 'I agree with Richard, Dad. Our supposition should be: Whoever finds out or tries to find out what Will knew faces the same danger as he did. We need to be very discreet in our researches.'

Philip's face showed slight dismay, but he raised no objection. Worse changed the subject.

'Philip, over at St Eke's, I notice there's a door with very old wrought-iron strap hinges on the sexton's entrance to the bell tower. Would there have been a door in mediaeval times?'

Millie picked up their copy of Oldrice, which was on the sofa between her and Worse.

'I recall a descriptive passage in here ...' She found the page. '... when the Weaver and the Abbess were looking for the Worsener, and I quote: "Looking through the sexton's open doorway they saw the Worsener". What does that suggest?'

'It's ambiguous, really,' said Worse.

'I expect,' said Philip, 'they favoured being able to close off the tower in those days for the same reasons they do now: One, for effective demarcation. The sexton's space hardly compares in decorum with the church proper. It's a workroom. And, two, for warmth. Any attempt to heat the nave in winter would be hopelessly compromised by a draught. Remember, that tower with its bell-openings high up acts like a chimney. It would suck warmth out of the main building.'

'Yes, it would,' said Worse. 'It also follows, from your point one, Philip, that if Geoffrey had gone to St Eke's that night to pray, he would have been found near the altar, not in the tower.'

'Why do you ask, Richard? About the door?' said Millie.

'I was thinking about the odour point you made earlier. The pungent smell of Hades,' said Worse. 'And containment.'

'It's hard to judge how reliable a witness Oldrice was,' said Philip, 'but there's something else in that description that we should take note of. I quote: "He bled not." That's informative.'

'He was dead before the sword pierced him,' said Worse. He had inferred that on first reading, but verbalizing the thought left him repulsed.

'Exactly,' said Philip. 'How?'

All three were silent. Worse had a view, but was not ready to share it.

'To be determined,' said Millie. 'In relation to that,' she continued, 'the Worsener, in his speech, refers to, quote, "a wretched spy and felon in our midst", who was very likely the perpetrator later in the night. So, we are led to believe that we have thirty-six other pilgrims to choose from—'

'Plus many ancillary folk on a journey like that,' said Philip.

'Yes,' said Millie. 'But there's another possibility. He could have been thinking of someone based in the village, someone they had simply caught up with on arriving.'

Millie consulted the text again. 'When he says: "one whose design is not our holy end", we naturally interpret that to mean evil intentions, but it could simply mean that the individual is not on the pilgrimage.'

'A villager. Steeple Resting gets less attractive by the century,' said Philip.

'That's very interesting, Millie,' said Worse. 'Could you read the line where he says he doesn't know who that person is?'

'He says "Of whom I speak, I cannot tell". Again, does that mean that he didn't know, or that he knew and wasn't permitted to say, for some reason?' said Millie.

'We would need to look at Oldrice's original language to know if that ambiguity existed at the time,' said Philip.

'Whom does that supply as suspects?' said Worse. 'You mentioned the parish vicar. There's the unnamed innkeeper, and ostler, and Hobble the messenger. It doesn't give us a lot.'

'Alternatively, it gives us the whole wretched village to choose from. I could try to find out who the vicars were over 1369 and 1370,' offered Philip.

'That might be very useful,' said Worse. 'Philip, why can't they be exact about the dating of this pilgrimage? Isn't Geoffrey Magnacart's date of death recorded?'

'It is. It is. But differently in different places. We can't use it with any confidence.'

Worse was struck by that. Surely every human being deserved to have their passing truthfully noted, at the very least by a proper mark on the calendar. The sense of obligation that he had identified in the sitting room returned, but its heaviness felt different. Now, he was also profoundly saddened, and affronted on his ancestor's behalf.

'Where is he buried?' he asked.

'We don't know, Worse.'

Philip's tone was almost apologetic. He understood the import of this to a Magnacart.

Millie read the mood shift in Worse. She gave it time then changed topic.

'Just to satisfy my curiosity here, we know that the pilgrimage actually happened, that Geoffrey Magnacart was a real person, but how much of his Tale, the story of Christianus, should we believe?'

'I can answer that,' said Philip. 'There's no doubt that Christianus is historical and that his journey east was real. I think the evidence is strong that he did reach the Ferendes, given the mention of *Centrum Mysticum*, and the natural history observations that accord with our modern knowledge— the weaver fish, Asiatic condors, the Bergamot Sea, and so on. We do owe a debt to Darian for elucidating some of that. On the other hand, we need to remain sceptical of parts. Anything appearing supernatural, obviously.'

'Like speaking with the birds, for example?' said Millie.

'That, yes. And visitations of the Phlox. Though you should know that in the Middle Ages there were common mystic traditions about the language of the birds being gifted to certain individuals. The ability ascribed to Christianus is not so extraordinary for the times.'

Worse brightened at the lesson. 'And in that is contained excellent advice for historians, as well as archaeo-logicians, as we might view ourselves. An individual's beliefs strongly determine that person's actions. Therefore, to understand the actions, or to theorize where we are ignorant, we should always take account of prevailing superstitions and the general credulity of the times.'[1]

Millie glanced at her watch, and looked up. 'Richard, my current incredulity of the time is that it's nearly six, and you're on pappardelle duty. My mother is expecting something amazing, and I don't want you to disappoint her.'

---

[1] [EXERCISE Missing Pieces] Worse's argument here is enthymematic. The conscientious reader might prove its validity by formal completion. A mediaeval clue to the classical method can be found in the index.

10 PAPPARDELLE

'Richard, I was persuaded by you-know-whom to have high expectations of your cooking, but this has exceeded every fantasy. Thank you.'

'Yes, very good, Worse. Delicious,' said Philip.

'It's not all mine. You-know-who helped,' said Worse.

'Well, thank you to both,' added Philip.

'It's Richard's entirely,' protested Millie, 'and I can tell you that every time he cooks like this, I renew my vows.'

'Do you hear that, Philip?' said Veronica. 'I might discover my own vows dangerously malnourished, to be vivified only by a suitor's devotional cooking.'

Philip mimed alarm. 'Slip me the recipe, could you Worse?'

—

'There are some points that Millie raised in our afternoon discussion that we haven't taken up,' said Worse.

They were still sitting at the dining table, though the pappardelle was long vanished. Worse's statement announced a move to business, and Veronica stood up.

'If you will all excuse me, I'll be in my study. I had a very messy afternoon requiring some computational clean-ups, I'm afraid.'

'That would be digital remastering, as the sound engineers have it,' said Worse.

'It is. Finding a doctoral signal in a great deal of noise is my perennial labour. You two leave the dishes for later. Philip and I will do them.'

'Clean-up to clean-up. Are you sure?' said Millie.

'Yes, I'm sure. We'll take care of it, won't we, Philip?'

Philip gave a passable impression of browbeaten. 'Yes, Veronica.' His voice was comically flat.

Veronica grinned from the door. 'If anyone makes coffee, I'd love one, Philip.' She stressed his name.

—

'Was William a superstitious man, Philip?' asked Worse.

'No, I wouldn't say so. Not that he indicated to me. He wasn't religious, anyway; certainly not churchgoing.'

'Why do you ask?' said Millie.

'Oh. Applying this afternoon's lesson that belief predicates the act. Trying to imagine why he went to St Eke's that night.'

Philip and Millie nodded.

'Are you thinking it possible, Richard, that Geoffrey and Will were drawn to the tower for the same reason, six hundred and fifty years apart?' asked Millie.

'Same or similar. I do think it possible.'

'And that reason would be?' said Philip.

'A belief,' said Worse. 'Another question, Philip. Did William read Middle English?'

'Yes.'

'So when you were studying the *Wey*, for its significance to local history, he would have comfortably gone to original texts?'

'Quite definitely. Will was a professional. A purist.'

'And when he showed you that first calling card, was he aware of the meaning that you ascribed to it? That it was bogus Arabic, and it meant sixteen?'

'Absolutely. He was amused by its amateurishness.'

'A terrible misjudgement,' said Worse. 'Millie, is there anything you want to take up?'

'Yes. Who's had any thoughts on the "pungent smell of Hades" when Geoffrey was found?'

'What are your thoughts, Millie?' said Worse.

'Well, it was clearly noticeable enough to warrant comment by the witnesses. As we can be sure that the Worsener didn't die by the sword, let's suppose he was poisoned. Then in a grotesque, humiliating act his killer plunged the sword in and propped him up.'

'His killer, or a third party,' said Worse.

'In a parody of genuflexion,' said Philip.

'For those times, some would say the act of an Antichrist,' said Worse. He looked at the others. 'So let's consider the obvious candidate: sulphur dioxide, produced on site by burning sulphur.'

'The original fire and brimstone,' said Philip.

'Burnstone, indeed,' said Worse. 'Imagine Geoffrey was lured into the tower, probably up to the bell. His killer sets up a pan of burning sulphur below, goes out and bolts the door. Geoffrey descends to the tower base in an attempt to escape, only to find his exit blocked. When the killer is sure the poison has done its work and safely dispersed, he re-enters, performs that terrible act, and removes himself and the sulphur apparatus.'

'Was sulphur, elemental sulphur, around then?' asked Millie.

'Definitely. It was a favourite substrate for alchemists, but had been known for millennia before them,' said Worse. 'So we have a working hypothesis for Geoffrey. For William, a strikingly similar modus, using hydrogen sulphide. Millie, other issues?'

'We don't know much about Simon's death, do we?' she said. 'Dad, did you and Will research that topic?'

'Not thoroughly yet. There's clearly not much to go on, though we do have a date of death on his gravestone.'

'Is the historical belief that he was murdered?' asked Millie.

'That seems to be so,' said Philip. 'Would either of you like a coffee?'

Both declined. Philip left for the kitchen to make one for Veronica but was able to stay in the conversation.

'Would there be any contemporary records from 1280 relating to Simon's death, Dad? If so, where would one look?'

'I wish we had Will to answer that,' said Philip. 'We know from Oldrice that Simon joined Christianus from the English

Priory at Constantinople. His epithet, Acolytēs, might be taken to suggest he was not a senior in the Church, in which case his death would not excite great interest. On the other hand, his method of dying in itself could well have, if it were scandalous enough. As we discussed, the *Malison* was fully established by 1280, and a death in the tower would surely have fed into that. In terms of any records, such as they might be, I would expect them to be in Canterbury.'

'What about other deaths, through the years? In the tower; there must have been some,' said Millie.

'Oh yes,' said Philip. 'I remember about eight years ago having to rush across the road when one of the volunteer sextons had a heart attack on the job. Poor fellow.'

'I would expect that sort of thing to happen intercurrently many times over the centuries,' said Worse. 'Anything else, Millie?'

'I take it that we all dismiss the Phlox as a fable, as we would a phoenix in the present day.'

'Of course,' said Worse. 'But what is real and what is believed to be real are different things. And, as we have said, the act evidences the belief, not necessarily what is real.'

Philip came back to the dining room holding a coffee.

'Excuse me while I take this to Veronica.'

'And what did you make of the *Documento*, Richard? Real or fable?' said Millie.

'I'm not decided,' said Worse. 'Any scepticism about mediaeval speakers of the language of the birds needs to take account of the advances that Nicholas and others are making. When I was last at the LDI station, he was optimistic that humans would soon be communicating meaningfully with swints.'

Worse paused, looking at Millie. 'You must know all that. It's your brother leading the world. You're in touch with his work, aren't you?'

'Yes of course. So you're proposing that a person like Christianus might possibly have had that skill, somehow?'

'I'm saying my scepticism is softer than it would be if I didn't know about Nicholas's progress decoding birdsong,' said Worse.

'If we accept that Christianus did have that gift, we would be much more inclined to believe in the *Documento*, the Book of Swints, wouldn't we?' said Millie.

'It follows,' said Worse.

'So the question becomes: Given it existed, what happened to it?'

Philip caught the closing words as he returned from Veronica's study.

'What happened to what, Millie?'

'The *Documento*.'

Worse looked at Philip. 'We were just talking about Nicholas's work with swint language perhaps giving credence to the idea that a freakish individual in the 1260s might well have had the gift ascribed to Christianus, and that, in turn, giving credence to the existence of the Book of Swints described by Geoffrey in his Tale.'

'Yes. But I must say it does all sound rather fantastical,' said Philip.

Stated like that, Worse and Millie found themselves agreeing.

'How's Mum doing?' asked Millie.

'Intense,' said Philip. 'I expect caffeine will slow her down to stimulated.'

—

'It's hard to believe we've only been here, what, fifty-six hours?' said Millie. 'Yesterday's funeral feels like a week ago.'

They had said good night to Philip and Veronica, and returned to their rooms in the Surgery. Worse answered from the shower.

'It is hard to believe. Have you suffered at all from jetlag, would you say?'

'Not at all. But then, I have adhered conscientiously to the rules of recovery.'

'What are they?'

'Eat like crazy, snack between meals, sleep whenever, preference wine over water, play all night—not an arduous regimen, I find.'

'You should publish it,' said Worse. '*Clock Shock: The Emily Remedy*.'

'Perhaps I will. What about you?' asked Millie.

'I'm fine. My rules are not quite so stringent. Ready to hop in?'

Worse stepped away from the shower and Millie took his place.

'How have you found your father these last few days? Are you as concerned still as you were after the first dinner?'

'I don't think I am, actually. We haven't seen that moroseness again, have we? Mum thinks his mood has improved from having us here, and being part of the action solving Will's murder. He's found purpose, and feels he can make a contribution.'

'He can certainly make a contribution,' said Worse. 'He's the closest witness to what William was researching, and also to his state of mind. Incidentally, we haven't heard much from your mother about William, though given the time he and your dad spent together, she must have insights, observations that might help.'

'Absolutely. I think it's just that she's very busy at the moment with supervision. Perhaps you should make an appointment to interview her, under caution, handcuffs jangling from your belt. The third degree.'

'Emily Misgivingston; please speak clearly for the recording. Is that your personal fantasy?'

Millie turned off the shower, walked to Worse and embraced him, soaking wet.

'No belt required, I think.'

Millie's brother, Nicholas Misgivingston, is a volunteer mathematician attached to the Language Diversity Initiative research station in the remote South Joseph Plateau in the Ferendes. LDI was founded by the

Cambridge linguist (and renowned dream theorist) Edvard Tøssentern, who remains its director, with the aim of conserving endangered languages throughout the world. The LDI Charter in the Ferendes specifies the study of the origins of indigenous dialects and their convergence into modern Ferent. A parallel academic interest of Nicholas has been decipherment of birdsong, which is most advanced in the case of the swint (*S. tinctoria*).

(This migratory species, unique in its characteristic thricing behaviour—the flock count invariably is exactly 3-divisible—maintains a staging colony in a newly discovered Plateau caldera, where enormous numbers feed on the fruit of abundant seki vines. These supply the precious metal substrate, concentrated from volcanic soils, from which the swint synthesizes gold-heteroglobin, essential to the oxygen-carrying capacity of its blood xanthocytes.)

Some of the challenges of this research for computational linguistics are described informally by Misgivingston in the contemporary history *Bad to Worse* (attrib. A B C Darian). The science has been rapidly progressed by a single astonishing insight: that the minuscule silences (technically, Parsan gaps) separating words in human speech confer excess bandwidth for information content, a facility believed to be exploited unconsciously in many languages. A similar phenomenon appears certain in birdsong, at least for swints, in which a vocabulary of several dozen signifiers, including those for low integers, is now agreed. A recent review article by Thurdleigh and Misgivingston in *J. Numerical Ornith.* provides a comprehensive introduction for readers unfamiliar with the subject.

11 SUNDAY SERVICE

[Sunday]

Sunday morning at the Misgivingstons' began lazily. Worse and Millie were up first, and the aroma of their brewing coffee drew Philip and Veronica to the kitchen, if only in a primitive state of sentience seemingly confined to the olfactory. The bustle of others, plus croissants warming in the oven, along with quiet morning radio, slowly extended cortical arousal to vision, taste, hearing, and eventually conversation.

'What are the plans for today, everyone?' asked Philip.

'Lazy day,' said Millie, clearly asserting her need.

'Gardening, charity baking, reading,' said Veronica.

'What about you, Worse?' said Philip.

'Another coffee. Then some interviews, and a search warrant to execute.'

Worse looked at Philip. 'I was hoping that you might take me to William's shop this afternoon, for an informal look through.'

'Certainly.'

It was slightly delayed, and Philip looked as though his lazy Sunday had been confiscated by the form master. He glanced at Millie for assistance, but Worse was there before him.

'And it would be really helpful if Millie joined us.'

Now both were equal in defeat. Worse brightened.

'That's wonderful. But the really big thing for us all today is to attend the eleven o'clock service at St Eke's.'

Any residual sleepiness in Millie's parents was instantly erased by emergency self-preservation planning. Veronica was first.

'Oh, I'm sorry, Richard. That will be quite impossible for me.'

Worse continued as if he hadn't heard her. 'I expect there will be some kind of tribute to William.'

'Worse, I'm—I'm...' Philip was struggling, for anything, '...indisposed at that time.'

Worse managed to imitate crestfallen, without overdoing it. 'All right. I just imagined it as a family outing. A morality picnic, one might say. Bringing us together. Mostly for William.'

—

'Richard! That was blatant emotional blackmail, and you know it!'

Millie and Worse had carried second coffees back to the Surgery.

'No it wasn't.'

Worse could tell from Millie's expression that for their day to advance peaceably, an immediate concession was necessary.

'Well, a shade off-white, I admit. But the sentiments were genuine.'

'Why do you want to go?'

The tone was still severe, but less so.

'I think Simony will give an interesting sermon. And it rather annoys me, to be honest, that your father is closed off to the man personally, rather than separating the individual from the institution. And he does seem inordinately critical, if not curiously bitter, in my view.'

Millie said nothing.

—

PC Rence had obtained a key to Mansion's flat, as authorized by their search warrant. By arrangement, he and Worse met outside the Old Vicarage at 9.30, and walked down the side of the building to a rear entrance. Out of habit, Rence courteously knocked before unlocking the door.

The interior was rather austere, and their search was deemed complete after twenty minutes. They walked back to the front of the Old Vicarage.

'Do you know Mansion, Constable? Personally or professionally?'

'Neither, Chief Inspector. Only by sight as the verger.'

'What did you make of his living space, in general?'

'Honestly? A rather dull fellow's place. No books, for a start. No music. No computer.'

'What does it suggest to you?'

Rence hesitated, as if he knew he was about to be taught something.

'As I say, he's dull. Lives only for work. Doesn't entertain. Perhaps no friends.'

Worse nodded in agreement.

'Yes, all very likely. Or it might suggest he has somewhere else to live, besides this flat.'

—

At 10.15, Worse interviewed David Fielding, the pastor, in a vacant committee room in the Old Vicarage. Fielding's testimony agreed with that of Mary Coppicer. He denied entering the tower room at any time on the Sunday evening. His role at St Eke's was voluntary; professionally, he was a partner in a small accountancy practice in the village.

'What other occupations have you had in life?' asked Worse.

'Nothing, really. I did accountancy as my first degree, and never left it.'

'Have you ever served in the military, or police, for example?'

'No.'

'How well do you know the verger, Mansion?'

'Speaking terms in the church. Otherwise, not well at all.'

'Are you aware he is missing? Evading interview?'

'No.'

'Do you know where he might be?'

'No.'

'Did you note the presence of, or have any contact with, William Whencely at any time during the twenty-four hours leading up to the discovery of his body?'

'No.'

—

Worse let Fielding return to his duties at the church. Still in the committee room, he phoned Cecile Simony and introduced himself.

A day earlier, the intention would have been to check on her husband's account of events, utilizing questioning techniques designed to unmask collusion. But Worse had since concluded that Simony was a truthful witness and not a person of interest. His purpose now was to be reassuring, and request that she be in contact should anything occur to her that could assist in the investigation.

—

Worse and Millie entered St Eke's and sat on the rearmost pew on the south side, where Worse had previously spoken to Simony.

'Will your parents be joining us?'

'I've no idea. After your unscrupulous manipulation at breakfast, I would imagine their inner conflict has been unbearable.'

'There's nothing wrong with inner conflict,' said Worse. 'Isn't that precisely how the moral compass sets true worth, and the soul finds peace? Eventually, I mean.'

'We'll see,' said Millie, glancing over her shoulder towards the door.

After a few moments, she added a touch of dryness. 'Perhaps you should be giving the sermon, Richard.'

—

It seemed that the two souls found their peace in the affirmative as, a minute later, Philip and Veronica slipped along their pew to sit beside them.

—

'Today, I offer my words in memory of William Dale Whencely, of this parish, a scholar, historian, linguist, and bibliophile, who died within these walls one week ago. As many of you know, a service for William was held at St Eke's this Friday past, following which he was laid to eternal rest at the North Ground.

'At that time, I was unaware that William's death was unnatural.'

Simony paused while many in the congregation were unable

to suppress their shock. He repeated the news.

'On Friday, I was unaware that William's death was not natural. At this point, we cannot know why he should suffer treachery at the hand of another, more especially why such an act would be committed in this holy place. We can be grateful that very senior personnel are conducting a police investigation, and we wish for a speedy resolution. I urge all amongst you to cooperate, to come forward if you have any information that might assist Chief Inspector Worse in his endeavour to rid St Eke's of this stain of wickedness, and to seek justice for William Whencely.'

Simony again paused, rearranging papers on his pulpit lectern. He looked up. 'I shall start with a reading from *2 Syllabines*, Chapter 2, beginning Verse 1. When you hear these words, ending, *Therefore, offer water to the Roman*, I would ask that you keep in your thoughts the life and untimely passing of William Whencely.'

For Worse, this was interesting: he had always admired St Ignorius' *Second Letter to the Syllabines* for its human insight and lack of apostolic pretension. He glanced sideways.

Philip was paying attention.

—

Towards the end of the service, Rence texted to inform Worse that Mansion had returned to Steeple Resting and was nearing the church.

Seated as he was, in front of the squeaky door, it wasn't difficult for Worse to observe Mansion enter by the south-west porch and immediately go to the tower, presumably to ring the midday bell.

When formalities in the chancel had finished, Worse excused himself from Millie's family and went to the tower room. He found the verger standing by the bell rope.

Mansion spoke. 'This room is closed to the public. Get out.'

Worse let the door close behind him, and walked to the sexton's bench. He leaned against it, chose a pair of protective earmuffs, and held them in one hand.

'I am not the public. I am the police. Listen to me carefully. I will allow you to finish this ringing. Then I will question you. If you lie or do not cooperate, I will arrest you for obstruction. If you resist arrest, you will be shot. I am obliged to inform you that, as a matter of course in terrorism cases, such shootings are stipulated to be lethal. I have no discretion to vary that, other than in respect of the number of lethal shots fired. That number, beyond the first, will be of no interest to you—it is solely determined by the annoyance and distaste and sense of satisfaction that I feel at the time. Up until, but obviously not including, that point, I do stress that you retain the right to seek clarification on any matter we have discussed, as do I.'

Mansion's expression morphed from dark sullen to black foul.

'On the other hand, if you cooperate, you will be able to leave this room and continue your verger duties, with only modest restrictions on your movements that will be specified when relevant. You might use the next few minutes deciding which outcome suits you better.'

—

When Worse left the tower room, he found Canon Simony still in the south-west porch greeting departing congregants. The Misgivingstons had apparently gone home. Worse waited in line to speak to Simony.

'I enjoyed the sermon. *Syllabines* is one of my favourite texts. And a very apt tribute to William Whencely.'

They shook hands.

'Among my favourites, also. Very good to see you, Chief Inspector. And to have the Misgivingstons attend. Was that, am I to think, under police escort?'

'Not at all. Delivered by moral compass, I'm sure.'

Simony smiled. 'Good day, Chief Inspector.'

—

Worse crossed the lane and used the private entrance to the Surgery. Millie was in their sitting room, looking through a box of her childhood schoolwork, proudly conserved by her mother. She had guessed the purpose of Worse's disappearance into the tower room, and looked up.

'How did it go with the verger?'

'Coarsely. How did it go with the canon?'

'Interesting. I think Dad was impressed with the sermon, but he's not saying so. He and Mum are in their studies, staying very quiet.'

'I might prepare lunch for everyone, as a kind of making up. Do you think they would enjoy that?'

'Yes, I do. More importantly, I would enjoy it.'

—

Philip drove Millie and Worse in Veronica's car. The square was busy with Sunday tourists, and they parked in one of the reserved doctors' bays at Philip's old practice. More than once, he said, 'We should have walked.'

Inside the bookshop, there was little indication that the place had been burgled, suggesting that intruders knew what they wanted and where to find it.

Worse was most interested in looking for signs of recent activities, papers, unshelved books, mail—anything that William might have been focused on in the days before his death. He began by scanning everything on view or within reach.

All this was taking time, and Worse soon sensed that Philip and Millie were losing enthusiasm.

'Why don't you two have a coffee in the square while I work here? I'll find you when I'm finished.'

No persuasion was needed. And it suited Worse to be alone; he wanted to search upstairs in William's flat, and thought that might be upsetting for Philip.

Forty-five minutes later he joined the others. Millie noticed that his hands were empty.

'What did you find?' she asked.

Worse glanced at Philip before answering. 'Much undone, sadly.'

12 STĒPEL MALISON

[Monday]

Worse awoke with a start, to the loud ringing of a church bell. He sat upright, pushing down bedclothes, confused, still moments from functional consciousness.

All was quiet. Millie was sleeping beside him, unmoved by the call to worship. There were no people sounds, no distant vehicle noise, not even a reveille of birdsong. Worse checked the time on his phone: 3.10.

Of course, in full wakefulness, Worse recognized that the mighty dream-peal was very different from the ring of St Eke's. That was a relief, but also disturbing. Disturbing, because a dream is the inner-world narration of events and connections and reasons that we don't quite see. Disturbing enough that he got out of bed, crossed to the window, and drew back the curtain.

Unsurprisingly, the church and the Old Vicarage were in darkness. In subdued moonlight, the fabric of St Eke's—its stone, metal plumbing, roof slate, and lead-came windows—presented a palette of silvers and shadow that Worse found almost hypnotically beautiful. The three south-facing steeple windows high in the belfry, behind which Worse's dream would have placed the carillon of a phantom bell-ringer, were obsidian black.

As always happened from this aspect, his gaze shifted to the right, into the darkness that obscured the North Ground, and he thought of William Whencely's final hours. To Worse, it seemed that the greater mystery was why Whencely was in the church at that time, rather than who was his murderer. In his thinking, he had categorized the main possibilities as these: to meet someone; to search for something; or to conceal something.

His eyes were focused nowhere in particular when he thought he saw a dim flash of light behind the right-hand steeple window. Worse stared at the point, wondering if it could be explained by moonlight, some anomaly of reflection, perhaps off the bell. Nothing further happened, except an evolving tonal variegation of the scene caused by clouds crossing the moon.

Worse was fighting an impulse to dismiss the impression and regain his bed. But he knew that sleep would not easily return, that his curiosity would be satisfied only by crossing the road and looking for himself.

He dressed quietly, packed a torch and his mobile phone into pockets of his jacket, and took the Totengräber from his bedside cabinet. Millie was still sleeping soundly; before leaving, he unsilenced her phone which was on a battery charger close by, thinking that he might need to make contact.

—

Worse entered through the south-west portico; the main door was unlatched. He shone the torch beam around the interior of the nave, checking side to side as he walked forward to the chancel steps. Nothing seemed out of place.

He returned to the tower door. The loud hinge squeak on pulling it open obviated further efforts at stealth; he called out.

'Is anyone here?'

There was no reply. Worse would have been more surprised if there had been. He switched on the light. After a quick survey, he decided the room looked much as it had on previous visits. He returned to the door and, using a coat hanger borrowed from the Wistful Wardrobe, wedged it open. Now, if anyone had designs to bolt shut the door and trap him in the tower, at least he would hear the hinge.

Worse crossed to the spiral staircase. Twice on the way up, he stopped for several seconds to listen. Before stepping onto the platform, he ran his torch around the space, including upwards into the spire. Then he explored.

The only new finding was a modern, steel-box toolkit on the floor near the rope aperture. Worse shone his torch into it. The contents were largely conventional, plus two expensive-looking torsion spanners, along with a lubricant gun. None of this was out of place to Worse; after all, the swinging peak machinery was quite complex, and moving parts needed maintenance and safety checks.

It was very clear that the phantom bell-ringer had not materialized from Worse's dream. The faint impression of light that registered in peripheral vision had some different, entirely innocent explanation. Worse felt the absurdity: here he was, armed, reconnoitring an empty village belfry in the dead of night. He certainly would not want the Canon to hear about it.

At least it was beautiful up there. Worse looked out from one of the south-facing windows, across to the Misgivingston house. He pictured Millie, asleep as he left her. She wouldn't be troubled to wake up and find him out of bed. At home, he was often up early, working somewhere in the apartment.

The air was cold and pure. He leaned forward, almost to the outer edge of the stonework, and took deep breaths, as if drawing into his being the vitality not of air, but of atmosphere. He thought of mediaeval pilgrims who might have ventured up this tower, seen the night village, and inhaled the same experience. Perhaps one was Geoffrey Magnacart.

He turned back from the window.

The contrast could not have been more stark. The air inside had become unbearably foul. Worse experienced immediate nausea; his eyes started smarting. Below, he heard the squeaky hinge followed by the door slamming shut, and knew exactly what was happening: he was being poisoned. Imprisoned and poisoned.

Worse instinctively returned to the window, hanging forward, gasping for fresh air, any air, leaning so far out that he was in danger of falling. He knew he was becoming confused. The Misgivingston house, seen clearly only seconds before, was losing focus. He needed to get out. He wanted to fly.

And then he conceived of the next best thing.

Worse hyperventilated for several seconds, held his breath, and ran to the platform aperture. He grasped the bell rope, pulling it upwards as quickly as he was able. Twice, using the weight of the toolbox, he needed to secure the coils at his feet from slithering back into the tower void while he escaped to a window for fresh air.

At last, he was holding the ferruled end. This he looped through the handle of the toolbox and made a knot. He carried it to the centre window on the east wall and heaved it through. The rope coil on the floor beside him leapt away. Worse heard the toolbox smash into the slates below, then rumble down the steep nave roof, still drawing the rope with it. He was already on the window ledge, breathing exterior air now itself polluted by escaping toxic gas.

Worse lowered himself into free space, grasping the rope in a crude version of the abseil. Each time he thrust back from the wall, the bell emitted a complaining, tuneless note. Despite his physiological state of compromise, and possibly because of confusion, Worse found himself amused. No properly behaved church bell would be expected to make that sound, he was sure.

The pitched fall of the toolbox had been arrested on the south parapet, and the bell rope delivered Worse to a relatively safe rest at the box gutter just inside. There he made himself comfortable, breathing deeply and slowly. The headache that had struck as he crouched to tie the rope was subsiding.

From this height, there was insufficient rope length to reach the aisle roof below him, and beyond that, the ground, and Worse decided his only choice was to wait where he was for rescue. At one point, he pulled several times on the rope, partly in crazed celebration, but also to rouse the village to deliver help.

With progressive return of lucidity, and his vision, Worse

called a police emergency line in Canterbury. He ordered a cordon around St Eke's, a hazardous spills team, and detectives to locate individuals named on an Immediate Report list he kept constantly updated. That was intended to confirm the whereabouts of individuals during an incident like this. Almost as an afterthought, he described his plight high up on a crenellated parapet and requested a fire and rescue crew to get him down. He didn't ask for it, but he knew the response would include an ambulance, given his exposure to a toxic substance.

—

It was just after 4.30 am, still dark across the road in the Surgery. Worse phoned Millie. He saw the light go on in their bedroom.

'Richard?'

'I've been playing you a romantic melody on the St Eke's bell, and you didn't even stir.'

'Richard?' Millie repeated, as if it might instead have been a nuisance caller.

'Yes, it's me. I'm across the road, stuck on the wall of the church. The fire brigade are on their way with a suitable ladder.'

They could both hear sirens in the distance. Millie was now fully awake.

'What have you been up to? How could you be stuck on a roof?'

'Put on some warm clothes and come across to talk, but on no account enter the church. It's full of poisonous gas.'

Worse had a good idea of what that gas was, but he didn't say.

—

A few minutes later, he saw Millie running across the road and through the lychgate into the south graveyard. She was shining a torch at the church wall.

'Here,' shouted Worse, flashing his own torch to assist her finding him.

'Are you all right?' she asked.

'Yes, I'm fine,' said Worse. 'Just stuck in a ridiculous jam, semi-poisoned to half-dead, and I think I've failed my audition to be sexton of St Eke's.'

Millie sounded relieved. 'You might have chosen a more civil hour to cause a scene. I woke up Mum and Dad. Dad's making you coffee.'

Her parents appeared out of the darkness.

'Richard! Are you all right?' asked Veronica.

Before Worse could say something reassuring, Philip interrupted.

'Worse, get down from there. It's a church, for God's sake.'

'It is a church, I agree. But a particularly noxious one.'

Worse pulled on the bell rope.

'Tocsin for toxin, Philip. Witness the literal-thinking man's night on the tiles.'

—

The local fire brigade was the first unit to arrive. By now there were several curious villagers watching the drama under powerful floodlights. Worse ensured that everyone was told not to enter the church.

Before he descended the ladder, Worse untied the toolbox and handed it to his rescue escort on the ladder. The rope could be retrieved later through the tower window. The roof would need inspecting for broken slates, and the bell rocker was probably damaged.

The Kent police, a Canterbury ambulance, and the hazmat team all arrived within seconds of each other. A safety cordon was established around the entire church. Two hazmat officers, briefed by Worse, donned protective suits and breathing apparatus, and entered the building carrying a gas analyser. Worse wanted to suit up and go in with them, but was persuaded out of the idea. Instead, they promised to video their progress into the tower, and every detail in the ground-level room, particularly whether its door was bolted.

Worse was checked out in the ambulance, with Millie waiting outside. The emergency physician was introduced as Dr Malleson, which Worse found privately amusing. She had Worse's details on a screen, and spoke while drawing a blood sample.

'I see you're a doctor. What's your area of practice?'

Worse had been fascinated by an early comment of Philip's, delivered with an ambiguous glibness, that nevertheless resonated for him. He decided impulsively to try it on himself.

'I don't practise. I studied medicine for its vocabulary,' he said.

It felt right, but not completely right. Perhaps 'breadth of education' or 'self-knowledge' were more accurate.

'Truly?' she asked.

'Not entirely. Not sure. I'm still sorting out the reasons for everything.'

His physician nodded seriously. 'What do you think it was?' she asked.

'Hydrogen sulphide. I'm certain of it,' said Worse.

'Then you're very lucky to be alive, Chief Inspector.'

'I think I'm lucky that church bells come with long ropes attached.'

For the first time, she smiled, placing a dressing on his venipuncture site.

Worse often found himself drawn to others who shared a life experience of the institutionalized traumas, and wonders, of medical school.

'What about you? Why emergency medicine?' he asked.

Neither could know that her answer, lightly intelligent as it sounded, would inject a kernel of interest into Worse's sensual curiosity. Nor that this casually delivered bon mot might one day erupt, without warning, into potentially whole-of-life discord.

'Oh, semantics wasn't so much my thing; more for the syntax, I would have to say.'

13 CASUAL SYNTAX

[Monday]

By six o'clock, the excitement was largely over. The flashing light operatics had drawn to a close as emergency services vehicles departed. Temporary steel fencing surrounded the church, and a bright blue tarpaulin was sheeted over the damaged roof slates.

Philip, Veronica, and Millie were sitting around the kitchen table. Worse had excused himself to make a courtesy call to Canon Simony, informing him of the state of affairs at St Eke's. When he returned to the kitchen, the others were curious as to how the news had been received.

'Very composed, I would have to say. And concerned for me; his first question was whether I was unharmed.'

'Our Canon has discovered a fibre of pastoral caring,' said Philip, with too-viscous sarcasm.

Worse fixed an evaluative stare on Philip. It did seem to him that Millie's father was a harsh critic of their vicar.

'I took it to be a kindness,' he said, speaking directly to Philip. It created an awkward silence, broken by Millie.

'Well, I'll take breakfast orders, shall I? Mother, what will it be?'

—

Quite suddenly, Worse found company irritating. Compared with his recent experience, talk of eggs Benedict versus Florentine seemed unbearably trivial. He also recognized in himself a degree of trauma that he needed to deal with.

Taking a mug of tea, he gave apologies, and went to the sitting room in the Surgery. Through the window he could see his escape rope still hanging from the belfry opening. It looked absurd, like something disgorged, but also brought an appearance of dereliction to the place, which, fenced off, resembled a demolition site.

Dr Malleson's words, 'very lucky to be alive', came back to Worse. He knew it was true, but also felt oddly unemotional, almost separated from his starring role of hours before. He pictured the event remotely, with an unknown actor in the distance slipping down the rope to survival. Or it might have been Geoffrey Magnacart in 1369, making derring-do to safety, crushing his antagonists, and rejoining the pilgrimage with knightly aplomb.

But here the actor was Worse himself, the time was today, and he simply felt fortunate to have devised and executed a plan of escape before confusion supervened. So yes, he was very lucky.

Standing there, even in that mental place of detachment, Worse experienced again the connection to Geoffrey, as if this morning he had briefly inhabited the other's being, shared his same mortal danger, and assisted them both to safety.

That feeling of being connected to another, new to Worse just days earlier, had been returning intrusively, bringing each time a little more clarity. And right now, in front of the window, looking at the wreckage of St Eke's, Worse recognized distinctly the obligation delivered to him. It was something both ancient and present, for Geoffrey, for William, and for Worse himself. He didn't like it, but he owned it. It was a duty to avenge.

—

Worse sat down, wondering if he had been a little harsh with the others in the kitchen. He was reassured in thinking if that were the case, Millie would have followed him to the Surgery and said so. More likely, she had sensed his state of mind and understood his need to be alone.

An email arrived from one of the hazmat officers, who signed off—humorously, Worse supposed—as Hotel Charlie November. He confirmed that the tower contained high levels of hydrogen sulphide. There were no other toxic substances detected. Attached was the promised video recording of their exploration of the building. Worse studied it closely, then phoned HCN, thanked him for the information, and asked if it had been possible to identify a concentration gradient that might suggest a source. As Worse expected, the answer was no, other than that levels were highest close to the floor, unsurprising given the relative densities of hydrogen sulphide and air. They had not been able to safely ascend the spiral staircase because of the bulk of their protective gear and the gas analyser. The main body of the church had much smaller concentrations than the tower, fully explainable by leakage. A confirmation report would be sent to Worse when it was available.

No sooner had he finished that call than Dr Malleson phoned to check on him. She introduced herself as Jane. Worse was able to report that his eyes had stopped smarting, his headache had gone, and he simply felt tired. Her advice was, 'Rest.'

'Do you know how it happened?' she asked. 'How the place filled with hydrogen sulphide?'

'I'm working on that.'

'I'd be interested to find out. You're probably aware that most H_2S poisoning we see is non-fatal, from accidental low-level exposure in industry, sewerage plants, and so on. From what I've been told, the concentrations in the bell tower were way beyond lethal. That makes you worthy of a case report. How do you fancy being immortalized in the literature? De-identified, naturally.'

'Immortal would be good,' said Worse. 'Especially anonymously. And thank you for looking after me this morning.'

'No problem. You're welcome.'

It was a natural rest in which to conclude their call, but something tentative in Worse, slight but imperilling, returned him to the intelligence that he enjoyed earlier.

'Also, I should have confessed: I do like syntax as well. Though mostly because it's a very nice word.'

'Then it shall be deployed invisibly in the case report.'

Worse really was tired. He went to the bedroom and lay down. Yet again, he was disturbed by a call. This time it was PC Rence, advising that the church had been made secure and that no other suspicious activity had been reported in the night.

'There's one result from it all that will interest you. I think you'll be pleased,' added Rence.

'And that is?' asked Worse.

'Don't quote me exactly on this, but my superiors are going to take the Whencely case more seriously. Direct more resources your way. It's become a diocesan matter rather than village. Next level is national, and they would prefer that not to happen.'

Worse thanked him, and ended the call. He had mixed feelings about the news; he rather enjoyed the combination of autonomy and authority that Spoiling engineered for him. More resources could entail more annoyance, if not impediments.

For now, Worse wanted an answer to the obvious question raised by Jane Malleson: How was the tower filled with hydrogen sulphide so rapidly after his entry, without any evidence of its source remaining? A gas cylinder would be impossible to conceal, or to move in and out quickly. There were other questions. How was his presence detected? Was he actually lured there by the light that he saw? Was he specifically targeted? Who would be observing him at that time of night?

Naturally, he was keen to get back to the church and look around for himself, but there was something else on his mind. Again, it came from words used by Jane Malleson: 'concentrations way beyond lethal'. For many years, Worse had led a risky life, close to criminal figures for whom murder was everyday business. Of course, risky didn't mean reckless; Worse had a gift for making the most of chance and necessity equally. But now, after years of living alone, he also had Millie to consider, and she changed the risk equations fundamentally. Perhaps he should reconsider the work he did, move more into software security, embezzlement, identity theft, ransomware attack—investigatory roles that called less for routinely carrying a Totengräber.

Worse decided he would rest, but later. He sat up, intending to find Millie and restore relations in the kitchen. As he did so, Millie arrived with more tea and a toasted egg-and-ham sandwich.

'The family meeting resolved unanimously that the victim of poisoning should have something to eat,' she said.

She placed the tray on his bedside table, and moved around the bed to sit on her side. Worse eyed it doubtfully.

'Have you had some rest?' asked Millie.

'Not really; too many calls.'

Worse quickly updated her on developments. He tasted the sandwich.

'This is delicious! Thank you.'

Only in the act of eating did Worse become aware of the need, a lifelong appetitive disorder that always bemused his friends. A dietetic corollary was that he didn't easily recognize repletion also.

'Did I upset the kitchen party? Your father? About Simony? Was there a second unanimous resolution to expel me from the family?'

'Of course not, Richard.'

'Mm. From your tone I think you have taken the question more seriously than I intended.'

'My family loves you. Anyway, where you go, I go.'

Millie lay back on her pillows, placing an arm around Worse's chest. Worse also lay back, turning to face her.

'I could have lost you this morning,' she whispered.

And that is how the emotionality of the event, missing before, welled up inside him. He had known when he reached the parapet that he was lucky to be alive. Only now, he really felt it.

14 IN GOOD DOUBT

Worse showered and changed. He carried his sandwich plate and mug through to the kitchen and washed them. Millie had fallen asleep on their bed, and no one else seemed to be around.

He left by the main front door and headed across the road, then walked the full perimeter of St Eke's, staying outside the temporary fence. Every church door was stopped open for ventilation. HCN had told Worse that his team would be returning at midday for further analysis, but a site clearance was unlikely to be granted for a day or two.

Worse was less interested in an air quality clearance than in knowing how hydrogen sulphide came to be there in the first place. His concern was that if an attack could be mounted so suddenly, then it could happen again without warning.

He sat in the bus stop shelter outside the Misgivingston house, where he had a good view of the south façade. All was quiet behind the fence. The only activity was foreground—local traffic, delivery vans, dog walkers, and interested villagers. When he heard a bus approaching, he stood up, crossed back to the St Eke's side, and walked along to the Old Vicarage parish offices.

The staff in the front office seemed delighted to see him, expressing their relief that he was unharmed, and sharing their alarm at what had become of their church. For the moment, all administrative and secretarial work was clearly abandoned over the cause célèbre and its action hero.

When the commotion was at its loudest, Canon Simony appeared from inside the building. The decibel decline was minor and brief as he identified Worse and crossed the room to shake hands. He invited Worse to have tea in his office, and only when they both left the room was order restored to the reception area.

'They're a friendly lot,' said Worse, lowering himself into one of four leather chairs at Simony's invitation.

A secretary appeared at the door to take the tea order.

'They are relieved to see you appearing unscathed, as am I. There was much concern, despite my reassuring them at a staff meeting that I had spoken to you this morning.'

'I apologize for the broken slates.'

'That's not necessary. Any property damage is minimal considering the life-threatening situation you clearly faced. And a very small price to pay given that the ingenuity of your escape will enter village folklore, no doubt. It may even attract the curious into arm's reach of our collection plate.'

'To give, not take, it should be stated,' said Worse.

Simony smiled, lowering himself into another chair, to face Worse.

'Whoever would have thought, a bell rope having such multiplicity of functions[1],' he mused, then addressed Worse.

'I feel it is I who owe the apology, Chief Inspector, for the quite unfriendly reception I offered when we first met. I was ungracious, unworthy of my calling.'

Worse smiled acknowledgement, but said nothing.

'I can only plead, in mitigation, a reluctance to accept that such evil enters our church. It seems clear that you were correct in your judgement from the first.'

Simony met Worse's gaze, nodding slightly, and continued. 'Are we to take it that William Whencely died in that manner, from gas poisoning?'

'Yes,' said Worse.

There was a knock on the door, and Mary Coppicer entered with tea. Worse thanked her, and asked how she was. Her reply was more an admonishment.

'I warned you about the tower, Mr Worse.'

When she had left, Worse quietly completed the rebuke.

'... but you wouldn't listen.'

'She's a good soul, Mary,' said Simony. 'That tower aversion comes from her husband, you know. He doesn't enter the church out of superstition.'

Before speaking, Worse weighed irony against offence. 'Some might say, to the contrary, that others do enter out of superstition.'

'Ah. In that case we refer to it as faith, Chief Inspector.'

Worse tasted his tea. 'Have you any idea how a perpetrator could fill the tower with a toxic gas and not have the necessary paraphernalia noticed?'

'No, I do not. Our bell-ringers enter several times each day. It's even accessible to the public—though, as you were made aware, that is not encouraged.'

'Why is that?'

'Oh. It's not a strong prohibition. Simply because it is a work area. It's also used for storage. You would have noticed the spare chairs in there. I believe there's a repository of retired silverware as well, which I must examine one day.'

'I have seen it,' said Worse.

'And that space is not heated. The staircase may well be a public safety issue. You declared the electrics to be wanting. In fact, the more I think about it, the more inclined I am to declare it out of bounds to all but staff.'

'That would be a good idea. Anyway, for the moment it is a crime scene.'

Worse finished his tea and placed the cup and saucer on a side table.

'I take it that you are well acquainted with the history of St Eke's?'

'I believe so,' said Simony. 'May we offer you more tea?'

'Thank you, no; I'm fine. What can you tell me about the *Malison*?'

'Oh yes. The *Malison*. That unfortunate belief will be reignited from today.'

'Whatever the motive for an attack on me, a foreseeable consequence, as you observed, will be a revival of that belief.

Can you imagine any individual, or organization, who could conceivably be advantaged by that happening? And what that advantage might be?'

Simony sat back in his chair. 'That's an interesting line of reasoning, Chief Inspector. If we could answer that, I daresay we would rid our steeple of the curse. Unfortunately, nothing comes to mind.'

'When did you first become aware of the *Malison*?' asked Worse.

'I mentioned to you that I was posted here as assistant curate, early in my training for the ministry. Any number of people told me about it. As far as I know, there have been no adverse events for centuries that could possibly justify the belief. It's kept alive generationally by individuals like Mr Coppicer in our community, much to the dismay of the realists amongst us.'

'What is the diocesan view, officially?'

'That it is nonsense.'

'You imply that, centuries ago, there were indeed adverse events that supported the belief in a curse. Can you give me any details on those?'

'Before my calling, I was destined to become a mediaevalist. Rather extraordinarily, given my future living, St Eke's figures prominently in one of the great poems of the period. Perhaps you know it: Henry Oldrice's fourteenth-century *Th Pylgrymes Wey*.'

Worse was given no time to respond.

'This village was called Stēpel Raest at the time,' Simony continued. 'Rather inexplicably, the village fathers at some point adopted the gerund, giving the name more length and less sense.'

Worse smiled at the complaint. 'In the nature of history itself,' he said.

'Quite so. Anyway,' said Simony, 'Oldrice recounts the shocking murder of a pilgrim knight in our very own tower. And that wasn't the first. Many years earlier, another pilgrim died suspiciously, also in the tower. He is interred in our churchyard. Of course, over the centuries, there have been other deaths in or near the tower, but natural causes always provided sufficient explanation. Nevertheless, the myth of a curse managed to survive.'

Worse had stayed silent, taking in Simony's information. He decided to test the Canon's reaction to his own knowledge.

'You mentioned the historian Darian the other day. Are you aware that he has published a new, annotated translation of the *Wey*?'

Simony showed interest. 'No, I was not aware. Perhaps the man will find redemption through honest scholarship. Though judging from the work I referred to when we spoke, he has a great deal of atonement to suffer before finding the Kingdom of God.'

'Salvation may not be his life wish, of course. But I agree: he is not my favourite individual, either,' said Worse. 'On the other hand, he is a meticulous historian. His commentaries on Oldrice are fascinating.'

Worse stood up. 'Thank you for the tea, and our interesting conversation. If you have further thoughts on our problem, please call me.'

He took from his pocket the al-Sedeqim business card, and held it before Simony. 'Does this word mean anything to you?'

Simony looked at it for several seconds, finally pronouncing it.

'No. Should it?'

'I don't know,' said Worse. 'Where would I find Simon Acolytēs' grave?'

'I can point it out, but I think it will be inside the police fence for now.'

'Perhaps another time, then,' said Worse. 'Incidentally, in your—as it were—mediaeval period, did you have occasion to study the Oxford Passage in the *Wey*?'

'Oh yes. I remember that we were made to read it as best we could. It's basically uninterpretable as I expect you know.

For undergraduates wanting in maturity, that exercise was an invitation to produce doggerel translations or some other garble, most often salacious, in the manner of male youth garrisoned in hall.'

'Have you ever revisited it, out of interest, as a challenge?' asked Worse.

'I confess not. The demands of theological literature supervened, I'm afraid, and retain their hold.'

'Perhaps the Passage is, in fact, theological,' said Worse.

Simony looked surprised, then pleased. 'An interesting possibility, Chief Inspector. I take it your point is that we cannot know one way or the other until we translate it.'

'Thank you again,' said Worse, crossing to the door.

'Chief Inspector.'

Simony raised a hand to delay Worse's leaving. He was still sitting, facing Worse.

'You leave me curious. Are you a man of faith?'

'More a man of doubt, Canon Simony.'

Simony nodded, holding Worse's gaze. 'Though perhaps not entirely, I conclude.' Simony stood up. 'Doubt is good. Doubt is foundational to faith—for the greater the uncertainty to start, the stronger the faith that overcomes it.'

Worse was interested in the argument. He was also warming to Simony as a person.

'Go on,' he said.

'You know, it was never faith that drove those pilgrims to Canterbury; it was always doubt. About God's presence for some; about God's absence for others.'

'Even for the Worsener?'

'Ah yes, the Worsener. I would say especially for the Worsener.'

'What do you know about him?'

'I regret to say, only what I learned from the Oldrice poem, and even that, I fear, is rather forgotten over the years.'

'Why do you say "especially" in his case?'

'Only because the Worsener's calling was half priest, half knight. Part forgiveness, part vengeance. That's not fully Christian, it goes without saying.'

'Speaking of forgiveness, I understand there was another chivalric order in those times, called the Mercifuls. Can you tell me about them?'

'Ah yes,' Simony repeated, 'The Sixteen—'

'Sixteen?' interrupted Worse.

'There were Sixteen Graces, by which they ostensibly lived. When I studied the Order at university, it seemed these referred obliquely to sixteen ways of killing, rather than anything noble or religious. That was the cynical view of my tutor, in any case, who considered the purported physician role to be an instrument of power and influence.'

'But they provided hospice services?'

'That is well recorded, yes.'

'And what has happened to them?'

'Now? Goodness, Chief Inspector. They disappeared centuries ago, along with chivalry itself. Why your interest?'

'That business card that I just showed you; the word almost certainly signifies "sixteen". It was delivered anonymously to William Whencely a few weeks ago, followed by others simply bearing that number in Roman numerals. I'm interpreting them as messages of threat.'

'Are there other explanations?' asked Simony.

'Presumably there are. Can you suggest any?'

'I think not, at this stage, unhappily.'

'On another matter,' said Worse, 'do you know anything of the stories about Thomas Becket making secret visits to this church, escorted at night by Worseners?'

Simony looked amused.

'No, I do not. But I would be happy to advertise such a fiction if only to attract brethren to our services. Incidentally, his escorts would not be Worseners, who were too loyal to the King. It is much more likely that they were Mercifuls.'

Worse was still standing with his back to the door. He reached behind to grasp the handle.

'I've enjoyed this, and thank you again for the tea. But now I am the one left curious. Are you a man of doubt?'

Simony smiled. He glanced ironically around the room as if searching out eavesdroppers. Or perhaps it was to draw contrast with the elegance and appointments that would furnish a Cathedral office.

'Chief Inspector, is it not clear? For my faith, I am made canon. For my doubt, I am vicar of St Eke's.'

---

[1] Many would have thought—see note 1, Chapter 39.

15 THE CHEMISTRY LESSON

[Monday]

Worse left in a contemplative mood. The impression he had formed of Simony on the day of the funeral, and subsequently when interviewing him, now seemed quite false. He wondered if he had allowed himself to be prejudiced by Philip's negativity.

It was strange how one's view of another person could change, even quickly. Either it was erroneous at the start, or there was subterfuge—then or now—or, as Simony had alluded to, there was forgivable emotionality intervening. Or, perhaps the person had genuinely changed; but in Worse's experience, when that happened, it was rarely for the better.

Worse corrected himself, reflectively. Another possibility was a shift in observer bias: perhaps Worse himself had changed. Given his recent experience, that wouldn't be out of the question either.

He was surprised, though, to find himself drawn to Simony, enjoying his conversation, appreciating his intellect, respecting his evidently unconventional place in the Church. The assertion—so contrary to orthodoxy—that every pilgrim is driven not by conviction, but by doubt, was almost brutally insightful of the confessant soul.

For Worse, it made immediate sense: the defining state of mind of the pilgrim was never certainty, but anxiety. And how natural that would be in the impressionable, compelled by spiritual authority to visit places inextricably connected, through prayer and reliquary, to death.

Again, it brought to mind that favourite religious text, used by Simony the previous day: the first-century *Second Letter to the Syllabines*, in which St Ignorius delivers to a long-extinct people a redemptive ode commending to God their civilizational perplexity and despair.

One thing did trouble Worse, when he realized that during their discussion about the Worsener he had not identified himself as a Magnacart. The omission wasn't deliberate; he had simply not thought to mention it. Nevertheless, he now felt the oversight was in some way incompletely honest. He would rectify that when they next met.

—

As Worse walked home, he noted an unfamiliar car outside the Misgivingston house, and wondered if Nicholas had arrived. That was quickly confirmed when he heard voices from the kitchen.

Nicholas sprang from his chair to embrace Worse, expressing his relief at Worse's safety, having been told of the morning's events.

'It was quite something,' said Worse. 'I've been keen for days to have a turn ringing the St Eke's bell, but didn't imagine it would be from outside the tower, dangling on a rope over the roof of the nave. In a toxic confusional state, to add indignity to ... inharmony.'

'Undoubtedly a first, in all of England, Worse,' said Philip.

'Not to mention all of campanology,' said Veronica.

'Richard, Nicholas has arrived with seemingly boundless energy, and suggests we all have a special Ferende meal out in Canterbury tonight,' said Millie.

'On the basis of a strong recommendation from some Madregalo *cuisinas* whom I know,' said Nicholas.

'We thought we would invite Xavier to join us,' said Veronica.

'That's a great idea,' said Worse. He addressed Millie.

'Has the family brought Nicholas up to date with our thinking on St Eke's?'

'I believe we have,' said Philip, before Millie could answer.

'In that case, wonderful as it is to be with you all, I think I need some rest after my night up.'

He was tired, but also expected that the four of them would enjoy pure Misgivingston time together.

'So you should,' said Veronica. 'We all had a quiet morning to sleep. You need to get your strength up for tonight.'

'I'll join you soon,' said Millie.

—

It was true that he was tired, but his mind was too active to admit sleep. Whether it was efficiently active, he couldn't judge, but he did feel a strong drive to answer some of the questions he had raised with Simony.

Worse reasoned that if he could discover how the tower was filled so quickly with hydrogen sulphide, he might be provided with a clue as to who could have been responsible.

He researched its commercial availability. There were suppliers of the compressed gas catering for certain industries, but the convenience of this source was offset by the size and weight of the strengthened cylinders in which it was transported, not to mention ancillary gear like reducing valves and gauges. It seemed impossible that this equipment could be quickly deployed, operated safely, and removed without drawing attention.

Worse's approach was to imagine himself the perpetrator, setting about finding methods to meet his needs. As was his habit, he returned to first principles, much as Grimly would; for current purposes these were to be found in elementary chemistry problems. He studied several candidate reactants, but only one, aluminium sulphide, offered the convenience he sought. Then he considered the feasibility of generating quantities of the gas sufficient to fill the tower to toxic levels.

By the time Millie came into the Surgery, expecting to find Worse asleep, he had schemed out a hypothesis on his notepad. She sat beside him while he explained his thoughts. When he had finished running through a yield calculation, she asked what equipment would be needed to contain the reaction.

'Very little. A bowl or tray of some kind. Metal, ceramic, plastic,' said Worse. 'The larger surface area of a tray or platter would promote rapid gas production.'

'So the murderer sets out a tray of aluminium sulphide, pours in the water, and runs to safety; then returns to clean up when the reaction's finished and the gas sufficiently dispersed?'

'That's my general thinking. If I were the villain, I would want the reassurance of a gas mask and a monitoring device. That gives slightly more bulk to conceal, but I would say it's possible.'

Millie ran her eye over Worse's calculations again.

'Very impressive, Richard. And who is the villain?'

'To be determined. So,' continued Worse, 'how are you finding Nicholas?'

'It's really lovely to see him. You two should have a good catch-up when you get the chance. Right now, you need to sleep, and Nicholas has driven Dad to Canterbury to check out his Saab at the panel beater. The family majority vote is that it should be written off, but he's defiantly attached to it.'

'I can understand that,' said Worse. 'Saabs were once my favourite, too.'

Worse's calculation, using rounded values, was approximately as follows. Hydrogen sulphide is generated when aluminium sulphide reacts with water

$$Al_2S_3 + 6H_2O \rightarrow 2Al(OH)_3 + 3H_2S \uparrow,$$

such that three moles (3 x 34.08 g = 102.24 g) of the gas are produced from one mole (150.16 g) of the metallic sulphide. At Standard Temperature and Pressure (STP), this mass of gas occupies 3 x 22.4 litres, or 67.2 l.

The floor area of the square sectioned tower was 5 x 5 m^2 and the height estimated to be 20 m, giving a volume of 500 m^3. Adding the volume of the steeple (modelled as a cone having base radius 2.5 m and height 10 m) gives a confined space volume of 565 m^3, or 565,000 litres.

Hydrogen sulphide is lethal in a concentration of 500–1000 ppm. Assuming containment and perfect mixing, the latter concentration would result from 565 l of H_2S released into the tower. At STP this equates to 565/22.4 = 25.22 moles, which is produced from 25.22/3 = 8.4 moles of aluminium sulphide. This has a mass of 8.4 x 150.16 = 1262 g. For completion, the reaction requires six moles of water per mole of aluminium sulphide, in this case being 6 x 8.4 x 18 = 907.2 g, or about

907 ml in volume. For a concentration of 500 ppm, the substrate quantities derived will be, of course, half those given.

It is obvious that a very toxic atmosphere would result from mixing about half a kilogram of aluminium sulphide and less than half a litre of water, amounts that would be easy to smuggle or conceal within, say, a backpack or even in coat pockets.

16 LUSANG MAJORK

[Monday]

Veronica's car was unable to accommodate all six safely, so it was decided that she and Philip would collect Xavier, while Nicholas drove Millie and Worse in his rental car. They managed to find parking within a few spaces of each other, and regrouped outside the restaurant. It was called King of Kent, after the ship that in 1816 first carried British naturalist Thomas MacAkerman[1] to what is now the harbour of Madregalo.

Before entering, introductions were made on the pavement. Xavier shook hands with Millie, Worse, and Nicholas. His body language was expressive, and he conveyed delight and interest with perfect sociability, all without speaking.

The restaurant interior was quite formal, having deep-pile carpet and well-spaced tables with white linen tablecloths and sterling silver cutlery. Moreover, there was no background music. Veronica was pleased that it was suitable acoustically for a party of six to hold a conversation; she thought, if Xavier spoke, they had a chance of hearing him. Their table was circular, and by forward planning, they placed Xavier between Worse and Millie. Clockwise, Nicholas was next to Millie, then Philip, then Veronica.

The menus brought to their table were in Ferent, with rather scanty English explanations. Nicholas interpreted for the others as each sought to understand the choices. Eventually, to the relief of all, he offered to order a sharing banquet for the table.

When their waitperson returned, Nicholas conducted a dialogue in rapid Ferent while holding up and waving around his copy of the menu. It was almost melodramatic, in a way that those who knew him would see as out of character.

They concluded that gesticulation was an inherent manner of the language. The waitperson behaved similarly, nodding vigorously. She cast her eyes around the table, and left.

'What was that about, Nicholas?' asked Philip.

Before Nicholas could answer, an immaculately presented chef appeared, hurrying up to the table. Nicholas stood and offered a handshake. They spoke in Ferent. The chef beamed, also casting his eyes around the table, and returned to the kitchen. Five inquisitive looks were directed at Nicholas as he took his seat.

'Something not on the menu; it involves a little extra time for special preparation. I hope you don't mind.'

'Mind? Nicholas, we're the lucky beneficiaries of your knowledge,' said Worse, to murmurs of agreement.

They were served drinks, including a special vintage seki wine, and a variety of traditional appetizers. Shortly after, their waitress returned to position a lazy Susan on the table. It was made of glass, and heavy, requiring an assistant to carry the tray separately from the base. When it was assembled, those two waitpersons stood back from the table, and the chef reappeared. Nicholas respectfully stood up, which allowed the chef to reach to the middle of the table and gently manoeuvre the tray, checking for smooth rotation and balance. Satisfied, he yet again cast his eyes around the table, smiled at Nicholas, nodded approval to the two waitpersons, and left.

Nicholas resumed his seat, looking pleased. He reached out and touched the tray, moving it back and forth a few degrees.

'Polished glass bearing. We are immensely fortunate. The glass is a tradition unique to this dish. Be very careful with it—they are usually heirlooms in the chef's family. To have it broken would bring great distress and shame. The establishment would close.'

Everyone stared at the table centrepiece.

—

Worse had arrived with a shoulder bag, which was slung over the back of his chair. He now took from it an A4 unruled pad and three ballpoint pens—blue, red and green. He folded the pad open at its first blank page, selected blue, and quickly sketched a network[2].

Now everyone stared at the pad.

Worse slid the pad a little to his left, in front of Xavier. Xavier examined it, chose the red pen, made a modification, and slid it back to Worse.

Worse's face showed appreciation. He further edited in blue, returning the pad to Xavier. Xavier added more red. This back and forth repeated at least a dozen times. Finally, Xavier, having noted that Millie was showing intense interest in the process, passed it to his left, at the same time offering her the green pen. Millie studied the page, running her pen as a pointer, through the network. She made alterations in green and passed it back. Xavier glanced at the page, then stared at Millie in evident admiration. She had added a vertex with a simple connectivity, and aggregated others. Xavier looked back at the page, resting his pen on the new element, thinking. Without altering anything, he passed it to Worse. Worse also stared at it, thinking. Then with his blue pen he drew, for emphasis, continuous rings around Millie's vertex, and sat back.

'Brilliant, Millie,' he said quietly. Not all heard it, but Xavier nodded.

The page now resembled a child's scribble drawing in three colours, but it was profoundly meaningful. For the entire exchange, not a word had been uttered.

'What was that deafening conversation about?' asked Philip.

Worse wanted to say 'Solving a murder', but that would be premature. Instead, he answered innocuously but truthfully.

'Xavier was kindly helping with an automaton problem.'

He closed the pad, collected the pens, and returned them to his bag. Millie knew what he was thinking.

Philip wasn't satisfied. As the non-mathematician at the table, he felt excluded.

'Perhaps that eloquent script should be signed, dated,

framed, and donated to the restaurant to hang at this table, in perpetuity,' he said, adding, 'Titled *Great Chatter Was Here.*'

'I would be happy to explain it, later,' said Worse.

There was a surprising edge to Worse's voice, conveying unamused. It was a subtle reprimand, and no one could have missed the fact.

Veronica certainly didn't. Sitting next to Worse, she had seen the network design evolve. She couldn't know what it represented, but believed if it held Xavier's interest, it was important. She gave Philip a disapproving glare.

—

The restaurant lights switched off and on three times. Nicholas requested that everyone be quiet. Patrons at other tables also fell silent, wondering what was happening.

'Here it comes,' he said. 'It's their most celebrated dish, and they're doing it properly.'

He turned to have a view of the kitchen. The door opened. Through it emerged the chef, now wearing a toque blanche, followed by a sous-chef and two waitpersons, each carrying a component of the banquet.

The procession reached their table, the chef directing his staff on where and how to set everything down. On the lazy Susan was placed a large ceramic lidded pot. This was all executed with meticulous attention to detail. When each assistant had completed their task, they stood back in a row, almost to attention.

Then the lights dimmed again, and stayed low. From the kitchen came another sous-chef, holding a flaming torch, which she passed to her chef with the solemnity of an Olympic handover. She then joined the row of her colleagues. Again, Nicholas vacated his chair for access. The chef removed the lid from the centre bowl and waved the torch through escaping aromatic vapours. There was a soft whoosh, flames leaping almost a metre high before subsiding into a bluish will-o'-the-wisp gentleness. During this time, the assembled staff provided a quiet, harmonized recitation, in Ferent. This continued until the flames were done, then with a small bow of the head they returned, in line, chef last, to the kitchen. The lights came up, with an effect similar to a stage curtain closing a performance. Nicholas sat down, and handed a serving ladle to Veronica.

'Mother, you go first.'

As Veronica served herself, everyone watched, mesmerized, as if she were an actor in the still unfolding ceremony. Veronica herself, aware of being the focus of the mood, broke the spell.

'What was the chorus about, Nicholas?'

'A prayer to Rep'husela, their first queen, giving thanks. We would call it a grace.'

'Well, I give thanks as well,' said Veronica, replacing the ladle and carefully spinning the plate to position it before Xavier.

—

'This is delicious, Nicholas,' said Millie. 'What gives it that exquisitely perfumed aroma? I can't quite identify it.'

She was reaching to the lazy Susan for another serving, liberally covering it with a spoonful of deep-red sauce.

Xavier agreed by facial expression. He hadn't said a word all evening.

Philip, too, had been very quiet for a while, following what must have felt like unexpected admonishment from Worse. It was a relief, particularly for Millie, when he regained his humour.

'It wasn't too spicy for anyone, I hope,' said Nicholas. He didn't take up Millie's question.

'Not at all,' said Worse. 'What do you call this dish?'

'*Lusang Majork*[3], spicy meatballs, roughly speaking,' said Nicholas, smiling.

'It's wonderful, Nicholas,' said Veronica. 'This has been more a lived dining experience than a meal out. I don't think I've ever seen anything so thespian in a restaurant.'

'Agreed,' said Philip, reaching over to grasp the ladle like a mallet and holding it in the air. 'The pure theatre of it couldn't be bettered at The Marlowe. Now, if everyone's had enough of the main, let's smash the lazy Susan. That's the custom, isn't it Nicholas?'

Xavier's eyes opened wide, he rose in his seat, and a restraining arm jerked forward.

'No-o-o!' he cried out.

Philip and Veronica grinned at each other.

---

[1] It was on this voyage that Thomas MacAkerman encountered the weaver fish, becoming the first European to describe the species, to which he assigned its common name. His account of the discovery is one of the treasures of pre-Victorian scientific literature.

[2] For purposes of design and discussion, Grimly compilers are conveniently represented in salient form as networks, using graph-theoretic notation and methods. Essentially, applying aggregation rules, analytics can be reduced to a small subset of Grimly that is relevant to a question of interest. (The validity of the approach is easily tested in a given case by sequential disaggregation.) It was by means of these diagrams and a standard symbol inventory that Worse and Millie communicated wordlessly with Xavier. Readers wanting an introduction to basic concepts of graph theory, as well as a glimpse of eighteenth-century promenade society, are encouraged to seek out the famous Königsberg bridge problem.

[3] A semi-secret traditional delicacy from the Madregalo region, much admired by the foreign epicure—though often less so when made aware of its name in translation: Great Bleeding Balls of Satan. A stage in its preparation is said to involve Bergamot Sea water, accounting possibly for Millie's comment on aroma. (See Prologue, note 16.)

17 A FACE IN THE BELFRY

It was almost ten o'clock when they left the King of Kent. Their departure drew more ceremony from the chef and a maître d', who had apparently been summoned to the premises during an evening of otherwise quiet patronage. Other diners must have wondered if they were seeing a party of Ferende royals or senior diplomats.

They split between the two cars, as before, for the ride back to Steeple Resting. Worse checked his mobile and found an email from Simony.

Chief Inspector

Provoked by our conversation this morning, and hoping to make amends for my deficiencies regarding the history of St Eke's, I spent much of the afternoon in the locked gallery of our Cathedral archives. There's a great deal of fascinating, and I should say surprising, material that I think you would find of interest, if not actual relevance in answering some of the questions you raised. I would be pleased to meet and discuss the same at your convenience. Meanwhile, I have instructed our senior archivist, Mrs Thelma Dewey, to grant you full access under my rights should you wish to peruse any records in your own time. I think you should know that Mrs Dewey informed me that Mr Whencely consulted the same archive in the weeks before his unfortunate death. As St Ignorius advises (*2 Syll.*): *Make of my words what you will.*

Kind regards

Wilfred Simony

Worse wondered if anything in the Canon's findings would accord with the Grimly analysis conducted at the dinner table. He decided to call Simony the following morning.

Nicholas, Millie and Worse arrived back at the house first, as Philip and Veronica stopped in the village to drop off Xavier. Worse offered to make tea, and the three sat around the kitchen table.

'I don't think you were well positioned to see, as it were, our conversation with Xavier tonight, Nicholas,' said Worse. 'I'm sorry about that.'

'Don't worry, Worse. I was entertained enough watching vicariously from a distance. As you would have noticed, logicians and others in their discussions go to some trouble to maintain clarity about whether they are referring to Grimly the person or Grimly the automaton. I feel I can contribute to the literature by reporting the two formally indistinguishable.'

Worse smiled. He had a strong sentimental connection to Nicholas, and he felt it now.

'It's very nice to see you, Nicholas. I want to hear more about developments at the LDI station. How is Paulo?'

'He's well; he sends his regards to you. What did you learn from Grimly?'

Worse smiled again. Nicholas wanted to be in the moment.

'It's easy to assume that at St Eke's, what we see is all there is, in respect of access and egress. That is, disregarding multiplicity of church doors, we can move back and forward between the exterior, the nave, and the bell tower only linearly.'

'But certain things are better explained by extra paths?' said Nicholas.

'Exactly,' said Worse. 'There's an unusual feature of the door between the tower and the nave that I find somewhat unsettling. It has bolts on both sides. Millie's network introduces a circuit to make sense of that, and much else. Unlikely as it appears when you're in there staring at those mighty Norman walls, Grimly posits another way in and out.'

'Which is how poisoner and victim meet and separate,' said Millie.

It was a curiously personalizing yet matter-of-fact statement, and the other two looked at her for some seconds. Worse wondered how abstractly her mind was working when she spoke; whether she imagined characters in the building, or was reading off the red, blue and green model of earlier.

'Can we explore the place tomorrow?' said Nicholas.

'We can,' said Worse. 'It's not officially cleared for entry, but I can get us in. I'm sure the air will be safe by now. And there's something that I particularly want to look at.'

'That being?' said Nicholas.

Worse had no time to reply, as at that moment they heard Philip and Veronica opening the front door. Millie called out that they should come to the kitchen.

'Any conversation to report?' she asked as they entered.

'Oh yes. A "Thank you" following a journey-long pause following "No" at the restaurant,' said Veronica. 'Altogether, an unbearable prolixity that leaves me craving more silence.'

Worse was less in the mood for light humour, especially at Xavier's expense. The particular something that he wanted to look for at St Eke's was a possibility that had been troubling him, more so—if indistinctly—since reading Simony's email. In Grimly terms, it was Millie's green vertex.

'Does anybody know if St Eke's has a crypt? Now or in the past?'

The question was answered with four blank faces.

'Well, that's something we need to find out,' he said.

—

Worse was still awake at midnight when his phone rang. Cecile Simony was profusely apologetic for ringing that late, but her distress underneath a stoicism was clear. Wilfred had not returned home and was not answering his phone. She knew he had been in touch with Worse that evening, and hoped Worse had knowledge of his whereabouts.

'Cecile, it's fine ringing me at any time. You haven't woken me. Where would your husband be normally on a Monday night?'

'He visits the parish hospices, and sometimes the sick at home, but he's never home later than nine. I always hold supper so that we eat together.'

'So he would be in Steeple Resting?'

'Not necessarily the village. Anywhere in the parish. Several hospices are converted manors, some quite isolated.'

'Did he say anything about his plans for the evening?'

'Only that he hoped to speak to you about the goings-on at St Eke's.'

'We didn't speak. I received an email from him at eight-thirty,' said Worse. 'When did you last see or speak to Wilfred, Cecile?'

'He had a quick lunch at home before going to work at the Cathedral. Then he phoned at about five to say he was returning to the village. That's when he said he wanted to speak to you.'

'Are you at home at present?'

'Yes.'

'Do you have anyone who can be with you for now?'

'My sister and her husband are coming over.'

'Good. I will start some enquiries. Would you be able to make a list of the hospices and so on that Wilfred would normally have on his Monday rounds?'

'Yes, I can do that. I will do it now.'

Worse provided his email address. He tried to be reassuring but was privately extremely concerned.

Millie had been woken by the call and was sitting up in bed.

'What's happened?' she asked, when Worse rang off.

Worse gave an account of Cecile's news as he got dressed.

'Where are you going?' she asked.

'I'll start by looking around St Eke's,' said Worse.

Millie jumped out of bed. 'I'm coming with you this time.'

'Bring the torches,' said Worse.

—

As they left by the Surgery front door, Worse phoned PC Rence to brief him on the development and request that he join them with keys to the security fence. He also asked that RTA reports for the evening be reviewed for involvement of the Canon's vehicle.

They crossed the road and headed west to the front of the Old Vicarage. Worse's heart sank when he recognized Simony's car parked in the vicar's reserved bay. He checked that it was locked. There were no lights on inside the building.

Worse had a bad feeling that they needed to be looking inside St Eke's itself, and he led Millie back to the lychgate to await Rence. The church was in total darkness, and at that distance their torches were unhelpful.

Worse strained to see the top of the tower. There wasn't enough light to make out the detail of the bell rope, but something about the opening from which he knew it emerged caught his attention. He walked eastward along the fence for a few metres, trying to find a better angle to see. There seemed to be a small patch of white on the sill.

Rence arrived with light flashing but no siren. Worse ran to the car and borrowed binoculars. He asked Rence to direct his roof-mounted spotlight onto the eastside bell tower windows, then to unlock the gate on the security fence.

Worse entered the graveyard and found the best place to scan the tower walls. It wasn't easy to make out, but something was definitely changed about that window. He called Rence over and handed him the binoculars, asking him to look at it.

'What do you make of it?' asked Worse.

'I can't be sure. We need more light, or we need to go up there.'

'Millie,' called Worse. 'Can you give an opinion on what you see here?'

Millie joined them and took the binoculars from Rence.

'It doesn't look good, Richard. It could be a person.'

'That's what I think,' said Worse. He spoke to Rence.

'Sound the general alarm. Everything. We may need a

giant cherry picker to get up there if it's toxic inside again. Meanwhile, I want a drone camera to check what we're seeing. Preferably one that can get through an opening and give us a look inside.'

Worse ran into the church through the open south door. He found the tower door bolted on the outside. When he slid this undone, he pulled on the door handle, only to find it was bolted on the inside as well.

He also smelt hydrogen sulphide.

Worse returned to the others outside the south-west porch and described his findings. Rence informed him that emergency response teams were on their way. A cherry picker was being sourced in Ashford.

—

The following minutes were something of a surreal re-run of events of the previous morning, though on a larger scale. The multitude of sirens converging on Old Forge Lane wakened the Misgivingston household, and probably the entire village. Philip crossed the road and found Worse.

'I see you're down from the parapet at least. What's happening this time?'

'There's hydrogen sulphide in the tower again, and we can't get access. There may be a victim up in the belfry.'

Given Philip's habitual cynicism about their vicar, Worse knew that what he said next might profoundly affect him. He placed a hand on Philip's shoulder.

'We can't see well enough, but I have reason to believe that it is Canon Simony.'

Philip looked stunned. Veronica gasped quietly, and put an arm around him.

'My God. My God,' said Philip, turning to look upward to the belfry.

'Excuse me,' said Worse.

Hazmat officers had already confirmed the presence of hydrogen sulphide leaking around the tower door into the nave. Worse observed two of them attempting to break the internal bolt using a battering ram. It looked like a hopeless exercise, and he stopped them.

'That door opens outwards, so you're working against the bolt and the doorjamb. It will need a power saw to take out a block. I think it best if we figure out a rescue solution from outside first.'

Worse hurried out to speak to the fire rescue commander, Méchelle Lachute. They conducted a hasty stand-up meeting with the senior hazmat officer and a police superintendent from Canterbury. Dr Jane Malleson arrived in her private car as they were conferring. She joined their group, acknowledging Worse with a nod.

'First priority: let's get some drone footage,' said Worse.

'Underway,' said Méchelle. 'We expect the cherry picker in thirty minutes.'

'If there are signs of life, we haven't got that time,' said Worse. Here are the options. If we cut out the tower door lock, every one's put at risk from gas. Anyway, we know from this morning that hazmats can't easily get up the spiral staircase in protective gear, and they certainly couldn't evacuate a patient that way. That leaves getting up on the outside. The bell rope took my weight yesterday, but we can't trust it again as its fixation may have been tampered with. The safest, quickest way up is to fire a grappling hook into the battlement and climb the rope.'

Méchelle agreed, and sent the command.

'I'll do the climb,' said Jane.

Worse was surprised, and turned to her, but she spoke first.

'As far as I know, you and I are the only doctors here who can certify death and take the urgency out of this operation, if appropriate. As your treating physician of yesterday, I won't permit you to do it. Re-exposure to H_2S so soon could be fatal.'

Worse knew the argument was sound, and simply nodded.

—

'Live streaming,' came the shout from one of Méchelle's team.

It was unmistakably Canon Simony.

'Hold it steady ... there,' said Worse. He watched intently for about a minute.

'Respiratory movement, what do you think?' he asked of Jane.

'Not convinced,' she said.

'Cyanosis?'

'Impossible to say confidently.'

Worse addressed the drone operator. 'Can you bring it down a little to look upwards at his face? We'd like to see the eyes.'

That manoeuvre wasn't successful.

Jane had already donned a climbing harness. 'I'm going up,' she said.

She hurried to the ambulance and loaded some items into a shoulder bag slung around her neck. As she passed back beside them she spoke to Méchelle.

'I won't need breathing apparatus. This will be quick.'

Méchelle's crew had a ladder up over the aisle roof to the nave parapet, where Worse had been stuck earlier. From there they had a roof ladder laid over the tarpaulin on the nave slates. The new rope was easily accessible from there.

Jane was up both ladders and onto the rope with amazing agility. Any reservation that Worse had felt about her taking on this task was dispelled by the sheer confidence of her climb.

At the top, she locked her harness to the rope to be hands-free, and pulled herself across to the middle opening. From there she could reach in beside Simony's head and feel for a temporal artery pulse.

Worse was watching her through binoculars and could follow her thinking. She was clearly dissatisfied with her access. He saw her grasp the bell rope and test its security. Then she moved her weight fully across and re-clamped. Now she could pass her hand past Simony's head to reach the carotid.

'He's got a pulse,' she shouted, without looking down. 'I want oxygen here now. Use the new rope.'

Resuscitation gear had already been stockpiled on the nave

parapet. Within twenty seconds a climber was taking a light oxygen cylinder upwards. He also clamped at the top, passing the mask and supply tubing to Jane.

'What's his name?' asked Worse.

'Ryan,' said Méchelle.

There were now several spotlights on the tower, from the array of emergency vehicles. They offered better illumination, of course, but a strange effect was the multiple shadows of two people dangling on ropes from high on the tower wall.

'Where's the platform?' called Jane. 'We need to get him out and intubated.'

'Five minutes,' shouted Méchelle.

The Canterbury police had set to moving some of their vehicles and disassembling part of the fence to improve access for the crane. The public, including Millie and her family, had been escorted well back, across Old Forge Lane.

Worse found Rence. 'Get me the Archdeacon on the phone, Constable.'

'Archdeacon of Canterbury?'

'I believe that would be the closest,' said Worse.

—

Worse phoned Cecile Simony. First, he ascertained that her sister was with her. Then he explained the situation succinctly. He told her that the Archdeacon would be at the Simony home within a few minutes. If she wished to come to St Eke's, the police would drive them both over. As soon as he knew more, he would be back in touch.

By the time Worse had finished those calls, the telescopic cherry picker was in position with outrigger jacks deployed. The platform driver stopped at the nave parapet to pick up a nurse and the resuscitation pack, along with a kitted-up hazmat officer. He drew up just below the left window for Ryan to join them, and for the hazmat officer to climb into the belfry. Then he moved the platform to the right, picking up Jane, and locking position just below Simony's head.

With the man inside lifting and pushing, and two men

pulling from the platform, they made progress, if slowly, extracting their patient. Jane and the nurse used the time to prepare airway gear. Jane's judgement was that every second counted for providing assisted ventilation and good oxygenation, and she would establish this on the platform. Comprehensive assessment and monitoring could wait until they were on the ground.

Cecile had decided she would rather come to St Eke's than stay in Canterbury awaiting news, and a police siren announced her arrival. Worse was helping Jane as Simony was stretchered from the platform to an ITU ambulance.

'Okay with you if I bring the Canon's wife in?' he asked Jane.

'Of course.'

Worse walked to where Cecile was alighting from the car. He introduced himself briefly to the Archdeacon, thanked her for responding as she had, then placed a hand on Cecile's elbow to guide her over to the ambulance. On the way, he prepared her for what she was about to see.

'Wilfred is alive. He is now in an induced coma until we can determine the effects of the poison. Don't be concerned when you see his breathing tube and some other lines and wires. Most of those are to monitor how he is. He's in excellent hands with Dr Malleson taking care of him. She's a specialist emergency medicine and intensive therapy physician.'

They arrived at the open end of the ambulance.

'Jane, this is Mrs Simony.'

'How do you do, Mrs Simony. I'm Dr Malleson.' Jane glanced up for the greeting but immediately looked back to her work. 'You can step inside for a second if you wish.'

Worse helped Cecile up the step. She stooped beside Wilfred's legs, touching his knees through a warming blanket. Jane smiled at her.

'Does Wilfred have any medical issues we should know about—heart problems, medications, allergies of any kind?'

'No, doctor, I don't believe so.'

Jane reached over to touch Cecile's hand.

'It'll be easier for you when we're in the ITU. Worse, I'm ready to move in three minutes. Mrs Simony, you can follow us in a car.'

'I'll take you back to the Archdeacon,' Worse said to Cecile.

'Is it the same poison that happened to you?' she asked as they neared her police car.

'Yes, it is, Cecile. It's good that Wilfred was able to get to the window for fresh air.'

Worse was aware that her question sought, and his answer provided, implicit optimism. But inside himself, he felt very little.

18 THE THINKING BUS

When the ambulance pulled away, it carried with it much of the urgency and slight franticness of the scene.

The platform had delivered a second hazmat officer into the belfry, and was on station to bring them down after they conducted gas analysis inside. A second team in the nave was using an angle grinder to cut out the bolt on the tower door. As Worse pointed out, the possibility of another victim inside needed to be excluded.

Worse approached their supervisor, who happened to be HCN from the previous morning.

'Your people know that we'll want prints and DNA swabs inside?'

'They know. They're careful. The outside of the door is done.'

'And I'd like the absolutely earliest clearance on this place that you can manage to justify,' he said.

'Understood. Good to see you looking well after your own drama, Chief Inspector.'

Worse thanked him.

'You have my number.'

At that moment, the number rang. It was the Archdeacon. Worse didn't spend time on greetings.

'How is Cecile?'

'As well as can be expected. Very composed. She's sitting beside Wilfred now that all the admission business has calmed down. The staff say he's stable.'

'That's a good start,' said Worse. 'I'm very grateful that you responded as you did. Cecile has a sister in Canterbury. Do you know if she's been brought up to date?'

'That's Margaret. I spoke to her at the Simony home. She's now on her way to the hospital.'

'What are your plans with St Eke's? Obviously, the building will be closed until we eliminate this risk.'

'I intend to meet with the parish staff and volunteers later this morning. Services will be held in the hall for the time being. I have in mind a temporary vicar who will fit in well with that community.'

'And how are you?' asked Worse.

There was a period of silence.

'I'm fine, thank you.'

—

When Worse felt he was no longer needed at the scene, he crossed the road to the Misgivingston house. The others had returned home when Simony was evacuated. Philip and Veronica had gone to their room; Millie and Nicholas were in the kitchen.

'How do you think he'll go?' asked Millie.

'It's too early to say. The issue is hypoxic brain damage. We don't know his duration of exposure, and how quickly he managed to get to the window. I'm hoping that the quite vigorous breeze we felt last evening would have dispersed the gas in the belfry quickly. Otherwise, I think he would have perished before we got there. There's not a lot of time with hydrogen sulphide.'

'How did he get in, through the locked gate?' asked Nicholas.

'There was an emergency key left at the Old Vicarage; Rence had one. Maybe the perpetrator let him in on some pretext.'

'When will we know how he is?' asked Millie.

'I expect they'll try him off the ventilator in the next twenty-four hours, maybe even tonight, to assess him neurologically. Then we'll have a better idea of prognosis.'

Millie looked at her watch.

'It's almost three-thirty. Why don't we all get some sleep?'

—

When Millie awoke, she found Worse standing in his dressing gown by the bedroom window, looking out at St Eke's. She had seen him like that several times over the days and come to realize that it served as some kind of thinking vista for him. She called out from the bed.

'How are you, Richard?'

Worse turned to her. 'I'm okay. Would you like tea?'

Millie sensed he was not okay. 'Yes, I would. But come here first.'

She made room for him to sit on the edge of the bed, close to her. Worse complied.

'How long have you been awake?'

'Half an hour or so.'

Millie could well imagine that he had been standing by the window all that time, staring out.

'You were thinking about Canon Simony?'

'I was.'

Millie placed a hand on his, and stayed quiet.

'I should have foreseen the risk,' added Worse.

'How could you possibly have done so?' said Millie. 'Two attacks in two nights is crazy. And the vicar, of all people. No one would expect that. The place was fenced off with warning signs everywhere. Nothing more could have been done.'

'Even so, I missed something,' said Worse. 'Remember what I said in Perth? About assuming the worst case?'

'Of course I do—it was confronting. But self-recrimination is not your thing, Richard. You're a forward thinker.'

'Precisely. Anticipation is where I failed.'

'For heaven's sake, Richard, you have not failed.'

Worse met Millie's gaze, with no indication of how her assurance was received. He stood up.

'I'll bring you tea.'

—

Worse returned to find Millie standing by the bedroom window, as he had been. He suggested that they have their tea in the sitting room.

'Is anyone else up?' she asked.

'The kettle was warm; I didn't see anyone.'

Worse poured the tea.

'Do you have any news about the Canon?' Millie asked.

'At this very moment, he is being reviewed at the ITU morning handover. They'll be in touch as soon as his management plan is agreed.'

Millie nodded. Worse continued.

'He's been stable since admission, apparently. They did a brain CT overnight; that was satisfactory.'

'That sounds promising?'

'Yes. It does.'

Millie drank from her mug. 'You've come to like the canon, haven't you, Richard?'

'He's an interesting man,' said Worse. 'I certainly respect him. Actually, I do like him, yes. Why do you ask?'

'Oh, because I want to understand you. How you are. How you are being affected.'

Worse appreciated her caring. But he had a question.

'Why do you think your father is so negative about him?'

'I really don't know,' said Millie, 'other than a constitutional disdain for religion generally and a level of horror at past failings of the Church. I suppose he's always been an inveterate rationalist, anyway.'

'You know, Millie, Simony is far from irrational,' said Worse.

—

Worse walked over to the Old Vicarage, letting himself in using the key code. He wanted to be there before the staff arrived at 9.00 am, in order to provide news and some reassurance regarding the attack on their vicar, and address natural safety concerns about St Eke's.

In the meantime, he made a quick search of the Canon's office, particularly the desk, hoping there might be some indication in the form of notes or archival copies pointing to Simony's email remarks about surprising findings in Canterbury. And, more especially, anything to suggest why he had made an unscheduled visit to the tower at night.

There was nothing helpful along those lines, but Worse did spend a few minutes looking through a desk diary, which accorded with Cecile's information about the usual Monday evening hospice calls.

—

Rence's intelligence of the previous day, that in view of the attack on Worse, Kent Police were planning to direct more resources to the Whencely case, proved accurate. Now the shocking murder attempt on Simony only added impetus.

Around midmorning, Worse received a call from an Inspector Wirrier, who explained that he had been tasked with setting up an investigatory team, under Worse's command, to assist in what was referred to as the St Eke's matters. He requested that Worse and he meet in person later in the day for initial planning.

Worse next phoned Rence, asking that he question Mansion on his whereabouts overnight. It had struck Worse as odd, given his role as verger, and living on site, that he hadn't responded to the commotion at the church.

'By the way, Constable, you were correct in thinking there might be a priority shift in high-level material support for investigations here. We will be addressing that today. Would you like to be a member of the new team?'

'I would like that very much, Chief Inspector. Thank you.'

—

Wirrier came to Simony's office at midday. They introduced themselves at the door, shaking hands. Worse invited him to sit down.

'I'm sure that Canon Simony would not be distressed if we use his office temporarily,' said Worse. 'Do you know the Canon?'

'Yes.'

There was no unnecessary elaboration, a characteristic that Worse generally liked in people.

Wirrier handed Worse a printed list of personnel that

he recommended be recruited, going through the names highlighting the strengths they would bring. When he had finished, he asked if Worse had any questions.

'When can they start?'

'I took the liberty of assigning some to duties earlier today. We're covering forensics on the Canon's car and clothes, accessing phone records, checking last known whereabouts, as well as determining his business with the Cathedral archivist yesterday afternoon. I believe we should give first priority to his attack, on the grounds that the leads will be freshest. Of course, the attempt on your life, and the murder of Mr Whencely, will be integral. I propose that we have a full meeting at eight pm, for you to meet the other officers. That will be well after the prayer service in the hall. Some will want to attend.'

'Excellent,' said Worse. 'One thing: I would like our local PC Rence to be part of the team. He's been very helpful to me, is keen, and has good local knowledge.'

'I will contact him,' said Wirrier. 'I will also arrange relief officers to cover his station duties.'

'Do you know Rence?' asked Worse.

'Yes.'

There it was again. Succinct, nothing superfluous, bordering on shutdown.

'One final thing,' Wirrier added. 'The privilege of naming the task force belongs to you.'

Worse thought for a few seconds. 'Campanile,' he said.

—

At 1.00 pm, Worse walked home. He wasn't hungry, but he knew the others would be meeting up for lunch. He joined them briefly in the kitchen, relaying the news about Task Force Campanile.

Millie read Worse's mood perfectly.

'Are you needing some quiet time, Richard?'

Worse seized the permission, more abruptly than he intended, by jumping up from the table.

'I do, yes. Excuse me, everyone.'

At the door, he turned. 'The local bus that stops out the front: where does it go?'

'A circuit of the village, with a terminus just off the square. About fifty minutes for the round trip,' said Philip.

'Ask the driver to let you off at Bluebell Court, Richard. The public footpath through George Borrell's orchard starts there. It's beautiful. Parts of it are said to be the original pilgrims' way. If you choose left wherever it forks, you'll arrive back at the bus route,' said Veronica.

'Maze strategy. I will remember,' said Worse.

'Oh, Worse, he's known as Double-Borrell George for a reason. Stay on the path and don't be tempted by low-hanging fruit, as they say. Use my bus pass; it's on the side table inside the front door.'

19 INTERCESSIONAL PRAYERS

[Tuesday]

Worse arrived home at four o'clock, which allowed time for a shower and change before the special service for Canon Simony, scheduled for 5.30. Already, parked cars filled most available places in Old Forge Lane, and large groups of people were milling around outside the police barrier at St Eke's and along to the church hall.

He had phoned ahead to tell Millie he was on his way; she was standing by the front door waiting for him, and observing the gathering congregation. Worse gestured at the crowd.

'The Canon would be pleased to see this. He shared with me a ruefulness about declining attendance at St Eke's.'

'A rather extreme measure he's taken to summon the flock, don't you think?' said Millie.

Worse gave her a look that made her realize the irony was in poor taste.

'Sorry,' she said.

'No, no. It was amusing,' said Worse. 'Perhaps I didn't show it.'

Millie was left to wonder what he meant.

—

As they entered the house, Worse received a call from the Archdeacon. She described to Worse developments in Canterbury regarding the emergency at St Eke's. In return, Worse updated her, to an extent that would not be compromising, on his investigation's progress. Neither referred to Wilfred's medical status.

Then she changed the subject.

'Chief Inspector, when you address me as Archdeacon, I feel that I should clarify to you that I am acting in the role.'

We are all acting in our roles, thought Worse.

'I was briefed,' he said. 'How should I address you?'

'As Victoria Bray. My name.'

'People call me Worse. Victoria, I can't stress enough how grateful I am for your involvement this morning.'

'I'm pleased that I was called into the situation early,' she said. 'So, I take it you have chosen a reading for Wilfred's service?'

Worse wondered whether the question carried any anxiety about appropriateness—perfectly understandable if she had heard reports of his and Millie's Satroit presentation at William's funeral. He was reassuring.

'I have. It's short, but in its brevity I think it teaches that whatever one's affliction, there will be found, in one or other realm of argument—Divine for some—a compensating good that may be difficult to fathom. Difficult, but ultimately enlightening. I view it as a Lesson, and I hope that Wilfred's family finds comfort in it.'

It was clearly not an answer, or exposition, that the Archdeacon was expecting.

'I'm intrigued. Your reading is?'

'The dialogue concerning Bartimaeus from Leonardo di Boccardo's *Conversaziones e Silenzio*.'

'Oh. Yes. I was once familiar with it. A perceptive choice. Complex, dense, a touch subversive, but uplifting as I recall.'

She was quiet for several seconds.

'How do you know that work? Leonardo is not often read in the modern Church, if at all. If anywhere, for that matter.'

'But should be,' said Worse. 'No one these days is properly interested in how to be thankful, for example. Or challenged. Or trustful. Or mystified. Those things, at least, are taught in the *Conversaziones*, putting aside the wryness that you allude to. Which I value, by the way.'

'I agree,' said Victoria.

Worse pushed further. 'I've always thought that the subversive functions to refine our polity.'

There was no response. He kept pushing. 'On that basis, Leonardo could be regarded as a hero of the Church. If you have any influence in these matters, you might see fit to recommend he be canonized. The patron saint of the wide-eyed baffled, perhaps.'

There was another silence. Worse decided to lighten the exchange, if riskily. He liked to learn about people by testing boundaries.

'So it is Bray, as in Vicar of?' he said.

There followed what Worse would name for himself a Deaconess Delay. Eventually, it ended.

'You seem well informed about the scandals of the Church.'

'Only the amusing ones, though I confess to thinking of simony in recent days. I apologize. Naturally, my intention was a spelling check, for my visual memory.'

Again, Worse was left in suspense for several seconds.

'Apology accepted. Though I think you might credit me with the competence to spell my four-letter name on request. But yes, as in Vicar of. Or, in my father's more pretentious telling, *le cri de l'âne*—'

'My favourite quadruped,' interrupted Worse. 'Especially, *l'âne de Buridan*.'

She remained silent. Worse was concluding that, for Victoria Bray, the pregnant pause was a conversational necessity.

'Chief Inspector. Worse. If you'll forgive me for saying so, you don't sound like a normal policeman.'

Worse delighted in the opportunity to respond with a version of the Deaconess Delay. He returned a well-timed deliberative pause for no other reason than mischievous requital.

'Forgiven also. Then I should clarify to you that I am acting in the role,' he said.

—

Either by design, or providentially, the church hall had been built oriented as was St Eke's. This allowed, at the east end, a temporary altar to be fashioned from a trestle table and furnishings found in the hall and Old Vicarage stores. A sturdy music stand had been repurposed as a lectern, and this supported a beautiful, seventeenth-century King James Bible loaned from the Cathedral. In what might be called the chancel, several chairs were positioned for the use of Canterbury and parish dignitaries. To the left, an upright piano served as an organ substitute. On the right was a large flat-screen monitor, perched on an artist's easel, displaying the order of service. Snaking across the floor were several data cables and extension cords, bringing power to this, a microphone, and temporary lighting.

When Worse arrived, he estimated that the body of the hall seated about four hundred congregants. At least a hundred more were standing along aisles left free against the side walls.

He found seats reserved for himself, Millie, Nicholas, and her parents in the second front row. After sitting down, Worse turned to survey the world behind him. He saw Jane Malleson two rows back. She mouthed, 'How are you?' and Worse returned a silent 'Fine'. He texted her: 'Any news on Wilfred?' She replied, 'CT minimal cerebral oedema. Extubation trial this evening'. Worse looked around again to exchange smiles. That was neither good news nor bad.

Victoria Bray led the service. She began by welcoming Wilfred's family, noting that his wife, Cecile, had elected to remain by his bedside. Cecile wished to have conveyed to everyone present her appreciation for the prayers given up for her husband's recovery, and all the support she was personally receiving. With the forbearance of those participating, the proceedings were being videoed for Cecile's benefit at a later time.

There was no description given of what had befallen the Canon, which was widely known in any case, nor of his current condition in hospital. The tone was of thanksgiving for his service to the community of St Eke's, with an optimism bordering on joyful that the force of prayer and love in the room would restore their vicar to health.

—

The order of service identified Worse's reading simply as 'Dr Worse'. When he made his way to the lectern, the vengeful man who had spoken for William Whencely through the poet Satroit was not to be recognized.

Instead, Worse announced that the Lesson he would read addressed an intrinsic ambiguity in all of human fortune: That only in adversity is found hope; only in ignorance do we learn; and it is by way of paradox that we reach enlightenment. He named Leonardo as his scriptural source, reminding the audience of the blind supplicant Bartimaeus in the Gospel of St Mark. Then he placed his hands on the Bible, and recited without notes.

O Lord
There is made more sorrow in Judaea than solace.
What consolation comes to Bartimaeus
when given vision in the world
he wanted more his blindness?

My Son
Weigh not the night in talents of morning.
If Bartimaeus should see and also not see
he will dwell in two Jerichos, and so become
twice-knowing of Man, and therefore of God.

At the last line, Worse's voice threatened to break with emotion. When finished, he continued to rest his hands on the Bible, looking down. He was thinking of Wilfred Simony, alone in his night of coma; a solitary pilgrim enduring the trials of vision, blindness, faith, and doubt.

It was obvious to all that the man at the lectern was deeply moved, and an unnatural silence fell on the room. Millie felt an urge to race forward to rescue him, but Worse walked back to his seat with no further display of the deep melancholy that appeared to possess him only seconds before.

As he did so, his eyes were drawn to Jane's. Her look of

concern for him—intense, almost haunting, and suddenly beautiful—filled his thoughts while he sat down. He turned to her and mouthed, 'I'm fine'. Jane nodded, and smiled.

She was his physician, after all.

20 TASK FORCE CAMPANILE

[Tuesday]

At 8.00 pm, principal members of Campanile convened in Canon Simony's office.

Apart from Worse, the group comprised Inspector Wirrier, two detective sergeants each with an assistant constable, and, at Worse's request, Rence from the village station. Worse ran the meeting formally.

Sergeant Michelson presented her findings regarding Simony's movements on the previous evening. The pastoral visits ended at Priory Manor, a hospice situated three miles west of Steeple Resting. He was seen off at about 8.20 pm, and was expected to drive back through the village to his home in Canterbury. Instead, he stopped at the Old Vicarage, where Worse had found his car.

'Was he followed? Anything on traffic cameras?' asked Worse.

'Nothing,' said Michelson.

'Did he stop anywhere between the Manor and here?' asked Worse.

'Not that we have determined.'

'Mobile phone records?'

'His last activity was the email sent to you, at eight twenty-nine. Last phone call was to Mrs Simony, at approximately five pm.'

Worse spent a few seconds typing on his mobile.

'That email, I have just copied to you all. Please study it.'

He returned to Michelson. 'Who was his last personnel contact at Priory Manor?'

'There's an employed lay pastor who stays late on Monday evenings to discuss residents' issues with the Canon.'

'Named?' asked Worse.

'Michael Couchman.'

'Your impression?' asked Worse.

'Open. Believable. Smart,' said Michelson.

'I'd like to interview him,' said Worse. 'Do you have background?'

Michelson looked to her Constable, who scrolled to a page on his laptop.

'Born London, 1980. Qualified in clinical psychology in Brighton. After that, applied for training for the priesthood, was accepted, but withdrew. Lives in accommodation provided by the Manor. He's been in the role for two years.'

'Thank you, Constable,' said Worse. He returned to the Sergeant.

'Sergeant Michelson, who advised you that Couchman was the last contact? Couchman himself, or someone else?'

'The hospice director, who wasn't on site last evening, said it would be Couchman, who confirmed the fact.'

'The fact ...' echoed Worse slowly, to no one in particular. It may not be a fact, he was thinking. A confirmed assertion is still an assertion.

'And the director's name?'

'Dr Sleke,' said Michelson. She spelt it. 'First name, Arnold.'

Worse moved on.

'Sergeant Morley, was Mrs Dewey at the Cathedral helpful?'

'Very much so, Chief Inspector. She is so protective of her precious archives that she kept a close eye on everything that Canon Simony accessed and studied. She seemed to remember it all.'

'I imagine she was very distressed to know what happened to the Canon,' said Worse. 'It was only yesterday afternoon that he was sitting in her library.'

Morley seemed slightly put off by this redirection into the human story.

'Yes. Yes. She would have been. No doubt,' he said.

It was obvious that he hadn't given it a thought. Worse

caught a glance from Wirrier but didn't return it. Sergeant Morley would need to bring emotional intelligence into his work in order to succeed as an investigator.

Worse stared at Morley's constable, saying nothing. Eventually, the constable felt compelled to speak.

'Actually, she was crying when we left. I told her to leave work early and go home, and said I would vouch for her with the senior manager. I know the family; she lives with her elderly mother a short walk from the Cathedral Gate. I phoned just before this meeting, and she was more composed. She had managed to get to the Canon's service here, though I didn't see her. I asked her if she had remembered anything more about the Canon's questions in the library, but she had nothing to add.'

Morley sent his constable a murderous glare. It would have been comical if it weren't so awful.

'Perhaps check on her tomorrow,' said Worse. He looked back at Morley. 'You have copies of all the documents?'

'I do. Shall I send them to you?'

'To all of us, please,' said Worse. 'Everybody study them tonight, with a view to understanding what the Canon might have discovered, or realized, that explains, first, the content of his email to me; and second, why his life was immediately endangered. He may recover sufficiently to give us a full account of events, but we can't rely on that happening.'

Worse addressed Inspector Wirrier. 'Any reports from the police guard on Simony?'

'Nothing of consequence.'

There was a sense of relaxation that the meeting was concluding. Worse wasn't finished.

'You might consider this: given what I just said connecting the Canon's fate to the archival material, it is possible that Mrs Dewey is also at risk. I'll leave that assessment to you.'

Worse stood. 'Tomorrow, forensic report on Simony's clothes, and his car, please. I also expect St Eke's to be opened for us, so we'll put forensics in there too. I want night-vision security cameras looking at everything, inside the tower being the obvious priority. Let's have that operational by sunset tomorrow. Continue interviews. Bring in Couchman and Sleke. Sergeant Michelson, work backwards from Priory Manor to every other place he visited that evening. Before you go, has anyone here experience or knowledge of this sort of event? Of serial poison attacks within a church, including on clergy?'

There was a general murmur in the negative.

'Seven-thirty in the morning, then. This office. Please bring ideas, however wild, from your study of Sergeant Morley's document copies. There's something there. If Canon Simony saw it, between the seven of us, we should as well.'

The others stood up.

'By the way, Sergeant Michelson,' said Worse. 'You spoke of residents at Priory Manor. What would you say is common to them all?'

'I'm not sure, Chief Inspector. They're all sick, one way or another—or frail, requiring fully assisted care. Perhaps terminal illness.'

'Might it be religion, denomination? Professional affiliations? Background?' asked Worse.

'I don't know, sir.'

'Well, thank you, everyone,' said Worse. He gestured for the Inspector to stay behind as the others were leaving.

'Will Morley give his constable a hard time over that?'

'If I find out that he has, he'll be disciplined. He will know that.'

Having raised the question, Worse decided to keep his thoughts to himself.

'Mm. See you in the morning,' he said. Privately, he found it curious that Wirrier had hardly said a thing for the whole meeting. He wondered if there was an issue with seniority, Worse being an outsider.

It was important to Worse that he had in his team a senior officer whom he could trust implicitly. He decided he would ask Victor Spoiling to conduct a discreet check, just to be sure.

'Shall I see you out of the building? I expect there will be no other staff around at this time, and we can't assume it is a safe place.'

'Thank you for the concern, no,' said Worse. 'I'll read the archive files before going home.'

Wirrier wasn't to know that Worse now carried the concealed Totengräber at all times.

—

An hour later, Worse had completed a first, but thorough, reading. He now moved to the same leather chair where he had sat having morning tea with the Canon on the previous day. Somehow, that small degree of reconstruction helped with recall of their conversation. Because, almost certainly, reasoned Worse, something mentioned that morning had sent Simony to the archives.

At 11.15 his phone rang with a video call from Jane Malleson.

'What's the news?' he asked without greeting.

'Not good, Worse. His blood gases deteriorated late afternoon. Airway pressures trending up. They couldn't extubate him.'

'Decisions day to day, then,' said Worse.

'Quite.'

'Any indication of his neurological state?'

'Not really, without lightening him. That hasn't been possible.'

They both fell silent, still looking at each other.

Perhaps she was thinking about Simony, but it didn't feel that way. As the seconds passed, Worse became acutely unsettled. Each could have said good night and ended the call. But Jane didn't, and he didn't.

Her face had the same intense expression that captured his gaze during Wilfred's service. He couldn't look away.

'Where are you?' she asked.

The voice was changed, softened, from factual to tentative.

'In the parish office, at the Old Vicarage. We've had a team meeting here.'

She was quiet, looking at him.

Worse was looking at Jane, but not seeing her. In a scene erupted out of nowhere, he pictured a man teetering on the edge of risk, then plunging, into a future untied to his past. He didn't recognize the man.

At last, Jane spoke. 'Your Leonardo passage was beautiful.'

It brought Worse back to himself. It slowed the fall.

'Thank you.'

Silence.

'I'm glad you were there,' he said.

'Was that your wife, sitting with you?'

'My partner, Millie.'

Silence. Nothing in her expression changed.

'Where are you?' Worse knew that his question, in context, was intimate.

'At home. I live in Canterbury.'

The falling man in Worse wanted her to answer: 'In my car, outside the Old Vicarage. Come for a drive'.

It was as if Jane heard the thought, because at that moment she smiled.

'I should let you go,' she said. 'I'm pleased to see you looking well. I shall be discharging you from my care before long.'

So ethically we can be lovers, are you saying?

In the circumstances, it was a base thought, sprung from unreality, unworthy of Worse. He hoped, half hoped, she hadn't heard this one as well.

'Yes. Thanks for calling, Jane. Please keep me updated about Wilfred.'

'I will. Good night, Worse.'

'Good night, Jane.'

—

Worse remained sitting. Fifteen minutes prior, he had been visualizing Canon Simony and himself having tea, parsing their previous day's conversation for leads.

Now that calm was replaced by a diffuse, nervous arousal, seemingly of his whole person. He felt it as a tremulousness in his voice when he said good night. He felt it in his breathing, in his lost concentration.

Nothing like it had ever happened to Worse. Not even with Millie.

He thought of calling Jane back, to see her again.

But he didn't. It would be wrong. He was afraid.

At midnight he walked home, into the bedroom he shared with Millie.

21 WORSE

Millie was asleep, lying awkwardly in bed with an A4 pad of research algebra half clasped in one hand and a loose pencil astray on the sheet. Worse delicately removed these to a bedside table, and switched off her reading light. He undressed in the dark, put on a bathrobe, and went to the sitting room, aware that without thinking through what had happened, he would not sleep.

Was he falling in love? Tumultuous, precipitate, irrational love? If so, it was like nothing he recognized.

Was this seduction? Or something entirely imagined?

Was it just a dangerous, reckless infatuation?

Was it flirtatious play, touching on that hesitant dialectic of lovers-to-be?

Perhaps. Yet, since living with Millie, Worse had never, for one moment, thought of being with another woman. He found himself ashamed that the very idea of a liaison, unformed as it remained, had come to him at all.

He reflected on Millie. Living with her, he was happier than he had been for a very long time. He loved her, respected her, and trusted unconditionally in their mutual honesty as life partners.

He reflected on himself, on his values. Values that made it possible to live comfortably with the complex, some might say on occasions ruthless, person that he was. But whatever opinions people held of Worse, good or bad, qualities or faults, there were two character traits consistently agreed. He was analytical—and he was moral.

Tonight, sitting in the armchair staring at nothing, these became the strengths that rebalanced him. He made a resolution to put sexual thoughts of Jane away, to be scrupulously professional in his dealings with her.

And of course, *of course*, he would remain true to Millie.

And from that decision there followed, as if by way of absolution, a realization that brought to Worse a profound clarity and almost instant peace of mind. Its gift to him was emotional freeing, and a kind of self-exoneration from the fantasy near betrayal of earlier.

The insight was this: whatever had been happening to him during his interaction with Jane, compelling as it seemed at the time, he didn't enjoy it.

Knowing that, he was able to like himself again.

—

Worse stood up, went to the window, and held the curtain open slightly. St Eke's under moonlight looked a cold and forbidding place. He wondered if Geoffrey Magnacart had seen it like that.

Jane's report on Wilfred's condition was personally upsetting, naturally, but for the investigation it was also a major setback. The team had reasonably hoped that the Canon would recover sufficiently to explain why he went to the tower that evening, and what had happened. That possible breakthrough was clearly not to be.

Worse let the curtain fall. He walked to the bedroom, removed his bathrobe, and slipped into bed beside Millie. Of all his moments in a day, this was always the most luxurious. She rolled toward him, still asleep, and put an arm across his chest. He felt well loved, and he felt deserving of it once more.

—

As was his habit, Worse skipped breakfast. He entered Simony's office at 7.15, carrying a coffee from home. Morley's constable was already there, working at a laptop. He stood up for Worse.

'Good morning, Constable. Sit down, please. Continue your work.'

'Thank you, sir.'

Worse looked around the room, selecting a different seat from the one he occupied while speaking with Jane.

'What is your name, Constable?'

'Wells, sir.'

Worse smiled.

'I think you should feel very good about speaking up last evening for Thelma Dewey. I was impressed by your humanity.'

'Thank you, sir.'

'I will follow up with her myself today. One other thing: your sergeant. Gain what is good, but don't lose the qualities you have in yourself. In time, he'll move on and you'll move up. These are private remarks. Carry on.'

—

The others arrived punctually, and found seating. Worse watched carefully the body language between Morley and Wells. It wasn't warm, but nor was it uncivil.

'We seem to have got through a night without an attack in St Eke's,' said Worse. 'I suppose we can view that as progress of sorts.'

Everyone looked at Worse, unsure how to respond. He gave no guidance.

'One consequence of that breakthrough success,' continued Worse, 'is that we can expect entry clearance from hazmat in a few hours. Where are we up to with geophysics?'

Inspector Wirrier answered. 'I've sourced a team from London. Equipment ETA ten o'clock this morning. Personnel around the same time. I have assumed they can start the exterior perimeter study before the building's open.'

'I'm sure that is reasonable,' said Worse. 'Excellent.'

He looked at Sergeant Michelson. 'We have a timetable for interviews?'

'Organized. Starting eleven o'clock, this office. I will circulate the schedule, and any unavoidable revisions.'

'Security cameras?' asked Worse.

'Technicians on standby for building clearance,' said Wirrier.

'Forensics?'

'Preliminary reports promised this morning.'

'Phone records?'

'I have the Canon's, and those of individuals of interest from Priory Manor,' said Sergeant Michelson.

'Copy to all, please,' said Worse. 'Now, let's move on to last night's homework. What did Canon Simony see in the Cathedral papers that endangered his life?'

No one took the initiative.

'Let's go around the circle, shall we? I'll start.'

22 ANGELA

Worse had some free time. He left the Old Vicarage and walked east along Old Forge Lane, intending to pass in front of St Eke's before crossing to the Misgivingston house. He was keen to talk to Nicholas.

He stopped to look up at the tower. Now there were two ropes hanging incongruously from the belfry, the first from the bell itself, the second from the grappling hook. That scene, photographed from where he now stood, had been syndicated unhelpfully to news sites around the world. Each of those ropes had a human story attached, one his, one Simony's. But these were untold; in their place was shallow, sensationalist copy serving largely to indulge its by-liner.

Worse turned when his name was called. It was Nicholas, emerging from the house; he crossed the road to join Worse.

'We missed you last night, and this morning. Do you ever sleep, Worse?'

'It has been rather curtailed, but I try.' Worse looked directly at Nicholas. 'I'd hoped we might find more time together while you're here, Nicholas. I would very much value your input on some translation problems we need clarity on.'

'Happy to help if I can, Worse. Only, I'm slipping up to Cambridge now to report on LDI developments to Edvard.'

Worse had noted that Nicholas was fidgeting with his car keys.

'I'll be dining in hall at Nazarene this evening, and home late, I'm afraid. What's the translation? I can task it to Edvard—he's the best in the world.'

It was probably true: if Edvard Tøssentern couldn't manage, it was unlikely anyone else would.

'Tell him it's the Oxford Passage of Oldrice's *Wey*. He'll know of it. Pass on my regards please, Nicholas. To Anna as well.'

'I will. How's the Canon?'

'Not improving, as of last evening, I'm afraid.'

'I'm sorry to hear that. Maybe see you late tonight.'

—

Worse had been thinking over the days of visiting William Whencely's grave. Now that the opportunity to catch up with Nicholas was lost, this seemed a good time.

He walked around the police perimeter to the old east graveyard, unaware at first that someone was standing over on the North Ground near where William was buried. Not until he reached the bridge did he recognize Angela, William's ex-wife. They greeted each other as Worse approached.

The funeral flowers, five days old, were becoming brown and shrivelled, but a glass vase of fresh ones was embedded a few centimetres into William's earth.

'Yours?' said Worse, pointing to them.

Angela nodded. 'I'm here to mourn,' she said. 'Why are you here?'

Worse quite liked her directness. 'I'm here to think,' he said.

Angela glanced at him, then turned her gaze to the far distance. 'I'm sorry I haven't been in touch about the promised tea for you and Millie. I underestimated my need for solitude over these days.'

'Please don't feel apologetic. Would you prefer that I leave?' said Worse.

'No, no. Not at all. Why don't we sit down?'

They both fell silent, sitting on the grassy bank, looking across the river to St Eke's. Behind them, on the low ridge, a row of aspens whispered on the breeze.

'It is beautiful here,' she said.

Worse responded only in his thoughts. Yes. A melancholy beauty, however ... every headstone a testament to the inevitability and permanence of an undone day.

'You're not a talkative man,' Angela said, after a while.

'Between silences, I view myself too garrulous,' said Worse. They were quiet again.

'You haven't interviewed me about William. I feel over-looked,' she said.

Worse smiled. 'Most people would be relieved.'

Following that, Worse felt it not inappropriate, in the setting, to ask her some questions.

'I've been told that you play bridge with Cecile Simony. You know about Wilfred, I take it?'

'About Wilfred, about you, about William,' she said. 'Three nice men attacked. Though I'm not sure about you.'

'Properly so,' said Worse. 'I'm perfectly awful in my silences.'

'Best keep the conversation flowing, then.'

'There is something I wanted to check with you,' said Worse. 'When we spoke at William's wake, you expressed no curiosity at my choice of Satroit's requiem, on the theme of murder. Why was that not surprising to you?'

'I had strong suspicions. William shared with me that he received strange messages, in the form of calling cards. He dismissed them as a prank and a nuisance. I suggested they were threatening and implored him to report them to the police, to no avail. So, when you spoke at the funeral, I was relieved, in all honesty, to realize that you evidently were treating his death with the seriousness that I thought he deserved. At the wake, with all those people around—I didn't want to talk about it.'

—

'What work do you do, Angela?'

'I'm a clinical psychologist.'

'In private practice?'

'Largely, these days. I used to do some institutional work, much less so now.'

'Because?'

'Because I found I wasn't valued.'

'I'm interested,' said Worse. 'What institutions did you work at?'

'Oh. There are hospices, sanatoria, retirement homes all over these parts. Some provide very well for their residents, others less so. I worked two days per week for about three years at one, until they said budgetary constraints forced my release. That was fine, until one day I heard from Cecile that someone was appointed in my place almost immediately. Cecile knew because it was a hospice that Wilfred regularly visited on his rounds. I worked with him on many a case.'

'How long ago was that, that they let go of you?'

'Two years, or so.'

Worse was certain he knew the answer to his next question.

'And what was that particular institution?'

'A hospice called Priory Manor, about a three-mile drive from here.'

'Is the current director there the same one who dismissed you, do you know?'

'I believe so. Arnold Sleke. I'm sure that Cecile would have mentioned if he had left.'

'Have you ever received an explanation as to why you were given an apparently false reason for your termination?'

'No. Why would they admit to unfair dismissal? I suspect someone with influence didn't like me.'

'I was thinking, perhaps, from a separate party who might know.'

Angela thought for a few seconds. 'No. That hasn't happened. Why are you interested?'

Worse judged there was nothing to be lost in telling her. 'We have established that Priory Manor was the last place that Wilfred visited on his pastoral care round before stopping at St Eke's on Monday night, where he was attacked.'

'And that is important?'

'It is important until proven not to be,' said Worse. 'What name do you practise under, Angela?'

'Angela Ponting. I always have. I never adopted William's name.'

'So, given that you had been separated from William for

three years before you began working at Priory Manor, would the people there have been aware of your connection to him?'

Angela considered. 'In a village, everyone knows everything.'

Not everything, thought Worse. Beneath the unspoken, behind the unseen, there are always secrets.

'Priory Manor is rather cut off from here, though. So, I would say probably not. It never came up.'

She was speaking slowly. Worse waited.

'In fact, when I think about it, something odd happened one day. William visited the Manor seeking information about its history, and so on, for his research. He had made an appointment with Dr Sleke. I was working there that day, and naturally William and I met for tea in the staff cafeteria. I think our connection became public at that time.'

'How did Sleke treat William, do you know?'

'Cordially received, cleverly expelled. They were the words, essentially, that William used when he described his experience to me. The thing is, though, what was odd about it, was that Sleke treated me differently after that.'

Again, Worse was confident in his next question.

'And this visit, William's visit, occurred shortly before your removal?'

Angela turned to look at Worse. 'Yes, by a few days.'

'Angela,' said Worse, after a few seconds, 'are you comfortable enough, sitting here on the grass?'

'Yes. Why?'

'Because I would like you to tell me everything you can remember about Priory Manor. The place, and the people. Three years of clinically astute observation.'

—

Worse stood up with Angela as she made to leave. They shook hands. He watched her cross the wheatstone bridge and wend through the churchyard's melancholy beauty to Old Forge Lane. Here, the Anas was become her personal Styx; she had visited the Underworld for William, conferred, and safely rejoined the still-embodied souls of Steeple Resting.

Worse turned to look at William's grave.
Now listen by my swollen ground.
'Indeed I have, William,' he said quietly.

23 THE CONVERSATION

When Worse walked back to Old Forge Lane, he found the geophysics team unloading equipment from a van parked just outside the lychgate. He approached the woman who seemed to be supervising, and introduced himself. Her name was Phoebe Andrieus.

'I'm very grateful that you've all made the time to help us here,' he said.

'Glad to be of assistance,' said Phoebe. 'I only hope we make a contribution to solving this ghastly case. It's obviously more urgent than uncovering yet another trove of Roman coins.'

'Yes. Treasure is patient, but justice not,' said Worse. 'I suspect, anyway, that you will ultimately uncover both crime and history on this site.'

Worse outlined the subterranean architecture that he thought they might find, including the possibility that an ancient crypt might extend beyond the boundary walls of the present St Eke's. They would map the periphery, inside the police fence, looking especially for any tunnels, then move inside the church when it was declared safe to do so.

–

There was still time before the 11.00 am interviews, and Worse was keen to see Millie. He found her alone in Philip's study, and when he entered she gave him a lovely smile and stood up to embrace him. He felt supremely fortunate.

'I've been worrying about you,' she said. 'You're not sleeping enough.'

Worse started to speak but Millie placed a finger over his lips.

'I mean, with me.'

Worse pulled her close again. 'I think the same. I promise to rectify things this evening.'

The double entendre was not lost on a mathematician.

'By the way,' Worse added, 'last night when I got home, I rescued several pages of matrix algebra from certain crumple death in bed.'

'Thank you for that. As you could see, my consolation in solitude was perfectly chaste.'

'It was charming. Shall we have a quick cup of tea?' said Worse.

As they went to the kitchen, he asked what she was working on.

'The Perth project. It's challenging. How are things going across the road?'

'Progressing. Today we are searching for Millie's green vertex.'

'You think it's a forgotten crypt?'

'Not forgotten by everyone. On another matter, I want to ask you something. Last Friday, when I mentioned that William's ex-wife, Angela, suggested we come to tea, you and your mother exchanged meaningful glances. What was the meaning?'

'Oh. Nothing sinister. I think Mum and Dad found it difficult when Will and Angela split. Awkward, you know—Will being so close to Dad. Now that he's gone, I suppose there may be another adjustment around Angela.'

'But you all view her as a good person?'

'Oh yes. There's no question about that. Their separation was perfectly amicable, as I understand it.'

'Excuse me, Millie,' said Worse. His phone was ringing.

When he rang off, he smiled at her.

'Victor sends his best. It was good news for me. My inspector is ethically beyond reproach, signed off by Victor Spoiling.'

—

At 10.50, Campanile members met in Simony's office. They conferred briefly about the morning's progress, before Worse made it clear to the others that he, exclusively, would conduct the first interview, and requested no interruptions.

Rence brought Arnold Sleke into the room. Worse indicated where the director should sit, and introduced himself, but not the others present. He began.

'You are aware that we are investigating events taking place in St Eke's?'

'I imagined so.'

'Our interest in speaking to you relates to the fact that Priory Manor was the last stop made by Canon Simony on Monday evening before his arrival at St Eke's and the subsequent attack on his person. Do you understand?'

'Yes, I understand.'

'Did you see, or have any contact whatsoever with, Canon Simony this last Monday, between midday and midnight?'

'No.'

'During those same hours, did you have any dealings whatsoever with any third party who themselves had dealings with Canon Simony, dealings of which you were informed, or otherwise aware?'

'No.'

'During those same hours, what were your movements, precisely?'

Sleke was starting to look very uncomfortable. 'I was in my office till about five-thirty, I would say, then went to my home for the night.'

'Your home is?'

'I own a bungalow a short walk from the Manor, in the grounds.'

'Is there anyone who can corroborate your movements?'

'Well, I live alone. No, I suppose not.'

Worse shuffled some papers he held, appearing to study one with particular interest. He continued to look at it as he asked the next question. Sleke had no idea that it was pure theatre.

'Arnold Sleke. Did you have any involvement, or know of any other person's involvement, in the St Eke's attacks on William Whencely, Chief Inspector Worse, or Canon Simony?'

Sleke lost his temper. He stood up, speaking down at Worse. 'Look here. I'm not answering your questions. I'm leaving.'

Worse didn't move. 'Then turn around, look at the door you intend to use, and tell me what you see.'

Suspended from a coat hook was a pair of handcuffs, placed there by Rence at Worse's request.

'Need I inform you of their purpose?' said Worse. 'Please sit down.'

Sleke resumed his seat. 'I object to this. You are interviewing me without my lawyer present—'

'This is not an interview in the formal sense. It is a conversation. You are not entitled to a lawyer.'

Sleke thought he saw an advantage. He looked around the room for support.

'If this is not an interview, and I am not represented, nothing said here will be admissible.'

Worse placed the papers he had been holding on the floor beside his chair. He sat back, hands clasped, and seemed to smile. 'Admissible is not my concern.'

His voice was chilling. Sleke looked shocked. No one moved.

'Let me explain,' continued Worse. 'This case will not come to an ordinary court. There will be no legal loopholes. There will be no judicial niceties. There will be no technicality appeals. I consider the St Eke's gas attacks, having as they did the potential to kill multiple innocent citizens, to be domestic terror incidents. Ordinary law does not apply.'

Sleke's eyes were fixed on Worse, as if hypnotized.

'Having made that clear,' said Worse, 'you are obligated in our conversations to answer all questions fully and truthfully.'

Sleke said nothing.

'To encourage your good behaviour in that respect, and to illustrate what I mean by "ordinary law does not apply", I will tell you this. If I find you have lied to me, I will personally supervise the razing of your bungalow in execution of a thorough search warrant, authorized by myself.'

Worse glanced at his watch. 'Now, do you require a short break to gather your thoughts before we continue?'

The only response was a slight shake of the head.

'In that case,' said Worse, holding up the XVI business card, 'answer fully and truthfully. What does this mean to you?'

—

At midday, Worse received a text from HCN advising that the church was cleared for access, and he had already admitted the forensics team. Shortly after, Worse issued a caution to Sleke, terminated the interview, and let him go.

'You know what to do with him,' Worse said to the others. 'Full surveillance.'

They had been completely silent for over an hour.

'I need to check some things outside. Schedule Couchman for three pm. Same rules apply; I'll lead the conversation.'

—

Worse left the Old Vicarage and walked along to St Eke's. Parked across the road, just east of the bus bay, was Sleke's car, with Sleke in the driver's seat. He was speaking on his mobile.

Worse pretended not to notice. *We are listening, Sleke.*

Beside the lychgate, he stopped to look, for the first time carefully, at the public sign identifying the church, its denomination, its vicar, St Eke's feast day—being twenty-ninth December—and service times. There was the name: Canon Wilfred Simony MA. Yet again, Worse felt in himself that difficult fusion of emotion and urge: sadness, anger, duty, revenge.

Pasted across the base was a banner showing a large left arrow, advising that services were being temporarily held in the parish hall. At the top, arched in golden Gothic script on black enamel, was painted *St Eke's*. Perhaps it was seeing that name in print, or the church itself beyond, in the same sweeping vista where he had spied Sleke in his car and thought his name. Perhaps it had already been a nagging, subconscious association. However things came about, he was suddenly struck by the curious near-homology of Sleke and St Eke.

Worse sat on a bench in the lychgate, and phoned Nicholas.

'I need an urgent favour. Could you ask Edvard for an opinion on the origins of the family name Sleke'—Worse spelt it out—'and any connection it might have with St Eke?'

'Of course, Worse. He's right beside me, sending his best. He and Anna want you and Millie to come up to Cambridge and stay with them. By the way, on the Oxford Passage, Edvard has already done work on it. He says it's been a lifelong ambition to decipher that text. He believes he's made some progress, it seems.'

'Excellent,' said Worse. 'What progress? Can you say?'

'You'll never guess what he thinks it's about, and why he thinks it.'

'Let me try. About Becket, and because of thricing?' said Worse.

There were several seconds of silence.

'Jesus, Worse. How did you work that out?'

'Not sure. Thinking the worst of humanity generally advances our understanding of the world. Did Becket have a mistress?'

'Jesus, Worse. Wait!'

Worse could hear Nicholas conferring with Edvard. He returned to Worse.

'Edvard hasn't reached a conclusion on that. He says you're a rotten anti-papist scandalmonger and he's looking forward to sharing it all with you.'

'Don't forget the Sleke question please, Nicholas. Thinking ill of somebody as I find myself doing, I believe the answer may be important.'

24 DOUBLE HELIX

Worse stayed sitting in the lychgate. He phoned Thelma Dewey, the Cathedral archivist, and asked how she was. She confided that she was given to outbursts of tears about the Canon, but recent difficulties looking after her mother had kept her mind busy. Worse sympathized, and asked if there were any assistance the police could provide, through Constable Wells perhaps.

'No thank you, Chief Inspector. We shall be just fine. Tunny already does a lot for us. He's a fine young man.'

'Tunny?'

'Oh. His nickname[1]. From Tunbridge. An example of sophisticated Kentish humour. I don't expect you would have heard it used, but Tunny is like family to us.'

'Nicknames do make an interesting study,' said Worse. 'Mrs Dewey, I'm very grateful for the assistance you gave to Constable Wells and Sergeant Morley. I wonder if I could impose upon your memory on a related matter.'

'Of course, Chief Inspector.'

'I believe that William Whencely approached you some weeks ago regarding archival resources relevant, presumably, to his researches into Steeple Resting.'

'Yes, he did. Poor Mr Whencely. Would you like copies of the papers he showed interest in?'

'That would be very helpful. I am particularly interested in any subject materials that both Mr Whencely and Canon Simony consulted you about.'

'I understand. I will email you the information this afternoon.'

A van displaying the name and livery of a private security company pulled up outside. An array of ladders nestled on its roof rack. Worse ended his call to Thelma and walked over to the driver. He established that they were there to install the cameras he had requested, then explained that a forensic team needed to complete their work first, and they would be given the all-clear for entry as soon as possible.

Worse left them and entered the nave through the south-west porch. The senior forensics officer was just inside, near the door to the tower.

'I'm Worse,' Worse introduced himself. 'Can you give me an idea of when some technicians and the radar team can come in?'

'We'll be wrapped up in half an hour, Chief Inspector. You can come in, though.'

Worse thanked her, and walked back to the security van with the information. Then he crossed the graveyard to where Phoebe was managing the ground-penetrating radar study. She looked up from a laptop screen as he approached.

'We've covered, what, a quarter of the perimeter, and there's nothing resembling a tunnel. Or a crypt extension, for that matter,' she added.

'Whatever we learn from you will be helpful, very helpful,' said Worse. 'Forensics should be finished in half an hour. I'll be inside if you want me.'

—

In the tower room, Worse found that the chair he had unfolded the previous Saturday had been moved away from the stairs. This he repositioned close to the squeaky door, from where he could study the space anew from a different angle.

Worse sat there. His mind settled first on the simple curiosity of the squeaky door having bolts on both sides. Of course, in different circumstances, each could have a perfectly innocent function. Perhaps Mansion would bolt the inside to prevent tourists intruding on his bell-ringing. Then, he might bolt the outside to discourage those same tourists entering when he wasn't there. It could even be furnished with a padlock, though Worse had not seen one used.

But this was not an innocent room, and its door was not an innocent door. Worse entertained himself with two mysteries.

First, what purpose might be served in having both bolts shot at the same time? Well, for one thing, he imagined a victim in the tower, incapacitated by gas. Such an individual could neither escape nor be rescued through that door.

Second, how was it possible, in principle, for a single perpetrator to shoot both bolts, and not be trapped as well? This was the question answered by Grimly, man and automaton, over dinner at the King of Kent. Millie's logical network solution, the green vertex, must surely be a crypt beneath him. But what were her green connections? In other words, how could Worse get from where he sat to a crypt? And then, escape from the crypt into fresh air?

Worse's gaze returned to the Wistful Wardrobe. He walked over to it, and for perhaps the tenth time examined it thoroughly, percussing its panels and plinth for hollowness, testing for weakness or movement at joints and seams. He saw no possible way that it could conceal a secret passage, or serve somehow as a channel to deliver toxic gases.

He sat down again, thinking about the room.

The squeaky door behind Worse had been wedged open by the forensics team, for convenience. The senior officer spoke to Worse from the entrance.

'Chief Inspector. We're finished here for now. Others can come in.'

Worse stood up and thanked her. He left through the south-west door to walk down to the security technicians' van and let them know they were cleared to start work. As he returned to the porch, he noted that Phoebe and her team were now out of sight around the south-east corner of the chancel. He decided not to disturb her.

Worse re-entered the tower room and sat on his chair, surveying the room, searching for the route to a crypt he wasn't certain existed. Wherever he looked there was massive, impregnable stonework, and his attention always returned to the Wistful Wardrobe as the only anomalous object in the space. He resisted the urge to go over to examine it again.

His concentration was broken by one of the security technicians.

'Mind if I come in?'

'No. Do,' said Worse.

'I'm Matt, anyway.'

'I'm Worse.'

Matt was taking in the space. He looked upwards. 'You want a monitor up there, above that platform?'

'We do,' said Worse.

Matt touched the closest wall. 'No way we can chase into this all the way up. We'll need to make do with surface conduit. It won't be the prettiest. What do you think?'

'Absolutely fine,' said Worse. 'It's a workspace.'

'We'll snug it into that corner, and colour-match to the stone as best we can.' Matt pointed. 'Those stairs go up, I take it?'

'They do.'

'Easy then. We'll take a reel up the stairs, drill through the platform and drop the cable, then sheath conduit over it from below, and make things fast as we're able. Easy.'

'You have to be wired? You can't use battery units and bluetooth?'

'Not up there. More maintenance, less reliable.'

Worse enjoyed relating to people who were skilled in their trade.

'And cameras down here?' said Matt.

'Yes, please. Especially on the door and the staircase.'

'Easy. We've got work outside first, at the distribution board. I don't see power in here, only light. Doesn't look up to standard either,' he said, nodding toward the old switch.

'I thought the same,' said Worse.

'Jake out there's a sparky. We'll fix what's needed.'

Matt left, and Worse followed him as far as the doorway. Jake was negotiating an extension ladder through the porch.

—

Worse was back in his chair, studying the room. Again, his eyes were drawn to the wardrobe. He thought, tactically, about what was happening. When his attention became fixed repeatedly on one object, it could not be on everything else. That was a failing of observation. He decided to shift mindset by considering the Wistful Wardrobe positively eliminated from his enquiries.

Something strange happened. Instead of finding his attention liberated to roam systematically around the room, as he had expected, it became fixed again, but on something different.

Worse stared at the spiralled staircase, his eyes following one step over the other to where they disappeared from view. He recalled noting when he first climbed them their challenging steepness, thinking vaguely that Norman builders, eager to cut less stone, were a little inconsiderate to their patrons.

But now another explanation was taking form in Worse. It was inchoate, difficult, and something he had never before imagined. He continued sitting there, gaze fixed on the spiral staircase, determined to have conceptual mastery over a problem in solid geometry that had come to him.

After a few minutes, Worse stood up. It was time to test the mental construct with physical exploration, and he was confident of knowing where to start. He phoned PC Rence and asked him to come to the tower with a powerful torch.

When Rence arrived, Worse instructed him to stay by the squeaky door, and let no one into the room except the security technicians. He thanked Rence for the torch, and entered the spiral staircase.

—

Worse emerged onto the timber platform, and glanced around. The bell rope was still snaking out through the central east opening, and the bell itself was skewed unnaturally by the rope's weight and angulation. Otherwise, nothing seemed changed.

He looked upwards at the stairway encasement, extending a few metres above the platform and seating two parallel oak beams from which the bell rocker was suspended. Ideally, he would have a ladder to access and examine its top surface, and Worse figured that he could pull one up through the bell rope aperture in the platform. But he was impatient.

The masonry here was undressed and offered several rough projecting and sunken toeholds. Worse hoisted himself onto an adjoining windowsill, stood carefully, and leaned across. His fingers gripped the top edge of the encasement, and he found one foothold, then another, walking his weight up the wall. Eventually he was able to use his arms to pull himself upward, twisting as he did so, to find himself sitting safely on the capping.

It was too dark to be sure of what he was looking into, and he retrieved Rence's torch from a coat pocket. In a flash, Worse's mental model of earlier became physical reality. Winding downwards was a second staircase, in chiral and phase harmony with the first, both sharing the central newel. But like the faces of Janus, even in their intimacy each was forever invisible to the other.

---

[1] See note to Chapter 28.

25 GEOFFREY MAGNACART

Worse swung his legs over the capping and placed his weight on the top step. For the first time since arriving in Steeple Resting, he felt he was getting ahead of the criminal secrets of his adversaries. He also marvelled at the ingenuity and skill of mediaeval masons.

Unlike on the first staircase, there were no slits to admit light from the tower, and Worse needed his torch all the way. The ceiling height was also much less generous, and he found himself forced to stoop uncomfortably.

The lowest steps opened into a crypt that he quickly judged to be as large as the full footprint of the church itself. Wherever he shone the torch, the space was broken up by massive Norman pillars and arches supporting the stone vaulted ceiling, and of course the weight of St Eke's above that. Headroom in some places was barely adequate. The air was musty but not intolerable.

Worse knew that where he emerged from the spiral stairs was directly beneath the tower room. He planned to begin with a brief reconnoitre of the whole area, and moved in the direction of the nave, following it toward the chancel end. About halfway along, his torch picked out the glints of gold altar ware. Apart from this, there was little adornment.

To the left of the altar, in the chancel equivalent, was a stone tomb carrying the carved effigy of a woman. On its side facing the altar was an inscription. Using his mobile phone, Worse photographed the text for later decipherment.

He moved across to the foundations of the north aisle. To his surprise, at its east end, he found a stone staircase leading to a neat gap in the vaulting. It was clearly a way out into the aisle above; he would investigate that when it was time to leave.

Worse walked westward to the back of this aisle, then crossed the nave to move eastward along the south aisle. Again, something glistened in front of him, though less brightly than the altar gold. Despite his torch, he was very close before he could see what was there. It was another raised tomb, in black stone, this one with no effigy.

Worse was not a person given to gasps of surprise. But he did catch his breath at what he now looked upon. Penetrating the stone slab, at a point where a man's heart might lie, was a knight's longsword, protruding a quarter-length, hilt and handle glinting silver in Worse's torchlight.

—

There was no inscription. None was needed: here was *unnatural cause and bloody consequence* told in steel and stone.

Worse placed his hands on the slab. He felt such cold as he never had before. He moved his right hand to the sword, at first touching its handle lightly with his fingers. Then he grasped it fully as would a knight in battle. It too, was cold, but in a different way.

Worse recognized this one. It was the same connection cold that he felt when looking at St Eke's from across the lane. Now he knew: it had come from this tomb, from the crypt to the tower, thence by some mysterious transference through the Magnacart name, to him.

But in this place, at this moment, there was no mystery. Here, and now, he was in close conduction contact with its very source—a priest-knight's death cold, sent from the Worsener's heart to his sword, to Worse's hand, to Worse's heart.

Worse understood what was happening: between the living and the dead, gift or curse, there is no more powerful exchange. In grasping the sword, he had accepted a covenant. It entered him as a touch-prayer with a spell inside; and was made of kinship warmth and vengeance cold.

Worse let go and stepped back, leaning against a column. He switched off the torch but stayed looking toward the tomb. Somehow, darkness here was warmer than light, and the chill of meaning slowly lifted from his hand.

Why are you here?

Worse imagined events in 1369. Geoffrey Magnacart is aware of a secret held at St Eke's. He suspects that Simon Acolytēs was killed while looking for it. Geoffrey comes at night, expecting to be undisturbed. But the ever-vigilant protectors of the secret confine him in the tower, poison him with burning sulphur, and in an act of unspeakable violation they thrust his sword into his warm corpse. The murder is discovered too early by the Weaver and his company, and once they have gone, Geoffrey's body is hastily removed to conceal the crime. Then, alarmed by the miraculous appearance of Th'Imperishable Stain in Canterbury Cathedral, and foreseeing the possibility that his death might be investigated as a prelude to canonization, they make the concealment permanent in a corner of the crypt. And the superbly crafted sword penetration of the stone? A contritional act, commissioned for a saving ounce of penance, preserving truth in the darkness, never to allow the peace of forgetting.

Not much had changed. There was still a secret. It was still protected by murderers. They still used gas, though now it was the far more lethal hydrogen sulphide instead of a cumbersome sulphur-burning method.

Worse felt ready to leave. He switched on the torch, photographed the sword-tomb, and made his way back to the altar, thinking there might be historical records hidden there. He found nothing, but this time he did register something odd about the altar itself: it was circular.

He swung his torchlight back to the woman's tomb. *And who are you? What is your story?*

Then he returned to the staircase in the north aisle. At its top, he pressed on one side of a brass effigy moulding. It hinged upward and Worse stepped out into the aisle proper, closing the lid on a false tomb holding no remains of its advertised twelfth-century occupant, one Sir Gestine Duquel. No one was in sight.

—

Worse walked through the church, and casually appeared at the open door to the tower. As requested, Rence was guarding the entry. Worse was delighted by the look of confusion on his face. He spoke seriously.

'You look surprised, Constable. Did you not notice me coming out?'

Worse curtailed Rence's pain with a smile. 'Don't tell anybody about this, Constable. May we keep this here, for now?'

He placed Rence's torch on the sexton's shelf. 'Did anyone other than the two technicians try to enter?'

'No one else, except Dr Andrieus was looking for you a few minutes ago.'

'Thank you, Constable. I'll find her. You may go.'

—

Worse had been rethinking the utility of ground-penetrating radar mapping, now that he had confirmed the crypt's existence. He walked out of the church, and found Phoebe studying strata profiles on her laptop. She looked up.

'Not a lot to report. We've done the full perimeter, and there's no tunnel. Definitely no tunnel,' she said. 'Sundry utilities, pipes, power, and so on, I expect.'

'May I have copies of the mapping?' asked Worse.

'Emailing as we speak. Do you want us inside now?'

'Actually,' said Worse. 'I no longer believe that will be necessary. Thank you for all you've done.'

Phoebe looked puzzled, but Worse wanted to keep news of the crypt strictly contained for now.

'There is a question I have—for the future. Are you equipped to image the interiors of above-ground tombs?'

'Yes, we can do that. Lead lining is sometimes a problem, but most stone caskets are amenable. I would need to get the right gear down from London. Georadar is not the way.'

Worse made an immediate decision to take her into his confidence. He looked at her directly.

'Would you agree to having a discussion that remains, at least for the time being, confidential between us?'

'Of course.'

'While you were doing your survey, I found an entry to a crypt. Inside are two unidentified tombs. I would like to show them to you and have you advise on whether you can get the equipment you would need down some stairs. Obviously, technical crew would best be minimal to maintain secrecy.'

'Fascinating. Lead the way, Chief Inspector.'

26   ENTER THE LISTS

[Wednesday]

Worse walked back to the lychgate and sat down. The rather charming shelter was ideally positioned to function as a sort of outdoor site office, where he could watch the comings and goings at St Eke's.

He studied his photograph of the tomb inscription. There were recognizable Latin elements, but most of the text was unfamiliar to him. In particular, he was unable to identify anything that would likely represent expected constituent parts, being a person's name and a date.

He texted the image to Nicholas, with the message: 'Tomb inscription found in Millie's green vertex. Can you or Edvard translate it, please? (The effigy is female.)'

Then he opened the photograph of the Worsener's tomb, and looked at it for a long time.

—

The promised email arrived from Thelma Dewey. She had summarized by making two lists for him: *Matters researched by William Whencely*, and *Matters researched by Canon Simony*. There were several dozen files attached.

At this point, it was items in common that interested Worse. They were architectural plans for St Eke's, dating from before 1116, Becket's connection to St Eke's, and documentation relating to the Mercifuls.

Both men asked these questions. Both men visited the tower at night, and each quickly met a similar fate. The analyst in Worse was pleased. Mill's Canons were his friend.

He phoned Thelma Dewey to thank her, and express how helpful she had been. Thelma replied that she was glad to assist in any way.

'I do want to ask you something, Thelma, about access to archival materials. I know you have an excellent memory for what Mr Whencely and the Canon accessed, but is that actually recorded anywhere? What's the routine in that regard?'

'Oh yes, Chief Inspector. Every item is logged into and out of the reading room. Anything that's copied or photographed is registered as such.'

'And who is responsible for that? Who are the people who clerk that information, or can access the register?'

'Well, I'm responsible, of course. But there are others who assist.'

'Can you send me a list of their names, and roles in the Cathedral, please? Anyone who could have found out what our two friends were searching for. That's the essential question.'

'I will immediately.'

—

A few seconds before this conversation finished, Worse missed a call from Nicholas. He phoned back.

'Worse. What are you up to in Steeple Resting? You're putting Edvard into some kind of linguistic frenzy. Don't be concerned, he's loving it. That text—he recognized it instantly. It occurs in the Oxford Passage. He's never translated it, but knowing its origin as a memorial inscription will help enormously. He's hoping it will prove to be the key to the whole Passage.'

'Good,' said Worse.

'Good? Worse, it's fantastic!'

'Yes, it's fantastic. Thank Edvard very much from me. Are you still planning to drive home tonight?'

—

If Worse showed more distraction than enthusiasm, it was because he was looking ahead. Inevitably, this meant also that he was thinking into the past. He focused, for now, on questions of reliability regarding Oldrice's account of events in 1369.

The thirty-seventh Tale, contributed by the Worsener, was undoubtedly semi-true, given that Christianus and his travels were elsewhere spoken of. Moreover, place descriptions were uncannily accurate, bearing in mind that the Ferendes were not otherwise known to Europeans, at least with any certainty, until the second decade of the nineteenth century.

But semi-true means semi-false, and there was much in the Tale that was not credible to the modern intellect. All the same, Worse would keep an open mind until he knew what motive Geoffrey Magnacart had in relating it.

Or perhaps it was more the motive of Henry Oldrice that should be questioned. Was he a reliable reporter of the times, or simply an imaginative storyteller like his more famous successor? Given the parallels with current events in Steeple Resting, and the discovery of what was almost certainly the Worsener's tomb, Worse inclined to the former.

And if he was a reliable reporter of the times, then he was present. And if he was present, either he was a ghostly, unreferenced travelling witness within the *Wey*'s company, or he was an infiltrator disguised, or depicted, as a fellow pilgrim. This latter was the idea, attributed to Franz Hebe, mentioned by Darian in an endnote to his translation. And the likely candidate, suggested by Hebe, was the all-knowing Weaver.

What Worse had just been told by Nicholas implied that Henry Oldrice either learned of the inscription from someone else, or had personally entered the crypt, seen the secret tomb, then—in the flickering light of a tallow candle, Worse imagined—copied its text.

And survived.

As had Worse. He felt a new connection, this time to the resourceful author. He imagined being Henry Oldrice, masquerading as the Weaver to gain his companions' trust. He was their constable in charge that last morning before Canterbury. He was the first on the scene of Geoffrey's heinous murder. He later wrote about it in his *Wey*. But he didn't write everything. In all editions we know, except MS-Oxford, there is no mention of the inscription. Even there, in the Oxford

Passage, its meaning—and its source—is hidden in a secret language bequeathed unintelligible to the centuries.

Why, Henry Oldrice? What were you compelled to write, but also hide?

—

Worse was thinking about this when he received an email response from Thelma Dewey, listing nineteen names and job descriptions of people who assisted in diocesan library and archive services. She included the work roster for the current and previous month.

One name stood out: Michael Couchman, Volunteer Aide. He was at work two days before, the Monday afternoon that Simony was about his researches.

Worse phoned Thelma again.

'I can't thank you enough, Thelma. I wish everyone I dealt with had the meticulous skills of an archivist. Tell me if you can: on Monday, would the Canon and Michael Couchman have interacted? Would each have known the other was there?'

'Michael would have known; he was at the data entry desk, recording requested items out and in. Every borrower is identified. The Canon I can't speak for. Possibly not. He wouldn't ordinarily deal in person with that desk.'

'And how do you find Michael? As someone to work with?'

Worse detected the slightest of Deaconess Delays.

'We are grateful for all the volunteer assistance we get, Chief Inspector.'

27 COUCHMAN

As Worse left the lychgate, intending to head back to the Old Vicarage, a large, brightly coloured van pulled up. There was no doubting the expertise it transported. On its roof rack was an enormous semiotic bell in metallized fibreglass, and painted on the side panels was 'William Toll'.

The driver got out and moved around to open a sliding door on the passenger side. Worse approached him.

'William, is it?'

'Nah. Rocky.'

'William's the owner?'

'Nah. That would be Boriska.'

Rocky threw a sympathetic glance to Worse. 'I don't get it either.'

'You know this bell?' asked Worse, with mounting concern for its wellbeing.

'Oh yeah, oh yeah. St Eke's. Most precious bell in Kent. Most important. That's why they send the best. Rocky Ryngelle.'

'That's good. Why is it the most precious?'

All this time, Rocky had been dragging toolkits and gear around on the van floor. He stopped and turned to Worse.

'St Eke's. The cursed tower. Don't you know? Mistreat this bell and the ground will open up. I'm talking Hades, friend.'

Rocky's gaze ricocheted from Worse to the tarpaulin-covered roof behind him, and the bell rope hanging ingloriously over it. He looked shocked.

'What the fuck? Who's done that? They're gone to hell, for sure.'

'Can't say, for now,' said Worse. 'Police were onto it promptly, though.'

Worse joined his Campanile colleagues in Canon Simony's office. He logged into the task force intranet, scanning through transcripts of phone calls between Couchman and Sleke. At three o'clock, he asked for Couchman to be brought in.

'I trust you had the foresight to bring any essential medications with you this afternoon,' were Worse's first words.

Couchman could hardly miss the implication, but he didn't reply. Worse continued.

'Let me state the rules. You will answer my questions fully and truthfully. If you fail to answer fully, or if you lie to me, you may be detained from that moment. Do you understand?'

Couchman looked sullenly around the room, without replying.

'That was a question,' said Worse.

'I understand that I don't have to sit here and be treated like a criminal. I understand I have a right to remain silent, and I will choose to.'

'You have been misinformed. In this room, you enjoy no rights, including the right to leave. Look about you. This room was Canon Simony's office. What sympathy do you think these walls contain for the person who grievously attacked the Canon?'

'That wasn't me.'

Worse ignored the denial. 'Describe for the panel your movements from six in the morning this Monday last, over the following twenty-four hours.'

Couchman evidently reasoned it was safer to answer than test his interrogator's patience.

'I was at home, worked at the Manor hospice for the morning, drove to Canterbury around midday, had a quick lunch, then worked at the Records Office of the Cathedral from one o'clock to five, drove home, started my usual evening shift at the Manor at six, finished at nine, and walked home.'

'Where is home?'

'I have a flat in Manor Hall. That's staff accommodation in the Priory grounds.'

'Did you leave your home at any time after nine that evening?'

'No.'

'Who can verify that?'

'I live alone.'

'What do you do at the Records Office?'

'Whatever I'm asked to do. I'm a volunteer. Mostly in library services.'

'On Monday afternoon, did you have any contact with Canon Simony?'

'No.'

'But you were aware that he was accessing materials from the archives? You were logging those materials out to him by name?'

'Yes.'

'What impression did you form, as to the subject matter of those materials?'

'Nothing. I didn't think about it.'

'Can you recall what items you logged to Canon Simony?'

'No.'

'Then I shall remind you. In summary: they pertained to historical building plans for St Eke's, to documents connecting Thomas Becket to St Eke's, and to Cathedral records regarding an order of knights known in centuries past as the Mercifuls. Now, what do you imagine might have been on his mind that he would access that combination of items?'

'I have no idea.'

'When Canon Simony met with you later, in the evening at Priory Manor, did he raise any of these subjects, make comments or ask questions?'

'No. We talked only about patients.'

'Are you aware of whether he discussed any of those archive materials with another person that evening?'

'No.'

'Did Canon Simony indicate to you, or anyone else to your knowledge, his intention to stop in at St Eke's on his way home from Priory Manor that evening?'

'No.'

'Were you in contact with Dr Sleke, by any means at all, between beginning work at the Cathedral on Monday and beginning work at Priory Manor on Tuesday morning?'

'No.'

Worse sat back, looking at Couchman. He held up the XVI card and spoke slowly. 'Answer very carefully. What does this mean to you?'

—

Worse let Couchman go at 4.00 pm.

'What does everyone think? Let's start with our constables.'

The consensus opinion amongst the junior officers was that the witness was untrustworthy, but no one held an emphatic view.

'Inspector Wirrier?' asked Worse, finally.

'I find myself less equivocal than my colleagues. I thought he was evasive, or tried to be so, especially with sentinel questions where his answers might be proven self-incriminating or ultimately perjurious. I think he warrants high priority as a suspect.'

'I fully agree,' said Worse. 'He rather obviously marshalled his clinical psychology skills attempting to run the interview on his terms. It was interesting to watch. If all agree, we should obtain a warrant to search Priory Manor, including associated premises such as living quarters for staff. It should take the form of a surprise raid, as soon as possible. Are there any arguments against?'

There was no dissension.

'Inspector Wirrier, will you lead? Can we aim for midnight?'

'Yes to both,' said Wirrier. He addressed the others. 'Muster St Eke's parish hall, twenty-three hundred. Sergeant Michelson, could you provide us with architectural plans for the Manor, please?'

'Yes, sir. I'll post them to our site.'

'Including outbuildings and anything underground, cellars and so on,' said Worse. 'To bring you all up to date, our working hypothesis is that the tower attacks were committed by a group dedicated to preserving something highly sensitive at St Eke's. The perpetrators possibly identify themselves with the mediaeval order of hospice knights called the Mercifuls. It seems that the word or number "sixteen" is significant to them or, at least, its Roman numeral notation. We do not yet know how they manage to flood the tower so readily with hydrogen sulphide, and leave no trace of its source. I would appreciate you focusing on these questions when conducting your searches tonight. Obviously, we take possession of personal and administrative computers. If there is any serious resistance, make arrests. Thank you.'

The others began readying to leave when Worse raised a hand.

'Oh, by the way,' he added. 'We're still looking for a light-coloured van with a probable non-functioning rear brake light. It was used to run Dr Misgivingston off the Canterbury road on the night that William Whencely was murdered. It may be secreted on the Manor premises.'

28 ECCENE NAMES

Though not feeling ordinary hunger, Worse became aware that he hadn't eaten all day, and knew he probably should.

He was sitting in the lychgate, reflecting on the Couchman interview, and his colleagues' appraisal of it. Now that his second in command, Inspector Wirrier, was speaking up more, Worse appreciated his maturity as an investigator, his instincts and competence. He felt fortunate to have him on the team.

Rocky's van was still parked there. The bell rope was no longer on view, and Worse was tempted to visit the belfry to ask about progress, but decided against it.

Instead, he went home.

–

'Goodness, Richard, you have to sleep and eat. At least one or the other,' said Millie. She looked concerned for him.

Worse gave her a hug. 'I know. I'll eat. I'm afraid tonight's going to be late again. We've scheduled a surprise raid on a nearby property.'

Millie stood back slightly, and raised her arms sideways. 'In the course of your investigations, have you considered the merits of a surprise raid on a nearby mathematician?'

'Very frequently,' said Worse.

He took her hand and led the way to their bedroom.

–

It was nearly six o'clock when Worse awoke. Millie was sitting up in bed beside him, working on her laptop. She reached across to stroke his hair.

'That was a very nice police raid, thank you.'

Worse turned to her, head propped on an elbow. 'And thank you for your full cooperation, madam. It's helpful members of the public like yourself who make difficult police work so rewarding.'

Millie gave him a happy shove as she got out of bed. 'On yer flatfoots, mister.'

She walked around the bed and took his hand. 'Here's your schedule: shower, dinner. You're not going back on the case until you've eaten.'

—

'Richard! We've hardly seen you for days. We've been concerned. As far as I can tell, your last proper meal was at the King of Kent on Monday night.'

'I think you may be correct, Veronica,' said Worse. 'But it is only Wednesday. I've been fine, really fine. I have missed the family gatherings, though.'

'As the family gatherings have missed you, Worse,' said Philip. 'You know that Nicholas is not with us tonight?'

'I do. We've spoken during the day.'

Philip showed interest, but Worse ignored the cue.

'That smells delicious, Veronica.'

'And Philip,' said Philip.

'Philip is our herb gatherer and gourmet fine chopper this evening,' said Veronica.

'Ah yes. I'm certain now; it is the aromatic herbs I was detecting,' said Worse, 'and the perfection of their cutting.'

—

'And how is the Canon?' asked Philip.

'Still intubated, I expect. He had a setback last night, so his recovery won't be fast. I don't know about progress today, but I'll get news later tonight after their evening handover.'

The thought brought to mind Jane Malleson as his source of information. Worse was pleased he felt no emotional discomfort. His focus stayed on the Canon. The infatuation had not reawakened from earlier.

Veronica's phone rang.

'It's Nicholas,' she said, looking at the screen.

The others heard only Veronica's end. 'That's fine, darling.

Much safer. Yes, he's here.' She looked at Worse, handing over her phone. 'Nicholas wants a word.'

'Worse. You were right about Sleke and St Eke. And a whole lot of others, like Sneke, Speke, Stecke. Even Frecke and Squeke. Dozens. They're all Anglo-Saxon[1], apparently, with some Flemish imports. Edvard doesn't know the reasons, but the connection is quite clear. He also thinks Michael is a candidate, through Hebrew, Greek and Latin, if that's of interest.'

'Thank you, Nicholas. And thank Edvard for me. The other matter?'

'We'll be working on it all night. Worse, at your end, stay out of trouble, won't you?'

'I look forward to a comprehensive translation, explaining everything, solving our case,' said Worse, ending the call and handing back the phone.

'Nicholas will stay in Cambridge tonight, and return home in the morning,' announced Veronica.

'After dining in College, I would think that's very sensible,' said Worse. 'For some, it is visibly unsafe simply rising from high table.'

'And after dining in the Misgivingston kitchen, I think you should have some steadying coffee before rising to detective work,' said Millie.

'Good thinking, as always,' said Worse. He turned to Philip.

'Philip, I was hoping you might help me with some theorizing. Both William and Wilfred did research in the Cathedral archives before heading to St Eke's, at night, and being attacked. I have electronic copies of the documents that each accessed, and I wondered if you could review them for me. The categories in common relate to St Eke's architecture, Becket, and the Mercifuls, but I haven't had time to study them in detail.'

'Of course. Glad to, Worse. Send them to me now.'

'Thank you. My news of the day is that St Eke's does indeed have a large crypt, accessed via secret staircases. It houses two raised tombs. One is of a woman, unidentified at present, but Nicholas and Edvard are working on the inscription. If the Becket rumours have substance, I suspect this will be key.'

Worse hesitated. 'The other is also unidentified, in the sense of having no markings, but is almost certainly that of Geoffrey Magnacart.'

'My God,' said Philip, staring at Worse. 'You have found him.'

Millie reached across the table to touch Worse's hand. Her eyes conveyed the empathy she felt.

It was Veronica who expressed in words the understanding they all had of how Worse must feel.

'You saw the Worsener's actual tomb? Geoffrey Magnacart, your ancestor? That must have been very moving, Richard.'

She placed a mug of coffee on the table in front of Worse, and put a hand on his shoulder.

'Yes. I would have to say, I was very much affected.'

He was also affected now. In Millie's family, he felt greatly cared for.

---

[1] Though Tøssentern is, of course, correct in determining this cache of Kentish surnames as Anglo-Saxon, their presumed parentage in *Eke* is altered Roman. The disciple saint, not otherwise named, was present at Jesus' emergence from the judgement hall, and is our primary source for Pilate's words *Ecce homo* (John 19:5). From Latin demonstrative *Ecce* comes Eke. The derivation has bearing on the occasional modern debate over the pronunciation of his name, being with a long or short first vowel, or even if in one or two syllables. As for much of ancient phonetics, the question is not settled. The adjectival form Eccene, pertaining to St Eke and, more generally, that epochal event in Christian history, is recent, and pronounced 'Eksene', except in New Zealand ('Iksin'). (For specialist scholars, a comprehensive residency in Eccene Studies is periodically offered by the Mount Sycamore School of Theology in the United States.) Note that ME *eek* or *eke* ('also') bears no etymological relation to the name Eke under discussion here (Enright), though it does give rise to our 'nickname'. On the other hand, interestingly, the name of the unfortunate St Alswāp (or Alsop) uncontestedly originates in OE *alswā* (also 'also').

29 REWIRED

It was close to 7.30 when Worse crossed the lane to St Eke's. The William Toll van was gone, but the security camera technicians were still working.

Worse found Matt sitting on a rear pew in the nave, a laptop on his knee.

'Evening. Final testing, and we'll be out of here. Jake's doing the rounds for the motion sensors.'

'Thanks for looking after us so promptly,' said Worse.

'No worries. I get that it's urgent. Terrible business. The Canon married my sister,' said Matt. 'If you know what I mean,' he added. 'You're in charge here?'

'Yes. Worse is the name.'

'I remember.' Matt handed Worse an information card. 'Here's your site address, access code and password.'

'Thank you,' said Worse.

'Any issues, my number's on this.'

Now Matt handed Worse a business card. Worse was looking around. He could see bright light coming through the doorway to the tower, and pointed.

'That's a vast improvement—the light in the belfry.'

'Yeah. It was bad. Illegal. Unsafe. Fire hazard too. It's all rewired now for the right amps. RCDs as well. We couldn't just do what you asked and leave the rest dangerous.'

'That's very good. Canon Simony will be pleased. Thanks for everything,' said Worse, moving away.

Matt called to Worse. 'By the way, did you know there are cameras already up there, high in the timber steeple? They're tucked in between the louvres, one facing east across the roof, one south to the lychgate. Not easy to see.'

'No, I did not,' said Worse, turning back. 'Operational?'

'Hard to say. Maybe eight, ten years old. I couldn't reach them, and I wasn't able to trace their feed. Same with the power supply. Everything disappeared into the stonework, somehow.'

—

The tower room was certainly brilliantly lit. Worse repositioned his familiar folding chair so that he looked back towards the squeaky door, which was still wedged open.

He imagined 1369. Whatever kind of entry fixture was there, if any, the Norman doorway itself had not changed. He saw the Weaver look in, hesitate to disturb Geoffrey in apparent prayer, confer with others, then finally enter to make his gruesome find. What happened after this, we are not told.

How truthful was Oldrice about this event?

The simple tenability of his account in the *Wey* was made questionable by the discovery that he could reproduce the secret tomb inscription in the Oxford Passage. To Worse, it required only one proven omission, or one falsehood, to establish unreliability in a witness. And once that is the case, everything else in their testimony must be treated with a higher level of scepticism.

Worse returned to a line of thinking that had been interrupted by Thelma Dewey's Couchman email. It began as a counterfactual exploration, but evolved into a simple completion argument, requiring just one contradiction in the record.

He started by assuming true Franz Hebe's hypothesis that Oldrice was present as the Weaver. The educated, literate, witty, and seemingly devout Oldrice behaved with the greatest respect toward the Worsener, thereby gaining his trust and becoming privy to his interest in St Eke's. That interest might have related to the rumours about Becket, or to suspicions over Simon Acolytēs' 1280 death in the tower. Or perhaps, given Simon's connection to the place, the Worsener had reason to think that the *Documento* of his Tale was concealed there.

Whatever the motive, during the night, Oldrice accompanied the Worsener to the tower. They found, and entered, the crypt. Oldrice returned promptly to the Canterbury Bell, leaving Geoffrey to investigate further, or to pray. Protectors of the crypt trapped him, overcame him using their favoured method of burning sulphur, then desecrated his body with the knight's own sword.

The one adjusting lie that this theory required was a dissembling on the part of Oldrice when they were searching for the Worsener, just prior to leaving Stēpel Raest. There, he attributes to the Abbess the idea of looking in St Eke's, when the same would surely be his own first impulse. In the circumstances of the clandestine night visit, their discovery of the crypt, and the subsequent murder, that revision in the telling would be understandable.

Worse recalled his conversation with Simony, about the compelling drive of the pilgrim being not devotion, but doubt. The thought occurred to him that perhaps, for the Worsener and possibly others in that company, their intention was never the pilgrimage to Canterbury at all. Instead, it was a journey of spiritual anxiety to St Eke's. To Becket's darkness, not his shrine.

And why would that be? The following year, 1370, was the bicentenary of Becket's murder, not to mention the tercentenary of the Cathedral's consecration. The pilgrimages would be massive, with celebration and reverence greater than ever before. For the doubters, now was the time to establish their case, confirm the old rumours, and expose, if they could, a flawed saint.

—

Worse remained sitting. He had been vaguely troubled by something Nicholas said, relaying Edvard's hope that the tomb inscription might be key to translating the whole Oxford Passage. If that proved so, it raised the question of how Oldrice could have known that language, given its assumed origins at least two centuries prior, and its evident purpose of secrecy. The alternative possibility, that Oldrice had invented the language of the Passage for his own protection and, in reportage, inserted a therefore foreign inscription verbatim, would hardly be consistent.

—

'We're done here,' Matt called from the entrance. 'Everything checks out. Good luck with finding the bastards.'

Behind Matt, Worse saw Jake manoeuvring the long ladder out of the building.

'Thank you again, Matt,' said Worse.

He heard a cymbal-clash of aluminium against stone as somewhere on his way Jake misjudged mediaeval dimensions. Their voices faded, the clatter-scrape of ladder seating on roof rack became a loud grunt of satisfaction, the van doors slammed shut, and an engine noise delivered itself to the night. St Eke's regained a little dignity.

Worse's thoughts settled on Matt's discovery of security cameras semi-hidden between the steeple louvres. If they were monitored in some way, it would explain how all three victims of poisoning—William, Worse himself, and the Canon—were known to be in the church at night.

He searched on his phone for Phoebe's georadar map showing the exterior boundary of the foundations of St Eke's. There weren't many underground service connections to find, but one was suspicious, leading from the north-west corner of the tower in the direction of the Old Vicarage.

Worse messaged Wirrier and Rence the new information, with the suggestion that the Old Vicarage, particularly Mansion's flat, warranted another search.

—

Still Worse sat there. The quiet would normally suit him, but tonight, in this tower room, it brought not tranquility, but unease. He had formed almost no relationship with the security team; yet, irrationally, their departure left him with a sense of emptiness.

Worse wondered about the feeling. He was sitting, brightly

lit, in the middle of a centuries-old crime scene. Through that doorway had come the innocents and the curious, for the bell, for the view, or in search of real or speculative history. And following, or waiting, were their killers, a guardian brotherhood of the crypt, sworn to defend whatever ungodly act it concealed.

Their method, hardly changed from mediaeval times, was by imitation of Hades, a sulphurous, tortured, suffocating death designed to frighten the credulous and perpetuate the useful myth of *Stēpel Malison*. Now, with stunning effrontery, the reverend custodian of everything that remained good in St Eke's, its very own vicar, was the subject of a blatant attack.

All this while, Worse was looking toward the doorway, his eyes naturally drawn to the one object brightly reflecting the newly generous wattage. It brought to mind Matt's remark about the old electrics: 'Fire hazard too'.

He looked around. What would burn? The sexton's shelf, the Wistful Wardrobe, the folding seats. And, of course, the bell rope; that was a natural fuse to catastrophe. If it caught fire, flame would be carried up to the belfry platform and then the timber steeple.

This was typical mental entertainment for Worse, exploring hypotheticals, running scenarios, planning risk mitigation. It was a habit of mind that had saved his life on numerous occasions.

His gaze returned, irresistibly, to the specular highlight on the glossy red fire extinguisher. The mental exercise advanced, with characteristic perverseness. When is an extinguisher itself a fire hazard?

In the instant that Worse posed himself this artificial, idly wondered riddle, he solved the mystery of the St Eke's poison attacks.

When it is not really a fire extinguisher.

When instead of retardant, it contains something flammable. A toxic, flammable gas.

He almost leapt out of his chair, and strode to the device.

It looked genuine, but the hypothesis was compelling. Having found the crypt, he had virtually eliminated the aluminium sulphide theory as there was no hidden paraphernalia to support it. And though he knew that hydrogen sulphide could be purchased in compressed-gas cylinders, these could not readily be transported and clandestinely stored. But here was concealment in broad daylight, as it were—effective, simple, and audacious.

Worse studied the fire extinguisher without touching it. In terms of the tank's colour-coded paintwork, specification tables, and instruction and safety semiotics, it looked real enough. So did the reducing valve assembly, handle, lever actuator, and trumpet.

He phoned the senior forensics officer to whom he had spoken earlier in the afternoon. She reassured him that her team had routinely swabbed the fire extinguisher for DNA. Next he phoned HCN, his contact in the police hazmat team, and explained the idea.

'Are you there now, in the tower?'

'I am,' said Worse.

'I can be with you in thirty minutes to collect it for testing.'

'I want this done very surreptitiously,' said Worse. 'Don't let anyone see what you're removing from the church.'

'Understood,' said HCN.

'Also, chain of custody is paramount for this item.'

'And safety, from what you're saying. All understood.'

When Worse had finished the call, he photographed the device without detaching it from the wall. Then he walked out to the patrol car stationed near the lychgate, introduced himself to the two constables on watch, and forewarned them of HCN's arrival.

After that, he returned to his thinking chair, and waited.

30 WORSENPREYERE

The feeling of unease that Worse had identified earlier was still there. His eye settled again on the fire extinguisher. Here was an item of universal building furniture, existing unremarkably in daily peripheral vision, afforded only the rarest promotion to foveal importance. And despite a brilliant-colour conspicuity, it was never the design interloper. Its presence in a public space was unfussily condoned, mandated in fact, by regulation. Style didn't come into it, only pure utility; and if, subliminally, its presence conveyed meaning, that was never threat, but safety.

The perfect sleeper, thought Worse; but his concerns were immediately more generalized. What other deceptions were hidden in plain sight, invisible to the lazy wavefront of expectation that we project upon the world?

He looked at the worn flagstone floor. There was another thing: the ground, present only impressionistically for most of our lives. Its persistence, its solidity, we assume step to step, without actually studying it. Yet it has secrets and dangers. Here, the crypt beneath, for example.

Worse repositioned his chair so that he was no longer seeing the fire extinguisher. He felt more comfortable not having the spiral staircase directly behind him. There was a reason for that. Both Geoffrey Magnacart and William Whencely were found facing those steps, as if from there, in their final seconds, they witnessed Death descend into their presence.

Perhaps in that moment, Geoffrey truly was praying, as Oldrice surmised. But it was no ordinary prayer. Who would choose to worship in this workaday room and not at the altar close by? *Ecce Satanas*. Only a man beholding the Devil, trapped here, breathing in the noxious air, breathing out his life.

Trapped. Worse's unease was identifying itself. The squeaky door was open, the church empty, the air clear; yet he felt confinement. Not physical, not intellectual, not wholly psychological. It was emotional, and only indistinctly real: the weight of obligation returning.

For someone who habitually modelled possible futures in terms of degrees of freedom, this was an unwelcome intrusion. Tonight, though, for the first time, Worse recognized its special nature. Here was no sundry duty noticed in passing, to be assumed or not as he felt able. This was obligation delivered, by inheritance, expressly to him, and today he had touched the tomb of the man from whom it came. It couldn't be put aside.

Perhaps Philip was right, about Worse and Worsener. The Magnacart connection to Geoffrey was not to be denied. Might it be true that his ancestry predestined a duty to make good, drew him to St Eke's, revealed to him the heinous mistreatment of his forebear, and thrust upon him the cumulative anger of the family generations to requite?

And along with the patrilineal names, Worse and Magnacart, did he inherit some descendent calling to the ancient office— to roam the world like Geoffrey, championing the wronged? Worse resisted the idea. It was not a role, not an identity, he would ever wish for.

He remembered Millie's amusement on the first evening: 'Now you'll have to do knightly deeds.' That was less than a week before, when he thought his coming to England was simply to reassure Millie of her father's safety, and assist peripherally with enquiries into William Whencely's death.

'Quench'n'temper!'

The theatrics didn't seem so funny now.

—

The sound of a vehicle door informed Worse of HCN's arrival. He left the tower, walked across the south aisle, and waited in the south-west porch. HCN was talking to the constables, who were presumably checking his identity and vehicle registration. They waved him on.

Worse was pleased to see him.

'Thank you, Sergeant. I appreciate this.'

'Glad to help. What was I doing, anyway? Paperwork.'

Worse required exactitude for visualization.

'Metaphorically, I take it. Meaning the electronic kind?'

'Yeah. Oh yeah. I'm not one for clutter. Bare desk; one laptop; vintage anglepoise; coffee mug.'

So, no paper at all. That better composed Worse's mental picture of the person. He liked the minimalism, as well.

'This one,' said Worse, stopping by the fire extinguisher.

HCN studied it closely, at first without touching it. 'Cleverly done, if you're right,' he said.

'When can you let me know?'

'Later tonight.'

HCN secured an evidence tag to the cylinder neck, and placed the whole in a hazmat service duffel bag. He had Worse sign it over to him.

'I'll be in touch, Chief Inspector,' he said.

—

Worse saw HCN out all the way to his car, then returned to the tower. He wanted to recover the feelings he had been exploring before the interruption. They were about connection to Geoffrey, obligation, and retribution. The more difficult thoughts, about himself, about unwanted destiny visited upon him, he would block from his mind.

And there was something else to think about: his repugnance at the Mercifuls' manipulative and exclusionary hold over the mysteries of St Eke's. Using murder and secrecy and superstition, they had seized and defended criminal ownership for centuries.

And for what? To protect a narrative of lies? The reputation of a mortal; even, possibly, of a flawed saint? To conceal some unforgivable, impious act? Or perhaps the Order of

Mercifuls had always worked for no other reason than venal profit, extorting power or wealth in exchange for safety and suppression.

Whatever their motivation, the woman of the crypt was key, and one day the world would be told why. At least her knight companion in their listening isolation was part-awakened and, through Worse, would expose and retaliate—for Magnacart honour, for revenge, and to rehabilitate the spiritual worth of this historic pilgrims' rest of St Eke's.

Worse was immediately irritated with himself. That was Worsener thinking, selfless, chivalric and idealistic perhaps. But also speciously heroic, falsified in paladin mythology, and a relic of violent masculinity portrayed as gallantry. He wanted no part of it.

—

Sitting in his meditation chair was fine for the analytics, but it didn't feel like achieving; it didn't feel like crime smashing. Worse jumped up, collected Rence's torch from the sexton's shelf, and entered the spiral staircase.

It was his now—the people's. Worse was reclaiming it from the Devil.

At the top, he climbed from the platform to the entry of the stairs to the crypt. There was only one thing he was looking for, and he found it five steps down. Concealed in a deep niche cut into the newel, and easily missed in the natural centrifugal sweep of a torch beam, was another fire extinguisher.

31 PRE-RAID

Worse retraced his steps to the tower room and sat down, looking at his mobile phone. Using Matt's information card, he accessed feed from the newly installed security cameras. Then he turned off the overhead light and walked around the room. The motion detection and night-vision clarity were excellent.

A text arrived from Jane, informing Worse that Wilfred had shown some improvement in gas exchange over the twenty-four hours, and that the ITU consultants were feeling encouraged by his progress. There was no hint of anything personal for Worse in the message, and for this he was grateful. He replied, thanking her for the news.

Worse left St Eke's by the south-west door, and noted lights on at the Misgivingston house across the lane. He decided to go home and see if Millie was still up.

—

Worse found Millie in Philip's study, talking to her father. The moment Worse entered the room, Philip addressed him.

'Worse. Those documents you sent me are a priceless resource for conspiracists and scandalmongers. How did you obtain them?'

'Through the goodwill of the Cathedral senior archivist, Thelma Dewey. She was terribly upset about Wilfred, and has been extremely helpful to us.'

'How is the Canon?' asked Millie. She had stood up to give Worse a quick welcome-home hug.

'A slight improvement today, according to my update of a few minutes ago.'

'Thank goodness for that,' said Millie, resuming her seat.

Worse looked at Philip. 'Any conclusions to draw?'

'Yes indeed, Worse. I can see why Will was interested in the Mercifuls. One could be excused for thinking they acted as a kind of off-the-books Praetorian Guard to the senior clergy. Whatever they did, they were generously rewarded with wealth. The diocese gifted their Order a number of properties, including the priory at Little Healing.'

'That would be Priory Manor, the hospice now?'

'Yes, it is. I made calls there, actually, when I was in practice. But anyway, the far more curious thing is that the Church ceded ownership in perpetuity of, guess what? Not St Eke's as such, but the *foundations* of St Eke's. How strange is that?'

'Do you have a date?' asked Worse.

'1156. Exactly forty years after consecration.'

Worse had been standing. He now sat next to Millie.

'Very strange, yes. So the diocese owns the land beneath, and the fabric above, but the Mercifuls control the foundations in between. That's an absurdly restrictive property contract to enter into. Was there any explanation for it?'

'Not that I could see,' said Philip.

'And it was never rescinded?' asked Worse.

'Again, not that I could see.'

'What do you think, Millie?' said Worse.

'I agree. Obviously, it seems irresponsible on behalf of the Church to let that happen. It would be easy to conclude they were forced into the agreement, by extortion, or threat of some kind.' She hesitated. 'Though, I wonder ...'

'You wonder what, Millie?' said Philip.

Worse had more patience, and was simply looking at her.

'Well, on the other hand, perhaps it was an agreement entered willingly. In which case, we should look for how the Church was, in fact, advantaged by ceding that control to a third party.'

'Love your Grimly thinking,' said Worse.

Millie continued. 'Let's suppose for the moment that this were the case, that it was an advantageous and very clever move by the Church. Then we need to understand why it was so.'

'They had a secret to hide, in the crypt, we now know. Perhaps the bishops trusted the Mercifuls to preserve it for them, more than they trusted future generations of churchmen,' said Philip.

'And that would be because ...?' asked Worse.

'Because ecclesiastic politics are notoriously internecine, and always have been,' said Philip.

'And because the secret was shockingly irreligious, in some way,' said Millie.

'Okay, yes. A case of contracting out the unconscionable,' said Worse. 'Shift, pay, forget: the moral economy in society at large. You are suggesting it applies to the Church equally?'

'No doubt it does, or has at times,' said Philip.

'Dad, what do you know about the founding ideals of the Mercifuls, their articles of conduct, and so on?'

'There's quite a lot of information in your files,' Philip gestured to Worse, 'Essentially, they were a monastic order, originally of physician knights, constituted to care for the sick, offer hospitality to travellers, protect the weak and pilgrims, and work for the betterment of Christ's flock, shall we say.'

'Were they militarist as well?' asked Millie.

'Oh yes. They became famous for rescuing the Templar garrison in the siege of Dar Sala-Roqun. There's a painting of the battle, from the school of Van Eyck, in the city museum in Ghent, I believe.'

'All that sounds honourable enough, for the times,' said Worse. 'Their allegiance was to the Church, I take it.'

'Very much so,' said Philip. 'And it would seem that, over the years, their knightly attentions refocused on protecting not the weak, but the Church, and accumulating great wealth in the process.'

Worse went quiet. He was thinking about the raid on Priory Manor that was about to commence. What he was learning gave him more confidence in its justification.

'What happened to the Order? Were they formally dissolved along the way?' he asked.

'Actually, there's no indication that they were, unlike the Templars, and others,' said Philip. 'There were named Mercifuls chapels for pilgrims well into the fifteenth century, and, of course, hospice accommodation here and there. But the Order largely retreated into itself, it would appear, or rather, into the shadow of the Church.'

'Content to manage their corporate wealth,' said Millie.

'So we are left to determine what metamorphoses might have occurred after that, and what form they may survive in today,' said Worse.

'I think we're agreed that they survive, at least in part, as the criminal sect still in possession of the St Eke's crypt and its unrevealed mystery,' said Philip.

Worse nodded. 'Very likely.'

His thoughts returned to Priory Manor. If that property had remained continuously with the Mercifuls and their successors for nine-hundred years or so, it might be serving as the repository for the Order's secret history.

'Tea, everyone?' offered Philip, and left to make it.

'You haven't mentioned the raid to Dad,' said Millie.

'This afternoon's, or tonight's?' said Worse, looking innocent. He didn't require an answer. 'Only because I see no need at present.'

'I take it the beneficiary of your attention is Priory Manor?'

'It is.'

'What time can I expect you home?' asked Millie.

'Very late. Take the matrix algebra to bed. Excuse me, Millie. I need to check something.'

At Inspector Wirrier's request, Sergeant Michelson had made architectural plans for Priory Manor available to the Campanile team. Studying them now, Worse could see no evidence of any underground structures. He phoned Michelson to confirm the finding. They concluded that it was extremely unlikely that such a building would not have at least a cellar.

'That's something to look for tonight, then,' said Worse. 'It may have a disguised entry. See you shortly.'

Philip came back with a tray of tea.

'Philip,' said Worse. 'You mentioned earlier that in the past you made GP visits to Priory Manor in Little Healing. What did you make of the place?'

'Oh. It's beautiful but depressing, in a way. That's typical of hospice facilities in the country, though this one is particularly privileged, I'd have to say.'

'And the staff, the administration, the director?'

'All inoffensive enough, if that's your line of enquiry. Sleke, the director, didn't relate to me very much. I had dealings with him when I needed to arrange ambulance transfers, provide a death certificate, that sort of thing.'

'Do you know anything about him, otherwise?' asked Worse.

'Not really. I never found reason, or opportunity, to be curious. You're aware he's not medical? The doctorate is in architectural history, I believe.'

'Anything unusual about the buildings, the way things operated?'

'Again, not really.'

'Is there a chapel in the hospice?'

'I don't know. If so, it was never pointed out to me.'

'Thank you, Philip. I'm very grateful for your work on the archive materials.'

'A pleasure, Worse. Don't let your tea get cold.'

32 PRIORY MANOR

[Wednesday/Thursday]

At 10.45 pm Worse walked from home to the parish hall, passing a dozen or so police vehicles parked in the lane. He found Rence in the vestibule, keeping an attendance record.

'Good evening, Constable. Would you mind giving me a ride to the action tonight?'

'That'd be an honour, Chief Inspector.'

Inside the hall proper, several chairs at the west end had been rearranged into a rough circle, to function as a briefing space. The temporary altar at the other end, in relative darkness, was a discordant presence so close to police business.

Inspector Wirrier brought the meeting to order.

'Attention all. Thank you for volunteering your time at minimal notice. Please unlock the briefing folder on your devices using the access code you have just been sent. Open File SE17.'

He waited for his instructions to be followed.

'This shows a modified Ordnance Survey map of our target property, which some of you will recognize as Priory Manor, in the village of Little Healing. We have reason to believe that personnel connected to this institution had direct or indirect involvement in the attacks at St Eke's. The principal persons of interest are the hospice director, named Arnold Sleke, and a staff counsellor named Michael Couchman. Both reside on the Manor estate, the director in a bungalow and Couchman in Hall accommodation. These are clearly identified on your maps. As many of you know, both individuals have been interviewed by Campanile, and are unable to provide essential alibis. I need to point out, for those of you who are not part of the task force, that a working hypothesis is that the hospice serves as a cover organization for a secret quasi-religious sect with historical connections to St Eke's that explain recent events. If that is true, it is very likely that other parties are involved, in addition to the two persons just mentioned. Our advice is to look especially for concealed spaces, including underground, that may be used for sect activities.'

Wirrier continued, giving further background to Campanile's case, and outlining the categories of material evidence that should be sought. He knew by name all those present, and was personable in forming teams for allocated tasks. When he had finished and taken questions, those teams mustered separately, took instructions from their senior officer, and headed out to their transport. Worse thanked Wirrier, before joining Rence for the ride.

—

The Manor estate was fully walled but for a main driveway entrance approached from the east, and two farm gates on the western perimeter. A patrol car was stationed at each of the latter, blocking exit.

At midnight, police teams swept through the main gate-arch and spread out to their assigned targets. The whole operation was conducted very quietly, with an emphasis on administrative offices in the Priory, staff accommodation at the Hall, Sleke's bungalow, and a variety of agricultural outhouses. Many of the elderly residents were completely oblivious to proceedings. Items seized were logged into police evidence vans parked directly in front of the Manor.

Staff on duty, and those in quarters, were all identity checked and either questioned immediately or summonsed to appear for interview. Worse scanned their names as they were added to the Campanile data page. Given Edvard's advice, he ordered those with names having any homology with 'St Eke', including a Speke and Sneke, to be detained. At no point did Sleke appear, and Worse decided to visit the director's bungalow to check with the search team.

He found Sergeant Morley and PC Wells in the kitchen, and

they exchanged greetings. Morley reported that their search was proving largely unproductive. There was no indication that Sleke had been present that evening.

Worse walked into the dining room. The table was long, with seating for five on each side plus a carver at each end. One carver faced a wide oak-beam lintelled entrance to the sitting room, the other a wall with a large framed historical map of Kent.

Worse sat in the second carver, and imagined chairing a meeting. His gaze lifted to the map. It was perfectly positioned to conceal a screen, and so it proved. Under the left-hand corner he found a spring release, which allowed the whole frame to swing open rightwards on secret hinges and reveal a flat-screen display. It was clear that a large recess had been created by partially infilling an old fireplace, leaving shelf space for a laptop as well. Power was provided from the wall, presumably ducted through the redundant chimney.

Worse called the others in and handed over the find. He didn't ask if they had been through this room already. He could read in Tunny's face that they had.

—

Worse was walking between buildings when he received a call from HCN.

'You were right, Chief Inspector. It's pure H_2S. From the tank weight we measured, we calculate there's enough to fill that tower to lethal levels maybe a hundred times over. Incredible.'

'I found another one after you left,' said Worse. 'And there may be more hidden around. I haven't been able to complete a thorough search.'

'Jeez. What were they thinking?' said HCN. 'One tank alone is enough to conduct a mass murder. We're talking thousands, potentially, given the right crowd density, containment, and egress limitations.'

'Any ideas about their supplier?' asked Worse.

'We're working on that.'

'Once you know, we need purchase and delivery details,'

said Worse. 'Incidentally, how will you dispose of it?'

'Return to supplier, once identified. Otherwise, we incinerate it.'

'Sulphur dioxide and water?'

'That'd be it.'

'Sergeant, there's something I need you to do urgently. Wake up whomever you need. Any issues, refer to me.'

Worse went on to explain his requirements in detail, and stressed the importance of secrecy.

'I'll meet you at St Eke's at zero three hundred. I can pass the second tank on to you then. Possibly more. Let me know if you need to change the time.' Worse paused. 'By the way, Sergeant, I know you as HCN. What is your name?'

'John Halcyon, sir.'

'Well, John, thank you for everything you're doing. Incidentally, that anglepoise you mentioned: how old is it, would you say?'

'Early 1970s.'

'Don't part with it. They're a design masterpiece ... I believe never bettered, fundamentally.'

—

Inspector Wirrier was coordinating the search from the Manor, and Worse found him in the director's office. He looked up from Sleke's desk as Worse appeared.

'Not a lot here, other than admission records, medical files, business accounts.'

'Staff files?' asked Worse.

'In the van.'

'I have a sense that the Mercifuls affairs are managed from Sleke's bungalow,' said Worse.

'Yes. Morley told me of your discovery over there.'

'I'm still keen to find something ceremonial, a chapel for instance; somewhere they keep historical artifacts, symbolic materials, vestments, and so on,' said Worse. 'Any ideas?'

'We may need to dig up these grounds,' said Wirrier.

—

All this time, Worse had been slightly distracted by the wish to resume his search of the crypt at St Eke's. One reason was that he felt sure there would be at least one more fire extinguisher to discover and, given his previous find, it was likely left close to the other exit, Sir Gestine's steps.

Another reason was this: Sleke and Couchman were almost certainly in hiding. If valuable historical, or incriminating, materials were stored in the crypt, the pair might attempt to recover them before fleeing to safety; Worse wanted to get there first. At 2.10 am, he arranged for Rence to drive him back to Steeple Resting.

When they stopped in Old Forge Lane, Worse informed the two patrol car officers stationed there that Sergeant Halcyon would be arriving in the next hour.

'What time did you do your last perimeter check?' Worse asked.

PC Banting, in the driver's seat, answered. 'That was zero two hundred, on the hour, sir.'

'From now on, I want your foot patrols staggered, randomized,' said Worse. 'Around four or five per hour. We have two fugitives, and reason to believe they may attempt entry here. Did you notice anything suspicious? Even slightly?'

'Nothing at all, sir.' This time, it was PC Best, from the passenger seat.

'I have asked Constable Rence to keep an eye on the north side while I'm in the building. You have his number?' said Worse.

Best scrolled a page on their dash-mounted touch screen. 'We do, sir.'

'All right. Thank you,' said Worse.

He waved to Rence as he headed into St Eke's by the south-west door.

—

Worse turned on the light in the bell tower, collected Rence's torch, and crossed the nave to the north aisle. He sat on a pew to review security camera feed on his phone; as expected there had been no activation except in response to his own and Sergeant Halcyon's movements.

In order to keep details of the crypt access contained for the present, he had not yet made the monitoring facility available to the Campanile team, and so he was able to raise the Duquel effigy without being observed.

At the bottom of the stairs, he began a systematic search of the full circumference of each nearby pillar. It was cleverly concealed, niched in deep shadow, but eventually he saw it: the expected third fire extinguisher.

33 THE ARRANGEMENT

[Thursday]

Worse slept till eight o'clock. He found Millie working in their sitting room. She looked up, both pleased to see him and concerned for his lack of rest; she put down her notes and stood up to kiss him.

'You were very late, Richard. Are you going back to sleep? Or just planning for an early night this evening?'

'No to the first question. Not sure to the second.'

Millie sat down. She was wearing a dressing gown. 'What happened last night, in the raid?'

'Very interesting. We have fourteen individuals in custody, pending further enquiries—'

'You know, Richard, you are beginning to sound like a real policeman,' interrupted Millie. 'I'm not sure if I should be worried.'

'We are unable to make further public comment on that question at the present time, while these matters are still under investigation,' said Worse.

Millie took a moment to realize he wasn't being serious.

'You're sharp, considering your night,' she said.

'It's interesting language. Not often when you speak can you sound bright and dull at the same time. I'm enjoying it.'

'That's a little unfair to your adopted profession, Richard. And to Victor.'

'It is. I apologize. It's a question of audience. Anyway, fourteen arrests, with two absconders, who happen to be persons of particular interest whom we had previously interviewed.'

'How did they get away?'

'By not being there. Despite surveillance. There was a process mishap.'

'A stuff-up, you mean?'

'No, no. A process mishap. Entirely different. No one's responsible.'

'Now I'm definitely worried for you.' Millie always absorbed numbers. 'Fourteen plus two: is the sixteen significant?'

'I no longer think it is,' said Worse. 'Not sure, but I don't think so.'

'Are you happy with the result, the raid?'

'Very much so. I'm fairly certain that Priory Manor is the control centre for the sect protecting the secrets of St Eke's. We'll have forensics in there for weeks, I expect. By the way, we found a vehicle matching the profile of the one that ran your father off the road. Right brake light inoperative. It was out of sight in a barn. We'll be able to search its movements on that Sunday night.'

'That's pleasing,' said Millie. 'What's happening to the patients, the residents, at Priory Manor?'

'Our excellent Archdeacon is mobilizing nursing and ancillary staff from across the diocese, and installing a temporary manager from her own office.'

'Don't tell me you phoned her in the middle of the night?'

Worse feigned a consuming interest in his fingernails.

'Well?' said Millie.

'You know, I've never been sure what the middle of the night is, technically. It's certainly not midnight, in most people's thinking. So, no, I can't say I did.'

'Richard ...'

'Millie ...' Worse tried to emulate, and return, the reproving tone, but capitulated.

'It was about two-thirty this morning, when the scale of our problem was becoming evident.'

'And what was your reception, calling her in the middle of the night?' Millie emphasized the closing phrase.

Worse ignored the sarcasm. 'She was fine. Extremely

accommodating, as she has been for this whole St Eke's business. Marvellous, actually; efficient, matter of fact.' Worse realized his opportunity for mischief. 'An altogether wonderful person. I really believe she waits by the phone for me to call in the night. I should, more often.'

Millie was looking at Worse, smiling. She stood up, loosening the tie on her bathrobe.

'You do remember that quaint expression, "spoken for"?' she said.

Worse gave a performance of racking his brain. 'Of course I do. As in: "Richthofen! Stop right there! You've spoken for three minutes, and now it's Immelmann's turn". In debating, I take it?'

Millie stepped toward him, her bathrobe falling open. 'So, a debate is it? And a ternary one at that? The proposition shall be: Should tea, shower, or an impromptu interrogation come first?'

—

Millie persuaded Worse that he should have something to eat, and he offered to make them both omelettes. While he was at the stove, Veronica entered the kitchen.

'Good morning, both. Is there coffee?'

'We've made tea, but I can get you a coffee,' said Millie.

'You're a darling. The news is that Philip's agreed to say goodbye to the old Saab; Nicholas phoned to say he'd be home around midday; and I will be in Canterbury for the afternoon, but I can make dinner. Now, what do you two have to report?'

'Richard has been out most of the night, conducting a dramatic police raid,' said Millie. 'And I have been dutifully keeping house for his late return.'

'Except you were unrousably asleep when I did get home,' said Worse.

He delivered Millie's omelette to the kitchen table.

'Excuse me.' Worse's phone was ringing.

He walked into the dining room to take the call. It was from Jane Malleson.

'Worse, how are you?'

'I'm well, thank you, Jane. How are you?'

'I'm fine. So you have no persisting effects from your exposure?'

'I feel completely well. Thank you for your care at the start. Do you have news of the Canon?'

'Improving, my intensivist colleagues tell me. Probable extubation today, and they're more hopeful that he's neurologically okay.'

'That's good news.'

'Worse, remember I mentioned the idea of writing up your experience as a case report? Two things: I'd be very pleased if you wished to be a co-author. With Canon Simony, we really have a case series of two, now. And secondly, I would like to visit the bell tower and take some measurements and photographs to use in the paper. Do you know when that would be possible?'

'It's still closed, but I can get you in past the police guard. The air will be safe. I need to be over there later today, in any case. If it suits, I could meet you there at twelve, say.'

'Midday I can do. I'm not working till three. Thank you, Worse.'

'About authorship,' said Worse. 'I will help in any way I can, but I'm happy not to have my name on it. Thanks for the offer though.'

'Okay. Most grateful. See you at twelve.'

After ringing off, Worse spent a few seconds examining his feelings. He liked Jane, but there was none of the sexual tension that arose out of nowhere on that earlier call. When was that, exactly? Tuesday night: it felt like weeks.

He returned to the kitchen. Millie was making his omelette, and he sat down.

'What are you smiling about?' she asked.

Worse had been reflecting on his accelerated Jane journey from artless adolescence to sensible adulthood in thirty-six hours. He was smiling at innate masculine naivety, and its ability to sabotage emotional composure at any age.

'That was Jane Malleson, the emergency physician who looked after me, and Wilfred.'

'Not bad news, I take it,' said Veronica.

'Wilfred? No, not at all. It seems that the treating team are more optimistic for his outcome.'

'That's a relief,' said Veronica.

'Anyway, she's coming to St Eke's at midday to get background specs on the tower, dimensions and so on, to write up the poisonings as case reports. Apparently, my survival story is something worth publishing, given the exposure concentrations they measured.'

'You've done all those space–volume and concentration estimates yourself, Richard,' said Millie, recalling Worse's aluminium sulphide calculations.

It was deeply buried, but Worse wondered if the remark contained a hint of disapproval at his arrangement to meet with Jane.

'Yes, I have. I'll share them if she's interested.'

'Are you meeting her there?' asked Millie.

'I am. Would you like to join us?'

'I would, yes. I feel out of touch with developments across the lane. Can I see the crypt?' said Millie.

'I can show you the crypt, but I'm not planning to tell Jane about it yet. I want to keep its discovery quiet for now.'

'Why?' asked Millie and Veronica, almost in unison.

'Because at least two suspects are still at large, and I want them to think our investigation is less advanced than it is. They're more likely to make judgement errors. Thank you for this; it's delicious.' Worse was finishing his omelette. 'Millie, why don't you meet me at the lychgate at eleven-thirty? I'll take you in and show you the secret staircase to the crypt. We'll be out before Jane arrives. It would be nice for you two to meet, and then you can stay as long as you like. I expect her interest will be fairly limited to the tower.'

'Great, eleven-thirty then,' said Millie.

'Bring a torch.'

'I'm sorry that I have to go to Canterbury,' said Veronica.

'The ageless rue-speak of a penitent,' said Worse.

Veronica smiled, with only a moment's puzzlement.

'Do you think, Millie,' he continued, playing with the idea, 'that your family's living in Steeple Resting has its origins in a stopover-made-permanent, for whatever reason? In other words, a Misgivingston pilgrimage remains unfinished, indefinitely paused in the night before Canterbury, and the family sins have simply compounded over the generations with no absolution sought or granted?'

Both women stared at Worse. Veronica sensed her personal immunity and was first to speak.

'Actually, that would explain all the unholy badness in my husband and children. Yes, a compelling hypothesis. Thank you, Richard. I'm reassured that my own business in Canterbury need not be confessional.'

Millie grimaced. 'Yes, thank you, Richard,' she echoed.

34 STAIRCASE DILEMMA

Inspector Wirrier had proposed, and Worse agreed, that personnel involved in the night raid, provided they had processed warrants and filed interim reports, could rest up for the morning and return to duty at midday. A second team had been tasked with the ongoing hunt for Sleke and Couchman.

Worse was not surprised, therefore, to arrive at Canon Simony's office at about eleven o'clock and find no members of Campanile working. Across the hall, though, he saw Victoria Bray on a landline call in the diocesan office. She motioned him to enter and sit down.

After replacing the handset, she said, 'I think the basic functions at Priory Manor are being met, thanks to our deep reserves of volunteers.' She looked up at Worse. 'Anyway, how are you?'

'I'm fine, thank you. I will be more at ease when our two missing persons of interest are located.'

'That is Sleke, and ...?'

'Couchman, the resident psychologist. With other roles, I suspect.'

'Oh yes, Couchman. Abandoned ordination for the secular soul. A relief for all parties when it happened, I am told. If it is of interest to you, he has worked from time to time at our small hospice facility in Reaching-on-Sea. It's called Sanctuary Woods.'

'That is of interest, yes. And you? How are you?'

'I'm well, thank you. I'm well.'

Worse smiled, and stood up to leave. 'I will report your good health to my partner, Millie, who thinks that I too often disturb your nights with onerous requests.'

'Reassure her,' said Victoria, without humour.

Worse moved across to Simony's office. He messaged Wirrier with the suggestion that Sanctuary Woods might warrant a visit. The Inspector texted in reply that the facility was under observation.

—

Worse thought it would be of most interest to Millie if he chose the entry to the crypt that he had first used, via the spiral staircase. Without explaining its double design, he led the way up to the loft, and helped her climb the casing. When they were both sitting on the ledge, he shone his torch downward on the secret stairs.

'Look at this trickery,' he said.

Millie required only a second to take it in. 'That is beautiful!' She looked at Worse. 'A double-strand, like DNA.'

'Exactly. The secret of inheritance was in St Eke's. We should have a drink at The Eagle and announce our find to the world.'

'How did you discover it?'

'Inferred, not discovered. Being Grimly. In a folding-seat version of armchair geometry, down where William was found.'

Worse thrust his weight forward. 'I'll lead. Conserve your battery for now.'

A few steps down, Worse directed his torch onto the fire extinguisher, without comment. When they emerged into the crypt, he took Millie's hand.

'First, I'll show you the other entrance, for safety. Mind your head on these arches. I suspect the mediaevals must have suffered frequent concussion in the darkness of crypts.'

'Explaining the slow dawn of the Renaissance,' said Millie.

He led her across to the west end of the north aisle space, then forward to the stairs under Duquel's tomb, demonstrating how the coffin lid could be pushed upwards. They both looked out from the tomb into the aisle proper.

'A casual observer might think us risen from the grave,' said Millie.

'Decoffinated, we say; remember?' said Worse.

'Only to return,' said Millie, as they retreated downwards.

Worse chose to leave the effigy hinged open, allowing some natural light into that corner of the crypt. As they moved toward the chancel, he noted the fire extinguisher, visible now without torchlight. He showed Millie the altar.

'I'd value any observations you may have,' said Worse.

'It's circular,' said Millie.

She switched on her torch, examining its structure as she walked fully around it. 'Otherwise unremarkable, I think.'

Millie then studied the objects positioned on the altar. 'These things make no sense to me, except for the cups and candlesticks.'

'I think I'm relieved to know you were never an altar girl. Come over here and meet the mystery woman,' said Worse, using his torch beam to guide her. He illuminated the plaque.

'Tell me what this means,' he said.

Millie turned off her torch, slipping it into a jacket pocket.

'Interesting,' she said after several seconds. 'I need hardly point out that I am not a mediaevalist, Richard. I haven't any idea. But if it's non-standard, we could ask Nicholas about AI translation. It's becoming a powerful tool, I understand. At the very least that might open up some pathways for us.'

'I did send it to Nicholas, to enlist Edvard's help as well. He suggested they would work through the night to crack it. I'm looking forward to hearing his news,' said Worse.

He gave Millie time to continue reading the inscription. When she looked away, he took her hand and led her to Geoffrey Magnacart's tomb. As Worse's torch beam pointed to the projecting sword, she gasped and let go of his hand.

'I felt the same,' he said. 'A monstrously inhumane delivery to the afterlife.'

Worse placed a hand, palm down, on the stone lid, holding it there as if through touch he might commune with the wronged ancestral soul within.

'Feel the cold, Millie. The temperature of infinite stillness[1].'

He turned to look into Millie's eyes. In the weak, scattered light of his torch her face was deeply shadowed, lined with concern.

'More than stillness,' he added. 'Infinite wanting. Infinite listening.'

Millie reached forward, not to touch the stone but to lift Worse's hand away and, in an almost prayer-like manner, enclose it flat between her own two upright palms.

'You feel, Richard, you feel: Geoffrey's cold and my warmth.'

It was loving, and quaintly declarative—for Worse, an assurance that Millie was his partner in the quest for historical amends.

'Let's move from here, for now,' she said.

—

They returned to the Duquel staircase, emerging into the north aisle. As Worse closed the false coffin behind them, he shared a thought that until then had seemed too idle to express.

'I wonder who Sir Gestine was, and where his missing remains lie[2]?'

—

It was by now a few minutes to midday, and Worse suggested that they wait outside on the lychgate seat for Jane to arrive. Before sitting, he waved to the police constables in the duty patrol car parked off the lane.

'What do you know about Jane?' asked Millie.

For the second time that day, Worse wondered whether Millie intuited an extraprofessional connection between patient and physician. For himself, he was certain that whatever risk might have existed, it had evaporated into the fanciful past.

'She's a good doctor, she lives in Canterbury, she roped up the bell tower very impressively, and she likes syntax. That's about all I know.'

It was true. For all that turmoil temporarily consuming him, the protagonist profile was thin indeed.

'Syntax? You do elicit the most exotic facts about people, Richard.'

'At the time, it seemed like mundane small talk over a venipuncture.'

Worse was pleased to find himself completely relaxed in the exchange.

—

A minute later, somewhat unexpectedly, Jane swept into the lychgate on a bicycle.

'Have you ridden from Canterbury?' asked Worse.

'Yes.'

Jane managed to make the question sound more surprising than the answer. Still astride the bike, she smiled at Millie, offering her hand.

'I saw you at the Canon's service. Nice actually to meet you. Millie, isn't it? I'm Jane.'

'Yes. Nice to meet you as well. I'm very grateful for your caring for Richard after the poisoning.'

'Oh, his stubbornness was the cure. I see it often. Are you medical, too, Millie?' Jane was securing her bike to a trellis post with a chain lock.

'No. Mathematician.'

'That's funny. So is my partner. She's taken my car for a day conference in Brighton.' Jane shrugged. 'I'm not sure how it happened—I thought I offered her the bike with a convincing argument that it wasn't really that far.'

It was the first Worse knew that Jane was partnered.

Jane detached a slim pannier, and held it up.

'Camera, laser rule, notebook. I won't need much time. Are you coming in as well?'

'We are,' said Worse. 'Millie hasn't had a chance to look around the tower before now.'

—

The squeaky door was still wedged open. Beside it, against the rear wall of the nave, some joinery supplies had been left in preparation for repairing the defect where the door bolts had been cut out during the rescue of Wilfred Simony. Worse entered the tower first, followed by Millie, then Jane.

'Worse, do you know yet how the hydrogen sulphide was pumped into the space?' asked Jane.

'Close to answering it,' said Worse, as she passed next to the fire extinguisher. 'By the time you're writing up the case, I'll be able to tell you.'

Jane took in her surroundings quickly. 'The security system is post-attack, I take it?'

'Yes,' said Worse.

'And that's access to the loft, obviously?' She pointed to the spiral stairs.

'Yes. Alternatively, your penchant for rope climbing could deliver you there,' said Worse, touching the bell rope.

'But not without much tintinnabulation—surely a favourite word, Worse. I'll get on with measuring.'

She placed the pannier on the sexton's shelf, sketched on a notepad the space in plan and elevation, and inserted dimensions as she determined them. Worse was showing Millie where William's body had been found, when Jane interrupted.

'Excuse me, Worse. What do you call this shape, the open floor plan here?'

'A gnomon.'

Jane smiled, without looking up from her sketch. Worse was left to wonder if his stated interest in vocabulary was being tested. He knew that to be the case when, a minute later, she brushed past Worse and Millie to enter the staircase.

'A telling time, it's shaping up to be. I'll just measure the loft, and be out of your way.'

'Jane,' said Millie. 'We're staying just across the lane. When you're done, why don't you come back to our place for a light lunch?'

Jane stopped and turned to answer, smiling warmly. 'That would be lovely, Millie. Won't be long.' She bounded up the steps.

'God, these are steep!' the others heard, as she disappeared.

'Okay with you, Richard?' Millie asked, when she felt sure of not being overheard.

'Of course. That will be nice.'

He led Millie to the Wistful Wardrobe.

—

A few minutes later there was a sudden scream and crashing noise from the loft above them.

'Worse! I'm being—Wooorse!' Jane sounded terrified.

Worse grasped Millie's shoulder, facing her toward the squeaky door.

'Get help from the patrol car outside. I'll go up.'

He raced into the spiral staircase, removing the Totengräber from his jacket. About halfway up, as he passed one of the natural-light slits in the masonry, he heard Millie's voice from below. She sounded desperate.

'Richard! Richard!'

Worse stopped, looking down through the opening. His field of view was limited by the thickness of the stonework. He was unable to see Millie or anyone else. He couldn't see even the edge of the flagstone floor.

'Richard!' from Millie.

'Worse!' from Jane.

Then a male voice from below. Worse recognized Sleke.

'Worse, you interfering fucker. I know you can hear me. You're going to pay dearly for taking on the Mercifuls.'

Worse kept silent. He managed to text Wirrier for urgent armed assistance.

'You don't have a chance against a thousand years of Mercifuls tradition.'

'Richard! He's got a gun!'

'I know who you are, Worse. I know where you are. Don't imagine you are hidden; you are trapped. Powerless. Halfway up, halfway down. Try saving one, we promise the other dies. And you'll hear it happening.'

'Worse! Save Millie!'

'Richard! Save us both!'

Even in the tension of the moment, Worse was touched by Millie's absolute trust in him. He heard more commotion from the platform above. The bell sounded a dull, damped ring. Jane was putting up a fight.

'There is no help to be had, Worse. But you can save them. Call off the investigation. Restore the status quo. We walk free. All Mercifuls protected. Ministerial guarantees. Then the women li—ugh. Fuck!'

No doubt that closure was a sign of Millie's undergraduate jujitsu career. Worse had sampled it himself in the absurd confusion of their first encounter as two investigative intruders, unaware of each other's presence, inside a criminal bank at night.

'Accept the terms, Worse. And don't even think about a double-cross. We have infallible countermeasures in place.'

Worse had experience of stand-offs like this. The best strategy was not to reveal intentions. The other party would invariably fill in the silence, and thereby erode their advantage, displaying frustration or impatience. Considering their circumstances, Sleke's proposal was insanely unrealistic. Desperate, even. And there was a clue to his state of mind in the inflated language: after all their failures, nothing about the Mercifuls could be judged infallible. To Worse, it signalled weakness and declining confidence. He stayed quiet.

'You have ten seconds to agree, Worse. Then this one dies. I'm counting.'

—

Worse never negotiated with criminals. Nor would he accept a dilemma manufactured to pincer his freedom of action. There were always countermeasure possibilities to be found, and they were usually surprising.

This time, it would be chaos.

Through the slit window, he had line of sight to only one feature of interest: the fire extinguisher attached to the opposite wall.

He levelled the Prussica gunsight, steadying the barrel against a masonry edge, and fired. A single round destroyed the regulator, rupturing it clear of the tank, which, then released from its wall yoke, dropped to the floor and out of Worse's view.

Out of sight, but not out of hearing. An explosive whoosh was followed by a fiercely loud hissing. From the banging sounds, Worse deduced that the cylinder was spinning and tumbling on the stone floor like a rogue rocket.

'Fuck! Fuck! Its gas! Get out, Couchman. Get out! Just leave her up there. Worse: you're all going to hell!'

Worse was already running down the stairs. He found Millie coming up toward him.

'Down again,' he instructed. 'Don't worry Millie. It's harmless. Sleke thinks it's H_2S, but I swapped them.'

Millie was forced to process the assurance of her safety, and the concept of the fire extinguisher playing a role in the poison attacks, all within a second.

In the tower room, Worse called out.

'Jane! Are you okay?'

Jane's face appeared at the bell rope gap in the platform.

'I'm okay. The bastard ran up the wall and disappeared from where he jumped on me. I managed to laser him in one eye, so he'll have trouble. I don't smell gas. What was that about?'

'Expectation. Assumption. They panicked. Come down. It's safe. I'll explain.'

Millie was pushing against the squeaky door, now closed. 'He's wedged it on the outside,' she said.

'To make sure we die. I'm not concerned,' said Worse. He was on his mobile to Wirrier, reporting their situation. The gas cylinder was now lying fully discharged on the floor.

Both Worse and Millie were standing with their backs to the bell rope, waiting for Jane to appear on the stairs. They heard a loud, dissonant peal, and turned to look up, only to find Jane standing behind them. She had fashioned a friction brake from her anorak to control her descent.

'That was fun. We could make a Sunday school activity[3] out of it.'

Rocky Ryngelle would not be pleased, thought Worse.

Jane was grinning. Perhaps the others' humourless expressions persuaded her that any such offence against the great bell of St Eke's needed more serious justification.

'Well, having had a madman leap out of the stonework up there and attack me, I thought those dark, winding stairs were unsafe by comparison.'

As if to assert the rightness of it all, she gave a little tug of gratitude on the bell rope, and grinned again.

---

[1] A rare instance of poetic hyperbole: Worse would certainly know that, theoretically, the temperature of infinite stillness is absolute zero.

[2] A penumbral consequence of Worse shining light into the foundations of St Eke's has been a concerted interest in the decoffinated personage of Sir Gestine Duquel—who he was, his connection to Stĕpel Raest, and, understandably, the true location of his final resting place. Promising research leads have consistently come to nought, fuelling the belief that Duquel was a twelfth-century invention of subterfuge with no other purpose in the world than to protect the secrecy of the north aisle access to the crypt. That theory is given weight, with radical implication, by consensus opinion that the effigy's visage is an exact likeness of none other than Thomas Becket himself.

[3] For a range of similarly unorthodox pastimes, see note to Chapter 39.

35 ON SIMILARITY

[Thursday]

The squeaky door was opened by PC Rence.

'Inspector Wirrier is at the lychgate, Chief Inspector.' He quickly surveyed the trio. 'All unharmed?'

'We're fine, thanks,' said Worse. 'Only one dead fire extinguisher to be discreetly undertaken, if I can put it that way. Gunshot to the neck.'

Rence looked around, momentarily confused, before continuing. 'We've made two arrests, Sleke and Couchman. They're with the Inspector.'

'Good. How did they get into St Eke's?' asked Worse.

'A process mishap, sir.'

Worse heard Millie snort with derision, then politely convert to a clearing of the throat.

'In what way, Constable?' asked Worse.

'The perpetrators were dressed as senior clergy. Hardly recognizable. Bluffed their way past the patrol officers saying they were sent by the Archbishop personally to assess cost of repairs for urgent budget business. And, that you had been told about it and given your approval.'

Rence's eyes conveyed: They're very junior officers. Unblemished records. Please don't be hard on them. They feel terrible.

'No doubt they are junior constables with blameless records. I shan't be hard on them for that,' said Worse. 'I imagine they feel terrible as it is.'

Rence looked as if he were in the presence of the messiah of coppers.

—

As they left by the south-west porch, Victoria Bray approached. Worse stopped.

'Victoria, I don't believe you have met my partner, Millie Misgivingston. And this is Dr Jane Malleson, who rescued Wilfred from the tower.' He gestured the introductions. 'This is Archdeacon Bray.'

'I'm Victoria,' she offered, shaking hands with the two women.

'Victoria has been unbelievably efficient managing the Cathedral end of everything we've needed this past week,' said Worse. 'Performed miracles, I would venture, in any other context.'

Victoria ignored his gentle provocation. 'I thought I heard something. More trouble at the tower, I see.' She was looking around at the array of police vehicles.

'I'm not confident that it's all over yet,' said Worse. 'If you want to go inside, please check with me first.'

Victoria acknowledged Worse, but spoke to Jane.

'Jane, do you have the latest news of Wilfred, may I ask? I sense the medical reports that come to us are rather guarded.'

'Guarded is appropriate when it comes to prognosis,' said Jane. 'My personal opinion is optimistic. I think there's a good chance that he will recover, possibly fully.'

'Victoria,' said Millie, 'the three of us were going over the road to my parents' house for some lunch. Would you like to join us?'

'That's very kind, Millie, but I shouldn't. I will be expected to describe this incident to Canterbury, without delay. I'm essentially seated by a hotline when I'm at St Eke's these days.' She turned to Worse. 'You have arrested the two miscreants, I take it?'

'Murderers,' said Worse. 'Yes. There's still a lot of follow-up investigation to complete, but I'm hopeful the killing may be over.'

Worse looked over toward the handcuffed prisoners held in

the lychgate. An ambulance officer was fitting Couchman with an eyepatch.

'I will interrogate those two this afternoon.'

It was a simple statement, but the steel in its voicing surprised all three.

He addressed Millie and Jane.

'You two go ahead. I'll be home in ten minutes. Victoria, if you would like me to brief Canterbury at any time, I am happy to do that. Excuse me.'

Worse was about halfway to the lychgate when Wirrier met him.

'Where did you find them?' asked Worse.

'They were huddled behind a gravestone over there.' Wirrier pointed. 'Easy to spot. I don't know how they thought they would get away.'

'They expected that all of us inside would be dead, with no alarm raised, and they would stroll out as priests on Cathedral business the way they strolled in,' said Worse.

Wirrier tried to read Worse's face. 'I deeply regret their getting past our patrol.'

'I know,' said Worse. 'Have the detainees been searched?'

'Yes. We have weapons and mobiles.'

'Handguns?'

'Found on both.'

'I want them fully stripped, here and now. Clothes bagged. Dress them in prison wear. Find out how they acquired that clerical garb. An accomplice might have helped them. Campanile team meeting in the Canon's office at fourteen hundred for interrogation. Couchman first. I'll have a brief word now. Are you happy with that?'

'Yes. Yes ... Chief Inspector—'

'Yes?' said Worse.

'I'm hugely relieved that none of you suffered injury in there.'

'Thank you. I'm grateful.'

Worse walked to the lychgate. The prisoners were seated, handcuffed, where he and Millie had waited for Jane. He ignored Couchman, and stared at Sleke.

'Why did you return to the tower?'

'For the unequalled view of Kent.'

Worse showed no reaction. He continued staring at his prisoner for a full minute. Sleke surrendered to his own curiosity and spoke first.

'How did you survive in there—the gas?'

Worse held eye contact for several more seconds before replying.

'By similarity[1].' He turned his back on the prisoners.

—

Nicholas had arrived home from Cambridge just before Old Forge Lane was yet again overrun with police and emergency vehicles. He was standing outside the Misgivingston house talking to Millie and Jane when Worse crossed from St Eke's to join them.

Worse addressed Nicholas without ceremony. 'Do you have news on the inscription and the Passage?'

'I'm sorry to disappoint you, Worse. Nothing so far.'

Worse did show disappointment. 'You and Edvard worked all night on it, as promised?'

If challenged on his manner, Worse would describe the question simply as direct. To the others, it sounded accusational.

'AI translators worked through the night, and are still at it. Grimly also laboured through the night. I permitted myself a few hours' sleep to be safe driving home.'

Nicholas's tone carried a reactive edge, as if he barely managed to censor himself from adding '... assuming that was all right with you.'

Worse detected it. 'My apologies, Nicholas.'

Worse turned to Jane. 'We're talking about some encrypted mediaeval texts that might help explain recent events in the tower. Nicholas, and Edvard Tøssentern in Cambridge, are the best chance in the world for deciphering them.'

'I guessed a relevance,' said Jane.

'That's far too generous of Worse, Jane. Actually, Worse, Edvard and I have enlisted some extra non-artificial intelligence as well. Franz Hebe, you will remember, the mediaevalist referred to in Darian's annotations; and Darian himself. He's obviously researched the *Wey* thoroughly. Edvard also contacted Lawrence Enright, but he hasn't replied yet, I understand.'

'Enright must be quite elderly now, I would have thought,' said Worse. 'He may have less energy for a major project.'

'I raised that idea with Edvard,' said Nicholas. 'His emphatic belief was that every linguist who ever lived would thrill at the possibility of cracking the Oxford Passage, even if the key to success revealed itself in their final minutes ... a deathbed apotheosis, as he put it.'

Worse smiled at the image. 'Obviously, that's what Edvard holds important for himself. Personally, I would rather be gifted remission of cause on my deathbed, in order to enjoy the triumph of translation at greater leisure.'

'That's too cunning, Worse,' said Nicholas.

'Thoroughly foxy,' agreed Jane.

There was a group silence. Perhaps all were focused on what could be the strategic cards to play in their own final hours.

'If it's a brains trust you are talking about, why not get Grimly the human² involved?' said Millie, at last.

'That's an excellent idea,' said Nicholas. He turned to Jane. 'We're neglecting our lunch guest. Please forgive the gatepost conferencing, Jane.'

'Yes, time to go inside,' said Millie.

–

Worse generally enjoyed the Misgivingston meetings around the kitchen table. This afternoon, Veronica was at work in Canterbury, but in her absence there was speculation over whether she might have encountered Hilary Gaisen, Jane's mathematician partner, in professional circles. Jane herself was an easy, quite spirited guest, relating to Philip on the woes of medical services funding, to Nicholas on the romance of linguistics research in remote parts of the world, and above all to Millie, about almost everything else.

The warmth of that conversing, between Jane and Millie, its humour and seriousness and candour, pleased Worse in a way he didn't immediately understand. But then, both women had just experienced the same terrifying assault and walked away, in a sense, as sisters in survival. Perhaps a kind of reactive euphoria explained it.

In contrast, Worse was quiet. He thought about his sharpness with Nicholas at the front gate. Disappointment had come out wrongly, as critical impatience, and Nicholas had reacted. That must have been hard for Millie, to witness friction between her partner and her brother. And it was to no avail. Nicholas would do his best with the decryption, and no one could do better.

Impatience with Nicholas wasn't fair, and Worse now realized what it really meant, and where it belonged. It was anger, mixed with contempt, toward the Mercifuls. He didn't expect Sleke to become cooperative, in which case their main hope of learning the story of the woman in the crypt, and exorcizing the *Malison*, was in the texts.

There was a larger disappointment around Nicholas, though, whom Worse considered a close friend. Worse had been looking forward to the two having some quiet, one-on-one conversational time, but it hadn't happened. That was partly from Worse's responsibility to the St Eke's crisis, and partly from Nicholas's totally understandable wish to spend time with his parents and Millie, and the need to visit Tøssentern for discussions about LDI matters.

Worse's meditation on these ideas had distanced him from the table. He was jolted back into its presence by Millie.

'You're not eating, Richard.'

'Oh. Yes. Very nice,' he responded, picking up cheese and bread from his plate. He was thankful that attention rapidly turned away from him. He was further thankful when his phone rang and he could excuse himself from the room.

—

'Worse speaking.'

'Chief Inspector; it's DS Michelson. We've completed another search of Mansion's flat and found a concealed CC cable feed from the steeple cameras to an accessory channel on his television monitor. Dumb but effective. IT thinks there is some kind of inline image signal monitor that triggers an alert when movement is detected.'

'I'm familiar with those stability sensors. Was there video recording?'

'Possible, but we haven't located any storage system yet.'

'And Mansion himself?' asked Worse.

'Nowhere to be found.'

'Has he cleared out his flat?'

'It doesn't have that appearance, Chief Inspector.'

'Hold the line please, Sergeant.'

A possibility was occurring to Worse, and he wanted a few seconds to think it through. Sleke's boast of 'infallible countermeasure', assuming it wasn't tactical bluster, suggested that a Mercifuls agent was still at large who was capable of redressing any double-cross. Could it be Mansion?

They had all viewed the sexton as very much a secondary figure, slightly oafish, not obviously numbered amongst the knights of the Order. On that basis, his background and identity checks had been routine but not extensive. He was written off as a bad-tempered, uncooperative player on the scene with a skill set limited to verger duties and little likelihood of high-level criminal involvement.

Perhaps they had been wrong. Mansion was ever-present at St Eke's, well placed to guard its secrets and mobilize as needed the forces from Priory Manor to counter threats. He was the one apparently monitoring the church grounds using the concealed steeple cameras. And he had been the first to find Whencely dead. Perhaps he was also the last to see him alive.

'Sergeant?'

'Yes, Chief Inspector?'

'Give Mansion highest priority. He'll be somewhere in the St Eke's locality. Assume he's dangerous. Place all available personnel onto it. We'll postpone the two o'clock interviews. Could you liaise with Inspector Wirrier on developments, please?'

'I will, sir.' No doubt Michelson was curious as to how Worse arrived at such an urgency over the seemingly dull sexton, but she didn't ask.

—

Worse returned to the kitchen in time to hear Nicholas explaining to Jane that in the case of swints, a flock is referred to as a tidings.

'Excuse me, Philip. May I have a word? And Jane, I think you left your pannier in the tower room. Did you leave anything up by the bell?'

'No, just the pannier, and my bike outside.'

'Have you completed your steeple measurements?' asked Worse.

'Enough, thanks. I'm not going back up there for a while.'

'When you go in to collect your pannier, I want to accompany you. We'll do that in a few minutes. Philip.'

Worse's tone made clear he would brook no disagreement.

Jane exchanged glances with Millie. Philip stood up to follow Worse. They spoke in the dining room, just outside the kitchen.

'Philip. Do you have the resources to research Mansion? Full background, family history, military service, ancestry, name changes; basically everything? I think the police check might have been incomplete.'

'Mansion? I'll do my best. There might be something in Will's papers.'

Philip hesitated. 'You do know that his role is peculiarly hereditary? At least, his father was there before him; I'm aware of that much.'

'No, I did not know that. Thanks Philip. It's urgent. I'll approach Thelma Dewey to see if the Cathedral archives are helpful.'

Philip looked into the kitchen to say goodbye to Jane, then went to his study. Worse rejoined the others.

'Let's go, Jane. I want to see you safely in and out of the tower. You can retrieve your bike and resume your conversation back here if you wish. In any case, I would prefer you were driven back to Canterbury. The situation is quite different from when you rode down earlier.'

'I can take you,' volunteered Nicholas, looking at Jane.

'Are you saying it's still not safe over there?' asked Millie.

'I'm not sure if it's safe anywhere yet,' said Worse.

---

[1] Consider false fire extinguishers F and true ones T. In what follows, similarity is defined on specified attributes, as is necessarily the case.

Recall that *Similarity* is a symmetric relation, S: symbolically, $FST \Rightarrow TSF$. In words, if F is similar to T, then T is similar to F. Colloquially, if you look similar to Jesse James, expect to get shot. On the other hand, if Jesse James looks similar to you, also expect to get shot.

The Mercifuls, in substituting T with F, made F indistinguishably similar to T, for the purpose of deception. When Worse, assisted by Sergeant Halcyon, reversed the switch, replacing F with T, the Mercifuls were themselves deceived. Darian states that all irony fundamentally arises from symmetry, one way or another, and this is a fine example.

Note that *Similarity* is not only symmetric but reflexive, TST. (Jesse James looks like himself. That's why he got shot.) This logical identity imprisons us all, despite the vanity industries advertising otherwise.

Note also that *Similarity* is (usually, not necessarily) a transitive relation, ASB and $BSC \Rightarrow ASC$. In words, if A is similar to B and B is similar to C, then A is similar to C. (If you look like Frank James, and Frank looks like his brother Jesse, expect to get shot.) Unlike the relation *Equivalence*, which is strictly conserved in transitivity, similarity can be expected to decay over multiple iterations. (If you are Jesse's third cousin, relax. Maybe.) An exception to this dissipative phenomenon is when the specified similarity attributes are made sufficiently abstract, a rich field of study in epistemology known as Thortelmann equivalence.

As observed above, the assertion A𝒮B and B𝒮C ⇒ A𝒮C is not guaran-teed true. Depending on commonality of attributes, we can have A𝒮B, B𝒮C, and A$\bar{𝒮}$C, where $\bar{𝒮}$ means not similar to. The presumption A𝒮C in this circumstance is the basis of a common fallacy, or (paranoid, for example) delusions.

It should be made clear that the concept of similarity is more important than matters of deception, or even being shot. We have that, if A𝒮B, then, very likely, G(A)𝒮G(B); that is, if A is similar to B, an operation G on A is likely to result in an outcome similar to the outcome of G on B. (In this context, A and B are referred to as *arguments* of G.) Letting G = 'Shoot regulator off', we conclude G(F)𝒮G(T), the common outcome being sudden release of compressed gas, noxious or otherwise.

G is quite general, here the only condition being that it operates on (at least) the specified attributes that define the similarity. From this, it should be evident that object similarity is the foundation of analogical reasoning, which is our most powerful intellectual and psychological tool for finding our way inductively in the world. In particular, it subserves prediction, and therefore survival.

We are now in a position to further generalize. Let G and G' be similar *operations*, G𝒮G', such that for any A, G(A)𝒮G'(A). Then, for A𝒮B (and not impossibly, for A$\bar{𝒮}$B) we have that, very likely, G(A)𝒮G'(B), and likewise G'(A)𝒮G(B).

[EXERCISE *Run, Hide, Ridicule, Betray*] Investigate arrangements of the arguments 'Jesse' and 'Reynard' and the operations G = 'Dispatch posse for' and G' = 'Dispatch fox-hunt for' in terms of outcomes similarity.

[REMARK *Artifice*] In the statement A𝒮B, A and B are not specified to be natural objects, or otherwise. In many cases, B is natural and A is synthetic, designed expressly to be similar to B for the purposes of representation, simplification, and manipulation. Examples of A would be mathematical models, maps, fiction, film sets, and the fatuously named 'virtual reality'.

[REMARK *U.S.A.*] Whilst properly perceived similarity is crucial to making sense of experience, it also underlies accidental misinterpretation (for example, mistaken identity, misheard speech, false arrest), in addition to deception with intent (forgery, disguise, camouflage, voter fraud), as illustrated for fire extinguishers.

It is estimated that, on average, similarity promotes comprehension in eighty per cent of humanity, eighty per cent of the time. For the rest, similarity misleads, implying that civilization teeters on a margin of reason over unreason of sixty-four per cent to thirty-six. For example, in a nation comprising, say, fifty separately governed states, thirty-two speak average sense and eighteen speak abject nonsense. Sobering as this must be, it is a mean measure; the sample ratio falls to alarming extremes in specified cluster populations identified by geography, education, and religiosity, as well as power, politics, presumption, and prejudice. Moreover, this spatial (inter-state) distribution of irrationality can shift suddenly and erratically over time. Add to all that the dissolution of individuals' capacity for independent thinking by intrusive, addictive and coercive instruments of social media, and the decline of intelligent society seems assured, at least in our hypothetical nation of fifty states.

(Regarding these expository fifty, in the interests of public safety it needs to be emphasized that although confounding similarity is a sufficient condition for absurdity, it is not a necessary one. In consequence, even if you bear no imaginable resemblance to Jesse James, expect to get shot.)

[2] Despite the fame of his automaton, Grimly the human reveals very little of his personality (and certainly nothing in conversation) to the interested public. One rare anecdote appears in a short biography in Pioniv's *Visionaries of Logic* [Lindenblüten], where Grimly describes how he came to be XX. His parents, knowing their expected to be a boy, each undertook to select a single given name, and keep it secret one from the other. At birth, they would open sealed envelopes, having agreed in a solemn vow to assign the names, whatever they might be, in forward or reverse alphabetical order, that to be determined by a coin toss. This algorithm was designed to ensure equal and equitable influence over their child's naming, and eliminate argument. In the event, they both identically chose Xavier, their ordering vow was axiomatically unfulfillable, and they argued forever over whose X came first.

As an aside, and apropos of *Equivalence* mentioned above, readers may recognize that biographer and subject here are further conjoined—at least, eponymously—in the widely applied Grimly–Pioniv non-replaceability theorem, which states that if either or both of two given entities (1) can be proven incomplete, or (2) cannot be proven complete, then the given entities cannot be proven equivalent. (They may still be *similar*. Indeed, they may yet be equivalent, but not provably so.) The result is important theoretically in validity analysis of substitution arguments, notably in moral philosophy, but serves also in challenging analogical reasoning more generally—for example, in economic policy, medical diagnosis and prognosis, or the doctrine of precedence in jurisprudence.

Where completeness rather than equivalence is the issue in question, a corollary of the G-P theorem is utilized: If two entities are equivalent, then they are complete. Comprehensive treatments of subtleties arising, and of the controversies surrounding so-called weak replaceability in applied logic, can be found in the specialist literature.

36   PC RENCE

Worse watched from the lychgate as Jane wheeled her bike across the lane to the Misgivingston front door, where Nicholas was waiting for her. He saw them enter the house together.

The two prisoners were still on site, screened off from the public while their clothes were changed.

PC Rence approached. 'Everything in order, Chief Inspector?'

'Could you get me Sleke's mobile phone, please?'

Rence returned a minute later with the device enclosed in a labelled evidence bag.

'Be my witness opening this, Constable.' Worse unsealed the bag and examined the phone. 'Come with me.'

Rence followed as Worse strode to the prisoners' privacy tent and swept back the fly. As he did so, Sleke looked up, only to find he was unlocking his own phone by face recognition. Worse turned to leave as abruptly as he had arrived. Sleke shouted after him.

'That's illegal, Worse. You can't use anything you find.'

Worse ignored him. 'Stay with me, Constable.'

Rence wanted some reassurance. 'Is he correct, Chief Inspector? Is there a legality problem?'

'No,' said Worse. 'Sleke hasn't any idea. He's up for domestic terrorism. Nothing is illegal. If you are ever asked, describe what I just did exactly as you saw it. Now find Mansion's mobile number for me.'

Worse accessed Sleke's last outgoing call. From the timing he determined that it was probably made when the two were pinned down in the graveyard.

'What is it?'

Rence read out the number they had for Mansion. It was

different from that for Sleke's last call. Worse wasn't surprised; Mansion would have a secure mobile for Mercifuls business.

'Note down this number, Constable. I want it located.'

Worse read it aloud as he pressed redial.

'What's happened?' It was Mansion's voice.

Worse stayed silent.

'Remember you report to me, you fucks. Tell me how the operation went.'

Worse held on until Mansion ended the call. He returned the mobile to its bag and handed it back to Rence.

'Reseal it in front of me, and sign the handling chit. Chain of evidence unbroken. Last outgoing was investigator's. It was Mansion who answered. Finding him is our top priority.'

Worse pointed to Sleke's mobile. 'Get this to IT forensics immediately. I want background noise in that call analysed for location pointers. Signal triangulation. Whatever they can do. Report to me and the Inspector.'

As Worse spoke, he was contacting Wirrier.

'You have more information, Chief Inspector?'

Worse didn't waste words. 'It appears that Mansion is in charge. He's probably armed, and certainly dangerous. Our absolute priority is to find him. I would be grateful if you take charge of that. PC Rence is organizing a phone trace on the number used by Sleke to contact Mansion. He will brief you. I need to go.'

Worse's mobile was notifying an incoming call from Thelma Dewey.

'Hello Thelma. Worse speaking.'

'Chief Inspector. I think you will find this interesting. We have the employment records for Mansion and previous incumbents in his position, including his father, as I expect you know, but going back some centuries. The name Mansion, or quite unambiguous variants, arises frequently. The earliest mention that I can find is 1470, but the curious thing is that a contract of employment signed in that year exists in two copies, identical except for the appointed sacristan's name. On one, it is Godfrey Mansionus; on the other—'

'Let me guess,' said Worse. 'A cognate of the word Eke?'

'Actually, yes. I suppose it is. Van Eyck, in fact. Like the painter. So that link allowed me to follow the line further back, to twelfth-century arrivals of the name from Bruges, largely, and Ghent. Almost exclusively, they came to Kent, as far as I can determine.'

'Do you have a record of who was sacristan at St Eke's in 1369?'

'Let me see ... if you have a few seconds, I can tell you ... Yes, one Roger Vaneek, appointed 1355, died in office 1375. During the Plague, before his tenure, incumbencies were tragically short, of course. He was fortunate.'

'Thelma, you are amazing. Can you send me information on Vaneek? And please continue the research, but I need to act on what you've just told me. I'll be in touch.'

Worse immediately phoned Philip with the news that the Mansion lineage connected to the name Van Eyck, and asked if there was any indication that William had known this, and had possibly become suspicious of Mansion. Philip promised to pursue the lead. He reminded Worse of their earlier conversation regarding the Dar Sala-Roqun painting, which linked the Dutch name with the Mercifuls.

—

Worse sat in the lychgate to think. The police activities surrounding him were scaling down, as personnel were redeployed to the urgent task of locating Mansion.

He hardly noticed when Sleke and Couchman were escorted, handcuffed, to a police lockup van, shouting obscenities at him. Before long, only two officers in the assigned patrol car were in view, plus Rence making calls from the south-west porch.

Worse reviewed the situation. He had not divulged his knowledge of the crypt to anyone except his Misgivingston family, and Phoebe Andrieus. Also, PC Rence must surely have inferred its existence, or something similar, from the trick Worse played on him the previous day. Therefore, in all probability, the Mercifuls believed that the crypt and tombs were still the Order's secret.

This belief, Worse reasoned, had weighted the risk calculus facing Sleke and Couchman in deciding to re-enter St Eke's. But that fact alone didn't provide a motive for them to do so. Worse fell back on his earlier basic supposition: they had something to conceal or something to recover.

And what was Mansion's thinking at this stage of developments? He would be sensing the disintegration of centuries of the Mercifuls' secret manipulation of St Eke's. The resources of Priory Manor had been exposed and seized. He would know that the current operation he had ordered, whatever that might be, had not been successfully executed by Sleke and Couchman. Now, communication with his lieutenants was lost, and without covert intelligence he could only guess their situation.

Worse imagined himself as Mansion. He was on the run. The Order was in historic collapse around him. He was facing shame. He was frustrated at that last mission's apparent failure. He was angry with everyone. And his thinking would be unbalanced by a distracting emotion that Worse had seen many times: the drive for revenge against perceived enemies.

Worse recalled their first interaction in the tower. The gruffness and vulgarity were almost comically in character for a provincial, rough-hewn gravedigger sort of verger, kept safely apart from the refined society of a scholarly Canon with direct links to the elite of Canterbury. There was no surprise that on Millie's and his first evening, at dinner, Philip had referred to Mansion as the steeple bulldog, which was rather how Worse had also found him.

Yet it seemed he was leader of the current-day Mercifuls—in ultimate command of professionals like Sleke and Couchman who, while fugitives themselves, acceded to a dangerous mission, incongruously armed with handguns and a willingness to murder. But they had not prevailed, and Mansion would be feeling acutely his responsibility to the ages to succeed in their place. His self-belief would be inflated by pride, by fear of failure, and disdain for his losing subordinates. If any canons of mediaeval knighthood had survived in the Order, they were not in evidence. Anyway, they would surely be extinguished by a consuming urge for revenge against the outsider who, in the course of a few days, had wreaked destruction on the secret life of St Eke's.

Worse considered an important possibility. Given the arrests at Priory Manor, and the capture of Sleke and Couchman, it was an easy supposition that Mansion might be the last of the Mercifuls out there. But really, Worse and his Campanile team had little intelligence at this stage on how extensive the modern sect was, or even where it was headquartered. Some days before, Millie, Philip and he had even wondered if an approach by William Whencely to a London historian connection had set in train events leading to his own murder.

There was one potential person of interest locally that Worse could think of, and a contact number was already stored in his mobile. He dialled it. Then he phoned Wirrier.

'I think we should locate David Fielding, the pastor. He's not picking up, though he undertook to be available to us at all times.'

'I will deal. Where are you at the moment?'

'Sitting in the lychgate at St Eke's.'

'Be cautious, Chief Inspector. I suspect Mansion will be furious enough to come after you. Can I assign more officers for protection?'

'I suspect the same. I'll be fine with Rence. Thank you.'

Worse spent the next few minutes viewing footage from the newly installed security system inside St Eke's. Sleke and Couchman, wearing clerical vestments, entered by the south-west door at 10.44 am, headed directly to the tower room, and ascended the spiral stairs. Immediately following, the loft camera showed them clambering up the casing and vanishing into the secret access to the crypt. The next movement on that feed was Jane appearing from below, beginning her laser measurements, and shortly thereafter being assaulted from the casing by Couchman.

At the same time, cameras in the nave caught Sleke running from the north aisle to the squeaky door. Inside the tower room, at 12.16 pm, another camera recorded his attack on Millie. Worse watched as the fire extinguisher bounced and spun on the floor. There was a glimpse of Sleke's panicked face as he ran from the room.

Watching the video of those attacks angered Worse, even more than when he was party to the drama as it happened. Sickening, as well, was the thought that those two assailants were concealed in the church for an hour and a half, probably in the shadows of the crypt, while Worse was showing Millie the tombs.

Why did they not attack Millie and him down there, under ideal conditions of location and surprise? Because they had a more important task, not yet completed, in being there. And why did they attack when they did? Because they had reported to Mansion the presence in the tower of Worse and two women, and he ordered it. That ridiculous negotiation for their freedom and immunity was a sham. They intended to kill. Torment and kill.

Worse decided it was time to make the camera feed available to the whole Campanile team. He requested that the junior officer in the onsite patrol car be primarily responsible for monitoring.

—

He was still thinking through these events, and trying to anticipate Mansion's likely actions, when he saw Nicholas and

Jane emerge from the Misgivingston house. He watched with amusement as each took turns to force Jane's bicycle into a configuration suited to the luggage tray of Nicholas's rented SUV. Eventually, they managed to close the rear hatch.

Worse stood up to see them off. He walked across the lane.

'That looked easy,' he said. 'Will you be able to extricate it in one piece?'

Nicholas grinned, but it was Jane who answered. She moved close to Worse and placed both hands lightly on his chest. He felt in himself a slight, protective recoil. Jane spoke seriously.

'Worse, it's only slowly coming to me what a bad situation I was in over there.' She nodded toward the church. 'Forget the bike; I have you to thank for extricating *me* in one piece.'

'Actually, I feel negligent in getting you into danger,' said Worse.

'I heard any negligence sat with the police officers who were meant to be guarding the place.'

Worse didn't answer. He stepped back. 'Drive carefully. Nicholas, don't stop on the way on any account. We still have at least one killer at large.'

As Worse watched Nicholas performing a U-turn in front of the Old Vicarage, Millie appeared at the front door.

'Can I make you a coffee, Richard? Proper homely mug?'

'Lovely. Could I have one for Rence as well? He's my companion field marshal this afternoon.'

—

Worse sat on the bus-stop bench until Millie returned, holding two mugs. He crossed back to the lychgate and balanced them carefully on a notices shelf. Rence was out of sight, and Worse phoned him.

'Where are you?'

'I'm up in the belfry, with a good view on all sides.'

'Come down to my gate lounge for a home-brewed coffee.'

—

'I take it you're armed?' said Worse.

They were sitting on opposite seats in the lychgate.

'Yes, Chief Inspector.'

'Show me.'

Rence put down his coffee and removed from his left shoulder holster a police-issue handgun. Worse observed closely the way that he handled it.

'You are practised?'

'Twice yearly. Range testing, safety, legals.'

'Thank you,' said Worse. 'Replace it.'

Worse had spent considerable time with Rence being driven around, and liked him.

'Constable. Imagine there is a gang of ten criminals, and you apprehend nine. What happens?'

Rence looked puzzled. 'There is one still at large.'

'True, but no longer the same one. For your own good, the thing to remember is that the one at large becomes ten times more dangerous. Approximately. Rhetorically speaking.'

Rence nodded. Worse continued.

'First desperate, then dangerous. There's something else to remember.'

Rence shook his head slightly, conceding to Worse.

'I might have been wrong in the first place, about the ten. So, we have Mansion out there, desperate and dangerous, and a real possibility that he's not alone. Excuse me.'

Worse's mobile was ringing. It was Wirrier.

'Fielding is a strong candidate. He hasn't shown up at his accountancy office today. We're looking into friends and family, last known movements, phone trace, and so on.'

Worse rang off. Rence was finishing his coffee. He hadn't heard the Inspector's part in the conversation.

'At the moment, we're guessing our eleventh man is Fielding,' shared Worse, 'the part-time pastor here. Warning two continues to apply, iteratively: there may be others yet again. Any suspicions on a twelfth?'

'Not immediately, sir. Fielding himself would be a surprise. I see him often in the square: cordial, pleasant to everyone, no issues with the law.'

'They're basic smarts, for a criminal under the radar, don't you think?'

'Very true. It makes suspicion a difficult art, doesn't it? There's not a lot of practice to be had in a village like Steeple Resting.'

'Why not practise on everyone?' said Worse.

—

The conversation set Worse thinking, about profiles of suspicion. All the detainees at Priory Manor were male. He excused himself to call Philip.

'Worse! I heard you saved my daughter's life yet again—'

'Millie acquitted herself very courageously. Philip, what can you tell me about the Mercifuls and gender? Was there any point in history when the Order admitted women?'

'Physician dames, not knights, you are suggesting? No, I've seen no evidence to support that. Mind you, they're not physicians any more, either, as you are finding out, so their constitution has definitely changed over time.'

'And they're not knights. Thanks, Philip. Could you keep the question in mind? Also, any progress on Mansion?'

'Nothing to report yet.'

Worse ended the call, and reached toward Rence.

'Let me take your mug, Constable.'

37 GRAVEDIGGERS

[Thursday]

Worse placed both coffee mugs on the noticeboard shelf, to be collected later. Rence was checking Campanile updates on his smartphone.

'Chief Inspector. The interviews are postponed for twenty-four hours.'

'Where will the prisoners be held in the interim, overnight?'

Rence scrolled through a document on his screen. 'The Inspector has requested they stay in the village.'

'At your station?' asked Worse, surprised. 'What facility do you have?'

'Two cells. Very secure. It says here that supervision will be afforded by task force officers.'

'It's a takeover,' smiled Worse.

'I'm not upset. I'd rather be here,' said Rence.

'Do you happen to know where exactly I could find the grave of a man called Simon Acolytēs, died 1280? The Canon indicated it was somewhere over there, inside the fence.' Worse gave a vaguely eastward wave.

'I'll look it up for you,' said Rence. 'They're mostly documented online these days, with exact location guides. Spelled as in acolyte?'

Worse nodded. A few seconds later, Rence stood up.

'Shall I take you there?'

—

Simon's headstone proved to be one of the largest in the graveyard. His name was well enough in evidence, but apart from the date of 1280, much of the inscription had weathered badly.

Rence returned to the church. Worse stayed at the grave for several minutes, trying to interpret the text, photographing it, and thinking.

In a way, he was paying respects to this person whom he knew only through the Worsener's Tale, a faithful servant of God who participated in one of the most arduous, fantastic journeys of geographic and intellectual exploration in human history. Only to arrive at St Eke's as a pilgrim and become, very likely, a victim of the Mercifuls.

Then to be here interred, beside where Worse was standing; and—were it not for the assiduous recording of Henry Oldrice in his *Wey*—fully forgotten over three-quarters of a millennium.

And perhaps Geoffrey Magnacart had stood on the same ground, in 1369, reading this very inscription, paying respects similarly to this one of the missionary Three.

Worse terminated the reverie deliberately, by looking over to the North Ground. Two gravediggers in traditional dress, with spades, were completing a filling quite close to William's site. The mourners had departed. Worse had been informed of this funeral, which was for the churchwarden Sylvia Hurt, as part of the daily intelligence report. According to that, the service was to be held in the church hall, with the procession using Old Forge Lane to bypass St Eke's en route to the wheatstone bridge.

He walked back toward the south-west porch pondering this: When the sole village florist dies, are there more or fewer flowers at her funeral?

Inside St Eke's, Rence was nowhere to be seen. Worse decided it was time to attend to something that he had hoped to do since arriving in Steeple Resting: satisfy his curiosity about the bell. He passed through the tower room, went up the spiral staircase, and set about a thorough examination. It was a lifelong interest, and he generally knew where to look for inscriptions, foundry stamps, and dating. Next, planning to record a soft peal for later harmonic analysis, he prepared his smartphone and swung the clapper.

As an acoustic sample, it proved non-ideal for the purpose. What he recorded was two gunshots from the tower room below him, and a cry of pain from Rence.

From the crypt access above him, he could hear Mansion, still out of sight, shouting.

'Did you get him, Fielding?'

Worse's priority was to help Rence, and deal with the others later. As Mansion appeared above, Worse leapt into the staircase leading down to the tower room.

—

Worse was planning his tactics as he raced down the steps, sometimes jumping two at a time despite their riser height. He could hear Mansion following, perhaps two windings behind. But a spiral staircase is no place for a gunfight.

In the tower room, he took in the scene quickly. Rence was on the floor, lying back against the opposite wall under the extinguisher yoke. He clearly had sustained gunshot wounds to the right shoulder and left lower leg. Worse judged them not to be immediately life-threatening, but they were immobilizing. Rence signalled a thumbs-up to Worse.

Instead of crossing the room to the squeaky door exit, Worse pulled open the Wistful Wardrobe and concealed himself inside. Through the slit in its chronically ajar door, he saw Mansion enter the room, pistol in hand, hesitate while looking at Rence, then race out to the nave.

Worse could hear Mansion shouting at Fielding. 'Which way did he go?'

'Who? No one came out here.'

'Fuck. How could he ...?'

By this time Worse had vacated the wardrobe, closed its door, and re-entered the spiral staircase, stopping just out of sight. When he heard Mansion and Fielding come back into the room, he moved suddenly into full view, but remained one step up. The Totengräber was held at eye level. He spoke clearly and quickly.

'Drop your weapons. Final warning.'

They didn't.

Fielding, behind Mansion, was the first to level for a shot, and died for the privilege. He jerked backwards, falling into the doorway, revolver spinning from his hand to clatter on the floor.

Worse spoke without emotion. 'Your accountant has seen fit to close the ledger, unreconciled though it be. Dressed for the occasion, too, I see—each of you properly suited to bury the other.'

Mansion looked confused, and frightened. Here, impossibly, was Death descending the bell-ringer's own staircase, coming for the faithful steeple keeper himself.

Worse read his face, and offered a thin smile. 'You should understand the importance of your role in today's proceedings. The wronged knight has awakened in the crypt, exchanged his longsword for a pistol, and is seeking retribution, twenty-two generations forward. You, as it happens, will serve to extinguish the Satan line of his longstanding legitimate grievance.'

Worse had thought it only fair that Mansion be informed of his fated place in history. Despite the explanation, the sexton's face showed no comprehension of events, nor curiosity. Worse ended the lesson.

'I once suggested that you cooperate with me, out of self-interest. This is the time. Lower the weapon slowly to the floor. Remember what I said about resisting arrest.'

'Fuck you.'

Mansion fired before taking aim, and the shot was wide. An instant later, he sank to his knees, eyes fixed on Worse in terminal bewilderment, a neat entry wound centred in his forehead. For a few seconds he balanced there, like Geoffrey. Then he collapsed to his left, like William.

Worse strode over to Rence. The bleeding wasn't dangerous, and he was fully conscious. Worse called an ambulance, then Wirrier.

'Let the team know that Mansion and Fielding are eliminated from our enquiries. PC Rence is wounded, not badly. Come to the tower room to see how it ended.'

He crouched down, looking at Rence. 'How's the pain?'

'Hardly feel a thing.'

'It was Fielding who shot you?'

'Yes.'

'Where's your pistol?'

'He took it.'

Worse walked over to Fielding and rolled his body over, using a foot. The police weapon was tucked into his belt. Worse retrieved it and returned to Rence.

'This is yours. How good is your aim, left-handed?'

'I practise. Not perfect.'

'When you can, train up with this.' Worse handed over his Totengräber. 'It's a gift. Brand new but for three shots down. Special Prussica sight. I've finished with it. You can do the licence necessaries.'

Rence's delight transformed into a wince as he moved his wounded shoulder unthinkingly.

'Rest up,' said Worse. He took back both pistols, placing them by the wall.

'You won't want these in the ambulance, and they'll be needed for the internal investigation. You'll find them held in the task-force evidence safe.'

–

By then, two constables from the patrol car stationed outside were standing at the doorway, gaping. Worse looked at them, without conveying his disapproval at yet another process mishap.

'PC Rence will be fine.' He pointed. 'These two probably assaulted the real gravediggers after the florist's funeral and stole their clothes. I suggest you start your search up behind the aspen row on the North Ground. They may have serious injuries. Report to Inspector Wirrier.'

–

A call relaying a police officer down rings high-level alarm bells. Instead of a standard ambulance dispatch, a mobile ITU was sent. Worse wasn't aware of this until Jane Malleson and her team rushed into the room.

'Worse! Jesus! My occupational nightmare! St Eke's and your antics are straining all of Kent's endurance. And mine.'

'I just entered the room and found poor PC Rence lying here. What was I supposed to do?'

'Very Samaritan of you. Any others injured?' She was checking vitals on Rence.

'Remains to be seen. Meaning, only this handsome pair you avoided on the way in.' Worse waved toward Mansion and Fielding, both disguised as gravediggers. 'As you intuitively determined, intensive care won't help them.'

Jane was paying full attention to her patient, and didn't react.

Worse smiled at Rence, receiving another thumbs-up in response.

'I'll be outside.'

'Oh Worse,' called Jane, still not looking up. 'The Canon's extubated. Lung function excellent, all things considered. And neurologically intact, it seems. Expected transfer to ward this evening, discharge home late tomorrow.'

'I'm pleased,' said Worse.

He stepped over Fielding's body and walked to the lychgate. He wanted to sit quietly and recompose events in his mind.

—

When Wirrier arrived, accompanied by Sergeant Michelson, Worse didn't look up to speak.

'Take a look inside. The firearms need tagging and securing, Sergeant. My T9 is a gift to Constable Rence.'

Worse returned to his train of thought.

Next came Rence, carried on a stretcher, oxygen mask in place and an IV running. As he passed, Rence managed a thank-you wave with his left hand. Worse responded with a nod.

He didn't look at Jane. He didn't watch the ambulance leaving. He just felt tired of it all.

Wirrier returned, sensed Worse's mood, and seemed to understand. He sat down where Rence had earlier been, and waited. Eventually, Worse spoke.

'I will file my report on this incident. Then I would be pleased if, in the coming days, I could hand over leadership to you.'

Only then did Worse look up and make eye contact.

'Of course.' Wirrier paused. 'That's quite a scene in there. Is there anything you need? Anything I can do for you?'

Worse was grateful for the solicitude. 'Thank you. I'm fine. I just need some time. Do you mind organizing the coroner and disposals?'

'Of course,' Wirrier repeated.

Worse stood up, collected the two coffee mugs, nodded toward Wirrier, and walked home.

38 NICHOLAS

Millie found Worse standing at the window in their sitting room. He seemed not to be aware of her arrival, and continued staring across to St Eke's. Over previous days, she had often seen him in that exact pose, and understood what it meant.

Once, looking out there, he had shared with her a meditation on William Whencely's cortège journey, from St Eke's to the North Ground, asking what might be the meaning of Satroit's *mourning substance*; what could the ethereal weigh; and where did it reside?

Millie had responded: 'You know those are metaphysical, religious, questions, Richard,' as if to say they were unanswerable, and both had fallen silent.

This time, Millie felt instinctively concerned. Worse was so deeply immersed in his thoughts that he made no acknowledgement of her presence, even when she crossed the room behind him. She chose to sit in one of the armchairs and wait.

It was another two or three minutes before Worse turned, showing no surprise to find her there. Millie saw something drawn in his face.

'Richard. Are you all right?' She stood up to be closer to him.

Worse didn't answer immediately. He was stopping himself from saying the reflexive *Yes, of course. I'm fine.*

'No, to be honest. Not completely. I'm thinking that I've had enough of this place.'

Millie sensed the seriousness of his mood. She embraced him.

Over Worse's shoulder, she had his view of a minute before. A contract workforce was removing security fencing. The

William Toll van was parked near the lychgate. A party of clergy, in rich maroon and purple vestments, were huddled outside the south-west porch. They were obliged to make way for two men, supervised by a woman, carrying heavy equipment into the church. Worse's rumination had been so intense, she wondered if he had seen any of it.

'We can leave, as soon as you want.'

She leaned back, to see into Worse's eyes.

'Tell me what it is, Richard.'

'Can we lie down? I'm tired.'

'Come with me.'

Millie led the way to their bedroom. Worse chose to lie on her side of the bed, on his back. Millie lay down facing him. She waited.

'St Eke's has got to me, Millie. When we arrived, it was picturesque, beautiful. I thought how fortunate your family was, having that outlook across the lane. Even William's unexplained death didn't really detract—there was no sense of the place, the building itself, or its whole history, being implicated in his fate. But with all that's been exposed, when I look over there now, do you know what I see?'

Millie shook her head.

'I see Geoffrey, dying, brutalized, as it happened. And I find myself grieving for him as if it were yesterday; as if he were my father. That close.'

Millie waited a few seconds before speaking.

'Are you wanting to go home, Richard?'

'I don't know. Possibly. I'm sorry, Millie.'

'You mustn't be sorry. We need to do what's best.'

'I'm thinking the *Malison* is retaliating, through its hold on Geoffrey. As if I troubled it and now, in revenge, it's troubling me.'

'We both know that is superstitious thinking, Richard. A curse has only as much power as you surrender to it.'

Millie placed a hand against Worse's cheek, turning his head to face her.

'Listen to me. You did more than trouble the *Malison*. You killed it. When you found the crypt, you killed it, like Heracles and the Hydra. Its den of vipers, Mansion and the others, lost all their poison from that point. It can't come back, to hurt you or anyone else.' Millie hesitated. 'Can I say something?'

Worse nodded.

'You, Richard Magnacart Worse, have truly avenged Geoffrey's murder. Remember that.'

In a way, her tone and cadence were almost parodically formal, as if her words were taken from an investiture speech. Worse smiled, and took her hand in his. At that moment, he was realizing something: For him, for Worse himself, it was Millie who would kill the *Malison*.

Worse turned his head back to face the ceiling, and closed his eyes. Millie wondered if she heard the very faintest chuckle.

—

He was awakened by the bell of St Eke's. It was probably a test peal by the technician Rocky Ryngelle.

Millie was still lying beside him, reading. 'How are you, Richard?'

'How long was I asleep?'

'A little over an hour.'

Worse sat up. 'I have work to do.'

'Wait, Richard. Wait! You have life to live as well. I know you've wanted some special time with Nicholas. Take that now.'

Worse hesitated, but Millie didn't. She phoned Nicholas.

'Where are you?'

'At home, in the kitchen. Where are you?'

'In the Surgery. I'm setting you up with a not-so-blind date. You are going to take Richard into the village and buy him coffee in the square with whatever specialty cake he wants, and you two will have a proper catch-up without the rest of us around. It's time you told my partner how happy you are that he's now your brother-in-law.'

'Love to. Send him along.'

—

'You would hardly recognize the place, Worse. Since you were there, thanks to Edvard's persuasive genius, Cambridge is setting up advanced research facilities. They're building most of the infrastructure along that path you walked once, from the LDI station to the Edge[1].'

Nicholas was describing developments at the Language Diversity Initiative field station, established on the Joseph[2] Plateau in the Ferendes. They were sitting at an outdoor table at the Black Ketill tearooms in the historic Steeple Resting marketplace. Across the square, Worse could see William's bookshop, not shuttered, but showing no life to the world either.

'What disciplines are up and running?' asked Worse.

'Edvard's favourite, of course. A decipherment team looking at the medallion[3] images. Plus spectroscopy, chemistry. The first priorities, though, were improving communications and transport into the place. That ghastly road to Madregalo has been upgraded by the government. Our teaching service has been given full national school status, so we have salaried staff along with our volunteers. Paulo[4] fought hard for that.'

'I'm sure he did. How is Paulo?'

'Still the same, except perhaps more entrepreneurial. Now that we have researchers coming to the station from Cambridge, Madregalo, Australia, Mount Sycamore—all over— he personally is less hands-on with the language programme. He's sort of de facto dean of everything.'

'And you, Nicholas. Are you still happy there?'

'Absolutely, Worse. I continue to manage my financial consultancies most mornings. That's much easier with our upgraded internet access. And there's a lot of interesting stuff happening, not just on the Station, but in the whole country. Are you going to eat that?'

Nicholas pointed to a savoury muffin in front of Worse.

'Oh yes. Thank you. What's changing in the country?'

'Everything, Worse. Everything changed when Nefari died. Prince Arnaba is more liberal than anyone anticipated. There's been a huge shift toward genuine democracy, and it's all peaceful for once. The Democrasi found the discipline to form a party and are in Parliament. The secret police have been cleaned out and APOSTA disbanded, human rights restored, the institutions modernized and given transparent governance. Oh, and remember Madam Kohl? That despicable government Secretary overseeing Paragraph 51, known underground as the Vanishing Act?'

'I do.'

Nicholas had warned Worse of the tentacular reach of the Ferende Internal Security Act during his first visit to Madregalo.

If a look can be made of purified irony, Nicholas had it.

'She was disappeared.'

Worse's expression didn't change. 'How just is Nemesis,' he said, without joy.

'And China?' Worse then asked. 'What about their interference, all that exploitation?'

'Curtailed, and they're progressively being expelled, much to the relief of the population.'

Nicholas paused. 'Actually, Worse, this will appeal to your revolutionary tendencies. There's a growing movement to regain Ferende sovereignty over their historical westernmost territory, Circumferentia[5], if you remember.'

'In mainland China. I do know about it,' said Worse.

'And with it, exclusive economic rights over the Circular Sea[6].'

'How realistic is all that?'

Nicholas behaved as if he should say nothing more, but really wanted to. He looked around, leaned in towards Worse, and whispered. 'Surprisingly so.'

—

At that moment, Angela Ponting passed between the tables behind Nicholas. She and Worse made eye contact, and she approached the pair. Worse raised himself politely in his chair to greet her.

'How are you, Worse?' said Angela. They shook hands.

'I'm well. You must know Nicholas?'

'Oh yes. How wonderful. It's been a long time.'

She offered her hand.

'Hello, Angela. I was sorry to learn about William. How are you going?'

'I'm managing, thank you.'

She turned to Worse.

'I hear that you are responsible for the upheaval at Priory Manor. I've been asked by their interim director to return as clinical psychologist.'

'And will you?' asked Worse.

'I'm considering it. My other news is that William left me the shop. I'm just on my way to look inside and work out the future. Actually,' she said to Nicholas, 'I was thinking that Philip might like to choose some books and maps and so on— whatever he wants. That would be William's wish. Mention it to your father, if you would, and I'll be in touch to make a suitable time.'

'I'm sure Dad would be very thrilled at that offer. Thank you, Angela.'

'Well, I'll get across there. Worse, are you eating that muffin? Or is it some kind of envy trap for opportunistic villains?'

—

'And how are the Ferent language studies going, Nicholas?'

'Brilliantly, Worse. UITA Press have commissioned the first comprehensive Ferent–English dictionary, with a five-year horizon. Edvard is editor-in-chief, of course.'

'What will your role be?'

'The usual. Computational cladistics and so on, for the etymologies. Actually, I've pulled back a little on that side of things. The swint language studies have largely taken over.'

'I'm not surprised, Nicholas. That's real breakthrough science. I admire you for it.'

Nicholas looked very pleased to hear Worse's compliment.

—

'The Plateau is opening up more, Worse. The government is determined to bring equitable social and health services to the remote villages. It's really excellent. One day, someone might even come across the wreckage of *Abel*[7].'

'That would be momentous for Edvard,' said Worse.

'Of course. There's a lot of resource exploration happening, which is bringing in people and construction, much of it far west of LDI. Someone discovered jungle swamps out there having high levels of oneirates[8], of all things.'

'Really? My understanding was that they're not plentiful in natural form anywhere in the world.'

'I know. But as you must have realized by now, Worse, the Ferendes is not part of the natural world. Anyway, they've established a low-level concentrating facility on site, and truck the sludge in tankers to La Ferste for refining. It will be a significant revenue earner for the government. Very significant.'

'Excuse me, Nicholas. I should check this.'

Worse had received an email notification. It was from Phoebe Andrieus, and the subject line read, simply, 'Surprise'. There were several attached images to study. Nicholas stayed silent until Worse looked up.

'You look sad, Worse.'

Worse nodded, almost imperceptibly.

'Sad in the twelfth century, Nicholas.'

Nicholas held Worse's gaze, without speaking. A waitperson passed by their table, and stopped.

'Finished, sir? Would you like me to remove your plate?'

---

[1] The southern rim of the Joseph Plateau, offering scenic views overlooking plains leading to the Bergamot Sea. Traditionally, LDI staff walk from the research station to a forest clearing at the Edge for relaxation and meditation.

[2] Named for Captain Joseph, Master of HMS *King of Kent*, which first anchored in what is now Madregalo Bay in 1816. Aboard was the naturalist Thomas MacAkerman, of weaver fish fame. See note 1, Chapter 16.

[3] Referred to informally as 'blotchings', these Neolithic disc-shaped patterns discovered deep within a Plateau cave system are believed to be the unique art form of the earliest Ferende civilization, known as Rep'huselans (or, in this context, Medallion People). The elucidation of the method of manufacture, and significance, of the images is an intriguing physico-chemical detective story recounted in the documentary *Bad to Worse*.

The Medallion Caves referenced here form part of an incompletely explored complex having troglofauna new to science (a startling example being the giant Shuffler crab), at least one extensive lake, and possible connections to hypothesized subsea lava tubes. In regard to swint language, recent excavation of a prehistoric fire pit in the first of two blotchings galleries unearthed several clay flute and ocarina-like objects, mostly fragmented.

A specimen of the second form, intact but very fragile, was scanned to produce a 3D-printed pattern for mould casting in locally sourced clay. A skilled flautist experimenting with this replica can generate sounds that impressively mimic swint song, strongly suggesting that the purpose of these artifacts was communication with the birds. A description of the finding is to appear in the journal *Syrinx*. See also note to Chapter 10.

[4] Paulo Cinnamonte, manager of the field station. Worse knows Paulo personally from a previous visit to LDI.

[5, 6] See Prologue, note 14.

[7] The research balloon, piloted by Edvard Tøssentern, lost in a storm during an expedition to capture weaver fish on the ocean surface. An account of the near tragedy is given in Darian's contemporary social history *The Weaver Fish*.

[8] A strategic source of oneiric acid, an important precursor reagent across several industries. Although readily synthesized in the laboratory, the method has never successfully been scaled up for industrial production, explaining what are regularly termed its nightmare price runs on commodity exchanges. Demand from the pharmaceutical industry is the latest development to put pressure on supply: oneiric acid enters the synthesis of a class of agents having completely novel chemistry, now referred to as REM compounds (for Re-singulated Electrodense Metametaminate). Some of these are psychoactive and show early promise for human therapeutics.

39 VICTORIA BRAY

Despite that mood, Worse felt buoyed as they walked home. He was pleased to have caught up with the science news from LDI, particularly Nicholas's advances with avian linguistics.

Now the conversation was more personal, between brothers-in-law, both sharing a love for Millie, for one as only sister, for the other as partner. In fact, it had been during Worse's visit to the LDI station that Nicholas made an oblique remark about Millie's and Worse's suitability for each other. At the time, it seemed not to have any effect on Worse, but it was to prove percipient, if not prescient. Worse valued his friend for that, amongst everything else. He was, in any conventional context, Worse's best man.

At the Misgivingston front gate, they independently chose to stop, looking over to St Eke's. Worse recognized that something had changed in himself from only hours earlier. Though still aware of a grieving for Geoffrey, he was unaffected by the bell tower itself, and impervious once more to the silliness of a building's curse.

'What do you think about the *Stēpel Malison*, Nicholas?'

'That silliness?'

Worse stopped him there with a raised hand. No more was needed.

He smiled with his old lightness, not at Nicholas, but at St Eke's.

—

Millie was in the front hall as they entered. She gave Worse a hug and stepped back, pointing to his hand.

'Who's that for?'

Worse had absent-mindedly carried home his uneaten muffin.

'Would you like it?' asked Worse, holding it forward.

'Mm.'

As Millie took ownership, Veronica appeared from her study.

'Who's that for?'

'Oh Mum, would you like to share it?'

'Mm.'

They all set off to the kitchen for the grand bisection. Philip was there, making tea.

'Mm. Is that for me?' he beamed, looking at Millie's hand.

–

Worse carried mugs of tea to the Surgery sitting room, with Millie following. As he placed them on a table, Victoria Bray phoned him. He signalled to Millie that he needed to take the call.

'I've been told that your involvement in investigations is drawing to a close, and that you will be leaving the parish shortly.'

'Both true,' said Worse. 'I was intending to brief you, of course. Are you available to meet in person?'

'Yes, I'd be very pleased to.' She paused. 'Worse, I have become aware of rumours spreading about St Eke's, and I would like to be properly informed of the facts.'

'Understandably,' said Worse. 'What are the rumours?'

'I am simply hearing that there are rumours, nothing of their content.'

'I see. Rumour of rumours. So only meta-rumours percolate upwards to senior clergy. A case of career advancement to the best-not-told, as in my profession. How frustrating for you.'

There followed a Deaconess Delay, while Victoria appraised Worse's tone.

'I would appreciate your enlightening me, Worse.'

Worse smiled at the cultured good manners tinctured with English mild bitters.

'Naturally. I know nothing of rumours. I can apprise you of the facts. Will you be in Steeple Resting at all today?'

'I shall be in the parish office from midday.'

'I'll find you there. We shall go to the temple, and together cast out the lie changers.'

Victoria expressed polite gratitude.

'Sorry,' said Worse to Millie as he ended the call. 'The Archdeacon.'

He drank his tea.

—

'Let's talk at St Eke's. I want to show you something that, for centuries, only criminal eyes looked upon.'

Worse led the way out to the lane and along to the church. He took Victoria into the tower room and up the spiral staircase. A few hours before, he had sourced a stepladder in a parish hall utility room, carried it to St Eke's, and drawn it up through the belfry platform by tying it to the bell rope[1]. It made reaching the top of the stonework and accessing the second stairway both easier and safer.

'Where are we going?' she asked, as Worse directed her to the ladder.

'To the St Eke's crypt.'

'Upwards to a crypt?'

'They were devious.'

—

In the crypt, Worse's guided tour was brisk. He took Victoria directly to the circular altar.

'What does this shape signify?' he asked.

'Circular speaks pagan to me, but I can't be sure.'

'Sacrifice? That sort of pagan?'

'I sincerely hope not. Shine your torch on these, please.'

Victoria leaned forward to study the altar pieces.

'These are Christian, definitely. But there's no cross, you'll notice.'

Worse nodded, rather pointlessly given the dark.

'Now come and look at this.'

He directed his torch onto the woman's effigy, pointed out the inscription, then showed her the Worsener's tomb in the south aisle. He heard her start when she took in the symbolic brutality of the penetrating sword.

'A wound for eternity,' she said. 'How could anyone do that?'

—

They left the crypt via the stairs selflessly endowed in absentia by Sir Gestine Duquel, and walked from the north aisle to the front of the nave. Worse stopped.

'There is something known only to one distinguished archaeologist and to me. At least, that is true of the innocent actors in our recent St Eke's dramas. Her name is Professor Phoebe Andrieus. She has given an undertaking not to share her findings without permission from you. I invited her to the crypt on that assurance. Even her technicians assisting are not aware.'

Victoria turned to Worse. 'And you are going to tell me?'

'It is something not easy to think about.'

Worse allowed a few seconds for the warning to have effect.

'Phoebe's imaging of the woman's tomb, very sadly, reveals two distinct skeletons. In her pelvis, quite unequivocally, are foetal bones. She died in advanced pregnancy.'

Possibly in obstructed labour, reasoned Worse, or from antepartum haemorrhage, or eclampsia, or sepsis, or any number of afflictions of the time. Or by murder. He didn't share the differential.

'O God. That is dreadful.'

Worse motioned for them both to sit down, on the front pew.

'Dreadful,' Victoria repeated. 'And we have no knowledge of her, no name?'

'No. We are hopeful that the inscription will be informative. So far, we have been unable to decipher it. Secret tomb, secret language.'

'That is an awful committal, to God and the world. Denied their lives into posterity.'

'I think the same,' said Worse. 'Something very unchristian has lain in the foundations of St Eke's.'

'Clearly. Yes. I wonder if the infant was named,' added Victoria, almost to herself.

Worse silenced a response: The mother never knew her child's sex.

'Are you able to explain it?' Her voice was still soft.

'The secrecy? I am fairly certain it wasn't a decision made in her interest.'

'Then in the interest of someone else, are you saying?'

'It follows,' said Worse. 'Another, or others.'

He waited, allowing Victoria to reach any conclusions in her own time. She remained silent. Worse spoke.

'The sword tomb, we are quite confident, dates to 1369. We have strong corroborative evidence for that in the writings of Henry Oldrice. Phoebe places the woman's one much earlier, in the mid-twelfth century, based on stone carving technique and effigy stylistics. Her advice is that we would need to open the tomb to obtain a reliable dating.'

'Is that happening?'

'I have not requested it. Nor do I intend to,' said Worse. 'You may.'

Victoria nodded slowly. She was looking at the altar. Again, Worse gave her the opportunity to process the information.

'Twelfth century ... What are your thoughts?' she asked.

Worse had intended to canvas all possibilities with her, however unpalatable. Now was the time.

'Are you aware of stories from that era of mysterious night-time visits to St Eke's by a man heavily cloaked for disguise, travelling by coach and escorted by knights on horseback? From Canterbury?'

'No, I am not,' Victoria said. She looked inquisitively at Worse.

'Stories, reports, rumours—who knows the truth in these things? Wilfred Simony had no knowledge of it either. But after I mentioned it to him, he researched that and related matters in the Cathedral closed archive, and was shortly thereafter attacked. A similar coincidence occurred with William Whencely.'

'And what is in the archive?'

'A surprisingly bulky dossier regarding events of the time. Reports of sightings, descriptions, letters, demands, character disparagement to and fro, bitterness and denial.'

Worse waited, before adding unsubtle emphasis. 'Denial from high levels.'

She looked at Worse. 'You're about to tell me it was Thomas Becket.'

'The subject of the rumours was Becket. Yes.'

Victoria looked back to the altar. She was shaking her head slightly. 'He came to St Eke's?'

'Someone came to St Eke's, or was rumoured to have done so.'

'To the crypt? To that tomb?'

'We don't know. Probably.'

'And the secrets surrounding those visits, and the existence of the tomb, have been protected by some order of knights over all that time? Willing to kill?'

'Order of misguided zealots. Most recently a ragtag militia, of sorts. But yes, that seems clear.'

'You are aware that Becket was in exile from 1164 till shortly before his death?' said Victoria.

'And the reported sightings are consistent with that hiatus,' said Worse. 'Which is hardly evidential, because we would expect them to be so in either case: truth or competent calumny.'

They heard voices from the rear of the nave, and Worse turned to check. As he thought, it was the slate repair team inspecting for roof damage interiorly. He looked back to Victoria.

'To add to the mystery, around that time the Church entered a very unusual property agreement with the Order of

Mercifuls. In 1156, it transferred controlling ownership of the foundations of St Eke's, meaning, obviously, the crypt, to the Order, without any documented consideration in exchange.'

'But that is inexplicable, surely.'

'Few worldly acts are truly inexplicable, I would suggest. It's just that some only make sense in a foreign morality. In disowning, so to speak, the crypt, the bishops disavowed its secrets. I think that was the motive.'

Victoria's eyes had been fixed on the altar. Worse was surprised at what she said next.

'This is your discovery. What do you intend to make public?'

'Other than those facts necessarily tabled in a police report, I have no intention of making anything public. I view that as your prerogative.'

Victoria was quiet for several seconds.

'What would you do, if you were in my position?'

Worse also looked towards the altar as he spoke. 'It seems proper that the crypt belongs to the parishioners of St Eke's, no less than the church built upon it does. I think that the mystery woman and the violated man deserve to be made known to the world, their lives honoured, and the centuries of their unnatural fate redressed at least by some form of re-consecration.'

'So, open the crypt to the public, are you saying?'

'Yes. Formally annul the 1156 transaction on two grounds: that, contrary to binding verbal undertakings of the time that are no longer contestable, the Mercifuls used the crypt for criminal activities, namely, actual and attempted murder and concealment; and secondly, that the Order as constituted at the time of that agreement no longer exists and has no legitimate claimant inheritors. Further, in alignment with modern corporate full transparency and accountability principles, your Archbishop will issue a declaration of *Culpa Ecclesiae* that expresses Canterbury's remorse for these newly uncovered failings of the mediaeval Church, assumes responsibility for all feasible restitutions, and apologizes unreservedly for the injustice done to the entombed persons and their heirs and successors through the ages.'

'You sound like a Cathedral solicitor.'

'It's formulaic imposter English, quite basic,' said Worse. 'I frequently employ it. As will your legal advisers when it suits, I'm sure.'

Victoria gave Worse a dubious look. He returned to the subject.

'Getting back to public opening, though: obtain a building survey; make it safe; install lighting, ventilation; provide better access; ensure regular maintenance; upgrade your public liability insurance. Invite in researchers, historians. One never knows—by fortuity, a gifted academic or a tourist savant might recognize and decipher the inscription.'

'You seem to have a comprehensive plan to leave with me, Chief Inspector.'

'Not really. I'm making it up as we speak. The important point is this: if the tombs are made public, they can never again become the criminally protected private domain of a sect like the Mercifuls.'

Worse had a further thought. 'Something else for your solicitors to contrive: return ownership of Priory Manor and its grounds to the diocese. The Mercifuls, however they are currently incorporated, should be left with no benefit from historical crimes.'

The Archdeacon shifted her weight, as if shouldering another burden. 'And Becket?'

'Becket belongs in Canterbury. He was never positively identified; there was only ever rumour, and that's over eight centuries old. The man can't defend himself. The woman can't testify. The alleged visits might not have happened. It might not have been Becket. The relationship, if there was one, might have been pure, spiritual. He might have been her confessor. He might have been family, or a true and honourable friend.

He might have come to mourn. On no account should her pregnancy be connected to an individual without proof.'

'Many mights,' said Victoria.

'Yes. Mighty are the works of reason. I expect our understanding will be advanced by two things: a thorough, unimpeded research of the archives, not just in Canterbury but across the mediaeval Christian world; and a successful translation of the inscription, along with another coded prose piece by Oldrice. It's found in a version of *Th Pylgrymes Wey*, and known as the Oxford Passage. Wilfred knew about it. We believe it is relevant.'

'So, leave Becket out of it?'

'That would be my approach. Quite definitely.'

'I will need the permission of my superiors to do anything.'

'That's disappointing. I gifted prerogative to you, not to others.'

'Worse, yes, thank you, thank you for everything, but listen to me. The Becket connection is ecclesiastical dynamite.'

'Victoria, there's no validated Becket connection. That has to be stressed, repeatedly if necessary. Nothing proven, nothing substantively postulated even. Shame on the rumour-mongers. If people above you claim that Becket's sainthood would be seriously at risk, it suggests they know something that the rest of us don't, because actual rumour content doesn't reach them up there in the rarefied theologisphere, does it?'

'Mm,' said Victoria. She needed more convincing.

'In any case, if the dynamite does threaten to explode, you can console your Archbishop with the reminder that Becket wasn't, you know, proper. Not Church of England.'

It was the first time since he met her that Worse saw the Archdeacon smile, however slightly.

'Pass it on to the Pope to handle, you're suggesting?'

Worse enjoyed the whiff of naughtiness in her thinking. He played with it. 'I can hardly believe you thought of that—you, Madam Machiavel, Archdeacon of Canterbury. A brilliantly tactical divestment! Declare all the revealed impieties of England to be pre-Reformation and straightaway export them to Rome ...'

Victoria looked shocked at the role she found herself defined in.

Worse ended her embarrassment abruptly. He decided to state his position bluntly. 'I think the Church has a duty to the people of the crypt, a duty of truthfulness. To bring them into the light, as it were.'

'I do see that. I do agree with that. Of course I see that.'

'Remembering that one of them, beneath where we're sitting, is a child. Not dignified in a proper infant coffin. Unborn, unbaptized, unembraced, unsuccoured in the world. Only, we can be certain, once mortally fearful in its mother's womb, existentially distressed, and dying there.'

'Oh Christ, Worse.'

Worse's voice had risen in emotion, if unintentionally. Victoria clasped her face in her hands. She might have been praying, or crying, or seeking forgiveness for that small solecism before the altar.

Worse rested his argument, both for her sake and his own calm, before finishing. It was several seconds before he spoke.

'Also, a duty of transparency to William Whencely and Canon Simony. Victims in our own time. On our watch, as they say.'

Victoria was nodding her head. She uncovered her face and turned to Worse. Her eyes were moist. 'And to you? You were attacked also.'

'Not to me.'

Victoria looked questioning. Worse spoke without emotion. 'For me, it is different. The man with a sword through his heart was a Knight Worsener to Edward the Third—a priest named Geoffrey Magnacart. We can be sure of that from events described by Oldrice. I, too, am a Magnacart. It is enough for me to have learned of my unquiet ancestor, found his resting place, and avenged his murder, however belatedly, by destroying the vestige sect of the hospice order responsible for it. The Church owes me nothing.'

---

[1] Needless to say, Worse's enlistment of the bell rope as a ladder hoist would not have been condoned by Rocky Ryngelle. However, Worse's earlier rappelling from the tower made national news, and in an ill-advised flirtation with the popular, the normally sedate *London Tribune* hosted a trite correspondence seeking readers' ideas on improvised uses of a parish church bell rope. Things began charmingly (if impracticably) enough—pendulum physics for students, gymnastic climbing, knotting for naval cadets, lasso fun, even cut-and-splice skilling—but soon darkened to include an arsonist's fire-fuse to a timber steeple (Worse's thought also), and restraining discordant choristers for punishment. When, with macabre enthusiasm, clergy hangings were suggested, citing approvingly the infamous murder of Fr Ixas in the bell tower of St Alonzo's in Madregalo, the entertainment was speedily withdrawn, its column inches repurposed to satirical SayDoCo in a brilliant segue conducted in total editorial silence.

40 BENEFIT OF CLERGY

Worse found Victoria Bray working in her diocesan office in the Old Vicarage. Since her visit to the crypt, he had been wondering whether the experience of being shown the tombs and learning of the infamy buried in St Eke's might have proved more distressing than she revealed at the time. He knocked on the open door.

'May I come in?'

'Please do.'

Victoria leaned back in her chair to give Worse undivided attention, and invited him to sit.

'You are well?' he asked.

'Yes.'

Worse got straight to the point. 'I'm visiting Wilfred and Cecile this afternoon in Canterbury. I take it you have caught up with them since his discharge home?'

'I have.'

'What can I expect?'

'This morning, there was still much physical frailty, not surprisingly. But he remains mentally sharp, I was very pleased to find. At least, his humour is restored.'

'Including the irony?'

'Yes, indeed. With the measured Simony opaqueness intact.'

Worse nodded, but waited for more.

'He said he was looking forward to seeing you, to catching up with—in his words—the man of faith in you. I admit for a moment that single remark set me questioning his cognitive recovery.'

Worse didn't react. 'You told him about the discovery of the crypt? About what you had seen there?'

'I did. I think he immediately wanted to throw off the rug and slippers and come to see for himself.'

'Let's hope he is able enough to do that soon; he will need to manage the Duquel stairs. Did he talk about the Monday night, why he came to the tower of St Eke's?'

'I asked, but he said he was saving that conversation to have with you.'

'He is aware of events at Priory Manor?'

'Yes.'

'And of the involvement of his verger and pastor?'

'Yes.'

'And the fate of those two?'

'Yes.'

'Why do you hold the view that there is no man of faith within me?'

It was a sudden shift in depth and direction, at pace, that caught Victoria off guard. She paused, not quite lost in a Deaconess Delay, but for several seconds.

'I apologize, Worse. That comment was facetious and uncalled for. I thought it was amusing. I was wrong. It was at your expense, and I am sorry. I should also make it clear that Wilfred's remark was entirely without irony.'

'But why?' asked Worse.

Victoria held Worse's gaze, and spoke with evident deliberation. 'There has been much ungodly happening at St Eke's these last few days.'

Worse waited. Victoria seemed to struggle articulating her thoughts.

'I was informed last evening that it was you personally who shot dead Mansion and Fielding. Whatever their evil, it is difficult for me to reconcile that knowledge with the man who nearly wept reading the Leonardo dialogue at Wilfred's service of Intercession.'

Worse nodded. 'In difficulty is design, often, don't you think?' he said. 'You may also recall that I spoke about the worth of contradiction at that time.' He offered no pause for her to respond. 'You know, Victoria, on occasions, necessarily, reason imports violence. So has faith, over millennia, as we are all taught. That fact renders them no less reason and faith.'

This time, Worse did pause, but Victoria said nothing. She looked relieved when he changed the subject.

'Did you discuss Wilfred's future at St Eke's, may I ask?'

'We did, and I know he would value teasing through some ideas with you. He as much as said so.'

'What does he want to do?'

'It depends somewhat on his physical recovery, of course; return of stamina, especially. St Eke's is a very demanding parish.'

'Might he return to St Eke's, but with greater assistance?'

'I made clear that the archdiocese would support him in that. He is undecided.'

'What were your impressions of him spiritually, psychologically?' asked Worse.

'Very strong, I am pleased to say. If there were any quality of ruthlessness to be found in Wilfred, it would be the critical self-examination of the soul. My impression is that he is reassessing his feelings about everything.'

'Including staying in the Church?' asked Worse.

'Well, that's a difficult one. I believe he will. I don't for a moment think that Wilfred has lost his faith through all of this.'

Or elevated his doubt, wondered Worse.

'Tell me: Was your conversation with Wilfred in Cecile's presence?'

'Yes. Why do you ask?'

'Cecile participated?'

'Yes.'

'It makes a difference,' said Worse. 'What other possibilities for a change of role within the Church does Canterbury have to offer?'

'We discussed some options. One would be to give up the ministry at St Eke's and join the Cathedral archives as a researcher. He would be very valuable in that role, working on the history of St Eke's and Eccene studies generally. He read mediaeval history before ordination, did you know?'

'I did know.'

'Anyway, he was quite delighted, excited, I thought, by that possibility.'

'You could arrange that?'

Victoria looked down for a few seconds. 'Do remember that my position is Acting, Worse. My authority in many matters is both tenuous and temporary.'

'I remember. But your leadership throughout this St Eke's scandal has been exemplary. Everyone can see that. In any case, I know you are not one to compromise a duty of care to Wilfred in the face of, shall we say, seniority challenges.'

'You are a confrontingly direct man, Worse. No, I am not.'

'Which reassures me that with or without the blessing of your superiors, you will look after Wilfred, as well as advance the posthumous interests of the Eccene Mother with Child, as we might call them. Also, I would hope, formalize some grant of absolution, as it were, to St Eke's itself. And as we discussed, throw open the crypt. Extirpate the *Malison* for eternity, for those who suffer a belief in it.'

Victoria leaned forward, placing her right-hand palm down on her desk as if taking an oath on the Bible. 'Be certain of it, Worse. I undertake to do my best.'

—

Cecile Simony led Worse to her sitting room, and gestured to a chair.

'Make yourself comfortable, Chief Inspector. I'll be a few minutes getting Wilfred along.'

Worse was more comfortable standing. 'I hope I am not imposing on you both. I realize that convalescence is a fatiguing business. Do say if you think it becomes too much for Wilfred.'

'Don't be concerned, Chief Inspector. Wilfred is most appreciative that you wanted to see him.'

'Actually, the delight is mine. By the way, Cecile, I am simply called Worse by my friends. Or Richard, if you prefer. In any case, the Chief Inspector title I intend to relinquish in the coming days.'

'Really? Retire from the police?'

'Yes,' said Worse. He looked around. It was more a library than a sitting room. 'May I look at your books?'

Worse was already surveying the closest shelf.

'Of course. You may borrow any, if you wish.'

'Wilfred told me you are a bridge player. I see you have quite a reference library on the subject.'

'For my occupation. I write a syndicated bridge diary, plus some other pieces. "Occasionals", they're called, though the demands on my time are far from occasional.'

'Under what name?' asked Worse.

Cecile showed surprise at the question. 'A range of pseudonyms, actually. Adapted from not-so-famous span bridges. Not Tower, not Golden Gate, for example. I enjoy the obscurity. A silly conceit, I know, but at least I myself am entertained.'

'Not silly at all. I relish obscurity in all its forms.'

Worse recalled Victoria's word for Wilfred. Opaqueness and obscurity made a nice couple.

'Is "Wheatstone" one?' he asked.

Cecile gave a non-committal smile. 'You are surprisingly informed about the grand brouhahas of Kent. Don't tell me you are a secret operative for our local OhHo campaign?'

She turned away, not expecting Worse to answer, but he did.

'Circuitously admitted, I say.'

'I'll get Wilfred.'

—

'My friend,' said Simony, as he entered the room. 'We are a fortunate two, are we not?'

'Indeed we are, Wilfred.'

Simony leaned on a stick in his left hand. He offered his right hand to shake Worse's. Cecile assisted him to a lounge chair.

'I believe my rescue was in large part due to you.'

'Not at all. Cecile sounded the alarm; that was the main thing.'

Simony settled into his chair. Worse sat in another.

'Well, I thank you most sincerely.'

The two men held each other's gaze for a few seconds, without speaking.

'You are recovering well? Stronger today than yesterday?' asked Worse.

'Without doubt.'

That was enough of the preliminaries for Worse.

'But Wilfred, I had formed the view that you were never without doubt.'

Simony smiled. He, too, was not one to dwell in the quotidian.

'Ah, yes. Faith and doubt. I do remember our mutual confessional, Worse. I would say that both are stronger, be that possible within this enfeebled mortal frame that shelters them.'

Simony drew the handle of his walking stick up to tap his chest.

Cecile was still standing by a bookshelf. 'If you two will excuse me, I have a column to edit. But first I will bring tea.'

Both men thanked her. At the door, she turned before leaving.

'Richard, I told Wilfred your news about retiring from the police force.'

'Yes, Worse. A great shame. Why not settle here and rid the Garden of England of serpents?'

'I take that to be your role, Wilfred.'

'And I fear it has not been my strength of late.'

'The circumstances were without precedent, Wilfred.'

Simony seemed not to be comforted by the mitigation. 'You know, Worse, these last few days have brought up all sorts of feelings. I've been hearing the bell of St Eke's, in here,' Simony pointed at his temple, 'but now its sound is defiled by Mansion's dishonesty. I find it difficult to accept.'

'The honour and beauty and integrity of its ring were always there, Wilfred; they exist in the bell,' offered Worse. 'Not in the hand on the rope.'

As he spoke, Worse was unsure if he believed that himself, philosophically or even musically. He was trying to be helpful.

'And in the goodness of those who hear it,' he added.

Simony stayed ruminating. 'Every time, for him, it wasn't a joyous call to worship. He was celebrating his own wretched ascendency, his secret dominion over the tower and crypt. An appalling breach of faith.'

'More, I think, celebrating the dominion of the Mercifuls, in their broken, corrupted form. They ended up a pathetic, paranoid cult with no moral substance; only a myth of generational duty to a cause I suspect has been distorted and misunderstood for centuries. What did survive was a tradition of protection by threat and violence. Imagine their fall from grace: mediaeval physician-knight to terrorist racketeer.' Worse hesitated. He was about to say something provocative. 'Their services still retained, I might add, by the Church, if innocently enough, through the subsidizing of Priory Manor, and the position of sexton at St Eke's.'

Simony remained in the present. 'Are they ended, Worse?'

'We don't know. I think it is true for St Eke's. The wider picture will be the subject of ongoing enquiries. Our task force will continue, with Inspector Wirrier leading in my stead. I expect the investigation to run for at least a year.'

Cecile appeared with tea and plates on a tray.

'I took the liberty of making these earlier, Richard. I hope you don't view tea and scones with the vicar as an indigestible cliché. I know many do.'

She pronounced scone to rhyme with tone.

'I view it as an unforgettable delight, Cecile,' said Worse. 'Thank you.'

—

'Wilfred, tell me why you went to the tower that Monday night.'

'I was impatient to look for the crypt, Worse. To my

knowledge, there had never been the slightest suggestion that one existed, but my reading in the archives that afternoon convinced me that there was one, in some form, at least along the way. Your questions about the Mercifuls, Oldrice's *Wey*, and Becket really piqued my curiosity. Those Cathedral records are a cornucopia of surprises, I must say. I've also started reading, on your recommendation, that fellow Darian's annotated translation. I only wish it had been to hand in my undergraduate days. And I'm now wondering if I may have judged the man too harshly from his prior work.'

Worse absorbed the comment without responding. It brought to mind his own erroneous initial impressions about Simony himself.

'Apart from your email to me, did you mention your thoughts about a crypt to anyone before arriving at St Eke's?'

'Yes, I did, to Fielding. I was surprised to run into him at Priory Manor that evening, because he has no working role there. In fact, I enquired whether he was visiting a friend or family. Then it occurred to me that as my pastor he might have some knowledge of the subject, whereof I was ignorant simply because I had never asked.'

'What did he say?'

'That he was certain there was no such crypt at St Eke's. He was most emphatic.'

'Then what happened?'

'That was discouraging, of course, and I see now it was intended to be. But driving back, I kept thinking about what I had read in the archives, and made an impulsive decision to have a good look around for myself. I knew I wouldn't sleep if my excitement wasn't addressed with a little exploration.'

'I can understand that,' said Worse.

'The original plans for the 1116 construction are very confusing in relation to the staircase in the belfry, as are some subsequent survey drawings. That being the least clear feature in the design, I decided it was the place to explore first.'

'Did you discover the crypt that night?' asked Worse.

'No, I did not. And I don't believe I would have searched upwards in looking for it, as our Archdeacon described was to provide the answer.'

'So, you parked at the Old Vicarage: then what happened?'

'I went inside to retrieve the key to the police gate on their perimeter fence. All of us were told where to find it, in case of emergencies. I unlocked the gate, and was inside the south-west porch turning on lights when Mansion appeared.'

'From the police gate?'

'Yes.'

'Were you surprised?'

'Not excessively; he effectively lives onsite and is meant to act as a sort of security person.'

'What did he say?'

'He asked if I needed any assistance.'

'Did he ask why you were there at that time of night?'

'No.'

'We can take it that he knew already via a call from Fielding. All those phone records have been accessed. What happened next?'

'I had a thorough look in the tower room, in the wardrobe and so on, and could see no way to a crypt.'

'Did Mansion accompany you into the tower room?'

'Irritatingly, he did.'

'Did he bolt the door when you were both inside?'

'Actually, he did.'

'Did you find that odd?'

'He explained that it was for our own safety at that time of day, given that the police gate was left open to the public.'

'He lied. I found it locked. Then what happened?'

'Mansion disappeared up the stairs, while I searched the ground floor. He said he had some business with the bell.'

'And you?'

'On finding nothing of interest at ground level, I decided to go up the stairs as well. After all, they were the principal point of curiosity from the archived building plans. When I got to the top, it was the strangest thing—I couldn't see Mansion.'

'What happened next?'

'I called his name, thinking he must be up in the timber steeple, attending to something in the semi-dark.'

'He didn't respond?'

'No. Then immediately, I smelt that awful gas, and knew instinctively what it was. I thought of going downstairs, but lost my strength so quickly. Naturally, I remembered your escape, and stumbled to the same window with the bell rope going through. As it turned out, unlike you, I was not able to lift myself to safety.'

'You were exposed to higher concentrations, more quickly, I think,' said Worse. 'It was fortunate that you didn't go downstairs: you would have discovered the door bolted on the outside as well. In fact, it was that very finding, that the bolts were shot on both sides, that logically demanded another connection from the tower room to the nave. That proved to be the crypt.'

'So the Mercifuls, in trying to conceal its presence, unintentionally gave it away?' said Simony.

'In a failure of mental modelling, shall we say; yes. It is common for perpetrators to leave at a crime scene not fingerprints or DNA or, heaven forbid, a monogrammed jemmy, but something abstract, more invisible: a logical implication that proves ultimately helpful to us. Evidence not directly identifying the person as such, but the person's thought process. For example, what a burglar doesn't steal is sometimes more informative than what he does. We exploit these behavioural and inferential signatures frequently, as it happens, which is why criminal investigation is ten per cent looking and ninety per cent thinking.'

'Exactly as in finding one's faith, Worse,' said Simony.

—

'Victoria Bray and I spoke briefly this morning. She described to you, I think, the findings in the crypt?'

'Yes, she did. Most vividly. And informed me that you are a Magnacart, Worse, unquestionably descended from the knight Geoffrey. I'm not sure what form of condolence is suited to the time scale, but please accept whatever it is.'

'Thank you. Do you have any idea who the woman entombed there might be?'

'No idea, Worse, I'm sorry.'

'Her tomb inscription has not been deciphered. It is found repeated in Oldrice's Oxford Passage. I have a team of linguists and historians working on it, as well as your chess companion Xavier Grimly. I think, with your background in Middle English, you could make an important contribution.'

'That is most flattering, Worse, but those skills are long dormant.'

'Dormant perhaps, but primed for resurrection, might I put it. Would you be interested in becoming involved?'

'Most definitely.'

'Then I will forward you a photograph of the inscription shortly, and put you in touch with the others.'

—

'Wilfred, I am curious to know how you see your future. Will you return to St Eke's?'

'I really don't know, Worse. I love that parish, but going back will require quite an adjustment, the nature of which I am not sure. It will become clear in time, I trust. In difficulty, I have always found guidance in my heart.'

'I understand from Victoria that many opportunities are available to you. One that she mentioned is a role in Cathedral historical research. Does that appeal to you?'

'Certainly it does, but I'm not ready to make a choice just now.'

'Of course. I raise the subject because I think you would work well with my father-in-law in Steeple Resting. He's a competent amateur historian who's been extremely helpful in providing information to the investigating team. He worked closely with William Whencely over many years, and counts Xavier as a friend. You know Philip Misgivingston, I think?'

'Dr Misgivingston? Yes. A parishioner, but not, shall I say, an attending one, except for matins last Sunday, when I suspect you were the persuading force. For that reason, I am not kept informed of his state of wellbeing, spiritual or otherwise.'

Worse smiled. 'And for that same reason, it is the man of doubt within you who will forge the strongest intellectual bond.'

41 HERACLES IN KENT

Philip, Millie, Nicholas, and Worse were sitting in Philip's study. Worse and Millie had announced that they would be leaving in a few days, and Worse wanted to review their progress to date before handing over to Inspector Wirrier.

'Let's begin with William Whencely. Why was he at St Eke's, in the tower, that Sunday night?'

'Because he had strong suspicions about the place, probably from his researching the Cathedral archives, just as Canon Simony did,' said Philip. 'He possibly concluded that a crypt must exist. He was interested in the Becket connection. He was studying the Mercifuls, and might have wondered if there was a continuing presence.'

'If so, he was correct, as we know,' said Worse.

'Something to remember is that Will and I spoke only a few days before he died, and he made no mention of any ideas calling for an exploration of the church. And we always shared our theories. With Will, a good conversation was a sort of conjectural exchange.'

'So he arrived at some theory fairly suddenly, and felt compelled to investigate with relative urgency,' said Nicholas.

'At night? Why at night?' asked Worse.

'Perhaps that wasn't entirely his choice,' said Millie.

'Are you saying he was forced there?' asked Philip.

'Not necessarily. More, perhaps ... enticed. Everyone knew of his interest in what the Mercifuls regarded as their secrets. He was a methodical historian, asking questions, looking around the church, researching the Canterbury archives. All that made him the main exposure risk, from their point of view.'

'So,' said Philip, 'he was warned off with that calling card nonsense, and when that failed, they decided to dispose of him.'

'And to that end, enticed him to St Eke's with the promise of exciting discoveries,' said Millie.

'Premeditated murder, then,' said Worse. 'I agree that is the likely scenario, with Mansion the presumptive killer, hydrogen sulphide the method, and an added motive of reinforcing the *Malison* to the superstitious, for both explanation and deterrence.'

Worse allowed time for comments. There were none.

'Which brings us to Canon Simony. Fortunately, he is a reliable witness to events involving him. We know his reason for visiting St Eke's at night was his own curiosity, excited by his findings in the archives that afternoon. Mansion was his attacker. Fielding was an accomplice, in forewarning Mansion of the Canon's interests and intention. Everyone agreed?'

There was no dissent.

—

'There are a few matters we can dispose of quickly,' said Worse. We have established the involvement of the modern so-called Mercifuls. They are destroyed, or soon will be. We understand the hydrogen sulphide attacks, and have eliminated that risk. We have exposed their secret, being the crypt and its occupants. We discovered the role of Priory Manor and removed it from the criminal orbit.'

Again, Worse paused, but there was no comment.

—

'Let's move on to Geoffrey Magnacart. I suggest that the appearance of the sword tomb in the crypt is corroborative of Oldrice's account of the Worsener's death, and conversely, taken together, that account identifies the tomb as Geoffrey Magnacart's.'

'Wait, Worse. Isn't that a little circular?' said Nicholas.

'Understood. But within the totality of the Oldrice description and our discovery of the tomb there is internal consistency. We might view the tomb as physical evidence of the fact, circumstances, and nature of the Worsener's murder.'

Again, Worse paused for the others to speak. Nicholas was nodding in acceptance of Worse's argument.

'Tell me this,' continued Worse. 'Having read the *Wey*, does anyone doubt that the sword tomb belongs to the victim in the tower described by Oldrice and identified as Geoffrey Magnacart?'

'I don't,' said Philip, very definitely.

Millie and Nicholas concurred.

'Next, remember we were discussing the Worsener's reference to a spy in their midst, and the possibility that the individual belonged in the village rather than the pilgrims' party? We have a suspect: one Roger Vaneek, the sexton of St Eke's at that time.'

'The evidence being, Richard?' asked Millie.

'Not strong. A similarity argument. If we operate, in the main, by extrapolation to the future from the past, then, inversely, we should be comfortable hypothesizing events of the past from facts of the present.'

'Prediction justifying retrodiction, put simply,' said Nicholas.

'Historians do that all the time, even if implicitly,' said Philip. 'Will often mused on validity questions like that.'

Worse continued. 'It seems likely that, historically, there have been family lines of guardians dedicated to concealing the shame of St Eke's. Their ideally positioned incumbency was verger, or sexton, which afforded access, knowledge, and authority. The Mansion name can be traced back to Eke-related congeners, such as Van Eyck, or in this case Vaneek. Persons having such names figured prominently in the Priory Manor enclave.'

—

'Next, Simon Acolytēs. According to Geoffrey, as reported by Oldrice, Simon died in our steeple tower across the lane. We have a date, 1280. We have a grave, and presumably his remains, in the churchyard. His significance is this: Whereas the sword tomb is physical evidence for Oldrice's *Wey*, Simon's grave is, pending discovery of the *Documento* perhaps, our only physical link to the Worsener's Tale told within it.'

'Do we think he was murdered, like the others, Worse?' asked Nicholas.

'We haven't enough information to support that, or even suggest it with any confidence, but I'm hopeful that future research, particularly with Thelma Dewey's involvement, may help us there.'

Worse hesitated. He took from a pocket the second business card that had been sent to William, and lent to Worse by Philip.

'Personally, I do think there is a sinister link between the Mercifuls and Simon, for this reason. A few days ago, I looked at Simon's headstone. It's badly weathered, but there was something potentially very interesting.'

Worse passed the card to Philip.

'Read it, please, Philip.'

'X, V, I. Roman sixteen,' said Philip, placing it on the coffee table in front of him.

Worse continued looking at Philip, nodding slightly, but saying nothing. From across the table, Millie was seeing it upside down: IΛX.

'It's Greek! Iota Lambda Chi,' she exclaimed.

'Exactly,' said Worse. He loved Millie's intelligence. 'So, it turns out, nothing to do with sixteen. The same three letters, very faint, can be seen at the top of Simon's gravestone. That's his connection to the Mercifuls: the grave and the calling card.'

It was quite a significance shift from the theorizing they had done days before about the Roman numerals, invoking the Maiden of Fates or days of the Phlox.

'The sixteen, and the pseudo-Arabic were a mixed threat and decoy,' added Worse. 'A riddle, we might say, Philip.'

'What do you think the Greek means?' asked Nicholas.

'I don't know, but perhaps our question should be: What did it mean in the thirteenth century?' said Worse. 'We will need help answering that. I have sent the problem to Edvard, and we're awaiting his opinion.'

—

'Now, Philip. I had a very interesting talk with Canon Simony about what he may do with his career into the future. There's a reasonable chance that he will choose to pursue historical research, in which role I am assured by Archdeacon Bray he would be fully supported by the Church. I took the liberty of mentioning your name as a potential academic collaborator.'

'Worse?' It was mixed question, exclamation, dismay and admonishment.

Worse was unmoved. 'I think you would work well together. He read Middle English and mediaeval history before his calling: a perfect intellectual partner for your work.'

'Yes, Dad. That sounds ideal. Give it a try,' said Millie.

'He studied the *Wey* at university, and is now into Darian's translation,' said Worse. 'He's not at all evangelistic. In fact, on the subject of faith, we mostly discuss doubt.'

'Actually, talk about faith might do you good,' said Nicholas.

'Also, he plays chess with Xavier Grimly, so you share a non-denominational friend,' said Worse.

'And you'll enjoy privileged access to the secret archives in Canterbury,' said Millie. 'How amazing would that be?'

Philip raised both hands, palms forward, signaling a halt to the persuasion. 'I'll meet with him. I'll meet with him. Let's move on. Anything else to shock me with, Worse?'

—

'So, Philip. Millie and I will be returning to Perth, and Nicholas to the Ferendes. That leaves you as principal historian-investigator on the spot to solve the following outstanding problems that are not within the purview of the police. First, does the Tale's *Documento* exist, was Simon Acolytēs its final conveyor, and is it hidden in St Eke's? There is surely something of great value, otherwise why would Sleke and Couchman have been sent back, and Mansion himself return? I suggest a comprehensive search, especially of the crypt and its secret staircase, perhaps employing the services of Phoebe Andrieus, the archaeologist who conducted our georadar survey and tomb screening. Second, who is the Eccene Mother with Child, and what is her story? Third, and related to her, we need a translation of the Oxford Passage and her tomb inscription included. Nicholas, I took another liberty in inviting Wilfred Simony into that group project. Fourth, how real were the Becket rumours connecting him to St Eke's, and was he central to the Mercifuls appropriation of the place?'

The others were staring at Worse, contemplating the difficulties involved.

'So, just four tasks remain, not herculean for you, I'm sure, and no longer unreasonably life-threatening for an historian. The three of us will look forward to your thorough expositions.'

Philip wore the expression of a marooned sailor seeing his ship weigh anchor. It flashed to self-satisfaction when he discovered a potent counterpoint.

'Look forward, will you? Well, I might view it as a travesty against loved ones to deprive you of the anticipation,' he said.

—

'Was I unkind to your father, offloading those labours at the end?'

'Of course not, Richard. Under the pretend wounding, he will relish the challenges.'

'Do you think he will avail himself of Simony's expertise?'

'I do, actually. I think he knows it would be silly not to. Xavier was a good suggestion, too.'

Worse closed his eyes. They were lying, fully clothed, on their bed, resting before joining the others for dinner. Millie continued.

'I also think that an absorbing, difficult project like that is exactly what he needs to avoid those retirement doldrums we saw at the start.'

'Mm. Well, he's in charge now, and I'm pleased. I'm letting go of this place.'

'Not of me, I hope.'

'Not of you. Of course not of you. Not your family. Not your home. Letting go of the scene outside, William's final journey, across there.' Worse pointed to the window, without opening his eyes.

Millie rolled onto her side, placing an arm over Worse, as she often did in the night.

Worse enclosed her hand in his. 'Has this visit been good for you?' he asked.

'We'll have seventeen hours to talk on the plane. I'll think about it and let you know. However, at this point I can reveal that I'm smiling very happily.'

Worse opened his eyes. 'You feel fine about going straight home? Not accepting Edvard's and Anna's invitation to visit them in Cambridge?'

'Absolutely fine. We'll have many opportunities to be in Cambridge together,' said Millie.

'Promise me that I won't have to be a policeman on all our trips.'

'Only if you want to be. Every so often. Funny talk. Interrogations. Handcuffs jangling. I'll be your prime suspect.'

42   GLAD TIDINGS

Worse had given Wirrier several days' notice of his intention to hand over leadership of the investigation, and return to Australia. He had full confidence in the Inspector's ability to complete the task, and to exercise firmness with discretion where criminal leads touched on sensitivities of the Church. To facilitate communications, Worse had made a point of introducing him to Victoria Bray.

This morning, it was time. Core members of Campanile were gathered in the Canon's office when Worse arrived at 10.00 am. The news was already out, and a quiet round of applause greeted his entry. Worse quelled it with a raised hand.

'It is I who applaud you, as a team and as individual contributors. I want to thank you all for the hard work and long hours each of you has put in over these days. I think you deserve to be proud that the historic shame of this parish has been exposed, that its perpetrators, at least those proximate ones, are in custody or deceased. And that St Eke's is now a safe place—possibly for the first time since at least 1280, the year of Simon Acolytēs' death. I am very pleased to be leaving Campanile under the command of Inspector Wirrier, who will direct operations from this point on. Thank you, everyone, and good luck in your careers, and more importantly, your lives.'

Worse stepped back, and Wirrier moved forward to thank Worse on behalf of the task force, to wish him well, and safe travel home. Campanile would reconvene at 11.00 am to review progress and planning. When he had finished, he warmly shook hands with Worse, thanking him personally for his leadership and mentoring of the younger officers.

The rattle of crockery drew eyes to the door being opened, and Mary Coppicer pushing a tea trolley holding an oversized urn and lurching columns of stacked cups and saucers. She parked it with a sigh of triumph, as if no breakages were reason for congratulation. Then she made two cups of tea and brought them to Worse and Wirrier, who were standing to one side near a bookshelf.

'Don't you go thinking anything's changed, Mr Worse. I'm not going into that tower, ever. No I'm not.'

'I was sorry to learn of Sylvia Hurt's passing, Mary,' said Worse.

–

Wirrier excused himself, to consult with his sergeants. Worse approached Rence, who was standing alone beside the window. He was in civilian clothes, with his right arm in a sling made of brilliant police-chequer material. A crutch rested loosely under his left shoulder. Worse appreciated that he had taken the trouble of attending the handover while on medical leave.

'Is no one providing for the one-armed, one-legged, two-pistoled man? Can I get you a tea, Constable?'

'That would be very nice, thank you, Chief Inspector.'

–

Worse said goodbye to the Sunday parish staff as he passed through the front office. Once outside, still on the north side of the lane, he stopped to take in a deep breath.

He didn't need the air; he needed the ceremony. One breath was enough to be cleansed, and lightened. Cleansed of whatever institutional evil he had touched; lightened of the Worsener's burden that had fallen to him.

One breath, and they were gone. Breathed out.

–

He walked home feeling, for the first time since arriving, that he was on some sort of family holiday.

Millie, Nicholas, and their parents were in the kitchen. As Worse appeared at the door, they all stopped chattering and looked up expectantly, like a stage audience at the start of a performance. Worse obliged in a brief monologue.

'I've finished over there. Millie and I are now on vacation.'

There was a round of applause, louder, and from fewer, than at the handover. Millie hugged him.

'So that leaves us, what, twelve hours together on our romantic first overseas trip?'

'Yes, well. You did bring us to Kent Sin Central,' said Worse.

'I'm opening champagne,' said Philip.

—

Worse was very aware of the assistance he received from many people; he also valued the personal connections he had made. After lunch, he phoned Wilfred both to check on his recovery and to say goodbye. He spoke separately to Cecile.

'CoshEx.'

'I beg your pardon, Richard?'

'Obscure. Suspension bridge over the Peril River in La Ferste; part of the Marshal Yiscosh Expressway, axially and—'

'Orthographically. I see it.'

Worse was impressed. He had another suggestion. 'Perhaps also the Königsberg seven, for the well-connected stroller.'

—

In the course of the afternoon, he called Victoria, Jane, Angela, Thelma, HCN, and Phoebe Andrieus. All the conversations were short, but to Worse, important. He didn't foresee meeting with any of them again. To Xavier, he handwrote a brief letter, in Grimly red ink, and set it aside to post.

—

Towards evening, Nicholas came rushing into the Surgery where Worse and Millie were packing. He was excited.

'You're not going to believe this! Come outside!'

Philip and Veronica were already standing at the front gate, looking upwards.

'There!' said Nicholas, pointing at St Eke's.

A murmuration of swints had formed above the tower,

diminishing in size as member thrices progressively settled in the belfry. It was a public benediction, and a purification, far more authoritative than any incantatory statement from the Church could achieve.

Worse looked away. That was the picture of St Eke's to preserve, to carry home with him.

Charmed listener: See! They set you free!

He was thinking of Geoffrey, inside.

—

The airline limousine arrived early the next morning for their transfer to Heathrow. Worse and Millie sat in the back, and after a few sociable exchanges with their driver, both fell silent.

Worse's thoughts turned to that luxurious deep breath of the previous day, taken outside the Old Vicarage, when a slow, studied exhalation carried away the spiritual and moral contaminations of his work.

Now he saw in that act another meaning, primal, more generous, and unrecognized at the time; and it was not to do with breathing out.

It was about the breathing in, conceived as a gift, and sent through mourning substance into the past: a life-giving, sentinel first breath of the newborn, made for the Eccene Child, who on an undone day never had one.

—

About fifteen minutes out of Steeple Resting, still on minor roads leading to the A2, they crested a small rise where hedgerows had been removed.

'Richard, this is where we get the last glimpse of the steeple. Remember the first view we caught of St Eke's on the way in?'

Millie turned in her seat to look out the rear window.

Worse turned, to look at Millie.

THE END

AFTERWORD

Maken sinne an trecherie fram conscience ridden
Innen holi secrenesse, be wel anunder mitre hiden[1].

Despite Task Force Campanile—and, especially, the Church—exercising utmost discretion, this author is aware that certain events and discoveries chronicled here have found their way prematurely into uncritical public discourse, marred inevitably by distortion, exaggeration, or explicit untruths. It can only be hoped that publication of authoritatively accurate journaling, provided in this volume, will eliminate the more egregious of these rumours.

One of these concerns the sainthood of Thomas Becket. It is difficult to ignore the fact that Becket (bECKEt) belongs among those Eccene English surnames identified by Edvard Tøssentern as referencing St Eke, along with Worse's finding that the connection of this patronymic grouping to that particular parish of Kent has been, historically, invariably sinister.

Notwithstanding a temptation to draw sensationalist conclusions, if only from that incriminating suggestion of his name; or the recorded twelfth-century furtive night visits to St Eke's; or the mysterious Eccene Woman in the crypt; or her unborn Child; or their coded tomb inscription; or the unknown content of the Oxford Passage; or the undeniable likeness given to the phantom Sir Gestine Duquel's effigy; or the suspicious dispossession of the crypt by Canterbury; or the highly implicative fact that Becket's death was choreographed to occur on the feast day of St Eke; or the centuries of violent, cynical protection perpetrated by the Mercifuls, including the murder of innocents on consecrated land—notwithstanding all this sordid circumstance, we cannot conclusively make a case that a much-admired cleric's temporal and spiritual life was anything but of the highest sanctity.

Therefore, unless evidence to the contrary is uncovered, perhaps through fastidious researches of the Misgivingston–Simony collaboration, or from ongoing interrogation of Priory Manor detainees by Campanile officers, that view must remain the default position of all fair-minded readers. Only then, were it to become indicated, will an informed and impartial re-evaluation of Becket's deserts be possible.

Even so, already, impartial or not, voices are petitioning for a modern laical review of the character of the man, his connection to the Mercifuls, and related complicity sins of the mediaeval Church.

The public discourse alluded to above is not entirely without merit. A pseudonymous essay entitled 'Why Was Becket Canonized?', appearing in the *London Tribune* and subtly drawing on discoveries at Steeple Resting, has ignited serious, if predictably outraged, debate.

In masterly brushstrokes of casuistry layering upon no detectable fallacy, that writer's central question devolves to 'If Becket, why not Ixas?'—referring to Fr Atlo Ixas, rector of St Alonzo's in Madregalo, martyred by hanging in his own bell tower while defending the church from four 'knights' of Prince Nefari's despised APOSTA brigade.

Thence, forcefully, and unrepentantly, 'If not Ixas, why Becket?'

Suddenly, we are assimilating not a question, but an argument. Suddenly also, and unaware of it happening, the reader is become accessary to soft but erosive iconoclasm.

From that, elegantly, ineluctably, by lesson and logic, we are escorted through the mirrored halls of axiology, hagiography, and the problem of miracles, eventually into the great jurors' room reserved for Conferral and Annulment.

And there, amongst regretful Eccene spirits from a Judaean

hall of judgement, the essay leaves us, with no more guidance than an invitation to sit, deliberate, and decide.

Alas, it seems our assembly of earthly examiners comes too late—a determination from above is now before us, brought by the holiest of God's messengers. Swint sightings are drastically declining at Canterbury even as, commensurately, they increase in Steeple Resting. Apart from signifying all is not well in the church of Becket, this faith-migration raises a startling possibility: that the symbolic heart of the Anglican Communion must rightfully follow, city to village, grandeur to pastoral, Cathedral to St Eke's.

Perhaps it was always so, not least in 1369. That, unbeknownst to pilgrims on the *Wey*, their penance-place would be St Eke's; the spent, spent hours of unguarded confession the night before Canterbury; and the true saint of their absolution an infinite-listening Mother with Child[2], cruelly hidden from prayer and veneration.

Less momentous, but equally intriguing, has been a secondary correspondence in the *Tribune* seeking to uncover the identity of 'Nymphéa', the essay's author. A first confident assertion that it must surely be the rebel Archbishop Asporadikos of Ephthelion, based on 'textual clues' (reportedly, a syntactic idiosyncrasy), depth of scholarship, rhetorical sophistication, and known antipathies, was proven false. Other likely candidates have been suggested, all of whom have convincingly denied authorship.

So it is there, unresolved for the present, that the Nymphéa mystery rests. For Worse, though, there was a coincidence too far. Privately, he thinks he knows.

---

[1] This couplet, which introduces the Oxford Passage, is viewed by scholars as untypical of Oldricean satire, drawing on more hard-edged, unforgiving language, lacking a supporting context of crescendo irony, and being tonally humourless in the consensus ME reading. That mood displacement,

understandably, has been taken by many to prelude revelations of serious episcopal scandal in the coded Passage following, though there are emerging critiques warning that any such expectation bias, if erroneous, will have impeded decipherment to this point. For other possibilities, see Prologue, note 4. [*maken*: to cause; *innen*: into; *secrenesse*: secrecy; *anunder*: under]

[2] Not all is necessarily scandal: a prurient interest in paternity here is easily expelled under a presumption of Immaculate Conception ... No modern reader could fail to wonder whether these Eccene two of the crypt reprise corporeally the Virgin Mary and Child—with Stēpel Raest being the English Bethlehem to a miraculous Second Coming, capriciously ended in obstetric catastrophe.

INDEX OF FIRST AND FINAL MENTIONS

ACKNOWLEDGEMENTS

My maternal grandmother, Irene Sybil Patton, née Greenwood, introduced me at a very young age to Milton's 'On His Blindness'. Many years later, that initiation informed the lines that begin Chapter 1, and perhaps indirectly the Bartimaeus meditation of Chapter 19. She also gifted me an early appreciation of classical languages, together with a lifelong interest in English etymology.

To my parents, Oliver Francis Edeson and Joyce M C Edeson, née Patton, I am grateful for my childhood, my education, and a precious home schooling in my father's way of being observant in the world.

To my sister, Dorothy Irene Tribe, née Edeson, for her natural kindness, humour, and a shared delight in the cryptic.

To my partner, Lindy Jane Roberts:
  What spoken warmth could so anneal
  bright destiny, this late, impossible to real?

To Marian Patricia Giles, for our decades-long, forever interesting conversation—and the most thoughtful gift of Mayhew & Skeat at the start of this project.

To Sally Meryl Tayler, for those happy years of uniquely formative living and discovery together, including our adventure days in Canterbury.

To my children, Ruben Laurence Edeson, Gemma Tamsin McKibbin, and Imogen Mary Charlotte Edeson: three greatest blessings on my life.

I have been fortunate over the years in having good friends, fine colleagues, and many influential teachers, as well as a half-century of affecting acquaintances—some, patients; some, unnamed—found and lost at crossing points in the great world maze. In strange and largely indefinable ways, I think best imagined as a living convolution of odd-remembered things, all have entered this writer's person, and thereby possibly the work.

I thank the outstanding professional staff at Fremantle Press, especially my editor, Georgia Richter, for continued support of what critic Simon Vestry has labelled the 'indeterminate, frivolously light but riddling-dense' genre of ulterior fiction, with villainy inside.

ABOUT THE AUTHOR

Robert Edeson was born in Perth, Australia. He studied medicine at the University of Western Australia, has a research MPhil from the University of Cambridge, is a Fellow of the Australian and New Zealand College of Anaesthetists and a Diplomate of the Royal College of Obstetricians and Gynaecologists. Before becoming a novelist, he was a consultant anaesthetist and researcher, publishing in the neuroscience, biophysics, and mathematical literatures. His first novel, *The Weaver Fish* (2014), won the T.A.G. Hungerford Award. It was followed by *Bad to Worse* (2017). As a young doctor, he lived for some years in Canterbury, England; this region of Kent, home to anxious ghosts of pilgrims past, is the setting for *The Worsener's Tale*.